'Totally immersive, an utterly enjoyable experience. Here East, West and the Realm of Faye meet; three vivid and vastly different societies steeped in character, culture, conflict and alienation. A story full of ingenuity, humour, magic and wit. Zen Cho writes once more' ... ... en Lord

'I sat up all night racing to finish it (again). Another magnificent outing from Zen Cho, this is like a Blandings Castle with dragons (and I can't think of higher praise!). I selfishly hope for a new novel in the series every year from now till the end of time. Clever, funny, and compulsively readable – I loved it' **Lavie Tidhar**

'A lot of fun, ingeniously and carefully plotted, with some engaging and moving examples of the value of friendship and the moral dilemmas of power' *Locus*

'Cho continues to confront class and gender roles in an alternate Regency England while showcasing entertaining prose and characters. A delightful historical-fantasy novel that will capture readers in its layered storyline' *Booklist*

'Reading the clever deployment of weaponized manners never gets old; in Cho's charming prose, *The True Queen* weaves a very pleasant spell indeed' *NPR*

'A clever, thoughtful book . . . hopeful, and a genuine balm for the soul' *SFandFReviews*

Zen Cho was born and raised in Malaysia and now lives in the UK. She was a finalist for the John W. Campbell Award for Best New Writer for her short fiction and won the Crawford Award. Her debut novel, *Sorcerer to the Crown*, won the 2016 British Fantasy Society Award for Best Newcomer.

zencho.org
Twitter: @zenaldehyde
Facebook: zenchobooks

By Zen Cho

SORCERER TO THE CROWN
THE TRUE QUEEN

SPIRITS ABROAD

The True Queen

Zen Cho

PAN BOOKS

First published 2019 by Ace,
an imprint of Penguin Random House LLC,
a Penguin Random House Company, New York

First published in the UK 2019 by Macmillan

This paperback edition published 2019 by Pan Books
an imprint of Pan Macmillan
The Smithson, 6 Briset Street, London EC1M 5NR
Associated companies throughout the world
www.panmacmillan.com

ISBN 978-1-5098-0108-4

1 3 5 7 9 8 6 4 2

A CIP catalogue record for this book is available from the British Library.

Printed and bound by CPI Group (UK) Ltd, Croydon, CR0 4YY

Visit **www.panmacmillan.com** to read more about all our books
and to buy them. You will also find features, author interviews and
news of any author events, and you can sign up for e-newsletters
so that you're always first to hear about our new releases.

The TRUE QUEEN

PROLOGUE

At the beginning
On the shore

THE STORM WAS shattering.

Lightning struck a tree. The trunk split with extraordinary violence, but there was an inevitability to its destruction.

So, too, with her. As she was sundered in two, there was no surprise—only pain.

She heard herself crack, the ichor in her veins boiling, but then all noise was drowned out by the roar of the storm. In days past she had summoned lightning at a thought; the rain came and went at her command; the waves churned at her whim.

But those powers had been taken from her. Now it was she who was at the mercy of the elements, tossed about like a toy. She fought to hold on to the broken parts of herself, but they slipped out of her grasp.

Insensibility seized her. She was dragged down into darkness, not grateful, and yet relieved.

WHEN she opened her eyes, the first thing she saw was the dark bowl of the night sky. Faint stars were scattered across its curved surface, and a full white moon rode the clouds. The air smelt sweetly of rain, but the tempest had passed.

Now a hush held the world in the palm of its hand. A low voice rumbled through her bones, monotonous and familiar. It was the voice of the waves, running up the shore and receding.

She felt as if she had awakened after a deep, revivifying sleep. She could not remember what had happened before, but that she had suffered she did not doubt. All distress had passed with the storm, however. She felt pleasantly empty—weak, wrung out, but calm.

The sand whispered against her as she rose unsteadily to her feet. Before her was the sea. Behind her, the dark mass of the jungle loomed out of the night like a drowsing beast, only half-asleep.

She felt her way across the shore, going slowly, for her limbs felt new to her. The beach was scattered with the debris of the storm, and she tripped on a piece of wood, grazing her knee.

The silence of the world began to frighten her. She felt alone, abandoned by all she had known—even her own self, for she could not remember what she was called. Trees lined the shore, graceful assemblies of coconut palms and casuarinas. But when she addressed them, they did not answer.

She longed for a friendly voice, the touch of a hand she knew. She had been asleep for so long. If only someone would tell her what had happened . . .

Her foot knocked against something solid. This log seemed different—solid, but more yielding. She crouched down, reaching out, and felt warm flesh, the jutting edge of bone. The body was breathing. It stirred at her touch.

The girl opened her eyes. They gleamed as they caught the light of the moon, and they held the same look she must have had on her own face—a look of recognition and relief. "Muna."

"Is that my name?" said Muna, but she was not really questioning it. She had known at once that they belonged to each other. "I have forgotten yours."

"I was called Sakti, I think," said the other. "Help me up, *kak*," she said, calling Muna "sister," and from then on that was how they addressed each other.

1

MUNA

THE FORESTS OF Janda Baik were imposing even in the full glare of daylight. In the half-light of dawn they were something else altogether—an extrusion of another, inhuman world, beyond terror or awe.

The forests blanketed a large part of the island, but the villages clung to the coast. The people of the island went quietly in the shadow of the jungle, avoiding its notice. What came to pass in the jungle was the business of witches and spirits.

Of course, such business was precisely Mak Genggang's stock-in-trade. In appearance she was like any aged village woman to be found bent over cooking pots in a kitchen or selling vegetables in a market. Her manner, which combined warmth with an imperiousness that would not have been out of place in a palace, would not distinguish her from any other matriarch in her *batik* cloths.

Yet her appearance was deceptive. As everyone in Janda Baik knew, Mak Genggang was the foremost witch of the region, first among the magicians in the polities along the Straits. The King of Siam himself was said to have sought her counsel; she was renowned among practitioners of the magic arts in China and India; and she counted among her friends England's Sorceress Royal, who presided over the magicians of that distant country. Mak Genggang's name was known even in the Unseen Realm—the hidden world where the spirits live, next door to our own.

Despite her great powers she was a kindly woman, but as with many strong people who are not often afraid, it did not come naturally to her to take thought of the fears of the weak. It had been she who insisted that Muna and her sister Sakti depart at the start of the day, before the sun had quite risen.

"Magic is always strongest at a border," the witch had explained. "Whether it be between jungle and village, or earth and sea, or day and night."

Sakti's face had twitched. Muna had known just how she felt. Left to herself, Muna would not have set off any earlier than noon, when the sun would be high in the sky, its light inescapable.

"We will be guided by your judgment, of course, *mak cik*," Muna said. "But will not it be easier for us to see our way if we leave later in the day?"

"The sooner you are off, the better," said the witch firmly.

They had risen at dawn, when it was dark, and the sky was still a deep blue when they arrived at the edge of the jungle. Under the trees lay a shadowy world, full of mystery and discomfort— leeches, snakes, dangerous beasts . . . and magic. For through the jungle lay the shortest route to the Unseen Realm, the abode of djinns and spirits, whence all magic ultimately flowed.

"If we put you on a ship to England, it would be a year before you saw its shores," said Mak Genggang. "But the Unseen Realm borders all mortal lands, and it will take you no time at all to get there through the jungle. Any fool who wanders in the forest risks stumbling into the world of the spirits, if he does not take care."

Muna had heard all the usual stories of such fools, and the grisly ends to which they came. The tales were not such as to light in her any flame of desire to model herself on their heroes. "But is it safe to go this way, *mak cik?*"

"Of course it is not safe," said Mak Genggang impatiently. "But it would not be safe for you to remain here either. I shall make a path for you, and if you walk briskly, you will be in England before the Sorceress Royal has sat down to her breakfast."

The ceremony for the opening of the path was a simple one. Mak Genggang did not chant, nor work any great magic, so far as Muna could tell. She merely bowed her head, muttering and prodding the grass with a stick, as though she were searching for something she had lost.

Muna drew her shawl closer around her, shivering at the chill morning air. There must be more to the witch's activities than was apparent to unmagical eyes, for Sakti watched Mak Genggang with interest, seeming to forget her apprehension at the journey ahead.

There were only three of them at the forest's edge. No one else in Mak Genggang's household had been told of their departure. Of course Muna saw the need for discretion—it was no one's fault but their own that they were being sent away in secret.

Yet she regretted that she could not bid everyone good-bye. Like most persons of importance Mak Genggang boasted a numerous following, though hers was more variegated than was usual. In her substantial wooden house, set back from the rest of the village, resided a shifting population of witches, apprentices, servants, slaves, bondswomen, poor relations, strays of all descriptions and even a number of lamiae.

These last had alarmed Muna when she had first joined the witch's household, but use had accustomed her to them. They were not unlike mortal females—which was perhaps not surprising, for lamiae are nothing more than the spectres of women who die nursing a great grievance. The chief point that distinguished them from other women was their predilection for consuming the vitals of humans; they were particularly fond of infants. Those who lived under Mak Genggang's protection were tame, however, observing strict codes of proper behaviour. They were inordinately fond of gossip and prone to quarrelling among themselves—but these were foibles shared by most of the witch's dependents.

Yet Muna had grown attached to her fellow servants in the weeks since Mak Genggang had found her and Sakti wandering confused upon the shore, and taken them under her protection. Muna thought wistfully of the girl who slept on the pallet next to hers. She had often wished Puteh would not insist on repeating her conversations with a certain well-favoured youth in the village when Muna wished to sleep, but now she would miss that excitable voice buzzing in her ear. And she would miss Kak Lena, who reigned over Mak Genggang's kitchen. She had promised to teach Muna Mak Genggang's recipe for *sambal* (a secret as jealously guarded as any of the witch's magic spells), but Muna would never learn it now . . .

"Why do you sniff?" whispered Sakti, with what for her was unusual percipience.

"It is nothing," said Muna, embarrassed. She flicked her tears away with her shawl. "Only—I was thinking of everyone, you know! Aren't you sorry to leave, *adik*?"

"No," said Sakti. "You know I have been longing for something to happen!"

Muna sighed, but she had not really expected any other response from Sakti. She did not doubt they were sisters: how else could Sakti have known her name the moment they woke, though they remembered nothing else of their past lives? Certainly they looked alike—though Sakti was the prettier, with larger eyes, longer lashes and a clearer golden skin—but they seemed to share no other point of resemblance.

It was supposed they had been lost at sea during the storm—such a storm as Janda Baik had not seen in living memory, devastating crops and drowning several fishermen. But neither Muna nor Sakti could say what village they were from, nor name their family.

"The shock has chased these things out of your mind," Mak Genggang had said, "but you will remember in time and then we will find your people."

But they did not remember, though the days passed, turning insensibly into weeks.

The lapse of time had not worried Muna. It was inconvenient not to have memories, to be sure—yet life under Mak Genggang's protection was comfortable. Muna had been set to work in the kitchen, and since in the witch's household the art of cookery was as highly developed and esteemed as that of magic, she had found the work of absorbing interest. She had made friends among her fellow servants, and rapidly become part of the life of the house.

As for her sister, Sakti had been singled out by Mak Genggang from the outset for her remarkable magical gift. She had been elevated to the rank of apprentice and relieved of the greater part of her domestic duties so that she might devote her time to the study of magic.

Muna herself lacked any magical facility, but she was not exercised by this. Magic hardly seemed to make Sakti happy. To be admitted to Mak Genggang's lessons in magic was accounted a great honour—noblemen and princesses had eagerly sought the privilege—but Sakti did not value her good fortune as she ought. Hers was a restless temperament and she chafed under the burden of Mak Genggang's authority.

"The old woman is a tyrant!" she said to Muna. "I don't see how you can bring yourself to bow and scrape to her, and say *yes, mak cik* and *no, mak cik* as you do."

The truth was that Muna was fond of Mak Genggang. The witch could be overbearing, but it was natural that one so old and powerful should believe she knew what was best. But to say this to Sakti would only annoy her.

"I find that the fact she is a powerful magician is a great incentive to courtesy," said Muna mildly. "Besides, we are indebted to her. She was under no obligation to take us in."

Sakti could not deny that the witch had been kind. Mak Genggang had shown no impatience for their departure, as the time passed and they remained at her household. As for Muna, she knew there must be people wondering at their disappearance—family and friends waiting for their return—but since she could not remember them, she felt no urgent need of a reunion. She should happily have remained with Mak Genggang indefinitely . . . if not for the curse.

She glanced at Sakti's waist, but the evidence of the curse was concealed by Sakti's sarong. The recollection of the wound made Muna soften towards her sister. Why should Sakti regret to leave a place that had served her so ill? Muna could only hope that England would suit her better.

Mak Genggang straightened, tossing her stick away and clapping her hands. "There! That will keep you as safe as you can hope to be in djinn-country. And I have laid speech-magic on each of you, so you ought not to have any difficulty speaking with the English."

The path unfurled before their feet: a silver rope of light, winding across the grass and into the jungle. Sakti and Muna regarded it in some doubt. Mak Genggang's businesslike manner did not quite suffice to persuade them that to stroll into the Unseen World was nothing out of the ordinary way.

"What shall we do if we encounter any spirits?" ventured Sakti.

"I have taught you spells for defence. You will not have forgot them all, surely?" said Mak Genggang.

"No, but—"

"You should not have need of them in any event, so long as you keep to the path. Few spirits will offer to molest you if they know you are under *my* protection," said Mak Genggang. "You must be discreet, however. The Queen of the Djinns has never minded what we do here in Janda Baik, but she has quarrelled with the English, and that has made her particular about who may travel between her realm and England. But if you are quick and quiet there is no reason she should ever know you have passed through her lands.

"You had best get along," she added, when Muna and Sakti still evinced an inclination to linger. "I have other business to attend to—and we don't want the English to come and find you still here. It would be just like their wickedness to surprise us! Go in safety, and give my regards to the Sorceress Royal and her young man. And mind you look after your sister!"

It would have been natural for the witch to have been addressing Sakti, since it was Sakti who had magic and was best equipped to defend them against the various perils of the Unseen. Yet Mak Genggang looked at Muna.

"I shall watch over my sister, *mak cik*," said Muna. She hesitated. "Thank you. You have been very good to us!"

They set off. Muna did not mean to look back, for she had a suspicion she would disgrace herself if she did. Yet she turned despite herself.

Though they had only advanced a dozen steps into the jungle, already the crowding trees obscured her view. Through the gaps between the boles, she caught a glimpse of the witch still standing there—a small, upright figure, deceptively frail, shading her eyes with one hand.

2

I T WAS COOL in the shade of the trees, with only a few rays of sunlight breaking through the canopy. The light brightened as Muna and Sakti walked, and they were aided, too, by the eerie glow given off by the witch's path.

Soon the forest closed in around them, trees towering overhead on every side. The vast busy stillness of the jungle seemed to demand a respectful silence in response, and it was necessary to pay careful attention to one's feet to avoid stumbling over the various hindrances littering the jungle floor—snakelike creepers, fallen stalks of bamboo, rotting logs and tree stumps.

Muna trudged after her sister, absorbed in melancholy thoughts of all she was leaving. She could ascribe the blame for their departure to no one but herself, for it had been her disastrous venture that obliged them now to leave the island. Yet it did not seem to her that she could have done anything else. She had acted with the best of intentions. She had only wished to break the curse.

When Muna and Sakti had been at the witch's household for a fortnight without recovering their memories, Mak Genggang had conducted healing rites over them. These had consisted of extremely long, dull ceremonies, with much chanting and scattering of rice paste. Finally the witch had declared:

"Some wicked magician has been at you! You have been split apart like a mangosteen and the pulp pried out."

She gave Muna a thoughtful look. "I thought it strange that you should have no magic at all, when your sister has such an excess. But this accounts for it. It has been stolen."

Muna was dozy from several hours of fighting sleep while Mak Genggang wove spells over them, and it took her a moment to understand what the witch had said. "Stolen? But how could anyone steal a person's magic?"

"It is an evil magic, but easily done by a magician not overly burdened by scruples," said Mak Genggang. "They need only steal the vital part of the soul that is the seat of one's magic—what some call the heart. That is why many magicians keep their hearts outside their bodies, as a sensible precaution. Someone has taken yours. In other words, child, you have been cursed!"

"But why has only Muna been cursed?" said Sakti, sounding faintly indignant. "What could she have done to anyone? If I were an evil magician wishing to curse one of us, I should choose myself."

"Adik!" said Muna in reproof, though she secretly sympathised with the sentiment. It was not that she wished Sakti to suffer, but it seemed most unjust. It was one thing to believe that God in His wisdom had decided not to bestow magic upon her—another to hear that she had had magic, but it had been stolen away.

"You are both cursed," said Mak Genggang. "You do not have your memories either, do you?"

"But what has been stolen from me?" said Sakti. "I lack for nothing."

"Would you say so?" said Mak Genggang. "I can think of any number of things your enemy may have stolen from you. Your conscience, your manners, your respect for your elders . . ."

"Can you break the curse, *mak cik*?" said Muna, before Sakti could provide any further fuel for Mak Genggang's complaints.

Mak Genggang frowned. "I have tried, but I cannot seem to come at the trouble. There is something very odd about the spell! It is a subtle magic, or I should not have failed to see it before. And yet the breach is clumsily wrought. I cannot see how it was done, nor how it is to be undone."

It vexed the witch to be faced with something she could not do. She tapped her knee, glaring at Muna and Sakti.

"If I had the name of the enchanter, perhaps . . . Do you have *no* recollection of who might have done this to you?"

But neither of them had any notion of who their enemy could be.

Mak Genggang was not a woman to let a problem lie without seeking to solve it. She had her apprentices mix up stinking concoctions which Muna and Sakti were obliged to swallow, and taught them cryptic formulae they were to chant at sunset and sunrise, when the veil between the worlds wore thin.

But she lacked time to devote proper thought to the matter, for she was preoccupied with greater affairs. It was whispered that foreign powers had designs upon Janda Baik, which were giving the Sultan much anxiety. Whatever the truth of the matter, Mak Genggang spent most of her days at the palace, conferring with the Sultan and his advisers.

Once Muna had recovered from her first shock, the curse ceased to worry her. She was a practical soul and saw little good in fretting about what she could not change. Besides, the curse did not seem to impair her health, or Sakti's.

Or so she had thought, till Sakti came to her one day with the air of one who has a great secret.

"I have something to show you," said Sakti.

Muna had been charged with cooking a pot of rice and she would have preferred to be left to it. But Sakti lingered, winking and nodding, till Muna was obliged to take the hint. She begged Puteh to look after her pot and followed Sakti out to the veranda. "Could not you have shown me in the kitchen?"

"In front of Puteh?" said Sakti, with scorn. "No *tempayan* ever had a larger mouth. Anything I said in front of *her*, the witch would know by the evening."

This made Muna look more closely at her sister. Sakti was not quite her usual self; she radiated a brittle energy. There was a strange triumph in her eyes, mingled with anxiety.

"What's wrong?" said Muna, starting to feel worried, but Sakti refused to answer till they were on the outskirts of the orchard behind Mak Genggang's house.

Here, where the witch's fruit trees began to blend into the scrubby fringe of the jungle, there was little risk of being overheard. Even so, Sakti made Muna wait while she wove a spell to prevent any tree or zephyr from carrying tales.

"I don't think it's *true* that Mak Genggang talks to the trees," said Muna, but even as she spoke she recollected several instances of the witch scolding her garden as she might reprimand an erring servant. "That is, I doubt they talk back."

Sakti was not convinced. "It is you who are always telling me how she is the greatest magician east of India and west of China. I'd wager collecting rumours from trees is the least she does."

She clasped Muna's hand. "Swear you will not tell Mak Genggang what I show you now!"

"You have not stolen from the witch, have you?" said Muna, alarmed. Sakti was given to melodramatics, but this seemed to go beyond that.

Sakti drew herself up, ruffled. "Stolen from her! She has nothing

I desire," she said grandly. "Rather, it is she who is stealing the very life from me!"

"What can you mean?"

"Look!" said Sakti. She unwrapped her sarong with a flourish. Muna gasped.

"Isn't it horrible?" said Sakti, with grim relish.

Where her navel should have been, there was nothing whatsoever. It was as though a hole had been carved out of her person. There was no wound or bruise—the flesh simply faded into nothingness. Through the gap, Muna could glimpse the bushes behind Sakti.

Muna reached out, her hand trembling, but did not dare touch her sister. She felt sick. ". . . How did this come about?"

"I woke yesterday and found I had been hollowed out," said Sakti. "See, it goes right through me." She put two fingers through the gap.

"Oh, don't—don't!" said Muna, shuddering. "Does it hurt?"

"No," said Sakti. "I feel nothing." Her satisfaction at making a sensation was tempered with unease as she looked down at herself. "But I believe it is growing. It is larger today."

"The curse," breathed Muna. A pang of guilt shook her. She had been content to await Mak Genggang's pleasure, trusting that the witch would break the curse in good time. "I had no notion! Why didn't you tell me before?"

"I thought it might go away," said Sakti. "The witch taught us a great magic the day before yesterday; I thought perhaps this was the effect. But none of the other apprentices seem affected. It can only be the curse."

Muna pressed her hand against herself. Her finger dipped into her own navel, meeting reassuringly solid flesh. "But why should it affect you so, and not me?"

"I wondered," said Sakti. She wound her sarong around herself again, hiding the unnerving absence at her centre. "But the answer is obvious. The curseworker has already robbed you of your magic: that is why you have none, though magic generally runs in the family. Now that hateful woman has started on me—but a greater part of me is composed of magic. To drain me of my magic is to destroy me!"

"You have discovered who cursed us?" said Muna, startled. "It is a woman?"

"It does not take much guessing," said Sakti. "The answer is plain. Who else could it be but the witch?"

Muna stared. Weariness descended upon her.

"You cannot think *Mak Genggang* is the author of the curse!"

"Have not you ever thought it strange that she should be so powerful—an old woman of obscure birth like her?"

"She draws on the virtue of the island. Everyone says so."

Sakti dismissed this with a wave of her hand. "Superstitious nonsense! Who ever heard of an island being magical? Where would its magic have come from? Isn't it likelier that the witch steals her power from others? It explains why she should have taken us in, when we have no hold on her."

"But Mak Genggang's household includes a great many people who have no claim upon her," protested Muna. "Not all of them have magic. Indeed, most do nothing useful. You've said yourself their only talent seems to be that of sponging upon their friends."

"I expect she takes in the useless ones to disguise her true scheme," said Sakti, but Muna said severely:

"That is nonsense and you know it. Why should Mak Genggang have told us of the curse if she was the curseworker? We would never have known of it otherwise. Think of all the rice paste she has expended on breaking our curse, never asking for a single *wang* to defray the expense!"

"I don't believe rice paste is much of an expense," said Sakti. "As for why she told us, that is all part of her cunning. So long as we believed she meant to help us, we were not likely to suspect her. You must own it is strange that even after so many weeks, we should have no memory of who we are or what happened to us. If Mak Genggang were draining off our souls to increase her stocks of magic, that would explain it."

"There is a simpler explanation," said Muna. "We have been cursed, and it was Mak Genggang who told us so and is trying to break it!

"I think you are shockingly ungrateful," she added, with energy. "You need not have invented this absurd story, just because you do not like lessons, or the fact that Mak Genggang does not care how pretty you are but scolds you just as she scolds everyone else—"

"*Oh!*"

"You would have been better off telling Mak Genggang about your affliction," said Muna. "We ought to tell her now. I am sure she will find a means of reversing it."

She turned, intending to return to the house. But Sakti seized her arm in a frightful grip.

"Hush, or you will bring the whole village down upon us!" said Sakti over Muna's yelps. "If Mak Genggang knows we have seen through her deception, she will have no reason to restrain herself any longer. She must destroy us, or risk losing her good name. I expect she will have us murdered!"

"You have been listening to too many *syair* about depraved mothers-in-law," said Muna. She tried to tug her arm away. "Ow! Let go!"

"I shan't, till you swear you will not go to the witch. You promised you would not breathe a word of what I told you!"

"But—"

"I will seal your lips with magic if I must," said Sakti, "but I had rather not. I must conserve my soul-stuff. The more I use, the more I risk losing of myself."

This reminder of Sakti's affliction made Muna go limp in her sister's grasp. She searched Sakti's face. "Do you think the curse-worker has stolen your heart? Mak Genggang said he took mine."

Sakti looked grave. "I don't know what may have been done to me. But I fear I am fading away."

Muna felt a chill of apprehension. It overcame her frustration at her sister's obduracy.

"Let me go," she said. "I shan't say a word to Mak Genggang, since you don't wish it. But what do you propose we do instead?"

"Run away, of course," said Sakti, releasing her. "I should not wonder if I began to feel better directly once we were free of the witch's influence."

Muna's heart sank. Yet she should have foreseen this. Sakti's restlessness could have led to no other end.

"But what if you do not?" she said. "What if we find that Mak Genggang has nothing to do with the curse and it is still eating away at you? Then we will be alone, with nowhere to go and no one to turn to. What shall we do then?"

Sakti turned up her nose. "If you don't wish to come with me, you need only say so! I don't mind. I am perfectly happy to go alone."

This was pure bravado, for Muna could see that her sister was afraid. But Sakti was strong-willed and did not readily part with her prejudices. Since she had conceived one against the witch, she would be far happier to run away, even alone into unknown terrors, than to admit she was wrong.

Muna's mind raced. She must prevent Sakti from doing anything reckless, but how?

Her eyes fell on a wild banana tree. Banana trees were said to be haunted by lamiae—those lamiae, that is, who did not benefit from the hospitality of a sympathetic witch. The sight imparted the inspiration for which she had been looking.

"Of course I shall go wherever you will," said Muna. "But let us not depart quite yet. I have an idea."

"Oh yes?" said Sakti sceptically.

"What if we could break the curse ourselves?" said Muna.

3

MUNA

THE HOUSE OF the English raja of Malacca was an imposing building, fit for the series of foreign kings that had occupied it, for it had been built by the Dutch before the English had taken the city. Its brick construction gave it a heaviness that ordinary wooden houses lacked—an air of permanence and power. Sakti gasped as she took in the building's red roof, white walls and dazzling rows of windows.

"You could fit two of the Sultan's palace on Janda Baik in there!" she whispered.

Muna was beginning to regret the suggestion that had brought them there.

"They say the English king of Malacca is mad for magic," she had told Sakti. "He has a collection of magic spells and artefacts from England and India, as well as the countries hereabouts."

Sakti had been rather offended by the notion of Muna's knowing more of a magical matter than herself. "Who told you this?"

"I overheard the lamiae speaking of it," said Muna. "They were gossiping outside the kitchen and did not know I heard. It seems the English king is fond of collecting magic. Tuan Farquhar pays a *wang* for every magical verse he is given and more for whole formulae, so there is a great crowd of people outside his house every day, clamouring to sell him their spells. He has engaged two scribes and has them write the spells down in books."

"A *wang* for every verse!" said Sakti, intrigued.

Muna saw where her thoughts tended.

"Mak Genggang would be bound to find out if you attempted to sell her magic to the English," she said. "Even the lamiae would not do it, for fear of provoking her!"

"I did not think of selling him *real* magic, of course," said Sakti, injured. "A good spell is worth far more than a *wang*. But the English king is no magician, and one could easily invent a credible formula to take in a layman." At Muna's look, she said, "If the man has the impertinence to buy magic without being a magician, he deserves to be cheated. He ought to know his place."

"That is nonsense and you know it," said Muna, frowning.

"Oh, very well!" said Sakti. "But if you don't wish to profit from the Englishman's magic-madness, what do you mean by mentioning him?"

"Do not you see," said Muna, "if he has spells from England and India, he will have magic unknown even to Mak Genggang. Magic that could help us break the curse—cure your disease!"

Sakti was struck by the idea. Her look of scepticism fell away. Encouraged, Muna hurried on, "Perhaps it is not likely we will find the antidote to the curse, if it has proved beyond Mak Genggang's power to break it. But there may be a spell that would shed light on the nature of the curse, or its origins—a spell that would give us the curseworker's name."

Sakti gave her a pitying look. "We already know who the curse-worker is. It is only that you don't wish to credit it."

Muna raised her eyebrows. "Supposing you are right, can you tell me Mak Genggang's true name?"

"Why—" Sakti pursed her mouth, displeased. "No. But no one knows it."

"Well, shan't we need it if we are to break the curse?" demanded Muna. "When Mak Genggang is asked to cure any magical disease, the first thing *she* does is find out the name of whoever caused it."

This was an undeniable hit. Sakti looked vexed.

"That is only because one generally cures a magical illness by calling upon its author and threatening to break his head if he does not take the curse off," she said. "You don't mean to suggest we adopt *that* course with Mak Genggang?"

They both imagined it. Sakti looked rather pale.

"If we know her true name, we shall have other courses open to us," said Muna, but Sakti rolled her eyes.

"The truth is you do not think it is Mak Genggang at all!"

"Even if it is," said Muna, "we ought to make certain of it, rather than abandoning ourselves to the world on a mere suspicion! Come now, *adik*—would not you like to break the curse yourself, and tell Mak Genggang you had done it?"

Sakti had given in—more because an expedition across the Straits to the English king's house smacked appealingly of adventure than because she had had any real belief that it would teach them anything about the curse. As for Muna, she had been so anxious to distract Sakti from the idea of running away that her proposal had seemed less wild than it now appeared to her, hunkered down upon the grass outside the English king's house, with the sun beating on the back of her head.

Even Sakti's high spirits flagged at the sight of the King's house—and the armed sepoys guarding the entrance. "*Kak*, there are soldiers!"

Muna had not accounted for soldiers. This now seemed stupid to her. Vexed with herself, she said irritably, "Why, you did not think the King's own house would be left undefended?"

"I am sure you did not think we should have to battle sepoys when you said we should come," said Sakti, unimpressed. She reflected. "Perhaps we could turn ourselves into birds and fly in at an open window."

Disconcerted, Muna said, "Can you do that? Is not shapeshifting a very great magic? Mak Genggang says none but the most skilled magicians should attempt it."

"Oh, everything is 'Mak Genggang says' with you!" said Sakti. "I have never tried to change my form, but it cannot be that difficult. You would start by imagining yourself as a bird . . ."

She was already beginning to look rather beaky around the face. Muna shook her shoulder.

"Let us not!" she said. "I know what we ought to do."

It was Sakti's dismissive reference to Mak Genggang that had given her the idea. Sakti could call the witch wicked, but she could not deny that Mak Genggang was effective. What, Muna asked herself, would Mak Genggang do now?

Thinking this was like a sort of magic in itself. Muna suddenly saw the sepoys through new eyes. They were only bored young men stranded in a foreign country, perspiring in their regimentals.

Mak Genggang was of a thrifty disposition; she never used magic where force of character would do. Muna seized her sister's arm, brushing glossy black feathers off Sakti's head. "Come!"

Muna marched up to the entrance of the King's house, Sakti grumbling behind her. The sepoys looked doubtfully at them, but Muna was at the door and rapping energetically before they could issue any challenge. She frowned at the sepoys, as much as to say, *They had best not keep me waiting!*

The manservant who opened the door was a Malay, to Muna's secret relief. She had never spoken to a foreigner before and she was not altogether confident of her ability to mislead one into believing that she was a person of importance.

"Good morning, *adik*," said Muna in her stateliest manner, though the manservant looked of an age with her, and in common courtesy she ought to have addressed him as an elder, not a junior.

The manservant blinked, but he seemed to decide to overlook her lapse in manners. "Do you have a petition for the King? He has gone out."

"That is no inconvenience to me," said Muna graciously. "Tuan Farquhar desired me to come while he was away and put his library of spells in order. I am a witch," she explained, "and this is my assistant."

Sakti made an outraged noise, but Muna drove her elbow into her sister's side.

"Surely Tuan Farquhar told the household to expect me?" said Muna.

"You must be mistaken," said the manservant. "Tuan Farquhar cannot have asked for you. Perhaps you do not know, but the English abhor witches. Their customs prohibit the practice of magic by women."

"By Englishwomen, to be sure," said Muna. "But what business is that of mine? Tuan Farquhar sought one who understood our magic—one who could study the spells he has been sold and ensure that he has not been cheated—and he was given my name.

"I am sure his scribes have done their best," she added, in a tone of kind condescension, "but they are not witches. They are bound to have introduced errors while taking down the spells. I beg you will lead me to the King's collection. I am told it is extensive, and I must be off by the afternoon, for I have a healing ceremony to conduct."

"A case of possession by evil spirits," added Sakti. "Very sad!"

When the manservant hesitated, Muna fixed a stern eye on him.

"Unless you would like to account to Tuan Farquhar for turning me away?" she said. "You should know that witches are no fonder of Englishmen than Englishmen are of us. He is not likely to find another who is willing to assist."

The manservant wavered. Muna tossed her head, turning to Sakti.

"Let us go!" she said. "You were quite right to say we ought not to lower ourselves to help the Englishman. What business is it of ours if he has been cheated? Let him take false for true, the worthless for the valuable. It would serve him right for his servants' arrogance!"

Sakti was beginning to enjoy her role of witch's helper. "I cannot think why he paid us so many visits, begging for help, if he only meant to send us packing. It is a deliberate insult, depend upon it!"

"An insult not only to us, but to all witches," agreed Muna. "We had better spread the news abroad at once—tell everyone the English are not to be trusted."

"I beg your pardon," said the harassed manservant. "Pray come in! If you knew . . . but it is true Tuan Farquhar wished to know if the spells he collected were real magic. I meant no offence, *kak*."

Muna held her head high as they sailed through the door, but it was fortunate that the manservant did not look back at Sakti, for *she* did not trouble to keep her countenance at all.

* * *

THE English raja's collection was larger than Muna had expected. There were magical artefacts, in tall cabinets fronted with glass, but the main part of the collection consisted of spell books—rows and rows of these, stretching from floor to ceiling in the room where the manservant left them. Muna had not dreamt that there might be so many books in the world, much less books of magic.

"We shall never get through them all before that man returns!" she whispered, appalled.

"No," Sakti agreed, round-eyed. "Tuan Farquhar must have kept his scribes hard at it. I should think the people of Malacca have sold him all the magic they have."

But there were greater surprises in store. Muna had expected that they would be obliged to restrict themselves to investigating the spells Tuan Farquhar's scribes had taken down in Malay. No other language was used in Janda Baik, and there was no reason to suppose either Muna or Sakti could understand anything else.

When Muna took down her first spell book, however, reaching for the tome closest to hand, she found herself reading it with perfect ease. This was unexpected, for the book was not in Malay.

"That is English, I believe," said Sakti, when Muna showed her the book. "How curious that we should understand it!"

Their want of self-knowledge meant that Muna and Sakti often made surprising discoveries about themselves, but this was the most unexpected yet. Not all the books in the collection proved accessible—some defeated them, being written in scripts they did not recognise—but it appeared that in their past life they had made sufficient study of English and Arabic to be able to read both languages with ease.

Sakti was delighted. "How clever I am, and I never knew it!"

The revelation had given Muna's thoughts a different turn.

"Our family must have been wealthy, as well as liberal, to have educated their daughters," she said. "They must have been pious to have had us learn Arabic. And they must live here—in Malacca, ruled by the English. There is no reason why they should have had us learn English otherwise."

"Perhaps we are princesses!" said Sakti, brightening.

Muna would have thought it would be interesting to read about magic, but if the scholars of English magic were to be believed, their thaumaturgy was a very different beast from the magic that permeated the witch's household. Mak Genggang's magic was a wild, living force, as everyday as the weather and as untameable. The English made their magic sound exceedingly dull in comparison. To understand what they said of it demanded all of Muna's powers of concentration, so it was some time before she realised that Sakti had abandoned her books.

"*Adik*, what are you about?"

Sakti was standing by the cabinets, turning over an article in her hands with fascination. "Look! It is a dead imp. I wonder how they prevented it from rotting. I cannot tell that there is any magic on it to keep it sweet."

Muna recoiled, holding her book up before her. She would not put it down till Sakti had restored her find to its original place.

"You had best not touch anything else," said Muna. "For all you know there was a horrid curse on that imp, which could have rubbed off on you."

"Nonsense!" said Sakti, but she rather contradicted herself by adding, "We could always bathe in flowers later to cleanse ourselves of any bad luck."

"Yes, but you might *try* to avoid picking up any more bad luck. One curse is enough, surely," said Muna. "Come and look at the instructions for this spell." It was in a book of English spells—a device for discovering the author of an enchantment.

"You lay your hand on the enchantment and ask the spirits, *Whose magic is this?*" said Muna. "And if the spell succeeds, they tell you. Do you think you could cast it?"

"It sounds easy enough," said Sakti. Casting spells interested her more than reading about them. She became businesslike. "But how am I to lay my hand on the enchantment if it is *in* us?" She looked around, frowning.

"Is that a piece of string by you?"

She knotted the string around Muna's wrist, then held out her own to Muna. "If you tie it around me, too, that will do to mark the curse. What is the formula?"

Muna read it out from the book, Sakti repeating the syllables after her. When she said, *"Whose magic is this?"* the words themselves wound out of Sakti's mouth, written in green smoke. For a moment they hung in the air.

"Adik," said Muna, worried. It could not be healthy for a human to breathe smoke, surely?

Sakti coughed, dispersing the words of the spell. "What a strange effect!" she said cheerfully. "I have never seen that before." A look of surprise came over her face. She picked up a pen and wrote the words:

SAKTI MUNA

"What is that?" said Muna.

"The spirits' answer." Sakti looked put out. "But it is only our names!"

Muna reflected. "You asked the spirits *whose magic is this?*

Perhaps they misunderstood, and the spell is simply telling us what the source of your magic is."

"But *you* do not have any magic. Why should the spirits have named you?"

"The spell might have confused us. You could cast the spell on me alone," suggested Muna. "Since the curseworker stole my magic, the only magic remaining in me should be his—the magic of his curse."

Sakti slipped her wrist out of the loop of string, but the second attempt produced the same result.

"Perhaps the magic has not come off," said Muna. "Are you sure you have said the formula correctly?"

Sakti was not accustomed to her spells going awry. She said crossly, "Of course I did. Read out the instructions again. I expect you have missed a step."

"I have not," said Muna, but an inspiration had come to her. "I tell you what it is. Your question is too vague. I expect you are confusing the spirits. Could not you simply ask for the true name of the enchanter who cursed us?"

This time after speaking the spell, Sakti wrote a different word.

Muna read it out: "'Midsomer' . . . it must be an English name." She looked up, her eyes shining. "This could not possibly be Mak Genggang's true name. She is not the curseworker after all. I told you so!"

Sakti screwed up her face. She obviously meant to give an uncivil answer, but instead she gave a stifled shriek, staring at something behind Muna. The blood drained from her face.

Muna smelt frangipane—the small, sweet-smelling white blossoms people called grave flowers. She whirled around.

A ghoulish face hovered at the window. Long yellow nails

tapped the glass. The creature's mouth stretched wide, revealing yellow fangs and a scarlet tongue, but then the glowing eyes narrowed.

"Why, you are only natives!" exclaimed the lamia in disappointment. It was one of Mak Genggang's vampiresses.

Muna stumbled backwards, seizing Sakti's hand. Lamiae had poor vision during the day, their eyes being best adapted to the darkness of night. It was not too late. If they could only get away before the lamia recognised them . . .

Muna was nearly at the door when it swung open. She looked directly into the startled pink face of a foreign gentleman.

"What in heaven's name . . . ?"

With remarkable presence of mind, the lamia smashed the glass and leapt into the room. She seized Muna and Sakti and bounded out of the window again before the Englishman could do anything but gawp.

The air whistled in Muna's ears. The lamia flew over the city of Malacca, a sister under each arm. Behind them the Englishman leant out of the broken window, shouting, but his words were snatched away by the wind.

"If you keep writhing, I shall let go, see if I don't!" snapped the lamia.

"I shall make disgusting eating, I warn you!" shouted Sakti, struggling. "I have a bad disposition and everyone knows that turns mortal flesh rancid!"

"Where are you taking us?" said Muna. She shut her eyes, feeling queasy—they were a horrible vast distance from the ground.

"Where but the witch's house?" said the lamia. "If you were wise, you would beg me to drop you in the sea. That would be no worse punishment than Mak Genggang will deal when she hears what you have done!"

* * *

To be flown through the skies by a furious vampiress was terrifying, but the return to earth was even worse. Mak Genggang gave them such a scolding as seemed to shake the very timbers of her house.

Yet she did not throw Muna and Sakti off, as Muna had feared she might. They were charged with tedious tasks by way of penance—Muna was set to cleaning and Sakti to repairing the magic wards around the witch's house and orchard. But there was no suggestion that they should leave.

Two days passed; Muna and Sakti quarrelled seven times about whether they should tell Mak Genggang what they had learnt at the English king's house. The blemish at Sakti's navel had not improved, and she could not really believe any longer that it was Mak Genggang who was to blame for it. But Sakti would not own to being wrong, and Muna had yet to wear her down when Mak Genggang summoned them for an audience.

"I have received a messenger from the English," she told them. For once Mak Genggang's age, which one forgot in the full glare of her personality, was evident in her bearing. She looked tired, even frail. "He came to tell me that the Resident of Malacca—the English raja—caught women trespassing in his house two days ago. He has reason to believe they belong to my household and has demanded that I deliver them up. The intruders are thieves, or worse, says Tuan Farquhar, and they must be punished."

Muna and Sakti had been dreading another scolding, but this was a calamity neither had foreseen. They looked at each other in horror.

"But why does he want us, *mak cik*?" stammered Muna.

"Oh, it is not you they want," said Mak Genggang. "You are

only a pretext to seize control of Janda Baik. Tuan Farquhar knows I will not willingly give up any person under my protection, and when I refuse, well! He will not fail to make the most of it."

Muna was cold, though it was the middle of the afternoon, when the earth had been baked for hours in the relentless sunshine and the heat reached its zenith. Mak Genggang had every reason to surrender her and Sakti to the English. But . . . *when I refuse*, the witch had said. Surely Mak Genggang would not betray them.

"What does Tuan Farquhar want with Janda Baik?" said Sakti, baffled. "He has a great house, larger than our Sultan's palace, and reigns over a city many times the size of the island."

"They have need of a port for trade, and a base for their war against the French. Malacca is all very well, but the English seized it from the Dutch, and the Dutch are likely to want it back," said Mak Genggang. "What is more, Malacca does not have our magic."

"What did you say to the messenger, *mak cik*?" Muna said, in a voice she strove to keep even. She had no wish to insult the witch with her fear, but she could not help feeling nervous till Mak Genggang said:

"I sent him away, of course—impudent fellow! And I know what they will do now. Tuan Farquhar will say I am recalcitrant— we have no reason to defy him, unless you are spies and we intend an invasion of Malacca. He will say it is his clear duty to strike first. We will fight—he will pay a bitter price for victory—but we cannot hold out against the British forces; they are equal to the Dutch in sanguinariness, and they're superior in greed. The end of it will be that we shall be overrun!"

"No!" exclaimed Muna involuntarily. She thought of soldiers spilling onto the white shores of the island, savage men swarming the villages . . . "Oh, Mak Genggang, what can we do?"

"You might have refrained from going to the English king's

house and supplying him with an excuse for interference," said Mak Genggang drily. "But there! That is in the past—and all the magics for turning back time are best avoided, for they are liable to make worse muddles than they are designed to solve."

Sakti shifted restlessly, looking both guilty and irritated.

"We had no notion a brief call would cause such trouble," she said. "If we had known, of course . . . ! But we only wished to break our curse. It is not as though we took anything that would be missed. A formula may be cast any number of times."

Her manner was scarcely calculated to propitiate the witch, at a time when Mak Genggang had every reason to be vexed with them. But Mak Genggang only nodded, unsurprised. "It was for the curse you went, was it? I thought that was the case. What was this spell you cast, then?"

"It was an English spell," said Sakti. "But it is not as though we stole it!"

The consequences of their actions had shocked Sakti out of her obstinacy. After all her resistance to confiding in Mak Genggang, it was she who told the witch what they had discovered at the English king's house, though she omitted to mention her mysterious affliction.

When she told Mak Genggang the name the spell had given them, a faraway look came into the witch's eyes.

"'Midsomer,' did you say?" said Mak Genggang.

Muna looked hopefully at her. "Do you know this 'Midsomer,' *mak cik*? Is it an English name?"

"I believe it is." Mak Genggang frowned, tapping her knee. "I may have heard it before, but I cannot recollect . . . Midsomer, Midsomer!" Her tongue stumbled over the unfamiliar syllables. "These English names are impossible to keep in one's head."

She was vexed at her own forgetfulness. "It will come to me in time. I could ask the Sorceress Royal—but we shall already be at a disadvantage, for we must ask her to intervene with Tuan Farquhar on our behalf. I dislike begging for favours, but I do not see what else we can do."

Muna glanced at Sakti, but it seemed Sakti's ignorance on this point was as complete as her own. "Who is the Sorceress Royal?"

"It is what the English magicians call their chief—a witch of prodigious talent," said Mak Genggang. "She is notorious in her country, for she has established a school which educates females in their thaumaturgy, which is accounted a great scandal. Still, she wields considerable influence among the English and she is indebted to me, for I was able to do her a service or two before she attained her current position."

"A school for witches," echoed Muna. She sat upright, her eyes wide, as the seed of a notion began to sprout in her mind.

"But an Englishwoman will not help us against her countrymen, will she?" said Sakti. "Will not she take Tuan Farquhar's part against us?"

"Oh, we need have little fear of that!" said Mak Genggang. "If we were speaking of the young man who was Sorcerer Royal before, I might hesitate, indeed. Zacharias Wythe is burdened with a conscience—a fine thing to have, but dangerous in excess. But Prunella would never dream of allowing conscience to prevent her from helping her friends."

Still, she sighed. "Mind you, it sits ill with me to be beholden to any European. Prunella is a good warmhearted girl, but in these times I should rather have her in my debt than give her any hold over us. But it cannot be helped. When elephants battle, the mousedeer dies in the middle. It is this, or be trampled!"

She would have said more, but Muna broke in, saying, "*Mak cik,* may anyone attend the Sorceress Royal's school? That is to say, will she receive any female who desires to learn magic?"

Mak Genggang looked surprised. "I believe so. She wishes to open the practice of magic to persons of all kinds. The English as a whole are jealous of their magic; they hoard it as a miser hoards his gold."

"Then," said Muna, "why do not you send us there?"

The other two stared. Muna's heart was racing at her daring, but she must keep speaking before she lost her nerve, or was interrupted.

"Either we must give the English what they demand, or we must quarrel with them," she said. "We cannot afford to quarrel with them, so we must concede—or appear to. If you send us to the Sorceress Royal, that would take us out of Tuan Farquhar's reach. He could not accuse you of defying him, for after all you will only have done what he required. The English asked for us, therefore you sent us to England. Tuan Farquhar could not in decency complain of your preferring to entrust us to his countrywoman.

"It will be like rowing while going downriver," she added, "for it will put us in the way of making amends for our conduct. Perhaps we cannot equal the foreigners' ships and cannons, but in magic Janda Baik need not consider itself the inferior of any mortal kingdom. I daresay my sister will learn English magic quickly, and that will teach her its weaknesses too, so we may help defend Janda Baik against their encroachment."

Mak Genggang regarded Muna for a long moment, her expression inscrutable. Muna pressed her damp palms against her sarong, trying to look like someone capable of spying on the English.

"It is an interesting notion!" said the witch finally. "But that is not all you hope to do, surely. You wish to break the curse. Do you believe this 'Midsomer' is to be found in England?"

Muna flushed under Mak Genggang's penetrating gaze. "You said Midsomer was an English name, *mak cik*."

"What will you do if you find him?"

Muna glanced at Sakti. Sakti was looking at her in wonder, as amazed as if Muna had suddenly revealed an ability to fly. Encouraged, Muna turned back to the witch.

"My sister was trained by no less a witch than Mak Genggang," she said. "We shall think of something."

"Hmph!" said Mak Genggang: but she was pleased. "It is not a bad notion. It will vex Tuan Farquhar exceedingly. And to send the Sorceress Royal a scholar will have less of an appearance of petitioning her for a favour. Prunella has pressed me for some time to explain Malay magics to her—she has a great interest in our enchantery.

"There is little enough good that can be said of you," she said to Sakti, "but you do have some understanding of our magics! What do you say to your sister's suggestion? You have not shown any extraordinary devotion to your studies so far. But perhaps it is only my tutelage to which you object?"

Muna was in terror lest Sakti should be too honest—a failure of tact could scuttle the proposal. But Sakti could be diplomatic when it suited her.

"I should like to go to England, if you think it wise, *mak cik*," she said. "I would be proud to tell the English of your magic! But how would we travel there? Isn't it very far away?"

But to Mak Genggang, the distance between countries was nothing. She dismissed it with a wave of her hand.

"You would need a year at least if you were obliged to travel by conventional means," she said. "But we are not subject to such limitations. It is only a short path through the Unseen Realm. With your youth, you will not need more than a day to traverse it."

A shiver of foreboding ran up Muna's spine. "The Unseen Realm? You don't mean we would have to travel through the world of the spirits, *mak cik*?"

"Oh yes. Nothing easier in the world!" said Mak Genggang. "I shall lay the path for you. There is no reason you should run into any trouble, provided you are sensible."

"It sounds perfectly straightforward," said Sakti, who had never been sensible in her life. "When do we leave?"

4

The next day
The forests of Janda Baik

MUNA

AVING DECIDED TO adopt Muna's proposal, Mak Genggang lost no time. The very day after the witch had received Tuan Farquhar's messenger, Muna and Sakti set off for England.

I should have known what would come of my having ideas! thought Muna, as she picked her way across the jungle floor, keeping an anxious eye on her sister's back. Now they were banished from Janda Baik, perhaps for good for all Muna knew—for Mak Genggang had not said when they might return.

But they went for Sakti, Muna reminded herself. It was selfish to repine, when Sakti still suffered from her injury—that unnatural absence, carved into her flesh. There had been no time to look at it again this morning.

Muna opened her mouth, but before she could ask to see the blemish, Sakti turned her head. Her eyes were alight.

"I have been thinking," she said, "of what it would be like to meet a weretiger!"

Muna glanced around nervously, though she had neither seen nor heard signs of any beast larger than a moth since they had entered the jungle. "There is no risk of that, is there?"

"Well, you know they say there are villages of the creatures deep in the jungle," said Sakti cheerfully. "Cities, indeed, larger than Malacca! But tigers are unsociable animals; perhaps they have concealed themselves with magic. Still, I am surprised we have not seen a single spirit yet. The *hantu tetek*, perhaps, flying down to seize us and smother us in her bosom—"

"Those are just a story to frighten children with."

"Or the *hantu langut*," said Sakti, "that has a dog's head and a man's body, and stalks the jungle with his face turned upwards. They say even to look upon him once brings death!

"I expect *you* would rather meet a *bunian*," she added, in a tone of faint condescension. "I would not mind it, but there is not much to distinguish them from mortals, save their being invisible."

Muna glared at Sakti. "I would rather meet *none* of those creatures—" But Muna swallowed her words, recollecting that they were in the jungle, treading earth that belonged more to spirits than mankind.

"I wish you would not speak so recklessly!" she added in a whisper. "What if you should draw the fine ones' attention? Recall that we are on the boundary of the Unseen Realm!"

"Oh, we have passed that," said Sakti nonchalantly. "We are in the Hidden World now! Cannot you smell it? The air is full of magic!" She took an appreciative breath of air.

Muna looked around again, but she saw nothing to mark their passage from the known world to the unknown. The same jungle surrounded them, populated by familiar trees. The only noise was the incessant background ringing of cicadas' voices, interrupted by the occasional birdcall.

She felt a mix of relief and disappointment. She had no desire to encounter a settlement of weretigers or any other spirits, so far from Mak Genggang's civilising influence, but it was somewhat of a comedown to find the Unseen World so little different from the mortal realm.

"I have never smelt magic before," said Muna, "so I suppose there is no reason why I should have started now."

"It is wonderfully invigorating," Sakti assured her. "No wonder the witch is so hale despite her great age, if she comes here often!"

Sakti's eyes did seem brighter. Since Sakti had disclosed her complaint, it had seemed to Muna in her anxiety that Sakti was fading visibly, her ill health evident in her pallor and thin limbs. Now, however, Sakti's face looked round and full; a healthy colour tinted her cheeks. Muna recollected that she had meant to ask after Sakti's injury.

"What of your wound, *adik*?" she said. "I have not looked at it yet today."

Sakti raised her eyes to the canopy, but she began to unknot her sarong. "There will hardly be anything new to see," she said, "only more nothing—oh!"

"What is it?" said Muna, but then she saw what had made Sakti cry out.

The unnatural absence was restored. In its place was Sakti's flesh, whole and unblemished.

"I am cured!" said Sakti, delighted.

It was no illusion—when Muna reached out, she touched Sakti's warm, living flesh, as solid as Muna's own. Muna had not realised till then what a burden of anxiety she had been carrying. Relief washed over her; tears sprang to her eyes.

"But this is wonderful," she cried, embracing her sister. *"Alhamdulillah!"*

"I told you I needed only to escape that woman's influence to be restored."

Muna lowered her arms, her joy abruptly dampened. "You cannot still think Mak Genggang put the curse on us? After all we learnt at the King's house? What about 'Midsomer'?"

Sakti tossed her head, looking mulish. "Perhaps the English magician is her accomplice. Indeed, now I think of it, nothing is likelier. She said the name sounded familiar, and even now we are being sent to her ally in England . . ."

"You know you do not believe that," said Muna crossly. "We are no farther from Mak Genggang's influence than we were when we went to Malacca, and your blemish did not disappear there." She had insisted on checking this upon their arrival in Malacca. "It is perfectly evident it is not a matter of distance from Mak Genggang."

"So you say," said Sakti, "but we are farther from her influence than we can ever have been since she found us. You forget that we are in the Unseen Realm now!"

A thought struck Muna. "Could you take us back to Janda Baik without getting lost?"

At Muna's insistence they retraced their steps through the trees, till Sakti said:

"This is Janda Baik again. But why did you wish to return? We shall be late arriving in England."

Muna ignored this; her suspicion had possessed her. "Your stomach, *adik*—let us see it!"

Sakti pressed a hand to her person with exaggerated patience, humouring Muna, but her expression altered at the touch. She untied her sarong slowly, revealing a hole at her navel. It was larger now, spreading up her torso, as though she were fading away from the centre.

Muna took a deep breath, pushing back her horror. She must be calm for Sakti's sake. "Let us go back, *adik*."

They did not speak again until they had recrossed the border between the Seen and Unseen Worlds. This time Muna knew when they had passed over into the realm of the spirits, for Sakti let out a sigh of relief.

"Are you restored?" said Muna.

Sakti nodded, patting the knot of her sarong.

"Whole again," she said, with a crooked smile, not in the least convincing.

They walked until the witch's path came into view, lighting the way through the Unseen Realm to England.

"I don't believe it is Mak Genggang's influence that has had this effect," said Muna finally. "It is being in the Unseen World that has cured you. Janda Baik—does not suit you."

Sakti nodded. She was more subdued than usual, shaken by what was happening to her. "I felt better directly once I breathed in this air. It must be the magic of the Unseen."

Muna nodded. "Perhaps mortal magic lacks the potency to lift the effects of the curse—even the magic of a witch of Mak Genggang's stature. You needed spirits' magic to heal."

She swallowed, for the thought that followed was unwelcome.

"But if that is right," she said, "you must not go to England."

Sakti blinked. "Why not?"

"You ought not to return to the mortal realm," said Muna. "Not till we have broken the curse and you may leave the Unseen World in safety. Who is to say the disease will not strike you again in England?"

"Do you mean we should stay here?" said Sakti. She brightened.

"I wonder that never occurred to me before. It will be far more interesting to explore the Unseen than to go to England!"

"I am glad you think so," said Muna, shivering. *She* did not at all like the thought. Perhaps if she were a witch there might have been some appeal to remaining in the Unseen, despite its dangers. She thought with wistful longing of the village they had left that morning, where they had been safe from wild magic and ravenous spirits.

But Janda Baik had only been a refuge for herself. Its safety had been an illusion, for it had been murdering her sister by degrees.

"We cannot stay *here*," she said, looking around at the wilderness. "But there must be civilised places even in the Unseen—villages where one could stay."

Sakti reflected. "Mak Genggang taught us a spell for calling out the rain. With a little alteration it should serve to summon spirits. We could befriend them—explain who we are, you know, and work upon their sympathies."

Muna was about to remind Sakti that the sort of spirits that haunted jungles were not known for their broad sympathies, nor for their tendency to look kindly upon mortals with the effrontery to demand their attendance. But Sakti stiffened, her eyes widening.

"I had nearly forgot! I have just the thing to help us."

They both bore bundles containing various necessaries, as well as gifts for their English hostess. Sakti drew from hers a brown bottle stoppered with a cork, passing it to Muna. "Look!"

"What is this?"

"A talisman," said Sakti. "Mak Genggang gave it to me. She made me promise I would not use it before we reached England, but if we are to remain here . . ."

"But what does it do?" said Muna. "Is it a potion?" She tilted the bottle, but there did not seem to be anything inside it.

"Oh no," said Sakti. "There is a sort of djinn inside the bottle."

"A djinn!" Muna held the bottle up to the light. The glass was murky, but on closer examination she glimpsed swirls of smoke in the bottle. "I had thought Mak Genggang disapproved of entering into compacts with spirits. She says it is an irreligious practice."

"I expect she is a hypocrite where it suits her," said Sakti. "Most powerful people are. She thought we might need magical assistance in England. The djinn has a good understanding of witchery and instructions to make itself useful, she said. Shall we summon it now?"

Before Muna could stop her, Sakti took the cork out of the bottle, peering into it.

"Quite empty!" said Sakti, but this did not disconcert her in the least. She made the noise one uses to call chickens to feed:

> *"Kur, soul! Come out!*
> *I know whence you sprang:*
> *Your mother was resentment;*
> *Your father was greed.*
> *If you do not come out, wild beasts will eat you.*
> *If you do not come out, you shall be a rebel in the sight of God.*
> *I bid thee come!"*

Nothing happened. Sakti shook the bottle and repeated the formula, to no apparent effect.

"Are you sure you recited the right verse?" said Muna.

"Certain," said Sakti. "It is a perfectly typical formula." She upended the bottle with a discontented look. "I tell you what it is. It is that wretched old female! Mak Genggang insisted I should only call forth the djinn in the mortal realm. She said the air of the Unseen would not suit it. I suppose she has put a block upon its being summoned before we reach England. I think that shows a nasty suspicious nature, don't you? She might have trusted me."

Muna could not help laughing at Sakti's pique. "She trusted you to act according to your nature, I suppose! I don't see what you thought the djinn might do for us, in any case."

"Why, it is a spirit, and we are in the land of spirits," said Sakti. "I thought it might act as a guide and interpreter. Perhaps it could even find us a place to stay . . ."

She paused, looking startled.

"Adik?" said Muna.

Sakti's face screwed up. She let loose an enormous sneeze, dropped the djinn's bottle, and vanished.

Muna had been reaching for the bottle, meaning to catch it. She crashed to the earth with the bottle in her hand, shrieking, *"Adik!"*

But Sakti was gone. Muna had been so close to her that she had felt the warmth from her sister's body, but between one breath and the next she had blinked out of existence.

Muna staggered to her feet, looking around wildly, but an impassive forest surrounded her on every side. She would almost have welcomed the appearance of a tiger or ghoul, for that at least would have been some clue to what had happened to Sakti. But there was nothing and no one—only Muna herself, abandoned in a spirituous jungle, alone with her horror.

"Adik," called Muna again, fighting back despair. "Sakti!" Her voice cracked on the name.

She knew there would be no answer. Wherever Sakti was now—if indeed she still lived—it was somewhere far beyond Muna's reach. This was the work of magic, but whose?

Was Sakti the victim of some spirit of the jungle who lurked beyond the limits of Muna's perception? Or was it their enemy who had wrought this—the curseworker who, growing impatient with draining the spirit from Sakti by degrees, had stolen her outright? Perhaps he had somehow realised that the effects of the curse were lifted once Sakti entered the Unseen Realm. In consequence he had snatched her away.

Muna's hands were trembling. She looked down at them and realised that she still held the djinn's bottle.

The cork was lost among the undergrowth, but this was of little consequence, for the bottle was as empty as Sakti had said. Looking into the bottle, Muna saw only a dark smear at its base. Her vision was blurred and she could not tell what it was, but when she wiped her tears away she saw the smear distinctly. It was a streak of dried blood.

"Blood magic," whispered Muna, with a thrill of dread. She might be no witch herself, but she could not have lived in Mak Genggang's household without learning something of witchery. This was the strongest sort of magic, mysterious and easily warped to evil ends.

An uncontrollable shivering seized her. She put up a hand to push back her hair. Her forehead was damp with perspiration.

If Sakti had not succeeded in summoning the djinn, it was not likely that Muna would. She recited the verse anyway, just in case, but she was not surprised when nothing happened.

Perhaps Sakti's disappearance was a mistake, the result of some oddity in the spell for summoning the djinn. Sakti would be back in a moment, miffish and on her dignity, as she always was when she suspected she had made herself look foolish.

But even as the idea flashed through her mind, Muna knew it for self-deception. She repeated the formula again, halfheartedly, for a dull conviction was settling on her. It had been no mistake. Sakti had been taken. Muna was alone, and the djinn would not come.

She raised her head, rubbing her eyes in some irritation. No matter how Muna dried them, they *would* keep filling up again, and it was necessary for her to see clearly. Ahead the witch's path still glowed silver, trailing away into the distance.

There was nothing she could do here for Sakti, and the longer she stayed the greater the risk of an encounter with some spirit or wild beast. Loath as she was to leave the place where she had last seen Sakti, her duty was clear—she must seek help.

Her inclination was to go back to Janda Baik, for Mak Genggang was familiar and Muna did not doubt the witch would aid her, for all the trouble Muna's reappearance would represent. But she had no confidence in her ability to navigate the trackless jungle that lay behind without Sakti's help. She could not risk getting lost, or stumbling into the spirit settlements of which Sakti had spoken.

In England there would be help. Even if she proved unable to summon Mak Genggang's djinn there, the English Sorceress Royal was said to be a witch of vast powers, and at the very least there would be some way to convey a message to Mak Genggang, to plead with her for succour. To these great magicians the intervening oceans and continents were as nothing—Mak Genggang had called up the image of the Sorceress Royal in a basin of water when she wished to speak with her. Muna had heard the English witch's voice herself—it had been as though the Sorceress Royal were in the next room.

Her mind made up, she stopped the mouth of the djinn's bottle with moss and shoved it into her bundle. She doubted that Sakti would return, yet just in case Muna marked the spot where her sister had vanished with a few stones and twigs, before she straightened up.

The way lay clear before her, illuminated by witch-light. Muna started to run.

5

Later that day
The Lady Maria Wythe Academy for the Instruction of
Females in Practical Thaumaturgy, England

HENRIETTA

THE SALOON OF the Sorceress Royal's Academy had once been a handsome apartment, and it possessed the bones of handsomeness still. Poverty had not brought down the high ceilings, nor shrunk the fine windows. In candlelight one could easily imagine its charms in days past.

In the unforgiving light of day, however, its deficiencies could not be concealed. It was impossible not to see that the mouldings, though finely wrought, were now rather grey than white, and the brocade drapes hung limp and faded. The overall effect was of a decayed grandeur, calculated to depress the spirits of any person of sensibility.

Miss Henrietta Stapleton had the misfortune to belong to this class. She was generally allowed to be a pretty girl, for though there was nothing remarkable about her features, she was young and fair, and the eldest daughter of one of the wealthiest men in

English magic. To these virtues were added a gentle manner and speaking grey eyes—eyes that were particularly wistful now, as she looked around the room.

"How squalid we are!" she sighed. "I wish we were able to give our guests a better account of ourselves. They will hardly expect to find England's first school for female magicians so shabby!"

The Sorceress Royal did not respond at once, for she was studying the floor.

The one alteration the Academy had made upon occupying the house was to tear up the carpets, for the timbers thereby exposed were useful for wonder-working. Two years later, these were covered with thaumaturgical signs and sigils, only half-effaced, for the most diligent scouring in the world could not remove the marks of some magics.

The Sorceress Royal added a final flourish to the newest mark chalked upon the floor, rising to her feet with the aid of her staff.

"Nonsense!" she said bracingly. Prunella Wythe (née Gentleman) had been Henrietta's friend from infancy: as girls they had both been at Mrs. Daubeney's School for Gentlewitches, where they had been taught to suppress their magical abilities, as befit gently born females. In neither had this early education had the desired effect, for they were now—in defiance of convention, and much to the disapproval of the best part of English thaumaturgy—practising *magiciennes*.

They were united in a desire to swell their ranks—to educate as many girls and women as wished to practise magic. It was for this reason that the Sorceress Royal had established her Academy and begged her old schoolfellow to join her as an instructress.

Yet no two women could have been more different. Prunella was as dark and sharp-tongued as Henrietta was fair and mild. Prunella was an orphan, while Henrietta was burdened with more family than was convenient for a *magicienne*. Prunella was a magical prodigy, commanding the services of two familiars, when the greatest sorcerers in thaumaturgical history could only boast of having one familiar. Though a mere female, she had attained the highest office in thaumaturgy, taking up the ancient staff of the Sorcerer Royal—chief and representative of Britain's magical profession. Henrietta, on the other hand, would never pass for a genius—she had just enough magic to make a thaumaturgess, but at times she doubted whether she was fit to teach others magic, when she felt she knew so little of it.

"It is not as though we were receiving anyone grand today," Prunella continued. "They are a simple people in Janda Baik, and I do not expect these girls will be in the least puffed up. Mak Genggang holds all persons of that sort in disgust. She would never burden us with fine ladies."

"I am sure you are right," said Henrietta. "Still . . ."

Prunella had many excellencies of character, as Henrietta occasionally found it necessary to remind herself, but she was an indifferent listener. She leapt to her feet, dusting herself off and interrupting Henrietta:

"I believe the wretched girls are only late, and it is nothing to do with any defect in our summoning circle. Mak Genggang was never remarkable for her punctuality, and I expect her protégées are just the same."

"You do not fear that some misadventure may have befallen them? The girls are coming to us from Fairy, after all."

"Yes, but Janda Baik is on better terms with the Fairy Court than we can claim to be," said Prunella. "*They* did not lure away dozens of the Fairy Queen's subjects to serve as their familiars. Mak Genggang visits Fairy frequently—knows a path there that takes one from her island to England in scarcely more time than it would take for you to walk home."

"But to send her apprentices there alone!" said Henrietta. "I wonder she dared to take such a risk. Above all at this time, when the Queen's temper is said to be so uncertain . . ."

Few English thaumaturges had seen Fairyland since the Fairy Court had closed the border between its realm and Britain half a century ago. There were still some persons, mortal and fairy alike, who managed to circumvent the ban to travel between the two kingdoms, as Mak Genggang's apprentices were to do. But on the whole, news from Fairy reached England at third- or fourth-hand, distilled from rumour and hearsay.

Prunella benefited from a source of reliable intelligence about Fairy, however, for she counted among her intimate friends Robert of Threlfall, a scion of one of the oldest and most powerful draconic clans in the realms of Fairy Within.

Rollo Threlfall lived mostly in the form of a mortal man, indistinguishable from any dandy to be seen on Bond Street, and few who saw him in his everyday guise would have suspected that he had begun life as a dragon, hatched out of an egg. Nonetheless Rollo could not avoid the occasional summons from his aunt Georgiana, from which visits he brought back gossip of Fairyland. The most recent report had been that the Fairy Queen, who reigned over the several realms of Fairy Within, had announced a splendid banquet, to be attended by all her subjects.

"Bad news," Rollo had said, shaking his head. "Her Majesty only announces a party when she suspects her allies of conspiring against her. She's sent to my uncle Harold for the Virtu, for she means to eat it at the banquet."

"The Virtu?" said Prunella.

"It's an amulet—one of the Queen's most prized possessions," said Rollo. "We look after it for her. No thief has succeeded in taking anything from Threlfall's hoards in thousands of years."

"But whyever does she wish to *eat* an amulet?"

"Why, it is the quickest way to absorb magic, you know. Works just as well with amulets as with people. The Queen feels the need for more power, I suppose. Well," said Rollo, with an air of resignation, "we were due a purge—she has one every other century—but it's all very unpleasant. I wouldn't be at the Court now for love or money!"

Recalling this exchange, Prunella said now, "The girls will not have gone anywhere near the Fairy Court—Mak Genggang knows better than *that*! Can you wait till they arrive, Henny? Does not your mamma expect you?"

Henrietta looked guilty. "Not precisely. We were to call upon my aunt at two o'clock."

"Why, it is half past!" said Prunella, glancing at the clock on the mantelpiece. "Will not she be on the rampage—baying for your blood?"

Henrietta coughed. "No," she said awkwardly. "She believes I am with her. I knew you would have need of me today, so I employed the enchantment you taught me to disguise my absence."

At Prunella's blank look, Henrietta added, "The spell for the creation of effigies. I used linen and a pillow, and when I had bound all together it looked just like me."

"Did it really?" said Prunella, delighted.

Before her marriage, Mrs. Wythe had had occasion to require the services of a chaperone. Having neither the funds to hire one nor any real desire for a duenna, she had invented a companion literally out of whole cloth.

"But you must have adapted my spell, if it is able to move and speak well enough to deceive your relations, though you are not there to watch over it," she said. "You must tell me what you did, Henny. If it has sufficient novelty, you might send it to the *Gazette*. Then you would have your first published spell—named for yourself and acknowledged as your invention. What will you call it? 'Stapleton's simulacrum' sounds well, I think."

Henrietta smiled weakly.

"It could not bear the name Stapleton, you know," she began.

But she was interrupted, for just then the chalk marks of the summoning circle burst into a brilliant green glow. The timbers warped and turned clear, a dark pool opening in the floor. The sounds of a tropical evening filled the saloon—the rustle of small creatures crawling through undergrowth, the monotonous scream of insects and the distant cries of unknown beasts.

A girl lurched out of the dark pool of the summoning circle, startling the *magiciennes*. She stumbled and would have fallen if Prunella had not leapt forward, steadying her.

"Here you are!" said Prunella. "I am Mrs. Wythe, and this is Miss Stapleton, who teaches the scholars here at the Academy—" She broke off, saying in quite a different tone, "Oh, but you are hurt!"

The new arrival was panting and dishevelled, with leaves tangled in her hair and scratches all over her brown arms. Her square face bore the signs of recent tears; her eyes were red; and her jacket and skirt of woven cloth were both the worse for wear. Altogether she made a piteous sight.

She formed a striking contrast to Prunella, who looked as charming as ever. Though Prunella's skirts were somewhat disordered from close contact with the floor, still the wine red dress set off her rich colouring remarkably—her mother had been Indian and Prunella was darker than the common run of Englishwomen. Yet she seemed to disappoint their guest.

"*You* are the Sorceress Royal?" she exclaimed. "But you are only a girl!" Her English was perfectly intelligible, though it was evident that she spoke with the aid of a translation spell.

Prunella shot Henrietta a puzzled look—it was certainly odd that she should be reproached for her youth by a girl who could not have been more than eighteen. Henrietta only pursed her lips, but theirs was an intimacy that rendered speech unnecessary for mutual understanding. She knew Prunella had caught her meaning, as much as if Henrietta had said aloud, "*It is beyond me!*"

"I am one-and-twenty, and Miss Stapleton has recently attained her nineteenth year," said Prunella to their guest. "You cannot be much older than that, surely!"

Colour rose in the visitor's dusky cheeks.

"I beg your pardon," she stammered. "I did not mean any discourtesy. It is only that I thought you must be a contemporary of Mak Genggang's."

Prunella bowed. "Pray think nothing of it, Miss . . . oh, but how absurd! Mak Genggang did not tell me your name. Would you be so good as to introduce yourself? And I believe there was a code you were to give me?"

"Yes, of course," said the girl. She seemed distracted, so that conversation demanded unusual exertion on her part, but she collected herself with a visible effort. "I am called Muna. The witch charged me to say: the sky's pink dress, the basket, the secret in your blood."

"Quite right," said Prunella. She had agreed with Mak Genggang a test by which the guests were to prove themselves—for, Mak Genggang had said darkly, who knew what strange creatures might seek to take advantage of the path she opened for her apprentices?

Muna had passed, for not many knew that Mak Genggang had

once made a gift to Prunella of a pink dress on the sky's advice; that Prunella had extricated the witch from an awkward situation by means of a basket; or that it was Mak Genggang who had taught Prunella what secrets might be unlocked by her blood.

"I am afraid you have had trouble on your way here," said Henrietta, looking at Muna in concern.

"But stay," said Prunella, "were not there to be two of you? I am sure Mak Genggang said she would be sending two. A witch and her companion."

Their guest's large dark eyes filled with tears. She dashed them away impatiently, saying in a trembling voice:

"Madam, she did. Two of us set out from Janda Baik. But as we were walking through Fairy, we were struck by misfortune—my sister vanished, snatched away by black magic! Though I searched, I could not find her. I do not know what has become of her, but I fear the worst!"

"Good heavens!" said Henrietta, appalled.

Muna fixed a pleading gaze upon the Sorceress Royal, but before she could say anything else, they were interrupted. A maid burst into the room, pink and agitated.

"I beg your pardon, Mrs. Wythe!" she gasped. "Mr. Stapleton insists upon seeing you. I said you were not at home, but he would not be put off on any account."

Though she addressed the Sorceress Royal, it was Henrietta she looked at with stricken eyes.

Henrietta blanched, seizing the Sorceress Royal's arm in a cold hand. "Papa! Oh, Prunella, what is to be done? He thinks I am with my mother."

"I don't see that there is any call to disabuse him of the belief," said Prunella, with unruffled calm. "Thank you, Sarah. I suppose those are Mr. Stapleton's footsteps? (I told you we should be glad of those creaking floorboards, Henny!) Would you be so good as to shut the doors, Sarah, and stand with your back against them? That ought to detain him for a moment."

Prunella turned to the foreign visitor. "I hope you don't dislike animals, Miss Muna?"

"I beg your pardon?"

"I don't mean wild beasts, you know," said Prunella, "or even horses, which are liable to frighten some ladies. But smaller, peaceable creatures—do you have any objection to them? Would you mind a chicken, say, or a rabbit?"

"No," said Muna, bemused. "There is no harm in a rabbit."

"Excellent," said Prunella. "Then we will take the liberty of imposing upon your good nature, Miss Muna."

"Prunella, what are you doing?" said Henrietta in an urgent whisper, as a knocking started at the doors.

"Sh!" said Prunella, frowning in concentration as she wove a spell.

Sarah shrieked, leaping out of the way just in time before the doors at the end of the saloon burst open. Prunella opened her hand, gabbling a formula.

Smoke rose in the air, engulfing them all, and for the second time that day Muna saw a person vanish before her eyes. The yellow-haired Englishwoman disappeared, leaving in her place a small light-furred beast, with long twitching ears and a startled expression.

6

PRUNELLA

WHAT WITH COUGHING and swearing, it was some time before the caller was able to make himself understood. Prunella apologised, but her professions of remorse were not at all convincing.

"Sarah did tell you I was occupied with spell work," she said. "You know, I am sure, Mr. Stapleton, how liable enchantery is to go awry when interrupted! Otherwise I should have been delighted to receive you, though you will allow me to observe that it is rather early for paying calls."

Mr. Stapleton did not return her smile. Henrietta and her father were not much alike to look at, save in colouring. He was just as fair, with the same grey eyes—eyes that fixed a decidedly wintry look upon Prunella.

"I came," he said, "because I received this." He brandished a crumpled sheet of paper at Prunella. "It is the notice of an application to eject a certain person from the Royal Society of Unnatural Philosophers. Signed by you, ma'am!"

Prunella examined the sheet.

"Why, this is my petition for Edmund Hobday to be struck off," she said, pleased. "So the Presiding Committee has published it after all! I had feared it might be conveniently forgotten."

Mr. Stapleton took the paper back, smoothing it out. A trace of embarrassment entered his manner. He cleared his throat, but despite the boldness of his entrance, he seemed at a loss for how to begin.

Prunella waited, allowing herself a furtive glance at the other two occupants of the room. Behind her Muna huddled on a settee, trying to shield the burden in her arms from view.

Mr. Stapleton was so taken up with the object of his visit that he did not seem to have noticed Muna or what she held. Perhaps he would go away without seeing them at all, and there would be no trouble. Prunella shifted slightly so as to block his line of sight.

"Perhaps you are wondering why I have taken it upon myself to address you on this subject, Mrs. Wythe," Mr. Stapleton said finally. "You may not know that Mr. Hobday is shortly to stand in such a relation to my family that any insult to him is likely to reflect upon my daughter Henrietta. In short, we hope soon to announce their engagement."

Prunella stared.

"Surely not!" she said, with more candour than tact. "He is a wholly indifferent thaumaturge—and forty if he is a day!"

Mr. Stapleton stiffened. "I would have thought Mr. Hobday's position in the world was deserving of more respect, even from the Sorceress Royal."

"I believe I value a large fortune as I ought," said Prunella. "But that counts for little when joined to a person who persecutes females for practising magic."

Mr. Stapleton snorted. "We come to the reason for this petition! Do you call it *persecution* for a gentleman to make a few trifling remarks?"

"I am told Mr. Hobday harangued the scholars of this Academy for a full half-hour on the street, and would not let them get away till he had reduced them to tears," said Prunella. "You may call that what you like, but *I* call it intolerable. Thaumaturges must learn they cannot ill-use the ladies under my protection. If they cannot be civil, I am pleased to teach them manners!"

Prunella had been outraged by the incident when she had first heard of it, and recounting the details vexed her afresh. She glared at Mr. Stapleton, as though she had half a mind to begin by educating *him* in proper behaviour.

Mr. Stapleton seemed to sense that he must alter his approach if he wished to win over the Sorceress Royal.

"I beg you will not mistake me," he said, abandoning his former peremptory tone. "I do not by any means commend Mr. Hobday's conduct. But he very handsomely acknowledges his error. He was in his cups when he encountered the"—he coughed—"the young ladies, and he did not expect decent females to be abroad at that time of night."

"They had been working lunar magics," said Prunella coldly.

"To ruin Mr. Hobday for a mere slip is surely disproportionate to his crime," said Mr. Stapleton. "If you will not consider his career, consider yours, Mrs. Wythe. You cannot be unaware of how your petition will appear to the Society. It will be said that you are venting your rancour for a petty offence."

"Yes, Mr. Wythe said the same," said Prunella. "When my husband was Sorcerer Royal, he always sought to conciliate the Society. But I am cast in a different mould! I *do* have a vindictive temper when provoked, and I *am* fond of getting my revenge. So there can be no harm in my gaining a reputation for being vengeful."

Mr. Stapleton gave her a look of disgust.

"I had hoped to make you see reason, Mrs. Wythe," he began,

"but there is a most unwomanly spirit of independence in you, which—good God! What is that?"

Mr. Stapleton had been aware of the young woman on the settee behind Prunella, a native of some description, but he had paid her little mind, supposing she was a maidservant. It was not she who drew his gaze now, but the creature in her arms, whose high-pitched squeak had interrupted his tirade.

The beast's head and legs were covered with fur the colour of sand, while its body bore a gay pattern of flowers and leaves, recalling sprig muslin. Most extraordinary of all, its round, alarmed eyes were precisely the same shade of grey as Mr. Stapleton's—but it was not to be expected that Mr. Stapleton would notice this, with so much else to marvel at.

"It is a rabbit," said the Sorceress Royal.

"It resembles no rabbit I have ever seen," said Mr. Stapleton, staring. "What is that on its head?"

"Well," said Prunella, hesitating. She had just noticed the blond curls clustering around the animal's ears, and she was dreadfully afraid that if she spoke she would burst into laughter. Fortunately her guest proved more resourceful than Prunella might have expected from the girl's youthful appearance.

"That is only the mark of its true nature, sir," said Muna. "This is no ordinary rabbit, but a spirit."

Mr. Stapleton started; he evidently had not expected to be understood by the native girl. Muna misinterpreted his reaction.

"You need not fear it will do you any harm," she said kindly. "It is a tame spirit and abides by my every command."

Collecting herself, Prunella said, "I ought to have presented you to our guest, sir. Miss Muna hails from the Malay archipelago and is to study thaumaturgy with us at the Academy. She has brought the—er—rabbit with her from her native shores."

She cast a look of appeal at Muna, who rose nobly to the occasion.

"Yes," she said. "My grandmother saved this spirit's life when she was a girl, and it swore eternal loyalty to her lineage. It is a family heirloom."

It was clear that Mr. Stapleton felt himself to be at a disadvantage. As the possessor of one of the largest fortunes in thaumaturgy, he was accustomed to far more deference than he had received from the Sorceress Royal. He gave Muna a look of resentment but did not lower himself so far as to address her.

"Your scholars keep fine society, Mrs. Wythe," he remarked. "As though it were not enough that gently bred females should be educated alongside kitchenmaids, they must now consort with natives! But this is all of a piece with what I have heard of this establishment."

The two years Prunella had passed as Sorceress Royal had accustomed her to being abused by her colleagues, and she had learnt to endure their incivility with a tolerable appearance of complaisance. There was only the slightest edge to her voice as she said:

"We count ourselves fortunate to consort with the witches of Janda Baik, you know! Their friendship is particularly valuable to Britain, for they are closely connected with Fairy. Miss Muna travelled through Fairy to honour us with her presence—a journey few English magicians now living can claim to have made. We hope to learn a great deal from her."

Muna had been smiling politely at the Englishman. At this reference to Fairy she winced, her smile breaking, but neither Mr. Stapleton nor the Sorceress Royal took notice of this.

A happy thought had struck Prunella. She said, "Would you be so good as to oblige us with a magical demonstration, Miss Muna?"

Muna gaped. "Me, do a demonstration?"

"You see, I know very little of Asiatic enchantery," explained Prunella, "and I am sure Mr. Stapleton has never seen an Asiatic spell. We should be delighted to see your magic.

"Miss Muna is an apprentice of Mak Genggang, a very great witch and a particular friend of mine," Prunella added to Mr. Stapleton. "Oh, but perhaps you will recall Mak Genggang, sir? She attended the Society's Spring Ball two years ago."

"I recollect the lady," said Mr. Stapleton grimly. He folded the sheet of paper bearing Prunella's petition, tucking it away in his coat. "I must not detain you, madam."

"Oh, are you going, sir? Will not you stay to see Miss Muna's demonstration?" said Prunella. "From what little I know of Malay magic, it is truly fascinating!"

"I saw quite enough of Malay magic at the Spring Ball," said Mr. Stapleton. "As I recall, the witch Mak Genggang employed it to threaten her own king, and caused Mrs. Geoffrey Midsomer to fall down in a swoon. I had never witnessed a more disgraceful scene—and in the Society's halls! No, thank you. English thaumaturgy suffices for *my* needs."

He picked up his hat, giving Prunella a severe look.

"I refrained from comment, Mrs. Wythe, when you were appointed the head of my profession," said Mr. Stapleton. "I knew my daughter Henrietta had an affection for you as her old schoolfellow. I thought it right to reserve my judgment till we had seen how you conducted yourself as Sorceress Royal. Well, you have had your chance. You have shown what you are—a mere headstrong girl, caring for nothing but her own way!"

Prunella opened her mouth, but Mr. Stapleton shook his head, forestalling her with a raised hand.

"I don't propose to impose upon you any longer," he said. "I shall address myself to the Presiding Committee, for I know that a thaumaturge and a gentleman may expect a fair hearing from *them*. I beg you will reflect upon what I have said, however. In time you may come to consider the matter rationally."

But his tone suggested that he had little hope of this. Jamming his hat upon his head, he swept off in high dudgeon, leaving the women staring after him.

T HE door had scarcely shut behind Mr. Stapleton when the rabbit leapt from Muna's arms. It transformed in mid-air, the hind legs elongating and the fur melting into the flesh.

Henrietta landed on the floor, panting.

"Oh, Prunella, how could you?" she gasped in tones of reproach. But then she looked down at herself and gave a stifled shriek—for, of course, when she had been metamorphosed into a rabbit it had been necessary to whisk away her clothes. Now that she had reverted to her own form, she wore nothing at all.

Muna averted her eyes, blushing, but the Sorceress Royal had less delicacy.

"Why, Henny, there is nothing to be ashamed of. It is not as though there were any gentlemen present, and I have seen you in far worse circumstances," she said. "Do not you recall the Countess's visit to Mrs. Daubeney's school, when you brought up your dinner over her shoes? How vexed she was!"

This reminiscence was not designed to allay Henrietta's distress. Muna ventured to suggest that perhaps Miss Stapleton would like to be dressed.

"She must be cold," she said, though Henrietta's brilliant colour rather suggested otherwise.

"*Yes*," said Henrietta, with feeling.

The maidservant Sarah had retreated while the Sorceress Royal entertained Mr. Stapleton, but the promptness with which she responded to a summons indicated that she had not gone very far. All conversation was suspended till she returned with a robe for Henrietta. While Henrietta restored herself to decency, Prunella turned to their guest.

"I am very much obliged to you," she said to Muna. "I thought Mr. Stapleton would never leave! It was a happy thought to propose that you demonstrate your magic. Mr. Stapleton disapproves of both women and foreigners having anything to do with thaumaturgy. I thought the prospect of seeing the magic of a woman *and* a foreigner would send him packing."

Henrietta could not like to hear her father spoken of in these terms, and yet after such a scene she could hardly defend him. She only said, "Oh, Prunella!"

"I am sorry to speak so of one so nearly connected to you, but it is only the truth," said Prunella. "How cross your papa made me! As for all that nonsense about your marrying Mr. Hobday, ought not you to disillusion him? I suppose you are hoping that Mr. Hobday will not offer, but perhaps he will, and if he does I should think it would be best to have given your papa notice of your intention to refuse."

Henrietta would not meet Prunella's eyes but drew her robe around herself, saying in a hurried manner, "What on earth possessed you to transform me into a rabbit?"

Prunella stared.

"You don't mean to say you *would* accept an offer from Hobday?" she demanded, scandalised.

"I did not say anything."

"But you cannot like him," said Prunella. "He is quite old and not at all handsome. And I must warn you, if you tell me he has other excellent qualities, I will not credit it in the least!"

"Prunella," said Henrietta, with dignity, "I understand your feelings, but surely we may speak of this at another time." She cast a meaningful look at Muna, who tried to pretend she had not understood anything of what had been said. "You have not answered my question. I had no notion you understood the art of metamorphosis."

"Damerell started teaching me before he left for Threlfall," Prunella explained. Rollo Threlfall had received a summons from his aunt Georgiana but a week ago, requiring him to visit his family's home in the Fairy province they governed on behalf of the Queen. This had so cast him down that his friend Damerell had agreed to accompany him, for though he was a mere mortal magician, Damerell's connection with Rollo was of long standing, and he was well regarded by Rollo's relations.

Which was all very well for Rollo, said Prunella, but it was highly inconvenient for *her*. Damerell was one of her few allies in English thaumaturgy; an old friend of her husband, Zacharias Wythe; and a sorcerer possessing not only a fund of magical ability but what was even more valuable to the Sorceress Royal—an understanding of thaumaturgical politics surpassed by none.

"But he had scarcely begun when he was obliged to depart," Prunella said now, sighing. "It is a wonder the spell came off! Was it very unpleasant? I confess I simply reached for the first charm that came to hand. I would not have done it if I had known you would not like it!"

"It felt excessively peculiar," said Henrietta. "Though of course I am obliged to you for concealing me from Papa. I thought I should *die* when I heard his voice! I tried to cast a spell myself—an invisibility spell—but it did not take, though I am sure I took the greatest care in pronouncing the formula."

Prunella looked thoughtful. "Perhaps it was your worry that

threw off the spell. If you cast it again now, we might study it and see if we can trace the flaw."

Muna had been watching the Englishwomen, waiting for an opportune moment to speak. She had supposed herself forgotten, but this was not so, for now the Sorceress Royal smiled at her.

"It will be an opportunity for Miss Muna to see an example of English magic, which I am sure she will like," said Prunella. "And then, Miss Muna, if you have no objection, perhaps you could demonstrate some of the magics with which you are acquainted?"

Muna would not have a better chance to plead her case—and Sakti's. "I should be delighted to tell you all I know of the magic of Mak Genggang, but—there is the matter of my sister, ma'am." Her voice quavered despite her best efforts.

A shadow fell across the Englishwomen's faces. Looking thoroughly ashamed, Prunella said, "Oh yes, of course! I am so sorry. What an appalling thing to have happened! You must think us entirely unfeeling. I can only beg your pardon."

"You will wish to rest," said Henrietta, touching Muna's elbow. "We have prepared a room for you. Shall I take you there now?"

"You are very good, but I am not tired in the least," said Muna. The way the Englishwomen spoke made her anxious—it was action she desired, not sympathy. "I could lead you now to the place where I last saw my sister, if you could open the way again. I marked the trees along the path as I came."

Henrietta glanced at Prunella. "Perhaps the summoning circle . . . After all, there is nothing to prevent *your* entering Fairy, Prunella."

The Sorceress Royal looked as though she could think of several reasons, but she said nothing, only going over to the summoning circle they had chalked upon the floor. She tapped her staff on the circle, but after a moment she shook her head, saying, "No, it is as I thought! The way is closed. Mak Genggang was always very tidy in all her workings."

She turned to Muna.

"I am afraid we here in Britain are allowed far less liberty in the matter of travelling to Fairy than you are in your country," said Prunella. "In Janda Baik, I hear, one may wander into the Other Realm by accident! But we had the misfortune of offending the Fairy Queen some years ago, and in consequence she closed the borders of her realm to Britain—no one may cross over without her permission. To travel here from Fairy is one thing—the Queen frowns upon it, but it is known to happen. But to go the other way is nearly impossible for a mortal. Of all the English only I may open the doors from Britain to the Other Realm."

It was as though there was an object stuck in Muna's throat, which made it difficult to speak. Nonetheless she managed to say, "Cannot you do it? Oh, Mrs. Wythe, I beg you! I should do anything—render any service in my power—"

"I could," said Prunella slowly. "But the realms of Fairy Within are various and extensive, and they do not behave as mortal lands do. That is why no mortal has ever succeeded in mapping Fairy. Even if I contrived to open a route into Fairy without attracting the Queen's attention, I could not promise to return you to the place where you lost your sister. Do you think she will have returned there?"

"Oh, Miss Muna," said Henrietta in a tone of pity. It was only then that Muna realised that her cheeks were wet with tears.

"No," said Muna, drawing her arm across her eyes and ignoring Henrietta's attempt to console her, "I doubt she will be where I lost her. But surely something can be done to find her!"

The Sorceress Royal looked grave. "Do you have any idea what can have taken her? Was it a fairy? Could you tell what magic had been employed?"

Muna explained what had occurred, though the more she said, the worse she felt. She might have been telling the Englishwomen that Sakti had been struck by lightning, or drowned at sea. The looks that passed between them said what they would not—that they believed Muna's sister to be lost beyond any hope of recovery.

"Could not a message be sent to Mak Genggang?" Muna said finally. The witch would be able to help, she thought. Mak Genggang was not one to submit to fate when fate's workings did not suit her.

"Oh yes, there is no question of that!" said Prunella, sounding relieved to be entrusted with a task she was able to perform. "She must be told what has become of your sister."

"Perhaps she will know of a way to find her," said Henrietta. "After all, she knows the Fairy realms far better than we do."

Muna could see that Henrietta meant well, but her very gentleness had a chilling effect. Nothing could have better conveyed the Englishwoman's absolute conviction that Sakti was gone forever, swallowed up by the mysterious forces of the Unseen Realm.

Muna was suddenly overcome by the weariness she had been so eager to deny. She had run the remainder of the path to England in her desperation, slowing her pace only to score the bark of the trees she passed so she might find them again. She had known that she risked offending the spirits of those trees by doing so, but what could she care for that when Sakti had been taken?

She swallowed.

"May I send a message to the witch myself?" she began to say, but a great booming noise, as of an explosion, drowned out her voice.

Screams rose from the street outside. For a moment the three women stared at one another, frozen in shock. Prunella dashed to the window.

She was pale when she looked around.

"Another one, Henny!" she said. "They grow bolder by the day. I wonder if we still have a door! Did not I tell you we should be sorry if we had been so extravagant as to paint it?"

She turned to Muna, saying, "I beg you will forgive me for leaving you with Miss Stapleton. She will see to it that you are settled in and answer all your questions. I must go now, but I shall come to you as soon as ever I can, and we shall summon up your mistress on the shewstone."

She did not wait for Muna to answer, but shot out of the room, calling out, "Tjandra! Youko! To me!"

A CRATER had been gouged out of the street below, just outside the Academy. It was smoking gently, glowing with a faint green light. Curious passers-by had gathered around it. As Muna and Henrietta watched from the window, the Sorceress Royal joined the crowd. She was not alone.

"What are those?" said Muna.

The Sorceress Royal was shooing people away from the crater, assisted by two animals. One was a deerlike creature with graceful antlers, its body covered in scales. The other was a bird with splendid emerald plumage, like a parrot, but rather larger. When it lifted its face, Muna saw that it had a human head—the elegant dark-haired head of a youth, with a sullen expression and a beak for a mouth. She gasped.

"Those are the Sorceress Royal's familiars," said Henrietta. "The unicorn is called Youko and the simurgh is Tjandra. She did not think they were needed for the enchantment we cast to receive you, for our part of the summoning was straightforward—Mak Genggang supplied most of the magic needed. But they serve Prunella in all magical matters and, by adding their magic to hers, entitle her to call herself a sorceress."

It was some diversion from Muna's misery to see the Sorceress Royal's familiar spirits as they crawled over the crater with their mistress, studying the effects of the hex. She had grown accustomed to the sight of lamiae when living under Mak Genggang's roof, but the lamiae looked so much like human women that it was easy to forget they were spirits with such unsavoury habits as preying upon pregnant women and devouring the viscera of unfortunate men. There was no mistaking the unicorn and the simurgh for anything but magical beings, however.

How Sakti would have liked to see them! thought Muna. This gave her a dreadful pang.

"What a welcome we have given you!" Henrietta was saying apologetically. "You must think we live in a state of perpetual excitement. But I assure you this is by no means a daily occurrence. We hardly have an attack more than once in a fortnight."

Muna said, to distract herself, "It is the effect of a curse—a deliberate attack? Who can have done this wicked thing?" But then she remembered that Mak Genggang had said the English were at war.

"They are a sanguinary people, the English," the witch had said. "They are not content with quarrelling with their neighbours, but must needs sail over the seas to trouble us too!"

"I suppose it is your enemies the French," Muna said now. "They must be heartless indeed, to prey upon defenceless females!"

"Oh, well!" said Henrietta, hesitating. "In these times one

ought not to leap to conclusions, and perhaps . . . But English thaumaturgy has entered into a treaty with France's *sorcieres*, under which neither will attack the other, and we have never yet found them out in a breach. So far as we know, the attacks upon the Academy have all been from Englishmen."

Muna stared. "Your own countrymen!"

"You are surprised," said Henrietta. "In your country, I am told, it is deemed perfectly natural in a woman to practise magic! But here the open practice of thaumaturgy by females is an innovation, and English society is not fond of innovations. There are some gentlemen who still object to our very existence." She gave Muna a shy sidelong look. She seemed embarrassed.

"Your education will not have prepared you for such a reception," said Henrietta. "No doubt Mak Genggang has never known such opposition!"

On the street outside, the Sorceress Royal had been joined by a man dressed like an Englishman, but with skin of a much darker hue than that of any Englishman Muna had yet seen. He leant upon a silver-topped cane, watching Prunella and her familiars at their work, and the Sorceress Royal smiled as she looked up at him.

"I believe she has," said Muna absently. "Any great witch will have her enemies." But her mind had turned to Sakti again, and the English witches' troubles interested her less than her own. She opened her mouth to speak, but Henrietta had caught sight of the dark gentleman.

"There is Mr. Wythe!" she exclaimed. A pink flush rose in her cheeks. She added, by way of explanation, "Zacharias Wythe is one of our foremost scholars of magic—a brilliant mind. He was Sorcerer Royal before the staff passed to Prunella, shortly before they were married."

Henrietta was deeply interested in the scene below. She lingered by the window, gazing in rapt attention as Mr. and Mrs. Wythe started to work an enchantment to restore the paving destroyed by the hex.

It was not polite to interrupt her, but Muna could not afford politeness. She said, "Miss Stapleton, Mrs. Wythe mentioned a shewstone, which might be used to convey a message to Mak Genggang. Would it be possible for me to address her now?"

This served to break Henrietta's absorption. She turned away from the window at once, looking concerned. "Of course, you will wish to speak with her as soon as possible. I should certainly summon Mak Genggang if it were in my power, but I am afraid the shewstone is reserved for the use of the Sorceress Royal. Its magic will not answer to any other master."

A thought struck her. "Unless . . . do *you* know of any magics that would enable us to speak with your mistress? Prunella says Mak Genggang does not have a shewstone herself. I am told she employs a basin of water to commune with magicians in other countries."

"No," said Muna. "Mak Genggang has not taught me that magic."

But the witch had not sent her and Sakti forth wholly unequipped. Muna's hand stole to her bundle, feeling the outline of the djinn's bottle.

"I confess I am a little tired," she said. She had not meant for her voice to waver, but perhaps there was no harm in it, for it made Henrietta look sorry for her.

"Anyone would be, after all you have undergone!" said the Englishwoman with ready sympathy. "Let me take you to your bedchamber and you may rest before dinner. We do not keep fashionable hours here at the Academy, but you can be sure of several hours of peace. And"—she hesitated, looking away—"I beg you will not worry about your sister. With the aid of two such *magiciennes* as Prunella and Mak Genggang, I should not be surprised if we soon found her!"

But she did not sound convinced.

7

MUNA

THE BEDCHAMBER ALLOTTED to Muna was a large apartment, scrupulously clean, but not at all cheerful. A thin grey light filtered through the windows; the drapes were threadbare and the wallpaper faded. A large bed sat brooding in the middle of the room like a shipwreck.

"I am afraid this is the best we could contrive," said Henrietta.

Muna was not inclined to be critical. Her chief desire was to be alone. "Very kind, I'm sure! What a handsome room!"

But Henrietta would not go. She seemed oppressed by the thought of the help she had not been able to render. By way of compensation she lingered at the door, pressing upon Muna every conceivable form of comfort, from a glass of wine to books of magic ("We have begun a collection here at the Academy—it is small as yet, but I daresay you may find something of interest in it nonetheless").

With polite obstinacy, Muna insisted that she was not hungry, was forbidden by the laws of her religion to drink wine, and was in no mood to read. Still, it seemed an age before she was able to shut the door behind the Englishwoman. Her face was stiff from smiling.

She locked the door and pushed a chair against it before

drawing the curtains, leaving the barest crack through which light could enter. Even then the room seemed alive with noise. The rumble of passing traffic and the babble of foreign voices rose from the streets, only slightly muted by the glass.

Rummaging in her bundle, Muna drew out the bottle Sakti had given her. In the dim light the brown glass looked wholly opaque. There was nothing to suggest the bottle held anything but air.

Muna was shivering from more than the cold English air, and her palms were damp. What would she do if the spell did not work, even now that she had left the Unseen? After all, she was no magician. It might not be enough to recite the verse, if the speaker had no magic with which to give effect to the summoning.

What if the spell *did* work? After all, Sakti had vanished after trying to summon the djinn. What if the spirit was the cause of her sister's disappearance?

But the thought brought a spark of anger with it, overcoming fear.

If it is the djinn's fault, I shall make it bring Sakti back! thought Muna.

"*Kur!*" she whispered.

As she spoke the final peremptory words of the formula, commanding the spirit to appear, the dark streak of blood at the base of the bottle flickered. It *moved*, squirming like a worm.

Muna sprang back with a shriek, dropping the bottle. It rolled onto the carpet as a plume of red smoke burst from its mouth.

She had never seen a djinn before, but she had a tolerably clear idea of what one ought to look like—eyes of flame in a bestial visage, accompanied by horns and claws and various other demonic appurtenances. Lurid red smoke fit perfectly with her expectations. But when the smoke dissipated it revealed a tiny woman.

If a djinn's age could be judged from its features, this one was no longer in her first youth, but nor did she look old. In figure and countenance she was like any village woman to be seen in Janda Baik, respectably dressed in flowered Javanese cloth. Muna's immediate impression was that she must have seen the djinn somewhere before—there was something so familiar about the small figure.

"Well met, O djinn!" stammered Muna.

The spirit squinted shortsightedly at Muna. "I am a *polong*, and no djinn," she said.

Her accent was that of Janda Baik, a reassuring sound so far from home, but Muna recoiled, horrified. "A *polong*!"

She had heard of *polong*—undead helpers raised by wicked magicians to do their bidding. To create a *polong* was a very dark magic, for one was obliged to use the blood of the victim of a murder. Mak Genggang had always set her face against all such malevolent spells, but here was evidence that the witch had indulged in one herself.

It was a blow Muna had not expected. For a moment she felt herself at sea, abandoned by certainties she needed now more than ever. As she struggled to master her disappointment, the *polong* swept the room with a suspicious gaze.

"What an ugly room!" the spirit remarked. "This is England, I suppose, and you must be the witch's apprentice—for what that is worth." She looked Muna over disdainfully. "I have never heard a summoning charm so mangled. Did not That Woman teach you how to recite a spell?"

The hectoring voice was familiar. Muna's eyes widened in incredulity as the realisation dawned upon her.

"I beg your pardon," she blurted out, "but surely you are Mak Genggang!"

Now that she knew what to look for, Muna could trace the

witch's features in the *polong*'s countenance without the least difficulty. The *polong* lacked Mak Genggang's grey hair and wrinkles,
but the voice and bearing were unmistakable.

"No!" snapped the *polong*.

But Muna's relief made her less respectful than she would otherwise have been, for using one's *own* blood in a spell was perfectly
acceptable. "You must be. Why, you look just like her—and sound
like her too! I wondered why she gave us such a talisman, when—"
When she has always had a disgust of spirits of your kind were the
words on the tip of Muna's tongue, but it struck her just in time
that the remark was somewhat tactless.

"But this explains all," she said instead. "She dispatched a part
of herself to watch over us!"

"Pray do not confuse me with That Woman," said the *polong*
haughtily. "I may have sprung from her blood, but that does not
mean I am a part of her, any more than you may be taken for your
mother, because you were born of her. That Woman is a mere
mortal, who will expire and be buried in the earth. Whereas I am
a spirit—a being of pure magic!"

"But she did not harvest anyone else's blood to make you,"
Muna persisted, too glad to be troubled by the spirit's pique. "And
she did send you to watch over us?"

"That Woman seems to think I am some sort of nursemaid,"
grumbled the *polong*. "She is always after me to work beneficent
magics, when that is not my rightful purpose at all. A *polong* is
nothing more than a fly-by-night, intended to steal trinkets and
plague her master's enemies."

Muna took this for an affirmative. "*Mak cik*, I beg you will help
us—"

"There is no need to call me aunt. That Woman was scarcely
thirty when she created me."

"*Kak*," said Muna prudently, "I beg you will help us—"

The *polong* interrupted, frowning, "You say 'us,' but where is your sister—the one that has no magic?"

"I am the one that has no magic. Calamity befell us when we were travelling through the Unseen." Muna's brief gladness faded at the recollection, and her voice shook as she said, "My sister Sakti was captured!"

The *polong* frowned. "Captured? What do you mean?"

Muna explained what had happened to Sakti in the jungle.

"And I do not know what has become of her," she concluded tearfully. "Not even whether she is dead or alive! The English magicians would not take me back to the Unseen; they have given up Sakti for lost. But there must be something that can be done!"

She dashed away her tears, gazing hopefully at the *polong*. The spirit's brow was furrowed in thought.

"Strange," murmured the *polong*. "That Woman will have hedged you around with protective charms before sending you off into the Unseen. This was a turn she did not predict. The curse-worker's hand was at work here.

"Come," she added, not unkindly, "it will hardly help your sister for you to howl! I should not be surprised if she has been devoured by ghouls, but if that is the case you may as well know the worst at once."

Muna gulped. "Can you find her?"

"I don't propose to plunge into the bowels of the Unseen to track her path," said the spirit. "But there are other ways."

She rebound the *batik* cloth around her waist, squaring her shoulders with the air of one nerving herself to a challenge. "I shall need a pool of water. Blood would do as well," she added as an afterthought.

Fortunately there was no need for blood, for there was a jug of water by the bed, along with a basin. At the spirit's instruction Muna poured the water into the basin till the *polong* said, "That is enough! Stand back."

The *polong* spoke no formula and performed no mystic gestures but merely hovered for a moment, staring at the water. The water started to glow with a red light. She beckoned at Muna. "Come and see. Is that your sister?"

Muna darted over to the *polong*'s side. The water was shining so brightly that she could hardly make out the image on the surface. Yet it only required a glance for Muna to say, disappointed, "No. *Kak*, surely that is a spirit?"

Muna could not see the woman's countenance clearly through the glare, but that it belonged to no ordinary mortal was evident. It was a beautiful, impassive face, every lineament perfectly regular, and a splendid mass of hair was swept up above the forehead, between two curving horns extending from the temples. On the hair rested a crown.

The *polong* made an irritated noise.

"What are you about, showing me a djinn?" the *polong* demanded. Muna started, but the *polong* was not addressing her. The spirit continued, "I asked you to show me her sister, didn't I? What do you mean, *which sister*? She only has the one. Sakti is the name. Show me where she is!"

There ensued such a long pause, while the water bubbled and the red light came and went, that Muna ventured to whisper, "Who were you speaking to, *kak*?"

"The fine ones," said the *polong*, without raising her eyes from the water. "Lazy wretches! Did Mak Genggang not tell you of them?"

"It was my sister who was Mak Genggang's apprentice," Muna reminded her. "I worked in the kitchen."

"The elements are peopled with the fine ones—invisible spirits, who are the stuff of which magic is made," said the *polong*. "All enchantery is effected only with their aid, but they are of such exceeding fineness that no mortal can perceive them. Even in the Unseen they are given little consideration. They like to be spoken to, however."

Muna doubted whether even such neglected creatures would enjoy conversation consisting of the sort of scoldings the *polong* had been giving them, but she kept these thoughts to herself. She bent over the murky water, longing to see Sakti.

"Do the English know you have no magic?" said the *polong*.

Muna blinked.

"They must," she began, but even as she spoke it seemed to her that she lied. The Englishwomen would hardly have begged her for a demonstration of Asiatic magics if they did not believe her to be a witch. Muna had been so taken up with Sakti's disappearance that she had given little thought to the misunderstanding. "I—no, I do not think I ever explained it was Sakti who was Mak Genggang's apprentice, not I."

"Leave them ignorant," said the *polong*. "Let them believe you are the apprentice who has come to learn magic. That Woman told the English sorceress she would be sending her a prodigy. If the Sorceress Royal were to discover that she has been cheated—that a mere laywoman was substituted for the magician she expected— I should not be surprised if she were to throw you out on the street. I hear she is an evil-tempered female who cares for nothing but her own interest."

Muna had heard a rather different account from Mak Genggang, but what little she had seen of the Sorceress Royal did not tend to contradict what the *polong* said. Mrs. Wythe had not seemed unkind, but she would see no reason for Muna to remain at her

Academy if she knew Muna was handier with a pestle and mortar than a wand.

"If the English sorceress comes to believe that Mak Genggang has tricked her on purpose, Janda Baik will lose a valuable friend," added the *polong*. "Not that I care for that! But preserving the island is all That Woman cares for."

The *polong* struck the water with her palm. The surface of the water rippled. "There! Is *that* your sister? The fine ones insist it is she."

Muna leant over the basin. There was a girl in a doorway, half-turning to look back. It was only a glimpse, but Muna knew her at once.

Muna's heart leapt. Till then she had not dared admit her worst fear to herself—that Sakti might be dead.

Sakti saw her too. Her eyes met Muna's, widening, and her mouth opened.

"*Adik!*" cried Muna, but just then the *polong* struck the water again. Smoke billowed out of the basin. Muna stumbled back, coughing. When she had dried her streaming eyes and was able to see again, the basin was empty.

She whirled around, fixing a reproachful gaze on the *polong*. "It was Sakti! Why did you break the vision?"

The *polong* was pale. "What can have possessed you to call out in that reckless way? I can only hope no one heard you!"

Muna stared, the excitement of seeing Sakti ebbing away. She rubbed her arms, for suddenly the room seemed to have turned colder than ever. "Why? *Kak*, where was that? Where is my sister?"

"Your sister is in the Palace of the Unseen," said the *polong*, "where lives the Queen of the Djinns—she whom the English call the Fairy Queen."

She looked morose. "That Woman! She ought to have taken better care. Am I a miracle worker, to rescue a girl from the Queen of the Djinns? No one can say I have not behaved correctly. I offered to rob That Woman's neighbours, or afflict her rivals with embarrassing diseases. If she desired an angel to assist her she ought to have studied her Qur'an, instead of raising a *polong*!"

Relief—even joy—still warmed Muna, for it was something to know her sister was alive. But this speech was scarcely calculated to reassure her.

"Is it so bad that she has found her way to the Palace of the Unseen? I had thought she might have been kidnapped by a weretiger, or taken by a ghoul."

"I should have been happier to see her in a village of weretigers," said the *polong*. "There are some decent gentlemanly creatures among those people, whereas one would need to search for many years before finding a true heart in the Queen's Court!"

But Muna's expression seemed to make her regret her candour. The *polong* said, "Come, child, I would not begin to despair quite yet. It is long past the days when the Queen of the Djinns devoured every mortal who had the ill judgment to enter her Palace. Your sister might be doing very well for herself. The Queen has been known to make favourites of certain mortal magicians, who enjoy great rewards—so long as they manage to retain her favour."

The more the *polong* said, the less reassured Muna felt. "But are not spirits famously changeable?"

"I will have you know that is an offensive generalisation," said the *polong*. "No one could accuse *me* of inconsistency. Even That Woman would allow that I know my mind and stick to it. Of course," she added, "the Queen of the Djinns is a different matter. *Her* caprice is only equalled by her cruelty. But she is not to be taken as representative of the rest of us."

"But my sister is in the Queen's Palace," pointed out Muna, "so it is the Queen's character that concerns me. If Sakti were in your power, *kak*, I would not be concerned. I would know I could rely upon your forbearance!"

The *polong* raised an eyebrow. "This sister of yours demands forbearance, does she?"

Warmth rose in Muna's cheeks. "She is clever, and she has a great magical gift," she said defensively. "It is no wonder if she is bold and sometimes speaks out of turn. All witches are like that."

"Well, take heart!" said the *polong*. "Such a sister will often have vexed you. It must be some comfort to know that she will likely never do so again."

It was necessary for Muna to remind herself that the *polong* was no mortal, but a different order of being. It could not be expected that she should understand the ordinary feelings of a human being. Still, Muna was obliged to swallow an indignant retort before she was able to speak with anything like civility.

"I should much rather be vexed than sisterless," she said. "Perhaps Sakti's manners do not do her justice, but she is my sister. She is all I have in this world." There was nothing more to be said; that must explain all. Muna folded her hands to still their trembling. "*Kak*, I ask no sacrifices of you, but could not you take me to her?"

"So that you can be devoured by the spirits as well?" said the *polong*. "I think not! I shall receive a scolding from That Woman as it is. Besides, you must know that the English have so aggrieved the Queen of the Djinns that they have been barred from entering her realm. To send you to the Hidden World from here would only risk attracting the Queen's wrath."

"Do you mean that even you could not enter the Unseen?"

"*I* am a different matter," said the *polong*. "The distinctions between the worlds matter less to me than to you. But I could not bring you there. A great galumphing piece of flesh like you! I might as well try to smuggle a water buffalo across the border."

"Then a message," said Muna desperately. "Could not you take a message to her?"

"That Woman only charged me to look after you and your sister in England," said the *polong*. "And that is what I shall do, no more and no less. The air of the Unseen is dangerous to spirits constituted as I am. I could have my memories and my freedom stolen from me, and end as a miserable slave, toiling in the Palace of the Unseen."

A band seemed to draw tight around Muna's chest, constricting her breath. She could not have travelled so far, only to fail now. "Will you do *nothing* to help me?"

"If there were anything sensible to be done . . ." The *polong* shook her head. "But there it is! Even the great spirits of the many worlds would hesitate to quarrel with the Queen of the Djinns. It is a pity, but you had best reconcile yourself to the loss of your sister.

"But there, do not look so upset!" she added. "I expect you will forget your sister in time, if you regulate your mind and do not allow yourself to dwell upon her fate. Mortals have short memories. Are you sure there is no more fitting service I could render? Perhaps I could steal a treasure from the Sorceress Royal—a jewel, perhaps, or a powerful enchantment?"

"No," said Muna. "We were only brought to this point because we stole that wretched spell! And it was my idea. If I had not thought of it, none of this would have happened!" She buried her face in her hands.

"If thievery is not to your liking, I could possess a mortal for you," said the *polong* hopefully. "I have never possessed a mortal before and I fancy I would enjoy it."

"Please, *kak*," said Muna, "go away!"

When she lowered her hands, wiping her face, she saw that she had finally managed to give a command with which the *polong* would comply. The spirit had vanished. There was nothing to suggest that she had ever been there—save for the depleted jug, the empty basin, and the bottle, lying on the floor where Muna had dropped it.

Muna hid the bottle. Then she climbed into bed, for lack of anything better to do. Her head felt as though it were filled with cotton wool. It seemed an age since she had risen in the half-light of morning in Janda Baik and left Mak Genggang's house.

The bed was not unlike a cage, with its canopy and four posters, and Muna lay in it like a captured animal, defeated for the moment by her fate. Weary as she was, her mind would not be quiet. The events of the past few days crowded out sleep.

If only she had preserved her silence, instead of suggesting that Mak Genggang send her and Sakti to England. If only she had not thought of going to the English king's house in the first place . . .

Now Muna was alone, her sister abandoned to all the perils of the Unseen Realm. Perhaps it was fortunate that Muna had no magic. If she could, she would have sought to turn back time, despite all Mak Genggang might say about such spells resulting in disastrous confusion.

As it was, she was at a stand. She did not know what to do.

Muna rolled over, bedewing her pillow with tears.

8

THINGS SEEMED BETTER in the morning—as, even at the worst of times, they often do. Once unconsciousness seized Muna, it held her through the afternoon and night. She woke only when the first light of the new day broke through the curtains. She thought, *I shall ask the Sorceress Royal how to tame the* polong.

She would not tell Mrs. Wythe about the spirit—Muna doubted whether Mak Genggang would wish the English to know she had such creatures at her command. But the question might easily be put in general terms. With two familiars, the Sorceress Royal must know how such spirits were to be dealt with. Even on her brief acquaintance with Mrs. Wythe, Muna felt certain the English-woman would not countenance the least insubordination in the creatures who served her.

Perhaps she would not need the *polong* in any case, Muna thought as she became more awake, for the Sorceress Royal had said she would arrange for a message to be sent to Mak Genggang. But the witch might not come at once. She would have liked to accompany Muna and Sakti through the Unseen Realm, but she could not afford to leave Janda Baik unguarded: "Like as not Tuan Farquhar would snap it up the moment my back was turned!"

The English remained a threat, as did the other polities around

Janda Baik. Mak Genggang had given them the *polong* for a reason. It would be best if Muna were able to manage with the *polong*'s help.

A princely breakfast, laid on in honour of her arrival, served to improve her spirits further. Henrietta alone shared it with her, for the Sorceress Royal had returned to her own quarters, but there was such a quantity of food as would have supplied the wants of the whole of Mak Genggang's numerous household. To drink there was coffee, tea and an astounding invention called chocolate, which Muna had never tasted before but of which she thoroughly approved. There were eggs, salted fish, several sweet cakes and as many bread rolls as anyone could want—hot and generously spread with fresh butter, these were very good. But Henrietta was proudest of the chops.

"Pork chops with mustard!" she announced when the dish was set down before Muna. "Though you must not grow accustomed to this luxury, Miss Muna; in general we dine simply at the Academy. But Mrs. Wythe and I thought a good meal would set you up after your long journey, particularly since you missed your dinner—you were sleeping so soundly we did not like to wake you."

Muna thanked her, but she looked from Henrietta's eager face to the dish in front of her in consternation.

"It smells wonderful," she said. She paused—but she saw no way out of disappointing Henrietta. It was clear Muna's hostess intended to watch every bite. "But I am afraid I cannot eat pork. The rules of my religion prohibit it."

"Oh," said Henrietta, stricken.

Muna felt as though she had murdered a kitten. "I am sorry."

"Not at all," said Henrietta bravely. "We ought to have asked you before forcing our pork chops upon you. Nothing so rude as hospitality you do not desire! Sarah, pray take the chops away. But

Miss Muna will have the kippers, I hope—can you take a kipper, Miss Muna?"

Contrite, Muna took the kippers, as well as the eggs, cakes and bread, in quantities slightly in excess of her capacity to consume them. By the time the meal was concluded Henrietta's good cheer was restored, and Muna was so full that she could almost imagine that there was no space left inside her for grief or worry.

She had not forgotten her decision that morning, however. While the servants bore away the plates, Muna said to Henrietta:

"Will Mrs. Wythe be teaching any lessons today?"

She had decided that she would plead weariness from the journey, and anxiety about her sister, if she were asked again to perform any demonstrations of magic. How long this excuse would continue to serve she did not know. But if she could only extract some useful guidance from the Sorceress Royal on making the *polong* heed her, she would soon be able to rely upon the *polong's* aid to pass herself off as a witch.

But Henrietta said, "Oh no! Term does not begin for several days, so you will have time to recoup your energies and acquaint yourself with the Academy before lessons begin. Mrs. Wythe does not often take classes in any case. Her duties as Sorceress Royal demand most of her time. Mr. Wythe and I divide the teaching between us, and Mr. Damerell assists when either of us is called away from the Academy. Unfortunately Mr. Damerell is absent at present—I scarcely know how we shall manage without him."

Henrietta's forehead wrinkled, the pale eyebrows drawing downwards over her grey eyes. But Mr. Damerell's absence did not interest Muna in the least.

"Then will Mrs. Wythe join us for dinner?" she said.

"No," said Henrietta. "I believe she dines with Lady Hertingford tonight. Lady Hertingford is vastly wealthy and proud of her reputation as an eccentric, and Prunella hopes she may be persuaded to become a patroness of the Academy."

She hesitated, then went on, "I am afraid I will not be present at dinner either, for I must go home shortly. I am sorry to abandon you, but a few of our scholars are arriving this evening, so you will not be entirely alone. I am obliged to attend upon my family, you see. Indeed, they expected me at breakfast, but I wished to see you settled in."

"Pray do not apologise," said Muna, touched by Henrietta's look of guilt. It was easy to reassure her, for it was not Henrietta's presence on which Muna's hopes were pinned. "I am very well able to amuse myself. But I should like to speak with the Sorceress Royal soon, if it is at all possible. I wish to ask her about sending a message to Mak Genggang."

Henrietta's face cleared. "You need not worry about that. Prunella will not have forgotten. I should not be surprised if she has already spoken to Mak Genggang and told her all you have told us."

Since there was a great deal more that Muna wished to tell Mak Genggang that she did not intend divulging to the English *magiciennes*, this was less of a comfort than Henrietta meant it for.

"Still, I should like to speak to Mak Genggang myself," Muna persisted. "And to the Sorceress Royal, for I also wish to ask her about—"

About familiar spirits, she meant to say, but abruptly her voice gave out and the sentence ended in a squeak.

Muna blinked. "I meant to say, I wished to ask her about—"

But it was no good. Her throat closed up, and the words would not come. The effect was so sudden and so decided that it felt almost like—like—

Like a spell, thought Muna.

Of course. Mak Genggang would not have placed such a powerful talisman in Sakti's hands without taking precautions. She had not relied upon Muna and Sakti's discretion alone to preserve the secret of the *polong*. She had not wished them to tell the English about the *polong*, and so they could not.

To confirm her suspicion, Muna said, "I desired to ask Mrs. Wythe's advice about a familiar spirit Mak Genggang entrusted to us, a *polong*."

Or rather, she tried to say this. She choked on the first word and began to cough with such violence that Henrietta looked alarmed. She forced Muna into a chair, bringing her a glass of water and pushing a handkerchief into Muna's hand.

"I beg your pardon," said Muna, when the coughing had subsided. Her voice was subdued, for she was overcome by a sense of betrayal.

Perhaps Sakti needed to be restrained, she thought, *but Mak Genggang might have trusted* me!

Henrietta was all concern.

"Pray don't worry; I am sure Prunella will call upon you as soon as ever she can," she said. "She does not wish to be remiss in any attention, I know, for truly it is impossible to overstate how highly she esteems your mistress. There is no magician she respects more—and that is saying a great deal, for I have known Prunella since we were both children, and she has not a highly developed organ of respect! She would have breakfasted with us today, but she was called away."

Henrietta paused. There was evidently more she might say, but she seemed to doubt whether she should speak. Finally she made up her mind and went on:

"Mrs. Wythe does not wish the news to be spread abroad, for she has not yet decided what she will do. But yesterday she received a message from an old schoolfellow of ours—for we attended the same school as girls," Henrietta added by way of explanation, "an establishment for gentlewitches. Clarissa wishes to join the Academy as an instructress, and Mr. and Mrs. Wythe are seeing her this morning."

Muna patted her eyes with Henrietta's handkerchief, for they were streaming after her fit of coughing. There was no other reason for the tears. Certainly she was not weeping because Mak Genggang had not trusted her to maintain a judicious silence about the *polong*, for that would have been a feeble thing to do.

With an effort she brought herself back to the present.

"That is very good, isn't it?" said Muna. "To find a new instructress, just when you are in need of help. And it is someone you know! It must be a weight off your mind."

"Yes," said Henrietta dubiously. "But that is the problem, you see. We do know Clarissa."

"Were not you friends?" said Muna, though she could guess the answer from Henrietta's expression.

"We were never on what I would call intimate terms," said Henrietta, but then her true sentiments broke through her reserve. "Well, one couldn't be friends with a girl like that! She despised Prunella for being poor and an orphan, and because her mother was a native. I believe she was jealous as well—Clarissa was, I mean—for Prunella was always pretty and fascinating, and more magical than the rest of us put together.

"But that is why it is so surprising that Clarissa should have applied to us. Her father has always decried women's magic. He was one of the chief opponents of the establishment of this Academy. They do say the family has changed since Clarissa's brother went to live in the Fairy Court—his mother, in particular, feels his loss greatly. But still . . ."

Muna raised her head, for she knew the Fairy Court was what the English called the Palace of the Unseen. "Her brother lives in Fairy? I had understood the Queen of the Djinns welcomed few mortals to her court."

Henrietta nodded. "Yes, but Geoffrey married a connection of the Queen's and followed his wife to the Fairy Court."

If he were a relation of the Queen, she would not molest him, thought Muna; his situation was not remotely equivalent to Sakti's, for Sakti had been brought there by force. Still she said eagerly, "And is he happy at the Court?"

"Well," said Henrietta, hesitating, "no one can say! Visits over the border are not allowed; no one in England has seen Geoffrey since he left. But his relations are naturally anxious about him. And when one thinks of the horrors that have befallen mortal magicians in the Fairy Court, one can hardly blame them."

"Oh," said Muna.

She had already known that the Queen was ill-tempered and changeable, and Sakti was in grave danger every moment she spent in the Queen's Court. Why should Muna feel Henrietta's words as a blow?

"Still, I cannot believe that can have altered his father's opinions on women's magic," Henrietta was saying. "I should have thought it would have the reverse effect, for it is said Geoffrey's family blame Prunella for his departure. If Clarissa is defying her family in coming to us, that will mean trouble."

Muna thought of the scene she had witnessed upon her arrival. So much had happened since that she had neither sought an explanation nor been proffered one, but she had contrived to gather that the irate gentleman who had scolded Mrs. Wythe was Henrietta's father. Briefly distracted from her misery, she said:

"Your father, Mr. Stapleton—does he mind that you are a witch?"

Henrietta crimsoned. "He does not know. I am obliged to practise in secrecy. That is why I must often absent myself from the Academy—and why I know what trouble it causes when one defies one's family for magic! My father is acquainted with the greater part of English thaumaturgy, and it would expose him to ridicule if it were known that I teach here at the Academy."

"But everyone knows Mrs. Wythe is Sorceress Royal, don't they?" said Muna, perplexed. "That cannot be a secret here. It is known even in Janda Baik."

"Oh, but that is Prunella!" said Henrietta, dismissing the Sorceress Royal with the wave of a hand. "She does not labour under the disadvantage of having parents." She sighed. "Relations are a terrible burden to a girl with magical ability."

This turned Muna's thoughts back to her own troubles. She did not think she had ever been a burden to Sakti, but she was not being much of an aid either. "Do you know when I might see the Sorceress Royal?"

"She has a great deal of business to settle before term commences," said Henrietta unpromisingly. Muna's face must have fallen, for Henrietta added kindly, "But I shall send her a message. If she cannot come away before, you will see her at the ball, at least."

"The ball?"

"Mrs. Wythe is hosting a party tomorrow for all her acquaintances," explained Henrietta. "It will be at the Sorceress Royal's quarters, a small distance from here. That is why we shall have a few of our scholars with us this evening, though term has not yet begun. Mrs. Wythe wishes to introduce them to some important persons who she hopes may be prevailed upon to become benefactors to the Academy. Prunella was anxious that you should attend the ball, too, if you do not object. It is not often that we can boast of hosting an Oriental enchantress!"

Muna was in no humour to attend any party, and she was about to concoct an excuse when a thought gave her pause. She had left Janda Baik and journeyed through the jungles of the Unseen to find the author of the curse. If Sakti was in the Palace of the Unseen, it seemed unlikely that the answer would lie in England—and yet there remained the fact that "Midsomer" was an English name.

Was not there still a chance that she might find out something useful about the curseworker while she was in England—or even track down the curseworker himself, this Midsomer who had used her and Sakti so cruelly? She should leave no stone unturned. Breaking the curse might yet be the means of recovering her sister.

"Will there be many magicians at the ball?" said Muna.

"Nearly all of English thaumaturgy will be in attendance," Henrietta assured her. "And I shall be there with my family—though not, of course, in the capacity of a *magicienne*—so you need not fear that you will know no one."

"Then I should be delighted to attend," said Muna.

After her disappointment in the *polong*, she felt quite equal to threatening to break the enchanter's head if she could only contrive to find him. It was the prospect of the ball itself, conducted along foreign lines, that was rather more daunting. Muna looked down at herself. "Though I am not sure I have brought suitable clothes."

"Oh, that will be no difficulty," said Henrietta. "Mrs. Wythe left orders for her gowns to be brought to you so you may choose one you like; you are much of a size."

"That is very kind," said Muna gratefully.

But despite her best efforts it was evident she had failed to conceal her lack of excitement at the idea of the ball. Henrietta gave her a worried look.

"I thought I might just show you our library before I leave," said Henrietta. "Our collection is small yet, but there are several books that may amuse you. And if you did wish to begin your studies now, it includes a treatise by Mr. Wythe which serves as an excellent introduction to basic thaumaturgical principles."

Muna was able to muster rather more genuine enthusiasm at this suggestion—perhaps there would be something in the Academy's library that would tell her more about the curse, or the *polong*, or the Palace of the Unseen. Relieved to have hit upon something that pleased her, Henrietta led Muna to a small book-lined study.

"It will be very interesting to learn about thaumaturgy," said Muna. "I should particularly like to know about curse-working—evil spells, you know, and their antidotes. There are some wicked people in Janda Baik who are given to cursing their enemies," she added, thinking her interest might require some explanation, "and it is always useful to learn about remedies. And are there any books on familiar spirits?"

There were several books on both subjects, as it turned out, and Henrietta picked out a few for Muna to read before she left.

Even with a fire crackling in the grate and a shawl wrapped around her, it was cold. Muna huddled down in her chair, reminded herself that Sakti might be suffering much worse in the Palace of the Unseen—a place no doubt colder and more unpleasant than Britain by far.

English thaumaturges might make excellent magicians, but Muna could not admire their prose; every sample she read was written in the same hopelessly dull style. Still she persevered, determined to extract what she could from the books. But the authors she read were fonder of embarking upon flights of theory than dispensing practical advice. She had worked her way through two tomes, gaining no insight that seemed pertinent to her situation, when she gave up, pushing the books aside.

She felt stupid, but she had developed a pounding headache and did not feel equal to continuing. If Sakti were here, it would be easier. Not that Sakti would have bothered studying these books, or stopped in the library for above five minutes.

Muna was almost alone in the Academy—most of the servants had gone to the Sorceress Royal's quarters to assist with preparations for the ball, Henrietta had said. It was too cold to go outside, but there was no reason Muna should not explore the building. She would not disturb anyone.

She opened the door and stood for a moment, listening. The house might have been empty, save for herself. A hush lay over it, though she could still hear the sounds of the city outside. Muna set off along the corridor.

She tried the doors as she passed, glimpsing rooms with rows of tables and chairs, which she supposed to be where Mr. Wythe and Miss Stapleton taught their classes. At some point a person of means had evidently occupied the building, and it was kept clean enough for the most fastidious taste, with polished floorboards smelling of beeswax.

But upon closer inspection Muna could see that the carpets were worn and the furnishings, though handsome, were rather old. It was no wonder the Sorceress Royal was kept busy seeking patronage for the Academy. Running a school seemed an expensive enterprise.

In time the corridor opened upon a long narrow room, not

much furnished, with rows of paintings lining the walls. Muna's steps slowed as she studied these.

They consisted exclusively of portraits of Englishmen, all of whom bore a strong likeness to one another. Most had white hair; several looked wicked, and more looked miserable. Muna would not have been surprised to be told that their subjects belonged to the same family, and when she read the labels on the paintings she saw that the same few names did indeed recur.

One of the names was Midsomer.

Muna's heart lurched.

There were two paintings bearing the name of Midsomer among the collection, but these both turned out to be depictions of the same person, a George Midsomer. This was a pale, lipless gentleman with reddish hair and a severe expression. In both portraits he wore an enormous white ruff, beneath which the rest of his person, clad in black, seemed to vanish into darkness.

"That is certainly a face capable of cursing people," said Muna aloud . . .

She had spoken Malay, but she was answered in English.

"I beg your pardon?" said the portrait. While Muna stared, transfixed with horror, the painted head moved. George Midsomer turned to look at her, his forehead creasing in a frown. "But you are a woman!"

Muna leapt back with a shriek, clutching at her chest.

"A native woman, at that," said George Midsomer in disgust.

"It is because of that female that calls herself the Sorceress Royal," said another painted Englishman next to him. This second thaumaturge looked to have been painted on his deathbed, so frail was he, but his pale eyes glared with a passion that seemed scarcely supportable by his aged frame. "They tell me she has taken on half a dozen black servants. I can only suppose she relishes being defrauded by her staff!"

"You forget, sir, that Prunella Wythe has native blood herself," drawled George Midsomer. "It is no surprise she is attached to her kind, since the creatures cannot by any superiority of manner or intellect put her to the blush."

One by one the painted thaumaturges stirred and came to life, craning their necks so they could glower at Muna.

Muna stood with her hand pressed to her breast, trying to calm herself. But her initial shock had faded and she saw what was afoot. The paintings were possessed by demons. Antique objects did often become the repositories of spirits. That these were the demonic type of spirit was evident from the men's appalling manners and bigoted language.

"It is not to be borne," cried the aged thaumaturge. "You, gel, go to your mistress and tell her we will not have natives in the Society!"

Warmth rose in Muna's cheeks, for she could not recall ever having been addressed in such a manner in her life. Mak Genggang might reprove her dependents, but she did not deal in insults or name-calling. Like all the islanders of Janda Baik, she prized civility as highly as virtue—indeed, to speak gently and with refinement was deemed a kind of virtue in itself.

"You are mistaken, sir," she said, for after all the man who had addressed her was very old and frail. "This is not the Society, but the Lady Maria Wythe Academy for the Instruction of Females in Practical Thaumaturgy." She and Sakti had learnt the name of the Sorceress Royal's establishment before they came to England, in case they were lost and were obliged to ask for directions to the Academy. They had had to repeat it to each other several times before they could remember.

"And I am no maidservant," Muna continued, throwing her head back, "but a witch of the island of Janda Baik, and an honoured guest of the Sorceress Royal!"

The portraits burst into coarse laughter, intermixed with jeers and hoots.

"A witch!" sneered one. "Did not I tell you so, Midsomer? I knew Mrs. Wythe should be obliged to invite all sorts of riffraff to make up numbers at her Academy. I told you no Englishman with any ordinary pride would allow his daughter to be taught magic by an upstart!"

George Midsomer did not answer but fixed a gaze on Muna, whose chill seemed to pierce through to her bones. "We know how to regard any guest of Prunella Wythe," he said. "Females meddling in what has nothing to do with them—shameless, depraved and unwomanly!"

"Nonsense," said Muna, firing up. "If God had intended women to have nothing to do with magic, there would be no such creatures as witches nor any female spirits, and everyone knows there are a great many of those!"

The paintings did not like being spoken to in this manner. They broke out into an ungodly uproar. Some restricted themselves to marvelling that anyone should rely upon fairies as an argument for women's magic ("When everyone knows the females of the fairy race are the maddest of all!"), but others shouted, "Hex her! Teach her a lesson!"

Muna stepped back, daunted—after all, she did not know what powers these spirits possessed. She glimpsed out of the corner of her eye a green door tucked away in the corner of the gallery. The door was nearer than the entrance through which she had come, and it had the advantage that she need not brave a gauntlet of disapproving painted faces to get to it.

"I shall not lower myself to quarrel with you," she said with dignity, inching by degrees towards the door. "But you should be ashamed of yourselves. I am a guest in your country; I am entitled to your hospitality, and instead you hoot like monkeys! You dishonour your white hair by your conduct. Men so old should know better!"

"It is only a wig," objected one of the newer-looking paintings. "I am not more than thirty."

Another thaumaturge produced a wand from within his coat, crying, "We will see if you are still as impertinent in the form of a frog!"

The doorknob was under Muna's hand.

"No, we won't!" she retorted. She gave the door a shove. It swung open, and Muna slipped through it, shutting out the magicians' angry voices behind her.

9

MUNA STOOD IN a high-ceilinged hall. Brilliant sunlight spilt through the windows stretching from dark stone floors to a vaulted ceiling. A table of gigantic proportions ran along the entire length of the hall.

She was no longer in Britain. The air betrayed this—it was a dry hot air; nothing less like the damp chill of Britain could be imagined. The light, too, was not the watery grey light of London but a harsh brassy glare, possessing all the intensity of the noonday sun in Janda Baik.

The windows looked out on a vast expanse of blue sky, unmarred by a single wisp of cloud. Below lay golden desert, stretching away as far as the eye could see. Mountains reared up in the distance, but Muna did not study these, for the herd of beasts thundering past distracted her.

She took these for deer, but as she approached the window this illusion fell away. While she could see that some species of deer might have blue fur and beards and even furry paws in place of hooves, she doubted whether any could boast tails of blue flame.

A vast black shadow fell over the herd. The beasts put on a burst of speed, vanishing into the distance.

Muna raised her head and saw the *naga*.

She had never seen a dragon before, but she knew it for what it was at once. It was flying quite low and so she could see that it was not large, so far as *naga* went. The creature was no larger than an elephant—it was the massive wings that cast the greatest part of the shadow.

As she watched, openmouthed, the *naga* turned its great golden head. Muna looked directly into an enormous blue eye—and it looked back at her.

The *naga* swerved and dived towards her.

Muna whipped around and ran helter-skelter along the hall, too frightened even to spare the breath to scream. It took a hideous age for her to cross the expanse of floor dividing her from the door. At any moment the *naga* would shatter the glass and rush into the room. She could almost feel the beast's hot breath stirring her hair, its talons gouging her flesh . . .

She could not help glancing back when she reached the door. The *naga* had landed outside the window. It lowered its head to peer through, puzzling over how it might enter. Muna slammed the door shut behind her.

She had expected to return to the gallery of ill-bred portraits, but she stumbled out into a different corridor. Before panic could overtake her, recognition came—she knew that painting of cows by the river. She was in the Academy, back in Britain. Sure enough, when she pushed open the door by the painting of cows, she found herself in her own bedchamber.

Her heart was still racing. She collapsed into a chair, panting.

The Sorceress Royal ought to put up a sign on that door, Muna thought in indignation. *Why, anyone might enter and be devoured!*

But then she went still, for a disquieting thought possessed her.

They had lied to her—the Sorceress Royal, Henrietta and the *polong*. Leonine deer with flaming tails and blue-eyed dragons were not to be found in deserts in the mortal world. Muna had just been in the Unseen Realm.

She sprang to her feet and rushed back to the gallery. It was still there, and the portraits recognised her at once.

"There is that gel again!" one began.

But Muna's wariness of the paintings had evaporated in the shock of seeing the *naga*. Painted demons hardly seemed to compare.

"Oh, hush!" she snapped. "I shall go away again directly. I have no more desire for your society than you have for mine!"

Her tone startled the paintings sufficiently that they subsided into discontented mutterings. Ignoring them, Muna went down to the end of the gallery, but it was as she had half-suspected. The green door she had seen before had vanished.

It had been the same in Mak Genggang's house. Doorways shifted about; new verandas occasionally sprouted without warning; and once an entire annexe had blossomed behind the main house to accommodate a family from the village whose own house had burnt down. It had gone away again once their house was rebuilt.

It was in the nature of magicians' houses that they were in a state of constant metamorphosis. But Muna knew what she had seen.

W HEN Muna returned to her bedroom she took out the *polong*'s bottle from under the bed where she had concealed it. She could not interrogate the English; she was sure she had seen what was not meant for her. But perhaps the spirit would be able to tell her where the green door had gone.

Though she repeated the summons twice, however, the *polong* did not appear.

"I know I was uncivil last night," said Muna, "but I beg you will forgive me, *kak*. Think how you would feel if you knew your sister was in the clutches of evil spirits and you were helpless to prevent it!"

Muna's plea was met with silence—a silence that had a distinctly stubborn quality.

"Oh, very well!" said Muna. Bitter words crowded her throat, but she swallowed them. It was not impossible that she might still prevail upon the *polong* to help her, once the spirit had recovered from her sulks.

Muna was troubled as she restored the bottle to its hiding place. It was all very well for the *polong* to counsel her to maintain the pretence of being a witch. How was she to continue to impose upon the English without the spirit's aid? And what would become of her if she was found out as a fraud?

She could not quite believe that she would be thrown out on the street. The Sorceress Royal might be ruthless enough to use her so, but surely Henrietta would intervene on her behalf—Muna could not imagine the blond Englishwoman, with her gentle eyes, doing anything so unkind. They might send her back to Janda Baik. That would not be so bad, for then she could ask Mak Genggang for help. But if she was obliged to travel there without the aid of magic, it would be a year before she saw the witch.

Who knew what a year would mean to Sakti? It was said that in the Unseen Realm time did not pass as it did in the mortal world, but still, Muna could not afford to leave her sister in the Palace of the Unseen—perhaps in the power of the very enchanter who had cursed them—for so long.

The thought of the curseworker reminded her of the painting she had seen of George Midsomer. Was *he* the Midsomer to whom the spell had referred? But why should an English magician trapped in a painting have cursed two girls from an island thousands of miles away? How could he have spirited Sakti away to the Palace of the Unseen, if he had not even the power to liberate himself from a picture frame? Besides, surely if he were their enemy he would have known Muna, and he had shown no sign of recognising her.

She had not enjoyed her exchange with Mr. Midsomer and if she were governed by her inclinations alone she would not soon have returned to the gallery. But duty must override inclination, and it was clearly her duty to question him and discover what she could. Muna rose from where she knelt by the bed, dusting herself off.

She was resolved to go back to the gallery directly, but when she opened the door she found the maidservant Sarah stood outside with her hand raised to knock.

"Oh, you startled me, miss!" gasped Sarah. "I beg your pardon, but dinner will be served in half an hour, and I came to see if I might help you dress. We shall have three of the scholars with us—Miss Edwards, Miss Campbell and Alice—Miss Pinder, that is. They have just arrived, and right pleased to see you, they will be."

"Thank you," said Muna, after a pause. "I can dress myself, though it is kind of you to offer, and I shall be delighted to meet the scholars."

There was no reason she should feel guilty, she told herself, for it would not help Sakti for Muna to fast. Besides, she owed it to her English hosts to make a decent show of gratitude and attend the meals they laid on for her. She would go back to the gallery later. And if she felt relieved that she need not confront George Midsomer just then, no one who had seen his manners would blame her.

The Academy's scholars were waiting for her at dinner. They proved a motley crew—Miss Edwards was six-and-twenty, a governess who had given her notice when she heard of Mrs. Wythe's Academy, whereas Miss Alice Pinder was not more than eight years old. It seemed her attendance at the Academy had caused considerable controversy, because her mother was a cook.

"But what is offensive about that?" said Muna, surprised. "To be a cook is a respectable profession."

"Oh, you cannot conceive the number of things that will offend an English thaumaturge," said Miss Campbell. "He is the touchiest creature alive!" Miss Campbell, a lively maiden of fourteen, was from Scotland and had little reverence to spare for the English.

"They ought not all to be tarred with the same brush, however," said Miss Edwards in defence of her countrymen. "Mr. Damerell is a Fellow of the Society, and he is a great friend to the Academy. Mr. Damerell is abroad," she explained to Muna, "visiting Threlfall, for his familiar is a dragon belonging to that clan. But he often teaches us when he is in England."

Muna had never heard of Threlfall, but the scholars were only too delighted to enlighten her about that ancient clan of dragons, who governed their own demesne in Fairyland and were feared even by the Fairy Queen herself. They told her of Mr. Damerell's friend and familiar Robert of Threlfall, who was occasionally to be seen in the Academy—a pleasant-spoken, gentlemanly creature, not in the least proud though he was so highborn.

"What is Threlfall like?" asked Muna, thinking of the sun-baked land she had glimpsed earlier that day, in the room where she had sought refuge from the talking paintings. Might the dragon she had seen have anything to do with these friends of the Sorceress Royal? "Is it a dry country, do you know?"

Miss Campbell shook her head. "Mr. Threlfall never speaks of his home. If you did not know, you might think he was a mortal born and bred. You never met anyone so English!"

But she and the others told Muna everything else they knew—about the Royal Society of Unnatural Philosophers that frowned upon them; the dashing Sorceress Royal who trailed scandal and excitement in her wake; and their instructors at the Academy (they referred fondly to Miss Stapleton as Henny, but it was for Mr. Wythe that they reserved their most ardent sentiments—they all seemed more than half in love with him).

Muna had feared that dinner would be a wearisome affair, but she was diverted by the girls' conversation, and touched by their pains to welcome a stranger. Their gossip was more than amusing; it proved instructive. For it was Miss Campbell who said, with an air of importance:

"And they say we are to have a new instructress this year."

"Who says so? Who is it?" cried Miss Edwards and Miss Pinder.

"The footman told me," said Miss Campbell. "He saw her at the Sorceress Royal's quarters."

"A *magicienne*?" said Miss Edwards. "I had not thought there were any others qualified to teach."

"Yes, and you will never guess who it is," said Miss Campbell. "It is the least likely person in the world—Miss Clarissa Midsomer!"

If she had hoped to create a sensation, she was amply rewarded by her audience. Alice, to be sure, said, "Who is that?" but Miss Edwards echoed, "Clarissa Midsomer?" in tones of incredulity, and Muna choked on her mouthful of whiting.

Fortunately the girls had no reason to believe the name "Midsomer" meant anything to Muna. They supposed she had swallowed a bone. When, anxious not to interrupt the conversation, she had reassured them, they returned to the subject of Clarissa Midsomer, questioning Miss Campbell eagerly.

"But I thought the Midsomers abhorred the Sorceress Royal," said Miss Edwards. "Was not it Miss Midsomer's father who applied to the Presiding Committee to strip Mrs. Wythe of her office?"

Miss Campbell nodded, her eyes bright. "And Mrs. Midsomer blames Mrs. Wythe for exiling her son Geoffrey to Fairyland. Such nonsense, when everyone knows Geoffrey Midsomer went to Fairy because of his wife! But Miss Midsomer was at school with Mrs. Wythe and Miss Stapleton. It seems she is not entirely of one mind with her mother and father."

She exchanged a knowing look with Miss Edwards, and even little Alice looked sage. It seemed it was not at all uncommon for female magicians to disagree with their relations.

"It will be good to have another instructress," Miss Edwards concluded. "Though I wonder how Miss Midsomer could have learnt enough magic to be able to teach! Mrs. Wythe and Miss Stapleton have always said they learnt nothing at their school but how to suppress their magic. It was Mr. Wythe who taught them thaumaturgy."

"The Midsomers are one of our oldest magical families," replied Miss Campbell. "There are ways and means for a determined female."

Everyone at the table knew she belonged to this class, and they shared a smile in recognition of this—save Muna. For the remainder of the meal she said very little. But she was excused, for the girls had been forewarned of the dreadful tragedy that had befallen their guest, and sudden fits of melancholy were only to be expected in one who had suffered the loss of a sister.

* * *

MUNA was in a ferment for the rest of the evening. It could not be mere coincidence that, by her second day at the Academy, she should have encountered one Midsomer and heard of another, both magicians. She had been led here by an intelligence greater than her own. For the first time since she had lost Sakti, Muna said her prayers in a spirit of true submissive gratitude.

But which Midsomer was the curseworker? She puzzled over the mystery for half the night, tossing and turning in her bed.

Surely she could discount George Midsomer. He was only a painting. If he had any real power, he would be casting hexes at the Sorceress Royal, not only aspersions.

But Clarissa Midsomer sounded a mere novice *magicienne*. Muna could not see how she could have wrought a curse capable of confounding such a powerful witch as Mak Genggang—nor what motive either could have had for afflicting two village girls from a distant island.

Muna rose the next morning more determined than ever to seek out George Midsomer and interrogate him—but it proved difficult to gain the necessary solitude now that the scholars had arrived. Miss Edwards, Miss Campbell and Miss Pinder were anxious that their guest should not be left alone to stew in her low spirits. They threatened to attach themselves to her, and it was only by claiming a sudden indisposition, requiring a return to bed, that Muna contrived to extricate herself from their hospitality.

She stole to her bedchamber, feeling guilty. God would forgive her for telling so many lies, she hoped, since she did it all for Sakti. She waited till the hands of the clock on the mantelpiece had described several rotations before creeping to the door and looking out cautiously.

There was a bustle in the house there had not been before—the scholars' return had brought the Academy to life—but there was no one around to see Muna leave her room. Nor did she encounter anyone on her way. But when she rounded the corner into the gallery with its rows of painted thaumaturges, she came upon a scene that threw her plan into disarray.

"Ah, Miss Muna!" cried Henrietta. "We were just speaking of you. Clarissa, this is the guest I told you of, from the island of Janda Baik. The arch-witch of that country, Mak Genggang, has done us the honour of entrusting her apprentice to our care. Miss Muna, may I present to you Miss Clarissa Midsomer? She has agreed to join the Academy as an instructress."

Miss Midsomer dropped a brief curtsey. After a moment Muna managed to collect herself sufficiently to respond in kind.

She was too taken aback to know what to say or how to look, but Miss Midsomer did not speak either. The Englishwoman gazed at Muna with her lip curled, in a way that would have been accounted unmannerly in Janda Baik.

Perhaps she is the curseworker after all, thought Muna, though Clarissa Midsomer looked scarcely old enough to be so powerful or so wicked. She was as youthful as Henrietta, though less pretty, having a great deal of sandy hair and a skin so pale she might have been a ghost. Her eyes were of an indeterminate light shade, watery and reddish; the effect they gave was not in the least occult.

Nonetheless there was something eerie about Miss Midsomer, ordinary as she looked. For the familial resemblance was remarkable. Muna's eyes darted towards the portrait of George Midsomer, looking disdainfully down on the three of them.

"Are you a relation of this gentleman, Miss Midsomer?" she said. "You look so much like him!"

It only struck her after the words were out that this might not be taken as a compliment, for *she* would not like to be told that she resembled a man so pale and sour-faced. But either George Midsomer was deemed handsome by English standards, or clan pride supplied all that was wanting in his features, for Miss Midsomer's hauteur dissolved. She flushed with pleasure.

"Yes," she said, "he is an ancestor of mine. One of the two Sorcerers Royal who bore the name Midsomer!"

She gestured at the painting. For the first time Muna noticed the staff in George Midsomer's left hand. It was made of a gnarled and ancient-looking wood, and it looked familiar.

"Why," Muna exclaimed, "that is Mrs. Wythe's staff!"

At the mention of the Sorceress Royal, Miss Midsomer froze up again. "It is the chief emblem of the Sorcerer Royal's office," she said stiffly, "and was held by many Englishmen before Prunella Wythe. It is not rightly *her* staff—it belongs just as much to her predecessors."

"As it will belong to those that succeed her," said Henrietta. "But Prunella is the Sorceress Royal at present, you know, so Miss Muna is quite correct to call the staff hers. Now I come to think of it," she added, "yours is not the only family that can claim the honour of producing more than one Sorcerer Royal. There have been *three* Sorcerers Royal named Wythe!"

She spoke in a perfectly pleasant tone, as though she was agreeing with Miss Midsomer, but Miss Midsomer bridled.

"I wonder I did not notice the staff in the painting before," said Muna. She paused, but there was no reason to hide the fact that she had been here already, and she wished to know why George Midsomer was so altered. Neither he nor any of the other thaumaturges had shown the least flicker of life. "Mr. Midsomer did not say he was Sorcerer Royal. No doubt that accounts for his lordly manners."

"What do you mean, he did not *say* he was Sorcerer Royal?" said Miss Midsomer sharply. "Did Mr. Midsomer speak to you?"

"Yes," said Muna. "I was never so astonished in my life! Do all your paintings speak, Miss Stapleton?"

Henrietta shook her head. "Oh dear, I ought to have warned you! These are the only paintings in the Academy that speak. They used to hang in the Society, but they made such a nuisance of themselves that—that is to say, the Sorceress Royal felt they would do better here. This part of the building is not much used." Henrietta gave Muna a worried look. "I hope the gentlemen did not say anything untoward? I am afraid they are sometimes wont to forget their manners."

"You might recall, Henrietta Stapleton, that my forefather is among them!" said Miss Midsomer.

"I am not likely to forget," Henrietta reassured her. "He is the worst for abusing the servants and threatening the scholars with being turned into frogs! But I do not mean any reflection upon your ancestor. Mr. Wythe says the paintings have little of their subjects in them—the life that animates them springs from the artist, and the artist's opinions of his subject cannot be taken as a wholly reliable guide to who they were. I am sure the real George Midsomer was much pleasanter than his likeness."

She did not sound convinced, however, and Miss Midsomer was not propitiated. She directed a glare at Muna, as though she resented the honour Muna had received in being insulted by Miss Midsomer's ancestor.

"I am afraid Miss Midsomer and I must discuss her duties," said Henrietta to Muna. "We shall see you again this evening at the

Sorceress Royal's ball, but for now we must take our leave of you. May I escort you to the library, Miss Muna? You have discovered already that there are a great many surprises in this building—not all of them pleasant!"

Muna thought of the grand hall into which she had stumbled the day before, with its foreign sunshine and magical beasts outside the window. The green door was still conspicuous by its absence; in its place was a featureless expanse of gold damask wallpaper.

"Yes," she said. But she declined Henrietta's offer of assistance. She was very much obliged, she said, but she knew where the library was to be found, and did not fear any misadventure befalling her while she covered that short distance.

She parted from the Englishwomen, answering Miss Midsomer's ungracious "Good day" with more courtesy than it merited. It was clear that Miss Midsomer shared some of her ancestor's views on natives, but she had shown no sign of recognising Muna, any more than George Midsomer. That suggested either that Miss Midsomer was an excellent actress—or that she could not be Muna's enemy.

Perhaps it was another Midsomer altogether. Miss Midsomer had a father, a mother, a brother . . . they might all be magicians, and any of them might be the curseworker.

Yet why should any of Miss Midsomer's kin wish to curse Muna and her sister? What crime could they have committed against any English magician?

It seemed an impossible tangle. Still, to have met two Midsomers was progress she had scarcely hoped for before. Muna would watch Clarissa Midsomer, and pursue every clue that presented itself, till the curse was broken and Sakti restored to her.

Mak Genggang might not have taught Muna magic, but the witch's conviction that the world had meaning, and that time was a pattern that God understood, was one Muna shared. All that had happened in the past two days was a reminder that nothing was impossible, even to one as powerless as Muna. She had not felt so hopeful since she had arrived in England.

10

THE MAIDSERVANT SARAH came to Muna a few hours before the Sorceress Royal's ball, her arms heaped with muslins, silks and satins of every hue of the rainbow. No one could have been kinder or more attentive: Sarah took infinite pains over Muna's appearance, curling Muna's hair before winding a turban around her head, and helping her into the dress they chose for her, a green silk gown with puffed sleeves and ruffles along the hem.

Nonetheless the maidservant left Muna woefully uncomfortable. Sarah had introduced a horrific invention called "stays," and though what she had done to Muna's hair was not unbecoming, the turban was in a rather more spectacular style than Muna would have chosen. She wished she could have kept her own sarong and jacket.

But Mak Genggang would say that it was proper for her to be dressed, here in England, as the other women were. At least Sakti was not there to make faces at her, she thought ruefully.

Mrs. Wythe's carriage was to be sent for Muna, Miss Midsomer and the scholars at eight o'clock—one could walk to the Sorceress Royal's quarters from the Academy, but the young ladies would hardly wish to do that in all their finery, said Sarah. Mrs. Wythe was already there, making the final preparations for the evening, and Henrietta had taken herself off earlier that day—she would be attending the ball with her family, for it was an occasion of sufficient importance that Mr. Stapleton had deigned to overlook his disagreement with the Sorceress Royal.

At half past seven Muna ventured downstairs to wait for the carriage. She was passed on the stairs by an agitated Miss Campbell, trailing a cloud of fragrance, her toilette only half-finished. But in the hallway there was a lone female, already dressed and waiting.

"Miss Edwards," said Muna, for from the woman's height she thought it must be the eldest of the scholars. But then the woman turned and the words died in Muna's throat. The face was the last she had expected to see here, in a strange land. It was as familiar to her as her own.

She had never known gladness could be so piercing that it could make you weep. Her chest seemed to open out with relief. Tears sprang to her eyes. She reached out her hands to Sakti.

"Adik," she cried. "I have been so worried! But the *polong* said you were in the Palace of the Unseen. How did you come here?"

"I beg your pardon?" said the woman.

All at once Muna's vision cleared; the world reordered itself. In Sakti's place stood Miss Clarissa Midsomer, pale and English. She was frowning as though she suspected Muna of insulting her, for of course Muna had spoken Malay. No one less like Sakti could be imagined—and yet for a thrilling, wonderful moment, Muna had *seen* her sister's face in the Englishwoman's.

Her conviction had been so strong that she could not immediately reconcile herself to the error. She passed her hand over her eyes, disappointment a hard knot in her throat. It was necessary for her to swallow twice before she could speak.

"I—I am sorry, Miss Midsomer," said Muna. "I mistook you for another. It is this dim light, no doubt."

Miss Midsomer inclined her head, still frowning. She was got up very fine for the ball. Her dress was simple, a white gown with flowers embroidered in pink and green silks across the front, but around her neck she wore a gold chain with a remarkable pendant. It was in the form of a snake with rubies for eyes and a blood-red tongue flicking out to taste the air. The scales covering its body were made of turquoise. For all its splendour, the shape of the snake was curiously inelegant—the serpentine coils ended in an incongruous stubby tail.

"What an extraordinary necklace!" said Muna, grateful for an excuse to change the subject. "I have never seen anything so beautiful in my life."

The compliment did not seem to give Miss Midsomer much pleasure.

"Thank you," she said in a forbidding tone. "It was a gift from my brother."

She would not be drawn to say any more, though Muna heaped admiration upon the pendant. Muna was not sorry when they were joined by the scholars, ready for the ball and bubbling over with excited chatter. Even Miss Midsomer's evident resolve not to enjoy their society or the evening's merriment could not quench the girls.

"I was persuaded that Miss Campbell would prevent our leaving in time," said Miss Edwards, once they were rattling way in the carriage. "She could not decide on which dress she meant to wear, though she had only two to choose from. She kept throwing one off and picking up the other, and then when we had got her into *that* dress she would insist the first was the best, after all. I had made up my mind that we should only arrive when the ball was nearly over, covered in disgrace. Mrs. Wythe hates unpunctuality."

Forgetting the dignity of her fourteen years, Miss Campbell stuck her tongue out at Miss Edwards. Muna was laughing when Miss Midsomer surprised them all by bursting out:

"'Hates unpunctuality'! When Prunella Gentleman was never early for anything in her life!"

"But she is Sorceress Royal, you know," said little Alice Pinder. "People of consequence may be as late as they like. When *I* am a sorceress I shall never rise before ten o'clock."

"Slugabed!" said Miss Campbell. "Why not sleep till noon?" She and Miss Edwards were delighted by this naked ambition in their young schoolfellow, but Miss Midsomer turned her face to the window with a long-suffering air.

They were none of them surprised when Miss Midsomer decamped upon their arrival at the Sorceress Royal's quarters. She paused only to say:

"I must ask you to refrain from addressing me or claiming my acquaintance this evening. My mother and father are present and they would prefer me to limit my association with the Academy to no more than is strictly necessary for the discharge of my duties."

She did not wait for an answer before vanishing into the crowd. The scholars gaped after her.

"She is very disagreeable!" said Alice Pinder, with the unhesitating judgment of childhood.

"Hush!" said Miss Edwards, but Miss Campbell said indignantly, "As though we *wished* to claim her acquaintance! I wonder why Mrs. Wythe agreed to take her."

"Shall we look for the Sorceress Royal?" said Miss Edwards to Muna. "I am sure she will wish to see you."

Muna had scarcely paid attention to Miss Midsomer's ill breeding in her amazement at her surroundings. The Sorceress Royal's quarters, decorated for a ball, showed her Britain in a new light. As she followed the scholars through the crowd, she felt as though she had strayed into yet another world—a world far more glamorous than the cold, shabby Academy. Surely the Palace of the Unseen itself could not boast a brighter blaze of lights, richer furnishings or more beautiful people, expensively dressed?

Save for one or two of the men, who were garbed in the same gorgeous uniform, she could not help noticing that everyone present was white. Muna was conspicuous among them for the darker hue of her skin, and she was sure she was not imagining the heads that turned as she passed.

After her first thrill of embarrassment, she flung her head back, meeting the eyes of the women who stared at her, until they looked away. Sakti would not have been afraid of being stared at; she would not have worried about being deemed provincial or ill-bred. She would have been confident that all she did was right, since it was she who did it. If Muna was to recover her sister, she must have her sister's own courage. She could not be so feeble as to falter on account of a mere party.

She heartened herself enough that by the time they found the Sorceress Royal, Muna was able to greet her with a tolerably convincing smile. Mrs. Wythe was standing with Henrietta and Mr. Wythe; they received Muna and the scholars with delight.

"How magnificent you are!" said Prunella, admiring Muna. "That is precisely the gown I should have chosen for you. And that turban! You have just the complexion for that shade. How clever of Sarah!"

Muna was able to return these compliments, for Mrs. Wythe was looking very well. She wore a pale lilac robe trimmed with gold embroidery and her dark curls were caught up in a fillet. In one hand she held a delicately carved ivory fan; in the other, the staff of the Sorcerer Royal—the same staff that George Midsomer held in his painting.

"It looks odd to bring this to a ball, I know," she said, when Muna glanced at the staff. "But thaumaturges are mad for all articles of the kind—pomp and pageantry—and I do not omit anything that might encourage them to be civil."

She presented her husband to Muna. Muna recognised the dark gentleman she had seen from afar; closer to, she saw why Henrietta blushed when she spoke his name, and the scholars harboured such a passion for him. Zacharias Wythe was not only tall but remarkably handsome, with a gentle manner that was peculiarly winning.

He bowed. "I regret that my duties called me elsewhere, or I should have been present to receive you. I was very sorry to hear of the misfortune you met on your journey here. An appalling tragedy—without precedent, Mak Genggang tells us."

Muna's head snapped up at this. "Mak Genggang told you . . . ? You spoke to my mistress?"

Mr. Wythe blinked. "We were anxious to inform her at once." He glanced at his wife. "Mrs. Wythe said you particularly desired that she should be told about your sister."

"What did she say?" said Muna, her heart in her throat. "Is she coming?"

She knew the answer at once from the look of pity and discomfort on Prunella's face.

If Mr. Wythe was equally dismayed, he was less transparent. He said gently, "You need not doubt she was exceedingly concerned. She wished me to assure you that she will do everything in her power to trace your sister. But she could not come away. Her duties in Janda Baik detain her. For the time being she begs you will remain with us."

Muna felt cold, though what with her stays and petticoats, and the smart white spencer Sarah had given her, she was more heavily covered than she had ever been in her life. She folded her arms, pressing her gloved hands into her elbows to warm them.

Mak Genggang does not know Sakti is in the Palace of the Unseen, she told herself. *If she did, perhaps . . .*

But even if Muna could tell Mak Genggang where Sakti was, would the witch risk an encounter with the Queen of the Djinns on Sakti's account? Muna and Sakti had already made trouble with the British; Janda Baik did not need another powerful adversary. After all, they were only two of the many people requiring Mak Genggang's protection. Not only the witch's household, but the villagers—indeed, the people of the island as a whole—depended upon her. Muna would be foolish to think Mak Genggang would abandon her obligations for one girl's sake.

Her eyes stung with unshed tears. There was no one Muna could rely upon—no one who would save her and her sister, unless it was Muna herself. And she was so ill-equipped to do it!

Mr. Wythe was still speaking.

"I have called up our records on Fairy and will study these for what guidance they may yield," he said. "We have not lost a magician in Fairy in many years, and even then . . . But if there is something we can do, it shall be done. Your sister will not be forgotten. I beg you will be patient, impossible as that will seem to you."

"Thank you," said Muna when she had swallowed the lump in her throat. She owed it to Sakti to keep trying, even if she doubted what help the witch could—or would—give. "May I speak with Mak Genggang myself?"

Mr. Wythe hesitated. "Yes, of course. If a suitable time can be found . . . As you know, she is a woman with many demands on her time."

"We told her all you have told us," Prunella assured Muna. She seemed about to say more, but then she raised her head, her expression changing.

"Why, there is your mamma, Henny!" she remarked. She sounded glad of the distraction. "You will forgive me, Miss Muna—I must pay my regards. I wonder what has made her look so cross!"

Muna turned to see a fair-haired Englishwoman bearing down upon them. She did indeed bear a strong resemblance to Henrietta, and must have been equally pretty in her youth. But the first detail that struck the observer was the fact that she was in a towering rage.

"Henrietta Stapleton!" she cried in a voice that drew startled looks from the other guests. "There you are!"

"Yes, Mamma," said Henrietta. She darted a look of perplexity at Prunella. The Sorceress Royal spread her hands, as much as to say *she* had no notion what was amiss. "I said I would look for Mrs. Wythe, you know, and you see I have found her."

"Are not you ashamed of yourself?" said Mrs. Stapleton, her bosom swelling. "I am surprised you can bring yourself to address me with such an air of innocence, when you have deceived me!"

The colour drained from Henrietta's face.

"Deceived you?" she echoed. "What—what can you mean?" But Henrietta was a poor actress: her face was a picture of guilt. Before she could continue, the Sorceress Royal stepped on her foot, as though by accident. Henrietta gulped, but said no more.

"You know just what I mean," said Mrs. Stapleton. "Or rather, I should say *who*! I am speaking, as you know perfectly well, of *her*!"

She flung out her hand, pointing at Muna.

"Of me?" said Muna, baffled, but the Englishwoman did not reply. She stood glaring at Henrietta.

"I do not understand," Henrietta faltered.

"You have been making up to a native sorceress," said Mrs. Stapleton. "And you never breathed a word of it to me!"

"But, Mamma—"

"To think I should have sacrificed so much on your account," said Mrs. Stapleton tearfully. "Attended such a number of dull parties—scraped to so many Honourables and Countesses! I thought only of you and your sisters. I was determined that you should hold the position in the world to which your beauty and worth entitled you. And this is the reward for my devotion!"

She flung out her hand again, compelling Muna to skip out of her way, or embarrass everyone by receiving an inadvertent slap from Henrietta's mother.

"How could you, Henny?" said Mrs. Stapleton in a throbbing voice. "Hiding a foreign sorceress in your bosom, when I have been racking my brains for a sensation to present at Amelia's coming out! You knew how I felt when your aunt received a *Comte* and would not allow anyone else to take him about. And when that cunning Mrs. Midsomer harboured a fairy daughter-in-law for months, telling no one, before it was announced in the manner best calculated to make a splash!

"To be sure, she came to no good end," she added piously. "Which just goes to show that pride comes before a fall. But a native sorceress is nearly as novel as a fairy, and you never told me of her! If your papa had not mentioned his encounter with her, I should not have known she existed."

Muna was meditating upon a discreet retreat when, to her

astonishment, Mrs. Stapleton seized her. The Englishwoman held her by the shoulders, inspecting her as though she were a goat for sale.

"She is quite perfect!" declared Mrs. Stapleton. "Not so pretty as to draw away attention that should rightfully be Amelia's, but presentable enough. The dress is disappointing. You would not guess she was an Oriental sorceress from her dress. The turban will do, however."

"I should hope it will do," said Prunella. She had been stifling giggles behind her fan while Mrs. Stapleton harangued her daughter, but at this liberty she froze up. "It is mine, as is the dress, and they were both shockingly dear. You will oblige me by releasing Miss Muna, Mrs. Stapleton. You will give her curious ideas of English manners!"

"Oh, I do not mind it," said Muna. She felt sorry for Henrietta, who looked stricken. Muna had often thought she would like to have a mother, but in her imaginings she had never conceived of having a mother like Mrs. Stapleton.

"Oh!" said Mrs. Stapleton, disconcerted. She let Muna go. "You speak English, do you?" She soon rallied, however. "Where is your familiar? Stapleton told me of it—you will recall my husband, Stapleton; he saw you when he called on Mrs. Wythe at the Academy the day before yesterday. I should like to see the creature. Stapleton said it was monstrously strange!"

Casting Henrietta an uneasy look, Muna said her familiar was resting. "It is not accustomed to English weather, and I have not ventured to expose it to the cold, for it is very delicate."

"In truth, ma'am," said Prunella, "it was I who asked Miss Stapleton to keep Miss Muna's arrival a secret. I knew Miss Muna was anxious to avoid notoriety."

"To become notorious is the last thing I desire," agreed Muna.

Mrs. Stapleton said, mollified, "That is natural, I suppose. To be made a fuss of is what I, too, cannot endure! Still, it was very wrong in Henrietta to deceive her own mother."

"I did not set out to deceive you, Mamma," Henrietta burst out. "If I had known you had any interest in foreign sorceresses, I should have told you about Miss Muna. But I thought you disapproved of *magiciennes*."

"Why, magic-making does not do for Englishwomen," said Mrs. Stapleton. "But I understand these affairs are conducted along different lines in foreign parts."

To Muna's relief, Mr. Wythe intervened, clearing his throat. "I beg your pardon, Mrs. Stapleton, but there are several people in attendance tonight whom I should like to present to Miss Muna." He said to Muna, "The Chairman of the Presiding Committee would very much like to meet you."

"Oh, is Lord Burrow here?" said Mrs. Stapleton. "You will be busy this evening, Mr. Wythe—nothing so wearisome as hosting a ball. You will be glad to have the sorceress—Miss Muna, is it?—taken off your hands. I should be pleased to present Lord Burrow to her. Come with me, my dear. You will not mind the liberty from a woman old enough to be your mother!"

"Mrs. Stapleton!" cried the Sorceress Royal, but Henrietta's mother was a match even for her. Muna found herself being hurried away before she knew what was happening. Behind her she heard Prunella whisper:

"Henny, if we leave Miss Muna in your mamma's clutches, we shall have Janda Baik declaring war upon us before we know what we are about!"

Mrs. Stapleton cleaved through the crowded room like a

galleon in full sail. Muna tried to wriggle out of her grasp, for she did not in the least desire to be forced upon the attention of strangers by a madwoman, but Mrs. Stapleton was stronger than she looked. Her hand on Muna's arm was like a vise.

When smoke started to billow from the other end of the room, Muna's first thought was that the Sorceress Royal and Henrietta must have resorted to magic to create a distraction. It was like the smoke that had attended the *polong*'s emergence from its bottle, save that that had been red, while this smoke was of various colours—the spectacular greens, yellows and purples of a bruise.

Mrs. Stapleton came to an abrupt stop, her grip loosening in surprise. Slipping away from her, Muna saw Prunella snatch up her staff, and knew the smoke was no hoax.

As it dissipated, it revealed a figure suspended in mid-air. The figure floated to the ground, landing as lightly as a leaf borne on a breeze.

The spirit—for it could be nothing else—stood a full head taller than anyone else in the room, with skin of a sable hue darker than Mr. Wythe's and a great quantity of long silver hair. He wore a robe of green velvet, stitched all over with tiny gleams of light like miniature stars.

He looked around the room with a quizzical smile, taking in the fainting ladies and red-faced gentlemen.

"So this is England!" he remarked. His gaze fell upon Prunella. "And you, madam, must be England's Sorceress Royal. You match her description exactly—the only tolerable-looking woman in the room, they said."

"I am the Sorceress Royal," said Prunella. She held her staff at the ready, her head raised and eyes alight. "But I do not believe we are acquainted, sir. May I know whom it is I have the honour of addressing?"

The spirit made a courtly bow.

"I am called the Duke of the Navel of the Seas," he said. "My mistress the Fairy Queen has sent me with a message for you—for Britain and all her friends are in terrible danger!"

11

PRUNELLA

T HE FAIRY'S ANNOUNCEMENT was followed by an astonished silence.

Out of the corner of her eye Prunella saw Zacharias lean over to Henrietta, addressing her. Henrietta nodded and slipped away.

That was some comfort, for Henrietta would see to it that the building was secured and the guests sent home as quickly as possible. All that was left for Prunella was to attend to the new arrival.

The Duke of the Navel of the Seas did not seem to feel the least awkwardness. He swept an admiring look over the room, remarking that it was very handsome—almost fit to be compared with some of the lesser chambers of his Queen's Palace. "I have always admired mortals' ingenuity in making use of the dimensions perceptible to them. It is remarkable how much is done with so little!"

"I take it very kind in Her Majesty to send us a warning," said Prunella, ignoring this. "But what is the danger that threatens us?"

"Oh, did I not say?" said the Duke. "It is us."

Prunella stared. "You?"

"Her Glorious Majesty the Fairy Queen desired me to send you her best compliments," said the Duke, "and explain that she means to kill all English magicians, burn your spell books and sack your miserable country. Her hunger for revenge will only be sated by the wholesale destruction of English thaumaturgy."

He concluded this proclamation with another graceful bow. When no answer was immediately forthcoming, he said, "May I take a message back to my mistress, madam?"

One who was less familiar with fairy manners might have concluded from the Duke's insouciant manner that he could not be serious. But as mistress of two familiars, Prunella was better acquainted with fairykind than most thaumaturges. She adjusted her grip on her staff, deriving some consolation from its solidity. She must not show any fear.

"I beg your pardon, sir, but there must be some mistake," she said. "Why should the Queen wish to kill *us*?"

"Oh! It is no slight upon you," said the Duke reassuringly. "Her Majesty desires the death of all kinds of people, some of the very first consideration. Of course, it is only natural you should have joined those ranks once you stole her Virtu."

Prunella gaped. "The Fairy Queen accuses me of a theft of her *virtue*?"

"Do you deny it?"

"But I have never met the Queen in my life!" said Prunella. "Besides, I thought only gentlemen could deprive others of their virtue. Surely a lady only loses hers."

Zacharias cleared his throat. "I believe His Excellency means that the Fairy Queen has lost an article of virtu." He turned to the fairy. "Have I understood you, sir?"

"Lost!" sneered the Duke. "It has been stolen, as you know better than anyone! For myself, I blame the family," he added. "They ought never to have allowed Robert of Threlfall to remain in Britain for so long. Too much exposure to mortals is liable to warp even the finest nature. And now we see the consequences—the scion of an ancient family forgetting himself so far as to rob Her Majesty!"

"You don't mean *Rollo* is accused of stealing the Queen's talisman?" said Prunella, astonished. "That can't be. Rollo Threlfall has been visiting his relations in Fairy for the past fortnight, and is entirely taken up with agreeing with his elders and being scolded for listing to the left when he flies."

The Duke raised his eyebrows. "Of course. But the Virtu was entrusted to his family's safeguarding in Threlfall, as you must know."

Prunella was about to protest that she had no idea of it, and no reason to have known, having never heard of the Virtu before that day. But then a memory floated to the surface of her mind.

Had not Rollo mentioned an amulet of the Fairy Queen's, before he left for Threlfall? Perhaps it had been called the Virtu— Prunella could not now recall. Rollo had said the article was in the care of some uncle or other.

She flushed, but said, undeterred, "But that just goes to show how unlikely it is he should have stolen it. Why should Rollo have stolen an article that his family guards for the Fairy Queen? He has the greatest abhorrence of scenes. He would never risk the censure of his relations by such a step."

"Ah!" said the Duke. "So he fears displeasing his friends, does he? You would call him biddable?"

"Rollo is the most amiable creature alive," said Prunella. "He would not dream of stealing from anyone, much less the Queen."

"Unless he was put up to it!" intoned the Duke. "Know, madam, that Her Majesty has seen all. She knows that Robert of Threlfall is merely a tool—a victim of the schemes of English thaumaturgy. His actions were not his alone, but directed by Britain!"

Prunella exchanged a look with Zacharias. His expression reflected all the dismay she felt. The Fairy Queen was infamously capricious and mistrustful; tales abounded of the once-favoured courtiers she had slaughtered upon suspicion of treachery, the wars she had launched against former allies for petty slights. And Britain was in no state to go to war with Fairy.

One *war is bad enough!* thought Prunella. If the Fairy Queen's enmity was added to Bonaparte's armies, the country would be altogether extinguished.

"So that is why you have come to us," she said. "I can only deny the charge. Fairy is a valued ally of Britain, whom we would never risk offending by such a crime.

"And," she added, "I cannot believe Rollo can have stolen the Queen's talisman either! You cannot be acquainted with him, sir, or you would know how very unlikely it is that he should do anything of the sort."

"On the contrary, I have met him before. A noble-looking beast, for all his folly." The Duke shook his head sadly. "I have never seen such an exquisite hide! I advised the Queen to display it at court after his execution, but Her Majesty is so vexed that I should not think there will be enough left for a display."

"Execution!" cried Zacharias. Prunella's hand flew to her mouth.

"The Queen has not *killed* Rollo?" she said, horrified.

"Not yet," said the Duke. "Her Majesty judged it best that punishment should be dealt at her banquet, in a week's time." He sighed. "The consumption of a Threlfall will supply some spectacle, at least, and by devouring him the Queen will take into herself all the magic he possesses. But without the Virtu the ceremony will not be half so effective as Her Majesty had planned.

"Come now, madam," he added. "Cannot I persuade you to

return the amulet? If you do so now, in a properly penitent spirit, the Queen may be moved to show you mercy. If not, I am afraid I shall be obliged to murder you all!"

He flung out his arms, then seemed to realise that the room had emptied out. Those guests who had not been put to flight by the appearance of a fairy bearing ominous warnings had departed the moment they understood the charges laid against Britain.

"Well, perhaps the Queen will be satisfied with the head of the Sorceress Royal alone," said the Duke.

"Sir, I *do not have* the Virtu," said Prunella. "And I wish you would explain why the Queen should suspect us of having conspired to steal it. We have no reason to wish to deprive her of a prized treasure, and every reason to desire to remain on good terms with the ruler of Fairy."

"I wish I could explain to you the iniquity that lives in the heart of mortal man, but I confess it is beyond my own understanding," said the Duke. "Perhaps you were jealous of Fairy's splendour, or believed you might profit from aiding the Queen's enemies. It is not for me to tell you what evil motives drove you. My duty is merely to recover the amulet—or deal out punishment."

He shook back his sleeves. His hands glowed with a green light.

"I shall regret terminating the existence of the charming Mrs. Wythe," he added, with a gallant bow. "But if I fail to return with either the Virtu or your carcass, the Queen will sentence me to unspeakable torments. You will appreciate that your death is much to be preferred to my own."

Zacharias took an involuntary step towards the Duke, though he knew as well as Prunella that she was of all thaumaturges in England best-equipped to defend herself against a vengeful fairy. Prunella felt a stab of fear, but this only made her crosser than ever.

She welcomed the hot rush of indignation, for it made it easier to be brave. She drew herself up, flinging back her head.

"Well, I never heard of such laziness in a Fairy courtier," she said. "You need not think you will conceal your failure to do your duty, however. The Queen will hear about this!"

This was clearly not the response the Duke had expected. He was so taken aback that he lowered his hands, the green glow fading. "What do you mean? I was sent to kill you and I am about to do it."

"Nonsense!" said Prunella snappishly. "If Her Majesty's amulet has disappeared, it is your duty to recover it—you said so yourself. But I cannot see that you have made the least push to look for it. Instead you rampage about, hurling wild threats at the Queen's allies. Why do not you undertake a proper search?"

"A search?"

"When I have mislaid my things, murder is not *my* first course of action," said Prunella. "What I do is look for them—and quite often I find them!

"I don't believe you will find this Virtu in Britain," she added, "for we had nothing to do with the theft. But if you think you might, it is your duty to investigate. We have no secrets from our friends in Fairy. You are welcome to turn the kingdom out, and I hope you will accept my hospitality while you are it. This house has hosted many of your kin in the past."

Her peremptory manner was having a salutary effect. The Duke was so nonplussed it did not seem to have occurred to him even to be offended at being harangued.

"You would like me to stay with you?" he said. "But I intend to kill you and all of your connections. Perhaps I did not make myself clear?"

"But that would not do anything to restore the Virtu to Her

Majesty," Prunella pointed out. "Surely it would be better for you to try to find the article? I should think having her treasure back would please Her Majesty better than our destruction."

The Duke looked doubtful. ". . . Her Majesty finds nothing so cheering as a spot of indiscriminate slaughter.

"Yet," he added, "there is something in what you say. The amulet must be found. Perhaps I will undertake a search *after* I have bedewed the soil of Britain with your blood . . ."

"Why, where is everybody?" cried a new voice. "Have they all gone? It is not even half past ten!"

Clarissa Midsomer stood at the door, as outraged as though it were a personal affront that the ball had concluded early. She blanched at the sight of the fairy.

Prunella glared at her old schoolfellow—Clarissa had always had an evil genius for making a nuisance of herself at the worst possible time. But then she saw the Duke's face. He had fallen silent, looking thunderstruck.

"There you are, Miss Midsomer!" said Prunella, concealing her wonder. "I meant to ask after your mother. I heard she was taken ill and was obliged to depart. I hope she has recovered?"

"It was nothing," said Clarissa. "My mother was only tired. I saw her home before returning."

She had not taken her eyes off the Duke, and—what was even more extraordinary—the Duke seemed equally transfixed. He was gazing at the pendant hanging from the chain around Clarissa's neck.

Perhaps it was no surprise that this should have drawn his attention. No other female in the room wore anything like it. The pendant seemed to belong far more to the alien splendour of Fairy than to English notions of elegance.

But the Duke seemed just as fascinated with Clarissa herself, for his eyes kept straying to her countenance. This struck Prunella as peculiar. She was not especially vain of her looks, but she knew she was accounted a remarkable beauty, whereas Clarissa was plain. If the Duke were to be struck with a sudden passion for anyone in the room, Clarissa Midsomer seemed an odd choice.

Prunella was not about to question the blessings of Providence, however. If Clarissa was capable of distracting the Duke from his murderous intentions, Prunella meant to make the most of it. She said to Clarissa:

"We have been honoured with a visit by an emissary of the Fairy Court, the Duke of the Navel of the Seas. I don't suppose your brother has ever spoken of him to you?"

To the Duke, Prunella explained, "Miss Midsomer's brother, Mr. Geoffrey Midsomer, has resided in Fairy as a guest of the Queen since his marriage to her niece Lorelei."

"I am acquainted with the gentleman," said the Duke, after a pause during which he seemed to have forgotten how to speak. He cleared his throat. "He never mentioned he had a sister!"

Under his rapt scrutiny, a pink flush began to creep over Clarissa's face.

"Did you say, madam, that the Virtu is not in Britain?" said the Duke, turning to Prunella with reluctance. "You are confident of this?"

"I doubt there is any English magician who could rob Threlfall and survive," said Prunella. "Threlfall's caves are the closest-guarded in Fairy, as you know, sir."

"And you have never seen the Virtu, I collect," said the Duke. "You do not know what it looks like?"

"I have never seen it in my life," said Prunella truthfully.

"It is not an object known to thaumaturgy," added Zacharias. "But if you described it, sir, we could assist in your search."

"There is no need for that," said the Duke, with the air of one who had reached a decision. He bowed to Prunella. "You are in the right of it, madam. It is my duty to undertake a thorough search for the amulet. The delay may vex Her Majesty, but if I find the Virtu, that would compensate for all! After all, I could always kill you then and bear your head back to her as a token of my loyalty."

"Quite," said Prunella, contriving not to grimace.

"I shall be pleased to accept the offer of your hospitality," said the Duke, apparently unconscious of having committed any failure in tact. "I have always had a great affection for Britain, and wished to know more of the country and its inhabitants."

The Duke glanced again at Clarissa. Miss Midsomer cast her eyes down, her colour deepening. For once she looked far from cross.

"This," said the Duke, "will be an ideal opportunity."

12

MUNA

IT WAS PAST midnight by the time Muna returned to the Academy from the Sorceress Royal's ball. As she undressed for bed, she felt as though she had aged a hundred years—as in the stories of the Unseen Realm, in which unwary villagers wandered into the jungle and emerged to find the world changed. Had the same day passed for Sakti, in the Palace of the Unseen?

Muna knew she should renew her attempts to persuade the *polong* to help her, not least as she would be subjected to lessons the next day. Henrietta had been anxious to assure the scholars that the Duke's appearance would not disrupt the routine of the Academy (rather to the girls' disappointment). But Muna had been out of sorts ever since she had arrived in England—sluggish and bemused, overtaken by fatigue early in the day. It was as though her body did not understand that she had left Janda Baik; it seemed still to be regulated by the sun of a different land. Extricating herself from her stays exhausted her last reserves.

She crawled into bed, promising herself she would rise early the next morning. She hoped she would feel equal to quarrelling with a wayward spirit then. She must take courage from the

Sorceress Royal's example. If Mrs. Wythe could face down a murderous ambassador from the Fairy Court, surely Muna could impose her will on a minor ghoul conjured forth from a few drops of blood.

When she fell asleep she dreamt of home—the heat of the day, the distant murmur of the sea and the coconut palms swaying in the breeze.

It was still dark when she opened her eyes. Her faculties were clouded with sleep, but she knew that something had woken her. She sat up and saw a gleam at the window.

Her first foggy thought was of Sakti. Perhaps it was a message— or even Sakti herself! Muna fell out of bed, stumbling towards the window, but she checked at the sight that met her eyes.

"Mrs. Wythe!" a glad voice cried, then: "Oh, I say! I beg you will forgive me. I must have got turned round on myself—mistaken you for another."

A golden head hovered outside the window. It was shaped like the head of a horse, save that it was larger, covered in scales, and bore not only antlers but long graceful whiskers floating on the breeze. Pale eyes peered at Muna, blinking.

"Oh," said Muna faintly.

"But I know you," exclaimed the dragon. "You're the girl that was in the window!"

Muna had recognised the creature too. It was the *naga* from which she had fled the day before. She froze.

The *naga* did not seem to notice her horror but said affably:

"This is a piece of good luck! I have been wishing I could beg your pardon. What you must have thought of me, lunging at you without so much as a how d'ye do! I ought to have introduced myself. Muggins!"

The *naga* paused, giving her an expectant look out of its great long-lashed blue eyes.

None of this was what one would expect from a monster intent upon one's destruction, even though the friendly words issued from a mouth so dreadfully full of teeth. Muna squeaked, with automatic courtesy:

"I—I am pleased to make your acquaintance, Mr. Muggins!"

"Oh no, my name ain't Muggins," said the *naga*. "That is only cant, you know. I am making a mull of this! Poggs would give me no end of a dressing if he heard it. I am Robert of Threlfall, at your service, miss."

Muna stared. "Robert of Threlfall," she stammered. "But then—you must be Mrs. Wythe's friend!"

"You are acquainted with the Sorceress Royal?" said the *naga* eagerly.

Muna introduced herself. "Mrs. Wythe has been so good as to receive me as a scholar at her Academy," she explained. "The other scholars told me of you."

"Then I *am* here!" said Robert of Threlfall, relieved. "My family have bound my magic—don't want me getting rid of the guard and spiriting Poggs away. I had just enough magic left to make a door to the mortal realm, but when that did not answer . . ."

A thought struck Muna. "Was it a green door?"

"That was the one!" said the *naga*. "I was hoping to find Mrs. Wythe—thought you was her when I saw you at the window earlier. I only knew my mistake when you fled. Mrs. Wythe ain't much given to fleeing."

"No," said Muna. "I can imagine she is not!" She felt called upon in ordinary courtesy to explain her own flight. "You see, you are the first *naga*—the first dragon—I have ever spoken to."

"Honoured!" said the *naga* politely. "Well, the door used up the last of my magic, so I could not make another. But I'm a great hand at dreamwalking though you mightn't think it, and I thought I might manage to enter Mrs. Wythe's dreams even without magic. It has been dashed hard to navigate, however. I suppose that is why I have entered your dreams instead of hers. I do beg your pardon!"

"My dreams?" said Muna, puzzled. "But I am awake."

The *naga* blinked. "No, you aren't. What's that on the bed, if you ain't asleep?"

Muna turned and saw, with an unpleasant thrill, her own self stretched out upon the bed. She was sleeping in a most unbecoming position, a frown distorting her face.

It was disagreeable to see her body from the outside, as though she were at her own funeral, but it was worse to look down and see that what felt like solid flesh was in fact transparent. The moonlight shone right through her legs.

"Hadn't you better sit down, miss?" said Robert of Threlfall solicitously.

"No," said Muna, gulping, "I am quite well, thank you! It is only that I had not expected—that is to say, I thought I was awake."

"Natural, I'm sure," said the *naga*. "I beg your pardon for intruding upon your dream. I shan't trouble you any longer. If you are at the Academy, Mrs. Wythe can't be far off. I should think I ought to be able to find my way into her head."

"But if you go to the Sorceress Royal, won't you risk being detected?" said Muna. Brief as her acquaintance with the *naga* had been, it had sufficed to persuade her of what Mrs. Wythe had vowed—that there was not the least harm in the *naga*. She did not like to think of the poor blundering creature flying into a trap. "The Duke of the Navel of the Seas is staying with her."

"Is he? That is very bad, I'm sure!" said the *naga*. He paused.

"Who *is* the Duke of the Navel of the Seas, if you don't mind telling me?"

"He is an emissary of the Palace of the Unseen—the Fairy Court, I mean," said Muna. "And he has come to England to take vengeance for your offence."

"My offence!" exclaimed the *naga*, looking anxious. "So the Queen knows the Virtu is lost, does she? There will be the devil to pay and no pitch hot! But what is this fellow doing at Zacharias's house?"

Muna explained what had happened at the ball. "I do not know how far the Duke's powers extend, but mightn't he notice if you go to Mrs. Wythe now?"

"Very likely he will," agreed the *naga*. "But what shall I do? I *must* speak with Mrs. Wythe, for they have got our friend under lock and key. And if she will not help us, I fear he won't be long for this world—or any other!"

Muna reflected for only a moment, for the solution was obvious.

"Why do not you entrust your message to me?" she suggested. "I shall see to it that Mrs. Wythe receives it." It was true she had not seen great success in her attempts to gain the Sorceress Royal's attention so far, but Mrs. Wythe would certainly wish to hear news of the alleged thief of the Virtu. And if Muna took the opportunity to interest Mrs. Wythe in her troubles then, who would blame her?

Robert of Threlfall looked thoughtful.

"That might do," he said. "Well, it will have to! I can't risk being captured now, with Poggs in their clutches. They mean to offer him up to the Fairy Queen, you see!"

"Poggs is the friend you mentioned?"

"Yes. Though you had best say Damerell when you speak to Mrs. Wythe," said Robert of Threlfall. "Paget Damerell is his proper name. Poggs is only what I call him. When we was first acquainted I had less of the English than I do now." He sighed. "It was many years ago. I had come to your realm looking for my aunt, but I ran into trouble and would have been done for if Damerell had not saved my life. I vowed to serve him to discharge my debt—the Code of Threlfall permitted nothing less—and that is how I came to live in England. It took me an age to learn to say Damerell's name as it ought to be said, however. And *he* has never been able to pronounce my real name."

Muna was intrigued. "What is your real name, sir?"

The *naga* said impressively, "If you can believe it, I was christened—Robert Henry Algernon!"

This seemed no worse to Muna than most English names, but then the *naga* let out a guttural roar, concluding in a spectacular gout of blue flame. She leapt back from the window, stifling a shriek.

"It is that last vowel that gives people difficulty," explained the *naga*. "Even dragons mistake it half the time, and make it an orange flame. To own the truth, I never liked my name above half—far too showy! I beg you will call me Rollo. Everyone does."

Muna said she would be pleased to call him Rollo, but she saw she must direct affairs if they were to get on.

"Why have they offered Mr. Poggs—Mr. Damerell to the Fairy Court?" she said. "And who are *they*?"

"Who else but my relations? No one else would be so wicked," said Rollo. "My aunt Georgiana fears that the Queen will revenge herself upon us for the theft of the Virtu, so she means to offer Poggs to Her Majesty, in exchange for a pardon for Threlfall. In the meantime Poggs has been confined to a cage in Aunt Georgiana's cave. My grandmother used to keep her princesses in it before she ate them."

Muna knew that there were several species of *naga* to be found in the many worlds. Some were noble, godlike beings who resided in bodies of water, granted wishes and blessed suitably respectful mortals with rain for their crops. Others were dangerous beasts, given to picking off maidens, hoarding gold and setting fire to villages that had displeased them. Evidently the Threlfalls belonged to the latter variety.

"Mr. Damerell must be very uncomfortable," Muna said cautiously.

"He don't like it in the least," agreed Rollo. "My grandmother always thought fermentation improved a princess's flavour. Aunt Georgiana has never been able to get the smell out of the cage."

While Muna absorbed this, he went on, "I begged to be surrendered instead, since it is me they have accused of stealing the Virtu, but Aunt Georgiana would not listen to me. She has far too much clan loyalty to allow a Threlfall to be sacrificed, even if she thinks I deserve it.

"I wish I had never brought Poggs out of England," Rollo said sorrowfully. "But when my aunt summoned me she insisted he should come along and be introduced to the family. It has always vexed her that he would not agree to a wedding."

"A *wedding*?" said Muna, thinking she had misheard. "Does your aunt wish to marry Mr. Damerell?"

It was extraordinary what powers of expression the *naga*'s reptilian face possessed. Rollo looked appalled. "Aunt Georgiana marry *Poggs*? Good heavens, no! She would like me and Poggs to be married. It is the usual thing for bondmates, and I don't think Poggs would object, though it ain't the custom in England for males to marry. But Poggs still has relations living that hope he may be prevailed upon to marry a mortal female—his cousin

Elizabeth promised to leave him her fortune if he would do it. He doesn't mean to oblige her, but he is loath to set a seal upon her disappointment by having a draconic wedding."

"Oh, indeed," said Muna. She was certainly learning a great deal about the world that had not been apparent in Janda Baik. "But, sir, you were telling me of how Mr. Damerell came to be imprisoned. Why does the Fairy Queen believe you stole her amulet?"

"Well, I tried to steal it, didn't I?" said Rollo judiciously. "Natural misunderstanding on Her Majesty's part. I don't say she has responded in anything like a sensible fashion, mind you. Absurd to raise such a storm over a gewgaw!"

"So you *did* steal the talisman?" Muna felt foolish. How naive she was to have trusted the *naga* so quickly, based on nothing more than an engaging manner!

"I must say that was very wrong of you," she said severely. "If you had heard Mrs. Wythe scolding the Duke on your behalf . . . ! She told him upon her honour that you would never have done such a thing."

"Nor would I," said Rollo, with feeling. "After all, to steal from your own uncle! Not the thing at all."

"Then why did you do it?" demanded Muna.

"It was this hell-fired banquet of the Queen's," explained Rollo. "That was where the trouble started. The Virtu was to be the centrepiece, so my uncle Harold was summoned to Court. The fact that the Queen appointed Threlfall as guardians of the Virtu is accounted a great honour within the clan; they hand it around the relations, and it happened to be Uncle Harold's turn. He has a large cave in the south of Threlfall, guarded by *rakshasa*, and he kept the Virtu in a chest made out of his own mother's rib cage.

"Well, my aunt Georgiana could not bear the thought of Uncle

Harold's having the glory of being invited to Court and perhaps having a taste of the Virtu himself." (Rollo's family were certainly the *hungry* sort of *naga*, thought Muna.) "She told him *she* would be mistress of ceremonies at the Queen's banquet, not an idle scobberlotcher that had never taken any thought for the clan. But when she demanded he give her the Virtu, Uncle Harold refused. He said he did not give a fig for the Queen's ceremonials, but he would be damned if he would miss a chance to do Aunt Georgiana an ill turn!"

"It is always sad when one's relations fall out," said Muna sympathetically.

"One grows accustomed to it in my family," said Rollo. "That is why I left for England." He shook his head. "There is no getting away from one's relations for good, however. Aunt Georgiana sent for me and desired me to pinch the Virtu, so as to show Uncle Harold he could not set her at defiance."

Muna said, nonplussed, "But why? Could not your aunt have done it herself? Not that I mean to question your suitability for the task . . ."

"No doubt about my suitability," said Rollo. "I was wholly unsuitable. Bungled the affair. Told her I would! But my aunt would not dream of dirtying her own talons with such a task. Anyone else would bite her in the neck as soon as her back was turned, but my aunt knew I would not play her false. More fool me!"

"But then it is not so bad," said Muna encouragingly. "You could go to the Duke now and explain that it was all a mistake. There has been no theft, for after all the Queen entrusted the Virtu to your family and there was never any intention that the article should leave its charge. You could return it and that would be an end to the matter."

"Return the Virtu!" said Rollo bitterly. "I jolly well wish I *could* return the Virtu. I haven't the faintest idea where the dashed thing is."

"But you said you stole it," cried Muna.

"I *tried* to steal it," Rollo corrected her. "And it is unjust of Aunt Georgiana to say I could not have tried very hard, for she did not see Uncle Harold's *rakshasa*! I was obliged to eat the poor chaps, for they wouldn't yield. Unpleasant—very!" A shiver went along the *naga*'s wings. "After all that, to open the chest and find that the Virtu was not there! I can tell you it gave me a shock."

"Oh," said Muna blankly.

"I must have looked tolerably silly when Uncle Harold's servants found me," said Rollo. "But no one would credit that the Virtu was missing when I got there. The family is persuaded I have sold it to discharge my debts of honour. Only Aunt Georgiana believes me, but that is no help, for she is just as vexed with me as all the others."

"Why don't you explain that it was she who put you up to it?"

Rollo drew back his head, giving her a look of reproof. "That would be shocking bad form, to peach upon one own's aunt! I should never be able to hold my head up again."

Muna could hardly reproach anyone else for loyalty to an exasperating relation. "What am I to ask Mrs. Wythe to do, then?"

"It is Poggs I fear for," said Rollo. "I can't break him out without my magic. But if Mrs. Wythe can only contrive to get him out of Threlfall, I can look to myself. My aunt has gone to the Fairy Court, so Mrs. Wythe need only contend with my brother Bartholomew. He has been set to guard Poggs, but she would make short work of him. Mortals possess a natural advantage in Fairy, though they mayn't know it."

"But even if Mrs. Wythe succeeded in rescuing Mr. Damerell,

where could she take him that would be beyond the reach of the Fairy Court?" said Muna. "Surely the Queen's wrath would follow him wherever he went."

"That don't worry me. It ain't Damerell the Queen is vexed with, but Threlfall," said Rollo. "If he is lost, Her Majesty's wrath will fall where it belongs—on *our* heads. But the Queen won't wish to risk a war with Threlfall, not when she has lost the Virtu."

"Why not? She must have other amulets."

"None like the Virtu," said Rollo. He lowered his voice. "No one likes to talk of it, for it was a great scandal at the time, but the Virtu holds the magic of a powerful fairy—an enemy of the Queen. She defeated them and locked their heart in a talisman. Anyone who holds the Virtu could challenge the Queen. She cannot afford a quarrel with Threlfall now.

"Even if she does declare war on Threlfall," he added, "I don't intend that Poggs will be sacrificed on our account. I told him when we were bonded that he should not suffer from the bond, and I mean to keep my word!"

Muna was disquieted to see a large crystal tear roll down from one blue eye.

"Come, there is no need to cry," she said briskly. She felt sorry for the *naga*, but Mak Genggang was always brisk when anyone gave way to tears, mingling scoldings with reassurances. It seemed to Muna that this was the right approach to adopt with Rollo. "I will tell Mrs. Wythe all you have told me and she will see to it that Mr. Damerell comes to no harm." She paused, thinking. "She will need directions to Threlfall, I expect."

"Directions alone won't suffice," said Rollo. "Aunt Georgiana has concealed her cave with magic arts, so it cannot be seen by anyone outside the family."

He hesitated. "Will you take a gift from me? You will need to open the window. I give you my word I shan't do you any harm."

Muna had already decided what she would do with the message Rollo had entrusted to her, if she could. She tamped down on her trepidation—*After all*, she told herself, *if he wished to do you any injury, he could have done it before!*—and opened the window.

The *naga* said, "Hold out your hand."

A golden scale dropped on Muna's palm.

"Give that to Mrs. Wythe," said Rollo. "If she swallows it, she will be able to see through the wards around Aunt Georgiana's cave, for it has some of my magic in it. My relations haven't bound Mrs. Wythe, so she ought to be able to use my magic, even if I can't. She can return the scale to me when she comes."

Muna stared down at the scale. "But you said this was a dream."

"Put it on your tongue, and when you wake it will still be there," said Rollo. "It is a part of *my* dream I have given you, you see. There ain't such a difference between dreaming and waking for me."

It was dark and quiet, with not a sound from the street, but suddenly the *naga* raised his head, as though he heard something. An alert look came over his face.

"I had better wake if I am not to be discovered," he said. "My body is sleeping in Aunt Georgiana's cave, but anyone who happens to look in is bound to notice my soul is out wandering. You will ask Mrs. Wythe to come as soon as she can? I don't know when my aunt will return from the Court." He began to fade, the great golden body dissolving into the air, starting from the tail.

"I will," promised Muna. "I don't doubt she will send help as soon as she can. The Duke's report has made her extremely concerned on your behalf."

"Oh, I am of no consequence. They won't eat *me*," said Rollo. "Only get Poggs away and I can slip off later, once the dust has settled." Only his head remained, but even that disappeared by degrees, so that his final defiant words issued from a disembodied jaw. "Then see if I ever return to Threlfall again—aunts or no aunts!"

13

MUNA WOKE IN the morning to the recollection that her first class in magic was to take place that day. She would be obliged to adopt the pretence of being a magical prodigy, possessed of sufficient power to attract the patronage of Mak Genggang.

The thought was so hideous that she sat bolt upright. From the quality of the light it was still early, but she had only a few hours before lessons began. She had made no provision to ensure that she did not disgrace herself. Why had she not given thought to the problem the night before?

"Idiot!" she said aloud.

A golden scale dropped from Muna's mouth onto the sheet, and her dream came back to her in a rush—the *naga* and his tale, and the scheme that had grown up in her mind as he spoke.

She snatched up the scale. There was a writing desk opposite the bed, in which Muna found pen and paper. She sat down and wrote a letter to the Sorceress Royal, scribbling in her haste to record everything she recalled before it was lost, for she knew dreams were soon forgotten in the light of day.

Only once the gist of what Robert of Threlfall had told her was fixed in writing did she pause, looking up.

She had propped the scale against the wall. Even in that dim room, faintly illuminated by the thin light of dawn, it shone with a wonderful brilliancy.

Muna was not doing anything *wrong*. It was true that Rollo had told her to give the scale to Mrs. Wythe, but it was not as though the Sorceress Royal could be spared for a rescue mission to Threlfall. While the Duke of the Navel of the Seas remained in Britain, so must she. Mrs. Wythe would not have occasion to use the scale herself.

Muna had promised Rollo she would convey his message to the Sorceress Royal and that was just what she would do. Indeed, she would do more—she would see to it herself that he received the help he so urgently desired.

She dashed off the last few lines and sealed her letter. Then she took the scale and put it on her tongue.

It did not taste of anything in particular, but it was an awkward shape to swallow. Muna choked it down with difficulty, the edges scraping the tender insides of her mouth.

Once she had got the scale down she inspected herself, then the room around her. But absorbing Robert of Threlfall's magic did not seem to have made any immediate difference. She could only hope it would give her the ability Rollo claimed for it when the time came.

There *was* an experiment she could carry out—a test that would show if she had absorbed the *naga*'s magic. She got on her knees, drawing out the bottle containing the *polong* from underneath the bed.

This time when Muna recited the verse, red smoke bubbled out of the bottle at once. It dissipated to reveal the *polong*, looking peevish.

"Where did you find the power to do that?" she demanded. "You said it was your sister that had the magic."

"So I do have magic now!" said Muna, pleased. "I hoped I might, but I could not tell that there was any difference. I have need of your aid, *kak*."

The *polong* eyed her balefully. "Do you wish me to torment an enemy?"

"No, but—"

"There is a theft you desire me to commit, then?"

"No theft, but—"

"I have told you I will have nothing to do with any reckless attempt to rescue your sister!"

Before the *polong* could dive back into her bottle, Muna said, "No, no, that is not why I called you. I need your help to perpetrate a—a fraud. That is a sort of wickedness, isn't it?"

To Muna's relief, the *polong* paused, a gleam of interest lighting her eyes.

"What sort of fraud?" she said cautiously.

"I am to begin my lessons in English thaumaturgy today," said Muna. "If I am not to disgrace myself before the English, I must convince them I am a witch."

The *polong* looked disappointed. "You have no need of my help for that. It is easily done. Simply mutter an *ayah* or two from the Qur'an and toss about some rice paste, and you will be as much of an enchanter as any of the dozens of charlatans who call themselves magicians back home."

Muna gave the *polong* a severe look. "Oh yes, that will give the English a fine impression of Malay magic! They are not villagers to be bamboozled by tricks, but magicians themselves. What will they think of Mak Genggang if the protégée she sent them is revealed to be nothing but a quack?"

The *polong* tossed her head. "It is of no account to me what anyone thinks of That Woman!"

Muna had expected that the reference to Mak Genggang would hold little weight with the *polong*, but that was not the chief weapon in her arsenal.

"But it is not just her reputation that is at stake," she reminded the spirit. "It is the fate of Janda Baik. The only reason the island has not been snapped up by greater powers is that they fear the cunning and magic of our witches. If the English conclude the witches of Janda Baik are neither cunning nor magical, what is to stop them from invading us? They have conquered Malacca and they mean to take Java, and everyone says Janda Baik will be next. You are a daughter of Janda Baik too, sister. You do not wish to see it overrun by foreigners, I am sure!"

"Why should not the English take the island if they want it?" said the *polong*. "One king is much like another, wherever they are from."

But Muna had swayed her. She spoke without conviction.

"It would be such a little thing for one of your great powers," said Muna coaxingly.

"What would you have me do?" said the *polong*. "It is not as though I could educate you in the whole corpus of Malay magic. That would take too much time—and more magic than you possess, even now. It is good strong spirit-stuff, your magic, but not nearly enough to make a real witch of you. You ought to have taken more."

"I did not steal any magic," said Muna with dignity, though her conscience pricked her. In swallowing the scale she had certainly appropriated what was not intended for her. It did not assuage her guilt to tell herself that she had greater need of the scale than the Sorceress Royal, so she pushed the thought away, turning her mind back to the business at hand. "I need not set myself up as an authority on Malay magic; I shall put them off if they ask for a demonstration. But they will expect me to learn their English spells. That is what worries me!"

"Is that all?" said the *polong*. "Why, that is nothing!"

For all her initial reluctance, the *polong* was clearly as fond of laying down the law as Mak Genggang. She grew more cheerful as she told Muna what she must do.

It seemed simple enough—so simple that Muna could not help feeling doubtful. "Surely that will never work? If magic were so easily performed, then everyone would do it."

"You are at liberty to ignore my counsel, of course," said the *polong* with awful civility. "I am sure you know best. Do whatever you think will impress the English. It makes no difference to me!"

The bottle leapt out of Muna's hand, clattering on the floor. The *polong* waved a haughty arm, drawing a circle of red smoke around herself.

"I did not mean to contradict you, *kak*," said Muna hastily. "Pray do not be offended! I am most grateful for your advice, and will do just as you say. There is another favour I would ask of you."

"Another favour!" said the *polong*. "You are like the Dutch asking for land."

"I have a letter for the Sorceress Royal," said Muna, ignoring this cutting remark. "I could entrust it to a servant, but it is a communication of considerable importance and *extremely* secret. It must not be seen by anyone but Mrs. Wythe, and there is a spirit at her house now who must not know anything of it."

The *polong* was intrigued despite herself. "What sort of spirit?"

"It is a very great spirit," said Muna. "An emissary from the Palace of the Unseen, sent by the Queen of the Djinns herself. The message cannot fall into his hands. Will you take it to Mrs. Wythe?"

Muna had decided upon this as the safest means of ensuring

that her message was conveyed to the Sorceress Royal without anyone else's coming to know of its contents, for she had learnt from the maid Sarah that several of the servants knew their letters. She thought it likely that for once the *polong* would not consider herself entitled to object to the task, for the carrying of messages was an errand eminently suited to spirits of her class—imps summoned forth from nothingness by magicians desiring a servant.

Muna was right. After a pause the *polong* said:

"Where is this letter?"

Muna showed it to her. "Pray beg the Sorceress Royal to read it at once. It is urgent."

The *polong* raised an eyebrow. "You do know the witch desired me to be kept secret from the English? I was not to betray my existence by the least sign."

"Then you will have to find some means of delivering my letter to the Sorceress Royal without giving away what you are," said Muna. "That is hardly beyond your powers!"

The *polong* gave her a sharp look, but it was not disapproving. "You are cleverer than you look, child. I wonder what mischief you are brewing!"

"You have the wrong sister for mischief, *kak*," said Muna. "I assure you, if Mak Genggang knew what I intended, she would approve."

"I doubt that very much!" said the *polong*—but it took the letter and vanished in a puff of smoke, without further argument.

THE Academy's lessons were conducted in a well-lit, airy room, not too large for the dozen scholars in it—for their numbers had been swelled by several day students. None were as old as Miss

Edwards nor as young as Miss Pinder, but their ages ranged from eleven to nineteen, and their abilities were as various as their personalities.

Muna thought that to teach such a class must be very trying. Henrietta, presiding over the lesson, looked anxious and weary, scarcely recovered from the exertions of the night before. Still, her smile when her eyes met Muna's wrought a remarkable change to her face, lending it an irresistible sweetness. Despite Muna's worry about the trials that lay ahead, she found herself smiling back.

"You have all met our guest Miss Muna," said Henrietta to the class. "Since she has travelled such a vast distance to study with us, I thought I would invite Miss Muna to choose the spell we shall learn today."

She turned to Muna. "You will already have some notion of English thaumaturgy from your reading. Was there any aspect that struck you particularly—any form of enchantery you would like best to understand?"

Muna would have liked to ask about curses and their correctives, but she doubted whether she would be able to introduce her curiosity about these naturally. She had no wish to divulge the true reason for her interest, for as an instructress Clarissa Midsomer was bound to hear of it—and Miss Midsomer might well be the curseworker in search of whom Muna had come to England.

She hesitated, conscious of Henrietta's expectant grey eyes on her.

"I should like to learn a magic for revelations," said Muna finally.

"Revelations?" echoed Henrietta.

Muna could not ask for a counterbane for the curse, nor for admission to the Unseen World. But it would be something to know what Sakti was doing, and how she was.

"Like a spell for divining the future," explained Muna. "But one that would tell you about—about the present."

Henrietta's eyes softened. "I understand you. You wish for news of your friends and family."

"Yes," said Muna, thinking of her fleeting glimpse of Sakti in the vision the *polong* had vouchsafed her. Perhaps it was unlikely that Henrietta knew such magic as would allow Muna to pierce the walls surrounding the Palace of the Queen of the Djinns and see Sakti—but Muna was very willing to be surprised.

"I am not acquainted with any enchantments that would achieve the effect you desire," said Henrietta. Before Muna could experience more than the briefest stab of disappointment, the Englishwoman went on, "But perhaps one could adapt a spell of augury for the purpose. I know one that might answer."

From a shelf behind her desk, she took down a tome bound in dark leather.

"It is a formulation of Isaacson's," she explained, flipping the pages carefully, for the paper was delicate, yellowed with age. "A scholar of the last century. Mr. Wythe has a particular regard for his work. It will be an interesting exercise, and instructive for all the scholars, for the spell is incomplete by design."

She read out the formula, which consisted of two lines in English:

Come forth, thou spirits, disclose thy design!
My heart will receive it, be it pure or malign.

"Mr. Isaacson was a better magician than he was a poet," she added in a tone of faint apology. "But it is an ingenious spell, for the enchanter is obliged to complete the poem himself with his own couplet, and that gives the magic its direction. Mr. Isaacson argued that its being incomplete imparted the looseness necessary for a spell of augury. Since the future is not fixed, he said, there can be no fixity in the magic used to foretell what will come."

It was charming to see how seriously the girls who had entertained Muna with their gossip took their magic. Perhaps it was to be expected of Miss Edwards that, as the eldest scholar, she should be a model student, hanging on Henrietta's every word. But even little Alice Pinder did not so much as fidget, and the high-spirited Miss Campbell's countenance was alive with interest.

"Presumably if you wished to study the present, you would only need to compose a suitable verse," said Miss Campbell.

Henrietta smiled. "Just so."

Not all the scholars were pleased to be called upon to compose poetry. Miss Pinder set to the task with all the unself-consciousness of youth, her tongue sticking out of the corner of her mouth, but Miss Edwards grew red and flustered as she worked at her couplet. She whispered to Muna that she did not know how she would read it out before the class without withering away from shame.

"I should not think the elegance of the poem will make any difference to the efficacy of the spell," said Muna, but this seemed little comfort to Miss Edwards.

Her distress perplexed Muna, for this part of the task, at least, gave her no anxiety. In Janda Baik versifying was a pursuit to which nearly everyone was addicted. She had only practised the art in Malay before, but she was grateful now for the mysterious education she had received before the curse, for supplying her with such a command of the English language that the words came almost as readily. Her couplet might not meet the English *magiciennes'* standard for elegance, since she was not familiar with the conventions that governed English poetry, but she did not fear disgracing herself—at least in the matter of composition.

Magic was a different matter; she was not nearly so confident of her powers in that regard. When Henrietta said, "Should you like to make the first attempt, Miss Muna?" Muna's stomach leapt about like a fish caught in a net.

"I should be delighted," said Muna, hoping her nervousness was not apparent. "Though I have never performed English magic before, so I beg you will not expect any wonders!"

She showed Henrietta the formula she had devised:

The storm hurls the boat upon the shore;
For a moment 'tis there—and then 'tis no more.
Come forth, thou spirits, disclose thy design!
My heart will receive it, be it pure or malign.

"But the spell is meant to *begin* with Mr. Isaacson's couplet," said Henrietta, frowning slightly. "And I confess I do not quite see what connection your verses bear to the original."

"It is a *pantun*," explained Muna. "That is one of the kinds of poems we like best in Janda Baik. The beginning need not have any obvious connection with the rest. The first half is an image, and the sense comes in at the end—that is why I used Mr. Isaacson's couplet to conclude the poem. If it is a spell that looks into the future, perhaps if one turns it around one will see . . . something else."

Henrietta held Muna's poem up to the light, studying it. "Well, we are wild for novelty here at the Academy," she said, smiling. "I should like to see what happens—and so will the girls, I am sure."

Not without some apprehension, Muna spoke the words of her formula. Then, as the *polong* had advised her, she added in the barest whisper:

"If you please!"

"I beg your pardon?" said Henrietta.

Muna did not answer, for she had perceived a flicker out of the corner of her eye.

She blinked. Sure enough, there it was—a distinct ripple in the air, like the patch of vagueness above a pot of boiling water. Narrowing her eyes, she could make out a face, half-transparent and ill-defined, its features continually shifting—the face of a strange spirit. She had succeeded in summoning one, after all!

Muna gulped, darting a glance at the English *magiciennes*. Some of the scholars were still scribbling away at their own formulae. Those who had completed their poems to their satisfaction—or had better manners—looked courteous and attentive, but there was nothing to suggest that they had noticed anything out of the ordinary. Henrietta's forehead was a little furrowed, as though she were trying to discern a faint melody playing in the distance, but she, too, showed no sign of having seen the face.

"What did you say?" said the face.

"Oh, er," said Muna. *"The storm hurls the boat upon the shore—"*

"Not that bilge!" said the spirit impatiently. "It was the words at the very end I meant. What did you say then?"

"'If you please'?"

"That was just it! And you were speaking to me?"

"Yes," said Muna.

The *polong* had told Muna to seek aid from the fine ones—the many lesser spirits, invisible and fleeting, which were the stuff of all magic.

"In magic, perception counts for as much as action," the *polong* had explained. "Mortals have little of the former. To ask them to cast a spell is like asking a blindfolded man to find a path. But with the spirits' magic you have stolen, you need have no anxiety on that score. You will be able to see the fine ones and address them, and gaining their ear is most of the battle. As for the rest, you will find a civil manner works wonders. The fine ones are so little used to being addressed with courtesy that I should think they will fall over themselves to help."

Muna could not quite believe magic could be achieved by mere flattery, and she was acutely conscious of the baffled stares of the English *magiciennes*, to whom it must appear that she was addressing nothing at all. But it was better to appear mad than powerless, she reassured herself; after all, most powerful witches were a little mad. Trying not to feel silly, Muna said:

"It was you I longed to see, O great spirit, for I knew you could assist your slave if you wished. I beg you will confer a favour upon this unworthy mortal, who can do nothing without your aid. Pray give effect to my spell!"

"Miss Muna, if I may ask," said Henrietta tentatively, "to whom are you speaking?"

"Sh!" said Muna. She waved her hand to show that she must not be interrupted.

"Well, that's doing the civil, ain't it?" said the fine one. Its voice was a mere faint rustle, so that Muna had to strain her ears to distinguish the words, but there was no mistaking the pleasure in it. "It is a change from being pushed about, I can tell you. There is no bully like a mortal waving a spell in his hand. And the gels are no politer than the men. They are just as given to ordering one about, without so much as a 'by your leave'! What is this spell you want doing? Give me the form of it."

Muna repeated her formula, glancing nervously at the perplexed Henrietta.

"Ah, it's prognostication you want, is it?" said the spirit. "But you have cast the spell the wrong way around, you know. With the best will in the world, I could not show you a vision of the future. However, if you don't much mind what you see, there are other visions I could grant you. What are you after?"

In truth Muna had already said what she wished to see. The image that began her poem, the reflection that foreshadowed the sense, was a transparent cipher. A storm had cast Muna upon the shore. Crawling over the sands, she had found Sakti—but now she had lost her.

"I should like to see my sister," she said in a low voice. "Can you show her to me, sir?"

The spirit hummed. "We shall have to go backwards, for that is the direction of the spell. But—ah! Here is a vision worth seeing. If you would be so good as to lend me your eyes . . ."

Before Muna had the opportunity either to consent or refuse, the creature pounced on her. It slithered into her nose and stole into the corners of her eyes.

It was like breathing in a lungful of Mak Genggang's *sambal* while it was frying in oil. The smell was extraordinarily pungent; it scalded the nostrils, bringing tears to the eyes. Muna bent over in a fit of coughing, her eyes stinging. She blinked away the tears and saw—

T HE light of home.

Muna was conscious that her physical form was in a foreign land—that her body breathed a cool damp air, surrounded by staring girls in a classroom. But the rest of her was no longer in England. She hovered in the unforgiving glare of the sun, as it shone on Janda Baik, brilliant and omnipresent.

The sky was a clear pale blue, with white clouds scattered across it like puffs of cotton. Janda Baik lay beneath her, a green gem cradled by the sea. The waves were a riot of reflected light.

If she had been there in person, she would have been obliged to look away from the glare, but in Muna's vision she was freed of mortal limitations. She saw, all at once, the island, the sea, the sky, and the dim world beneath the waves, where a mystery slumbered.

The surface of the sea became still, transparent as glass. A shoal of rock rose out of the seabed—but no, it was not rock, for the two points of red light were a pair of glowing eyes. It was an animal, but such an animal as Muna had never seen or dreamt of: a serpent out of myth, large enough to crush the island in its coils.

And yet . . . was it true she had never seen it before? There was something familiar about the serpent. Muna looked into its eyes and the skin on her arms prickled. She was visited by a sudden image of a narrow, pale face, above a jewelled pendant.

Miss Midsomer's necklace, thought Muna. A snake with red eyes and a broken-off tail. This giant serpent's body was submerged in the deeps, however. She could not tell what its tail looked like— and besides, what could Clarissa Midsomer have to do with a monster slumbering in the seas off the shores of Janda Baik?

Deep in the waters, the serpent was cold, but it did not regard the chill. It was only half-awake, and its thoughts were vague and slow. They consisted of a single refrain, repeated drowsily:

I have been wronged, thought the serpent. *I have been wronged*.

What had happened? A spirit so powerful did not lie on the seabed for unknown years to amuse itself. The serpent was not merely hibernating. It was ill—dying perhaps—or else it was . . .

Cursed, thought Muna.

SHE emerged from the vision gasping for air.

"Miss Muna? Miss Muna, do you hear me?"

"Yes," Muna tried to say, but she could not stop gasping long enough to speak. She attempted to rise, but she was thwarted by her legs giving away beneath her.

Ready hands reached out for Muna, guiding her kindly and firmly into a chair. She was not to worry—she must sit and rest—she must sniff some *sal volatile*. A bottle was thrust under Muna's nose, the scent of which would certainly have roused her if she were not already awake.

"Oh no, please!" said Muna, pushing the bottle away.

Someone had pressed a handkerchief into her hand. She raised it to her streaming eyes, and slowly England resettled around her, its soft colourless light blotting out the sunshine of Janda Baik. Muna became conscious of a pair of grey eyes fixed on her, expressive of the greatest concern.

"Pray do not worry, Miss Stapleton," she said. Her voice startled her—it was so thin and creaky.

"Oh, but you are wholly pale!" said Henrietta, distressed. "Pray let me ring for water, or wine."

"No, no," said Muna. "I am quite well." She looked around for the spirit that had helped her, but the face was nowhere to be seen. Nonetheless she said aloud:

"Thank you, great spirit! Your slave is grateful."

"Not at all," said the faint voice courteously, out of thin air. "Pleasure to meet a mortal as has any manners at all! I didn't know there was any such."

Muna allowed herself to droop in her chair. Her head was beginning to ache abominably.

She had asked to see her sister. The fine one must have been confused. It had granted her the wrong vision. It must have been a powerful magic that the fine one had wrought, for the serpent's slow, dragging thoughts had felt like Muna's own—as though she had repeated those very words to herself, over and over again, through numberless solitary years.

I have been wronged . . .

"Are you quite certain you are well?" said Henrietta.

Muna nodded, but she regretted it, for it made her head swim. "It was only a passing faintness. I am not used to your spirits," she added apologetically. "But they were most obliging! As hospitable as their mortal countryfellows."

Henrietta took a deep breath. "So you called upon the spirits for their aid. I thought that was what you must be doing. I have rarely felt such a burst of magic! I never had the pleasure of meeting Mak Genggang, but I see now Prunella did not overstate her powers, nor yours."

She looked at Muna with shining eyes, so admiring that Muna felt ashamed, for it was not her own powers that had enabled her to address the fine ones. Before she could mutter a disclaimer, Henrietta said eagerly:

"The spell caught, of course—I felt it. What did you see?"

The red gleam of the serpent's eyes, drowned in seawater.

"I saw the past," said Muna. She was grateful that it would seem natural to pause. What ought she to say? She scarcely understood the meaning of the vision she had been vouchsafed—but she must decide now what it was safe to confide in the English.

Conscious of the expectant eyes on her, Muna opened her mouth. But she was granted a reprieve, for just then the door burst open. The girls looked up at once, with all the alertness of school-children at any permissible distraction.

"I beg pardon for the intrusion, Henny," said Prunella, but she was looking at Muna. "Might I speak with Miss Muna? It concerns a matter of some urgency—I am told it cannot wait."

14

THE SORCERESS ROYAL held a letter in her hand as she led Muna out of the classroom—a letter Muna recognised. She followed Prunella into a sitting room, her heart beating quickly.

Prunella shut the door, turning to face her.

"I am sorry to have taken you away from your lesson, Miss Muna," she said. "But a zephyr gave me this message. It said it was urgent, and you were the author."

"I thought you would wish to know at once," explained Muna. She could not discern any anxiety in the Sorceress Royal's countenance. She felt a frisson of worry. The Sorceress Royal had spoken of Rollo with fondness, but would her affection extend so far as to risk herself—and Britain—on his behalf? Rollo had seemed to have no doubt of Prunella's readiness to help, but it was no small thing he asked.

"I doubted whether I would have the opportunity to see you," added Muna, "so I thought a letter would be best. I hope I did not do wrong?"

She was relieved to see a smile illuminate Prunella's countenance. Frustrated as Muna had been by the sorceress's elusiveness, she could not deny the effect of Prunella's smile—it was candid and warm, wholly disarming. Muna began to see how the Sorceress Royal had got away with setting English thaumaturgy at defiance.

"Oh no! I am very much obliged to you. It was an excellent notion and I daresay the letter is elegantly written. Only," said Prunella apologetically, "I am afraid I do not read Arabic." She unfolded the paper.

It was true. In Muna's hurry and distraction she had written in what came most naturally to her pen—the Jawi script that employed Arabic letters to represent Malay speech. The language was correct and courteous, but it was no wonder the Sorceress Royal had not understood it. Muna's hands flew to her cheeks.

"I am sorry! What a stupid thing to have done!"

"On the contrary," said Prunella, "it requires considerable wit to write a letter in the wrong language by mistake. But will you tell me what it says? I have been consumed with curiosity all morning! I should have come sooner if not for that plaguey Duke."

Muna acquainted her with Rollo's tale, and saw at once that she need not have feared that Prunella would feel any reluctance to act. The Sorceress Royal was all sympathy and indignation.

"Poor, *poor* Damerell!" she cried. "We must certainly help him. Thank heavens you had the presence of mind to warn Rollo not to seek me out. Suppose he had come and the Duke had caught him!" She shuddered. "We should never persuade the Duke we were not conspiring with Threlfall against the Queen then."

"Is the Duke at your house now?"

Prunella shook her head. "Lord Burrow is showing him the Society. If any thaumaturge were so idiotish as to steal the Fairy Queen's amulet, he might be just stupid enough to think the Society a good place to hide it. But I am certain the Duke will find nothing. And if he does, why, we shall simply be obliged to hang the thaumaturge that did it!"

She did not seem overly exercised by the prospect.

"Would not you *mind* hanging an Englishman?" ventured Muna.

Prunella looked contemplative. "Well! It would depend on the Englishman. I can think of several . . . but it is nothing to do with my preferences. We would hardly have a choice if it was that, or being embroiled in a war with Fairy. But we need not worry about it now. The question is, what shall we do about Damerell and Rollo?"

She rolled Muna's letter up and tapped her lips with it.

"What we need is a daring rescue!" declared the Sorceress Royal. "You said Rollo gave you the key to his aunt Georgiana's cavern?"

There was not the least shadow of doubt in Prunella's large eyes. Muna's conscience misgave her. She wished she had written her letter in English, for the falsehood had tripped off her pen more easily than it would come now.

But the thought of Sakti hardened her resolve. Even now her sister was lost in the Unseen Realm. Who knew what might have become of her? It was Muna's duty to adopt any course to get there, since the *polong* could not—or would not—take her. Any trickery, any underhand stratagem, was justified if it would help her find her sister.

She cast her eyes down, hoping this would be taken for maidenly embarrassment, or a foreigner's awkwardness, or anything but what it was—shame at deceiving her hostess.

"Mr. Threlfall told me to swallow it," she said. "He said that would unlock my eyes, so I would be able to see through the wards around his aunt's cave."

"I wonder he was willing to involve you in his difficulties!" said

Prunella. "It's most unlike Rollo. He is perfectly happy to impose upon his friends—poor Zacharias is always being dragged into his difficulties—but no one could be more disinclined to trouble a stranger."

Internally Muna writhed in torment, but she managed to summon up a smile in answer to the Sorceress Royal's clear-eyed gaze. "He thought I would be a useful addition to a delegation to Threlfall, since I have experience of the Unseen World."

This sounded pitiably weak to Muna, but Prunella only nodded. Her eyes were sparkling with excitement.

"Yes, indeed," she said; she was too distracted by the prospect of adventure to question Muna. "And will you come? No mortal has ever been admitted to Threlfall's caverns and lived to tell the tale! Save Damerell, of course—and one can hardly call *him* a mortal anymore, what with his connection with Rollo. He has not aged a day since he turned eight-and-thirty.

"You must not feel obliged to consent," Prunella added as an afterthought. "I should do all I could to keep you safe from harm, but you will know better than most what dangers lie in the Other Realm. You would be wholly within your rights to refuse."

"I should be pleased to come, only—" Muna hesitated. "Do you mean to go yourself, Mrs. Wythe?"

"Of course!" said Prunella, surprised. "I could not ask anyone else to risk themselves in Threlfall. Rollo's relations are the sort of dragons other dragons tell their children about, to frighten them into being good."

It was hardly Muna's place to remind the Sorceress Royal of her duties, and there would be certain advantages to being accompanied by a sorceress to the Unseen Realm. Still, thinking of the scholars she had left behind in the classroom, Muna said, "But will not you be needed here in England?"

"Zacharias can manage while I am away," said Prunella, dismissing England. "I shall be discreet; we must not risk provoking the Fairy Court further. Perhaps if I assume a disguise . . ."

"I have a better idea," said a voice, startling them both. "You ought to send *me*!"

Muna and Prunella whipped around. Henrietta stood in the doorway, flushed at her own boldness.

"Why, Henny," said Prunella, delighted, "were you listening at the door? How shocking!"

Henrietta flung back her head. "What if I was? I am sure I have caught you eavesdropping dozens of times!"

"But now you can never scold me for it again," said Prunella with satisfaction. "Pray shut the door; we don't want *all* the school insisting upon coming along. I should be pleased to have you if Damerell were here and could teach your classes. But what will the scholars do without you? For Zacharias will be busy dancing attendance upon the Duke, and it is not as though we could rely upon Clarissa. I should not have agreed to take her if I had not known you would be there to watch over her."

Henrietta closed the door. She did not join Prunella and Muna where they sat but hovered just inside the threshold, smoothing down her dress. She met the Sorceress Royal's eyes.

"I don't mean that I wish to come with you, Prunella," she said. "I meant that I should go in your place."

Prunella's eyebrows drew together in a manner that—even to Muna, who scarcely knew her—presaged a storm.

"In my place?" she repeated.

Henrietta looked desperately nervous, but she said, "Come, Prunella, you must see that the idea of your charging off to Threlfall is absurd!"

"Is it, indeed?" said Prunella silkily. "We shall see what Zacharias thinks about that!"

"THE Sorceress Royal to abandon England now, in her hour of need!" said Mr. Wythe. "It is out of the question. I am surprised you should have considered it for a moment."

Muna shrank back into the sofa, wincing. Not for the first time in the past trying hour, she wished she were really a witch, so that she could make herself invisible.

There had been some delay before Mr. Wythe arrived in response to his wife's summons, and in that time Prunella and Henrietta had quarrelled without pause, descending to astonishing depths of schoolgirl pettiness. It did not appear that this had in any way slaked Prunella's thirst for battle. She gave Zacharias a look of burning reproach.

"Will you allow Damerell to be sacrificed to the Fairy Queen?" she demanded. "He is your oldest friend!"

"By no means," said Zacharias. "But there is no reason you should go yourself."

"But Rollo asked for me," Prunella protested. "Miss Muna, *you* will confirm it! Rollo begged for my help, you said."

Muna had been dreading this. She cleared her throat.

"It is true Mr. Threlfall hoped you might come," she began.

"There!" said Prunella triumphantly.

Muna was relieved when Zacharias intervened.

"Be reasonable, Prunella," he said. "How could we account for your departure to the Duke? I would not be surprised if he took it as an admission of guilt. At the very least it would seem an insult."

"And what if Rollo's relations discovered you had aided

Mr. Damerell's escape?" said Henrietta eagerly. "Threlfall is a friend to Britain, but any friendly feeling could not survive such a blow. We must avoid provoking our Fairy allies, now of all times."

"You may scoff all you like, my love," said Zacharias, for the Sorceress Royal was scowling. "But you represent English thaumaturgy. Anything you do implicates our profession—indeed, the entire kingdom."

"It is as I said, you see," said Henrietta. "You are far too celebrated to undertake this venture, but I am dispensable—"

"Dispensable!"

"Yes, I am," snapped Henrietta, "and I shall shake you if you don't stop making that face, Prunella, see if I don't! It is most undignified in a sorceress. You have a duty to look after yourself and not hare off on any adventure that strikes your fancy. Do not *you* think so, Miss Muna?"

Miss Muna had no opinion on the matter that she wished to share. But fortunately she was not called upon to equivocate, for Prunella said:

"Oh yes, I am a monster of selfishness, not wishing to send my dearest friend into a nest of ravening dragons! You have not considered the danger, Henny."

"You might credit me with some modicum of sense," said Henrietta with hauteur. "I am not a complete mooncalf, and I have heard all the same stories of Fairy as you have."

Prunella opened her mouth, but before she could reply, Henrietta said passionately, "Think! If you were to die in Fairy, when do you think we should next have a Sorceress Royal? Or do you intend to be the last?"

Muna glanced at the Sorceress Royal. Prunella could not have looked more shocked if Henrietta had slapped her. She sat staring, her lips pale.

"No," she said finally. "You know I hope to be only the first of many *magiciennes*."

"Then I wish you would attend to your counsellors," said Henrietta. She took Prunella's hand, smiling. "Come, there's no call to look so mumchance! What did you become Sorceress Royal for, if not to be accounted more important than the rest of us?"

"You know perfectly well it was Zacharias who forced the staff upon me," said Prunella crossly, but she was defeated. After a moment she said, "You are always most provoking when you are right, Henny. Very well! Zacharias must go."

"No," said Henrietta, before Mr. Wythe could speak. "*I* shall go. The Fairy Court knows Mr. Wythe, since he was Sorcerer Royal before you. No one in Fairy has any notion who I am."

She raised defiant eyes to Mr. Wythe, who said:

"I have no doubt of your abilities, nor of your courage, Miss Stapleton. But you should know the nature of the venture to which you are committing yourself. We could give no assurances of your safety in Threlfall—and should you be discovered, we would be obliged to disclaim your actions. We cannot afford a war with Fairy now. To prevent that, any sacrifice must be made. Do you understand?"

Henrietta was pale, but she squared her shoulders, raising her chin. "Sir, I do."

It had not been the right time to speak before, but now Muna gathered up her courage.

"It is not as though Miss Stapleton will go alone," she said. "I shall accompany her."

She was touched by how Henrietta's face brightened at this.

"Will you?" said Henrietta, turning to her. "That is very good of you! It will be a great help, for of course you have been to Fairy before."

But this was the first time Mr. Wythe had heard that Muna was to go to Threlfall and the notion was evidently unwelcome to him. "There is no reason *you* should risk yourself in this enterprise!" he said.

"But we could not do it without her," said Prunella. "Oh, I forgot we did not tell you about the key to Georgiana's cavern!"

Mr. Wythe was not appeased by her explanation, however.

"I beg you will not think we are not grateful for your offer," he said to Muna. "But we have not, I hope, reached such straits as to need to send our scholars into danger. Mak Genggang entrusted you to our care, and she would not thank us for involving her protégée in our difficulties. I am sure we could extract the key from you easily enough."

Muna did not precisely wish to go to Threlfall; if she had not known before that the journey would be fraught with peril, the English magicians' argument would have enlightened her. They clearly thought it a desperate scheme. But it was Muna's best chance of returning to the Unseen Realm and finding her sister. If she did not go—if Sakti was lost to her forever—

Her mind shied away from the prospect. She had not been parted from Sakti since they had found each other on the shores of Janda Baik. Muna did not know who she was without Sakti; the thought that she might never see her sister again was intolerable. Her fear meant nothing compared to that.

"You will not take the key from me," she said. It was only when she saw the astonishment on the English magicians' faces that she realised she had clenched her fists. She unclenched them, adding, "Sir. Mr. Threlfall entrusted it to me. He felt my presence would be of use."

"It's clear Rollo has taken a liking to Miss Muna," said Prunella to Zacharias. "I expect he has persuaded himself she is a sort of lucky charm, and no rescue attempt could come off without she is there. You know how superstitious magical creatures are—my Youko and Tjandra are overcome by such presentiments all the time. Though it seems whimsical, it always answers to follow their instincts. I should not like to ignore Rollo's intuition—we should be sorry for it, depend upon it!"

"I don't wish to dismiss Rollo's instincts," said Zacharias, "but they are feeble grounds for sending Miss Muna into danger."

"You have forgotten one thing, sir," said Muna. She clasped her hands so they would not tremble and give her away. "I *wish* to go to Threlfall. I have longed to return to the Hidden World since I arrived."

"But why?" said Mr. Wythe, perplexed.

"Why not?" said Prunella.

Henrietta was the first to remember what reason Muna might have for wishing to return to the Unseen Realm. She said gently, "Miss Muna, you should know that Threlfall is one of the most heavily guarded provinces of Fairy Within. No mortal has ever entered that country without an invitation from one of the family. It is very unlikely your sister will be there."

Muna said in a low voice, "I know. Still, I should like to go."

"Oh!" said Prunella contritely. "I am sorry, Miss Muna! How stupid of us!"

Muna only nodded. She was watching Mr. Wythe, for she had seen the doubt that crossed his face.

To be sure, Mr. Wythe could not suspect her true object. Since the English did not know where Sakti was, none of them could have any inkling of Muna's ultimate destination. She intended nothing less than to storm the gates of the Palace of the Unseen.

Muna meant to keep her promise to Rollo, but once she had seen to it that this was discharged, she would abandon the party and make her way to the Palace of the Queen of the Djinns. She did not expect it would be easy. Perhaps it was impossible. From all Mak Genggang and the lamiae had said of the Unseen, it was at least as vast as the mortal world, containing lands and seas beyond her conception. She had no notion what distance lay between Threlfall and the Palace of the Unseen. But it would—must be—easier to close than the gap that lay between her and Sakti now, while they were divided by the veil between the seen and unseen worlds.

She must try any path that was open to her. Muna could not remain in safety in England while her sister was subjected to unknown torments in the abode of the spirits. But she could not allow Mr. Wythe to suspect the truth, or he would prevent her from going, and take Rollo's scale from her.

"I will do what I am told," said Muna. "You need not fear that I shall run wild in the Unseen Realm!" She allowed her fear to make her voice quaver. "But Mak Genggang has always attached a great deal of significance to dreams. I am sure there is a reason Mr. Threlfall appeared in mine. Since he came to me, I should go to him, and . . . it is unlikely, I know, but if I go, perhaps I will hear news of my sister."

She paused. Zacharias looked troubled, but at least she had been sufficiently convincing that she could discern no suspicion in his countenance.

"I fear you will be disappointed," he said. "You risk paying a heavy price for such a slim hope."

"Perhaps," said Muna. "But I have no alternative. Sir, do not forbid me! I could not live with myself if I did not try."

"No," said Zacharias, after a long pause. "I will not forbid you."

"Then that is decided," said Henrietta. She rose, as though she meant to go at once.

"We have agreed Miss Muna will go, but we have not said *you* would be allowed," said Prunella.

Henrietta bridled in a manner that was already wearisomely familiar to Muna. Muna found herself meeting Zacharias's eyes. They were full of fellow feeling—evidently Mr. Wythe was no stranger to the disagreements between his wife and her oldest friend.

"I know you are wont to forget this, Prunella," said Henrietta. "But you can claim no authority over me! Besides, you have not thought of what it will mean for me. How can I be worthy of being called a *magicienne* if I do not perform magic?"

"You do perform magic," Prunella objected. "What do you call your effigy, that you use to persuade your family you are with them?"

"Oh yes! Cheap trickery and parlour games!" said Henrietta in disgust. "You will not tell me that that is all I may expect to do? You founded this Academy to equip magical females to serve their nation. How long must we wait till we begin?"

"Miss Stapleton speaks a great deal of sense," said Zacharias. His tone was mild, but Prunella glared at him.

"The truth of the matter, Zacharias, is that you think it a very good notion!"

Zacharias inclined his head. "We have agreed you cannot go, but someone must—duty as well as friendship demands it. England can ill afford to lose a sorcerer like Damerell, and if he were to fall into the Fairy Queen's clutches, her magic would be amplified, making her a greater threat than ever. Miss Stapleton is England's best *magicienne* bar one; we can repose absolute confidence in her—and she wishes to go."

"But *anything* could happen!" said Prunella. "I wonder you are willing to risk it."

Mr. Wythe said, half-smiling, "If I did not believe in the occasional gamble, my love, I would not have surrendered the staff of the Sorcerer Royal to you!"

"And you have not heard my plan, Prunella," said Henrietta. "I have the French, you know, for my nurse was a Belgian lady. Even if I *were* caught there is no reason why Britain should be blamed."

Zacharias's brow furrowed, but the Sorceress Royal was quicker—or perhaps it was just that the suggestion was perfectly adapted to her manner of thinking.

"So if you are discovered you can persuade Threlfall it is the French that sought to kidnap Damerell," she said. "Oh, you cunning creature! I wish I'd thought of that. I would make a wonderful French spy."

"No, you would not," said Henrietta firmly. "You could not pass two minutes in Fairy without everyone's knowing who you were at once. But I am quite a different matter."

Prunella folded her arms, trying to frown, but she was so beguiled by the idea of cheating the French that the frown kept sliding off her face. She turned to Muna.

"Will you mind being accompanied by a French spy, Miss Muna?" she said. "I don't know what it will do for Janda Baik's credit with the world."

Muna would have agreed to any companion, so long as she was not prevented from going to the Unseen. "I should be honoured to travel with Miss Stapleton."

"Well, then!" said the Sorceress Royal. "Zacharias is so cautious upon the whole, I suppose we had best attend when he counsels recklessness. You *have* always spoke the most elegant French, Henny—Boney could not do better."

"Oh, Prunella!" cried Henrietta, transfigured. She flung her arms around Prunella. "I promise you will not regret this."

Prunella returned her embrace, but her mind was already on the practicalities of the undertaking.

"You can hardly walk into Threlfall as yourselves," she said. "Nor even as Frenchwomen, for no French spy would declare herself for what she was. How ought we to disguise them, do you think, Zacharias?"

15

Three days later
The Draconic Province of Threlfall, Fairyland

ROLLO

THRELFALL'S INTERNAL CONFLICTS were as bitterly fought as might be expected of such a warlike clan, but unlike its battles with outsiders, these private campaigns were waged with an intense and rancorous courtesy. The Code of Threlfall decreed that all should appear to be well between the various members of the family, no matter what bitter enmity reigned in their bosoms.

Every dragon in Threlfall's vast network of caverns therefore colluded in the pretence that there was nothing disquieting in the departure of Rollo's aunt Georgiana on a visit to the Fairy Court. They were even civil to Rollo, the wretched source of the trouble.

The only member of the clan who failed to exert himself was Rollo. No one ever saw a longer face on a dragon. It was generally agreed that this was shocking ingratitude, for it was not as though Rollo had been punished for his misconduct. To be sure, his magic had been suppressed, but no other restriction was placed upon him; he might fly around Threlfall as he wished. There was no fear that he might seek to escape while his soft-shelled bondmate was immured in Georgiana's spare bedroom.

That bondmate served as a salutary contrast to Rollo, for Damerell behaved with unimpeachable propriety, mere mortal though he was. He never complained of the stench, and his only request was for a desk to be installed inside his cage. Nor would he stand for any tragic airs from Rollo.

"If you think it amuses me to have you striking melancholy attitudes and asking if I am hungry a dozen times a day, you are mistaken," he said. "I beg you will take yourself off—go hunting, or terrorize a village, or do whatever it is dragons do for diversion. Since one of us has been allowed his liberty, you ought to make the most of it!"

Consequently Rollo went on long flights, though he was scarcely in the humour to enjoy them. When he could be sure of avoiding detection by his relations, he had drawn upon his last stores of magic to make a door to England, hoping to plead with Prunella and Zacharias for help. But the wards around the Sorceress Royal's quarters proved too much for him in his weakened state: the closest he had contrived to get was the Academy, and he had only succeeded in terrifying a stranger.

At least he had had the chance to apologise, reflected Rollo, for he was unlike most of his relations in that he derived no pleasure from persecuting human maidens. A nice girl, Miss Muna, though Rollo was beginning to think his trust in her had been misplaced. According to his reckoning, three days had passed in the mortal realm since he had entrusted his message to her, and still no one had come.

Rollo had not been able to dreamwalk again since the night he had spoken to Muna. Perhaps as a precaution, his brother

Bartholomew had begun sleeping next to him, and Bartholomew's dreams were so loud and bloody as to drown out Rollo's own. All Rollo could do was wait.

He had never been overly fond of the usual draconic pursuits and in the circumstances they lost all their savour. He could not bring himself to harry the unwary imps and spirits who strayed into Threlfall after dusk. At most he might dutifully pick off a unicorn that had wandered away from its herd, but he had not the heart to finish devouring the carcass before his appetite failed him.

If this goes on for much longer, I shall have to have my breeches taken in, he reflected on one such flight, glancing at his haunches. The thought was followed by a dreadful pang, for breeches could only be sported by a human form. In England Rollo wore both breeches and a human form regularly; after so many years he found the human body, with its compact size and convenient thumbs, almost more comfortable than his original draconic form. It was impossible for Rollo to assume the appearance of a mere mortal in Threlfall, however. Who knew when he might wear it—or breeches—again?

He was so engrossed in sorrowful thoughts that he did not even notice the clouds veiling the entrance to Aunt Georgiana's cavern. Threlfall was a dry country, composed mostly of desert; outside the brief rainy season it was unusual to see clouds in the sky, much less so close to the ground. They were peculiar clouds, too—denser-looking than clouds generally are, and striped with all the vivid hues of sunset: pink and orange and yellow.

It was only when Rollo had entered the cavern and cleaned the blood off his jaws with the scraper provided for the purpose that he realised they had company.

Rollo's brother Bartholomew sat before the narrow tunnel

leading to the chamber that was Damerell's prison. Two smaller figures, colourfully attired, stood by him.

"There you are, Rollo!" said Bartholomew crossly. They had never been on intimate terms even before Bartholomew assumed the role of Damerell's gaoler—the eldest of a dragon's litter traditionally ate its youngest sibling in the egg, and Bartholomew had never forgiven Rollo for hatching before he could be devoured. "Here is a pair of celestial fairies to call upon your bondmate. What does he mean by it? Don't he know visitors ain't allowed?"

"Celestial fairies?" said Rollo.

In common with most draconic residences, the Threlfall caverns were ill-lit, for darkness interspersed with only the occasional dramatic shaft of light was considered the best setting for a hoard of gold. Rollo was obliged to stoop closer to the new arrivals so that he could study their features. The visitors remained studiously immobile, but Rollo was less well prepared, and he recoiled.

"Those are never—!" But he swallowed the words just in time.

"One would think you had never seen our kind before," said the shorter of the two visitors disdainfully. "I am surprised to find such ignorance in Threlfall!"

Rollo only contrived to keep his countenance by a heroic exertion of will when he recognised the Miss Muna whose dream he had entered. The other fairy was Henrietta Stapleton—but a Henrietta Stapleton with hair so fantastically dressed and a person so swathed in layers of embroidered silk as to be wholly transformed.

"Those are never any acquaintances of Damerell's," said Rollo, gulping down his astonishment. "I did not think he knew any—any celestial fairies."

Surely it was evident even to a blockhead like Barty that the girls were mortal! But of course, like most members of the clan, Barty had spent hardly any time outside Fairy. Rollo's family thought him mad for choosing to reside in Britain. Even Georgiana was accounted eccentric for being fond of visiting the mortal realm.

Acting on instinct, Rollo lowered his head and glared at the visitors in feigned suspicion.

"Come to that," he said, "how d'you know they are celestial fairies? They look rum 'uns to me."

"Why, they rode into Threlfall upon clouds," said Bartholomew. "Did not you see their mounts outside?"

Here was another thing Rollo knew which his brother could not. Prunella Wythe was a proficient in cloud-riding, having been trained in the art by an archimage of the Orient, a friend of Zacharias's named Mr. Hsiang. She considered it such a useful skill that she instructed all her *magiciennes* in it.

"Even so, what can they have to do with Poggs?" Rollo demanded. "You never met anyone less celestial."

"That shows how little you know of it!" said Muna. She jabbed Henrietta in the side.

It had been agreed that Muna would hold her tongue and Henrietta do most of the talking, since Henrietta was better acquainted with Robert of Threlfall. But Henrietta had not said a word since they had arrived. Muna's worry was beginning to shade into panic.

What Muna did not know, and Prunella had not calculated upon, was that Henrietta did not recognise Rollo, for she had only ever seen him in the guise of a fair-haired young gentleman with better tailoring than brains. The golden dragon looming over her caused her to quake in her shoes—unlikely creations with a vertiginous wooden heel, on which she could hardly keep her balance.

These, like the remainder of the ladies' disguise, were on loan from the cloud-riding master Mr. Hsiang: being a gentleman, he had not thought to supply foot-gear that would enable them to run should they need to beat a hasty retreat.

Fortunately Muna's nudge recalled Henrietta to herself. She flung back her shoulders, lifting her chin.

"Stand not in our way, Lord Dragon!" she said imperiously. "We bear a message of great importance for the mortal Paget Damerell, as he is named in this life."

"Eh?" said Bartholomew, directing a look of accusation at his brother.

Those who loved Rollo best owned that he would never win any prizes for wit, but few had seen him in his native habitat. It had required cunning and perseverance for Rollo to escape Threlfall for his peaceful existence in England, undisturbed in the main by his relations or their notion of draconic duties. He drew on these unsuspected reserves now.

"I don't know that we ought to let these creatures trouble Poggs," he said with an air of doubt. "He has enough to worry him—and Aunt Georgiana would not like it.

"Of course," he added, "if I thought callers might do Poggs any good, I should allow it, and hang the consequences! But you will wish to think of your own neck, Barty. *You* won't wish to provoke Aunt Georgiana. I don't know that I wouldn't do the same in your position."

Bartholomew rose to the bait, just as Rollo had hoped.

"Oh, Aunt Georgiana don't worry me," he said loftily. "What she don't know won't hurt her. I have half a mind to let them in. I ha'n't had any sport since I was set to watch your wretched bond-mate. The First Dragon knows some entertainment would not go amiss!"

He turned to the putative fairies. "This message you have got for the mortal, what is it?"

"I am not about to tell you," said Henrietta, looking down her nose at him—an impressive feat, given how Bartholomew towered over her. "It is a secret, and I was charged to convey it to Paget Damerell and no one else. Even he has no suspicion of what it is!"

"But it is terribly interesting," added Muna.

Her comment hit its mark. Bartholomew was growing heartily bored of his charge. Damerell passed his time in confinement in reading and writing ("One never has a spare moment for study in London"). He would not be drawn into conversation, saying courteously that he would be remiss to distract Bartholomew from his duties. Nor was Damerell worried by jests about his likely fate on a banqueting table: "If I were not prepared for a future as someone's dinner, I should not have submitted to being bonded with a dragon. I never believe in crying over spilt milk."

In short, he had provided far less diversion than Bartholomew felt he had a right to expect. Bartholomew was not about to miss out on any fun to be extracted from the prisoner.

"You may have five minutes," said Bartholomew. "Mind you speak up when you deliver your message, and you need not think I shall hesitate to snap you up if I do not like what I hear!"

"I wish you would all let poor old Poggs alone!" cried Rollo. He followed the others, lifting his voice in conscientious complaint, while his heart beat fast beneath his ribs.

D AMERELL'S cage was as pleasant as a cage could be which had once contained the decomposing remains of princesses, for he had exerted himself to clean it. He was sitting at his bureau, swearing under his breath, when the party entered. He looked up, taking off his spectacles.

"Ah!" he said. If Henrietta Stapleton's presence had not given the game away, a glance at Rollo's countenance would have sufficed. Damerell knew what was afoot at once, but he betrayed it by neither look nor word. "To what do I owe this honour?"

"These fairies have a message for you, they say," said Bartholomew, adding with irony, "I hope we have not interrupted your work!" He glanced at the papers scattered upon the bureau.

"Not at all," said Damerell graciously. "I am grateful for the interruption." He turned to the two women. "I'm afraid to own I have succumbed to writing poetry to while away the hours. I am reconciled to producing poor stuff, but there are some depths to which no gentleman should descend. I was on the verge of rhyming *dragon* with *wagon* when you appeared."

"You are acquainted with these fairies, then?" said Bartholomew. Damerell's eyes passed over the women.

"I have not the least idea who these people are," he said.

Henrietta drew herself up, assuming a magisterial air.

"The hour is arrived," she boomed, "ye who were once known as Paget Damerell!"

Damerell's mouth twitched. Rollo quaked at the sight. Poggs had an inconvenient sense of humour and often found amusement in things no one else thought droll. If he should give way to laughter now . . . !

There was no need for Rollo to worry, however. Though he could not know it, Damerell was nearly as nervous as Rollo.

"The use of the past tense is rather worrying!" said Damerell.

"We bear a message from your sworn brother, the Supreme Emperor of the Dark Heavens," announced Henrietta. She paused.

In truth Henrietta was not altogether reconciled to the message Prunella and Zacharias had concocted with Mr. Hsiang's assistance; she doubted whether it was right to repeat such paganisms.

It was a view with which Muna had some sympathy, but the two *naga* breathing down her neck put paid to any reservations she might otherwise have had—it was true that one of them was friendly, but his teeth were just as large as the other's. Since Henrietta did not speak, Muna interjected:

"What Miss—my mistress means to say is, the Emperor sends his best compliments and he should be obliged if you would return to the heavens directly. You have suffered quite enough to atone for your sins and he begs you will come with us now to the northern skies. There you will be restored to your rightful position among the stars, looking down upon the trivial joys and sorrows of mankind."

Damerell received this extraordinary message with composure. "I should be honoured to accept your master's invitation. Permit me a moment to gather up my possessions."

He looked around his cage, then said, "Here is good news! I have nothing here that I wish to keep. We can be on our way directly."

"Don't you want your poetry?" said Muna.

"My dear madam, the opportunity to be free of my poetry is the greatest attraction of your master's offer," said Damerell.

"Here," said Bartholomew sharply, "what's all this about packing?"

"Your servant's manners leave much to be desired, sir," Henrietta told Damerell. She cast a withering look at Bartholomew. "You ought to have him whipped."

"I am not a servant!" said Bartholomew, but the visitors' demeanour and grand friends had impressed him. He said, with grudging civility, "You ought to know Damerell is Threlfall's prisoner, reserved for the Fairy Queen's delectation. I cannot agree to his leaving on any account."

Henrietta waved her arm, her vast sleeves lending a magnificent dismissiveness to the gesture. "I am not acquainted with the Fairy Queen, but want shall have to be her master. I suppose *you* think this gentlemen is a mere mortal!"

"Why, I know he is," said Bartholomew. "Looks like one. Smells like one." He looked wistfully at Damerell. "Tastes like one, too, I'd wager!"

"You are fortunate gaming is frowned upon in the northern heavens, for we should certainly profit from your error," said Henrietta. "This gentleman is not the mere puny Englishman he appears, but the Deity of the Unborn Star, robed for the brief span of a mortal life in human flesh. He was the childhood friend of the Supreme Emperor of the Dark Heavens and erstwhile favourite of that illustrious god, our master."

This revelation so astonished Damerell that he fell into a fit of coughing. It would not have convinced anyone who was familiar with mortal laughter—Rollo knew it for what it was, and glanced nervously at his brother. But the mortals Bartholomew encountered were rarely in a humour to laugh, and he took no notice.

"Ridiculous!" he sputtered. "Damerell was never a star. Was he?" There was a thread of doubt in Bartholomew's voice; this was Fairy, after all, where all manner of unlikely things might be true. He turned to Rollo. "It ain't true, is it?"

"Why," said Rollo reflectively, "it ain't uncommon, you know, this sort of thing. Don't you recall, Barty, how the Fairy Queen used to do the same to her friends and relations? When any of them displeased her, she would take their heart, depriving them of the best part of their magic, and pack them off into exile. She said it learnt 'em manners."

Muna had fixed a celestial expression upon her face, from which it was beginning to ache. For some reason Rollo's words made her shiver. A memory came back to her—of being submerged in the depths of the sea, watching the rippling image of the sun through the water . . .

She shook herself. The memory belonged to the serpent she had seen in her vision. There was no reason her heart should tremble in her chest, or her breath come short. Whatever had befallen the serpent had nothing to do with her. Yet she found herself speaking:

"Where did the Queen exile them—these friends and relations?"

"The mortal realm, generally," said Rollo. "Used to send a horde of them away on the seventh Tuesday of every month."

"The *seventh* Tuesday . . . ?" said Henrietta, frowning.

"But why did you never mention this before?" demanded Bartholomew. "It is just like you, Rollo, to let everyone believe you had united yourself with a mortal, when a word of explanation would have saved a world of trouble. When I think of the scandal you caused—the family conferences—the aunts' complaints—your want of consideration makes me sick!"

Two puffs of smoke rose from his nostrils. Henrietta and Muna edged away from him.

Alarmed, Rollo stammered, "Well, I can't say I knew, as such. I just meant that it don't seem unlikely."

But this only served to aggravate his brother further. "Do you mean to tell me you did not know your own bondmate was a constellation cast down to earth?"

Here Muna intervened, much to Rollo's relief.

"Really, sir, I am surprised at you," she said to Bartholomew. "The Deity of the Unborn Star was ignorant of his true nature—and if he knew nothing, how were his friends to have any idea of it? No one remembers their past lives. Our master took particular care to ensure that Mr. Damerell should be no exception. His mortal existence would have been no punishment if he could recall his former glories."

"I should have thought it would make the punishment all the worse," said Bartholomew. "I mean to say, I would feel it all the more if I were kicked out of Threlfall and knew it."

"But it is clear you, sir, are a being of keen sentiments and refined nature," said Henrietta. "Mr. Damerell was quite different. He was entirely reprobate. It was felt if he could look back upon his noble past, he would not feel his degradation as he ought."

"There is something in that," Bartholomew allowed. "But why was he degraded? I mean to say, what crime did he commit?"

Rollo saw Henrietta exchange a panicked look with Muna; it was clear they had never got so far as to invent a crime for Damerell to have committed. Before he could grow too anxious, however, Muna said:

"My mistress is loath to pollute the air of Threlfall with the name of his crime. I am afraid to say, sir, that Mr. Damerell was"— her voice dropped—"an inveterate gambler!"

Bartholomew nodded with a worldly-wise air. "Ah, the usual story! Gambled his way to ruin—lost all he had, I suppose?"

"On the contrary," said Damerell, "I begin to remember all. I won with such regularity that it impoverished all my acquaintance, and it was necessary to teach me a lesson. I am now chastened and regret being so unfeeling." He bowed to Henrietta and Muna. "Shall we return so that I may tender a suitably grovelling apology to my old friends?"

"But you can't go," objected Bartholomew. "I *said*."

"You don't mean to say you are willing to affront the Imperial

Lord—the Dark and Mysterious Sovereign of the Upper Heavens?" cried Henrietta.

Fairies were invariably snobbish and Rollo's family was no exception, but even these grand titles did not move Bartholomew. "That is just what I do mean," he said. "Either it is he or my aunt who is to be incensed, and I should much rather vex your Imperial Lord than my aunt Georgiana. And if you met my aunt, you would know the reason why! Do not you agree it is much the safest course, Rollo?"

He turned to his brother. As he gestured, it exposed the tender spot just below his foreleg.

Out of the corner of his eye Rollo saw Muna nudge Henrietta. But Henrietta was already drawing from beneath her voluminous robes an elegant filigree hairpin, inlaid with kingfisher feathers. She stepped forward and stabbed it into the soft flesh under Bartholomew's leg.

"Ow!" cried Bartholomew.

Muna seized Henrietta's arm, dragging her out of the way as the dragon whirled around, opening his jaw.

"We'll have none of that!" said Rollo. He caught his brother's jaw between his teeth, but they had scarcely begun to struggle together when Bartholomew staggered. His eyes rolled back in their sockets. For an endless moment he stood, swaying. Then, with all the ponderous majesty of an ancient tree being felled, he crashed into the dust.

Muna and Henrietta leapt away just in time. They huddled against the cave wall, panting.

"You ha'n't killed him?" said Rollo, awed.

Henrietta smoothed down her dress with shaking hands.

"Oh no!" she said. "That is to say, I hope not! We enchanted the hairpin, but it is only a sleeping charm. We used to sing it over the infants at Mrs. Daubeney's school. Mr. Wythe said it ought to work even upon grown dragons if we put some of Fairy's magic in it, since it is such stronger stuff than the atmospheric magic we have in England."

"Quite right," said Damerell from his cage. "That is why Rollo and I sought Mrs. Wythe's assistance. Mortal magicians are more powerful in Fairy than they realise, since they are so accustomed to making the most of thinner magic. The least breath of air in Fairy contains a stronger draught of magic than many thauma-turges will ever taste.

"It was an ingenious idea to employ one of your quaint school-girl charms, Miss Stapleton," he added, bowing to Henrietta. "No fairy would have expected that."

"Had not we better get you out of that cage, sir?" said Muna. "Surely we should get away as soon as we can." She glanced at Bartholomew's slumbering bulk.

"I am entirely of your mind, madam," said Damerell. "But first . . . Miss Stapleton, if you would allow me to examine your weapon?"

Henrietta gave him the hairpin. He brought it up to his eyes, saying to Muna, "We have not been introduced, but Rollo men-tioned you. We are very much obliged to you for passing our mes-sage to Mrs. Wythe. I must say I had not realised that the fame of our Academy had spread so far abroad as to draw our foreign col-leagues to us."

"The Sorceress Royal is the friend of my mistress, Mak Geng-gang," explained Muna.

"Indeed! I recollect the lady. A witch of considerable parts. Now, this is a fine piece," he said, admiring the hairpin. "And the charm is ingenious. Inducing sleep is not its only effect, I think?"

"Prunella altered it a little," said Henrietta. "She added an alexiteric to counteract the effects of any Fairy magic. Even if the dragon were to wake prematurely, he would find his magic inhibited for a time."

"Very clever," said Damerell. "The charm is not wholly exhausted, I think. What do you think, Rollo?"

Rollo lowered his head to the cage to study the hairpin. He saw Damerell's hand dart out between the bars, but he did not realise what it intended until he felt the pricking in his neck. He looked down, catching just a glimpse of the light gleaming off the silver pin embedded in his scales.

"Poggs!" he cried, but his tongue would not shape the words of reproach that sprang to it. Damerell's face dissolved into vagueness as insensibility drew Rollo into its embrace.

"OH, Mr. Damerell!" exclaimed Henrietta. She sounded as shocked as Muna felt.

Muna had planned to remain only till she had seen Mr. Damerell out of his cage; then she had meant to create a distraction and slip away. But she forgot her plan at the sorry sight of Rollo sinking to the ground. She leapt forward, drawing the hairpin out of Rollo's flesh, but it was too late. The *naga* stirred and whimpered but did not wake.

"How could you?" said Muna. She tucked the hairpin away in her robes, out of Damerell's reach.

But Damerell ignored her. "I beg you will take a step back. Two yards' distance should suffice."

To the women's astonishment, one side of the cage fell over at his touch. Damerell stepped out, as composed as though he were alighting from a hackney coach outside the Theurgist's Club.

"The air of liberty," he remarked. "All the sweeter for not being perfumed by the effluvium of princesses past!"

"Could you do that all along?" demanded Muna.

Damerell inclined his head. "It is an old cage, and the Threlfalls did not account for the operation of blood upon metal. Several of the bars have nearly rusted away. But if I had broken free before, I should not have enjoyed my liberty for long before Bartholomew devoured me.

"You need not feel sorry for Rollo, my dear girls," he added. "When he wakes he will agree that I only did what was necessary. His aunt stopped up his magic, you see, and unfortunately the nature of our contract meant that in consequence my magic, too, was bound. Mrs. Wythe's alexiteric will neutralize the fetters Rollo's aunt placed upon him, which should mean that I shall regain access to my own magic."

"But won't it cancel out your magic too?" said Muna, far from reconciled. It did seem hard on Rollo that he should have gone to such lengths to arrange Damerell's rescue, only to be downed ignominiously by the very man he sought to liberate.

"I think it will not," said Damerell. "I am still—mostly—mortal. I do not owe *all* my magic to Fairy." He rolled his shoulders and shook out his sleeves, breathing deeply. "I believe it has worked. I feel myself grow stronger already."

"Still, I don't see that there was any need to knock out poor Mr. Threlfall," Muna protested. "We could have supplied all the magic we needed."

"We are in the heart of Threlfall, madam," said Damerell. "We shall need all the magic we can get."

His tone was gentle, but it silenced Muna.

"But how are we to bring Mr. Threlfall away?" said Henrietta, gazing at Rollo in consternation. "I know he only wished us to free you, but we cannot leave him here!"

"No, indeed," said Damerell. He considered his fallen bond-mate. "But it is true he is rather unwieldy as he is now." He placed his hand on the *naga*'s head, muttering a formula under his breath.

Under the effect of the spell, Rollo changed. He lost his golden sheen, his scales sinking into his flesh and his hindquarters retracting into his person. By degrees he transformed into a young man—slight, blond and, since of course dragons did not generally wear anything but a ferocious expression, quite improper for a lady to look upon.

Henrietta and Muna sprang back with a shriek, covering their eyes. Damerell hoisted Rollo up and slung him over his shoulder.

"I beg you will not mention that you saw Rollo *en déshabillé*," said Damerell. "Poor fellow, he would be so abashed! We must hope it will not occur to him to wonder what happened after I struck him down. Come along."

But the words had scarcely left his lips when an enormous voice like a foghorn blared out, making Muna jump.

"Good morrow, Bartholomew!" cried the voice. "Is Rollo out a-flying?"

Henrietta and Damerell blanched, exchanging looks of dismay.

"Who is that?" said Muna, for recognition was patent on both English magicians' faces.

"Mr. Threlfall's aunt, Georgiana Without Ruth!" whispered Henrietta. "Oh, sir, what shall we do?"

"She was not supposed to return till the evening," said Damerell, vexed. "Damn! It is a judgment upon me. I was a fool to believe I had any hope of preserving this coat!"

16

GEORGIANA WITHOUT RUTH

HE DRAGONESS GEORGIANA Without Ruth heaved herself into her cavern with no very light heart. She had worn herself out in representations at the Fairy Court, but its stewards had remained obdurate. She had not even been admitted to the Fairy Queen's presence, for the Queen was busy, said the stewards.

The Queen had never been too busy to receive the chief representative of Threlfall before. But seeing protest was fruitless, Georgiana had left with what remained of her dignity.

"Well, Bartholomew, I have tried to put off the evil day, but there is nothing for it," she said. "We shall have to surrender our guest after all. What poison has been poured into the Queen's ear I do not know, but she is persuaded we mean to unseat her. We must assure her of Threlfall's loyalty, or we are lost! It is a pity—I had hoped to avoid the sacrifice—but it cannot be helped. Why, what's this?"

Bartholomew was stretched out upon the ground, lost to the world. A golden dragon crouched over him, its face in shadow.

A mortal might have thought the scene was hardly one to cheer a mind so burdened with cares as Georgiana's. But she cried out, in surprise mixed with delight:

"Rollo, do not tell me you have overpowered your brother!"

"We had a disagreement," said the golden dragon indistinctly. "Ought I to eat him? I confess I don't like the thought! Besides, I have caught my dinner already."

If not for the fact that the dragon's voice was muffled, Georgiana might have noticed that Rollo did not sound like his usual self. But he held three rabbits in his jaws, which could not but impede his speech. Besides, she was too overcome by his accomplishment to be detained by trifles.

"It is the convention to devour the defeated after a duel," said Georgiana. She looked at her nephew with new respect. "Those rabbits will hardly satisfy your appetite after your exertions. I must say I did not know you were capable of this. How came you to challenge your brother?"

The golden dragon seemed to feel none of Georgiana's pleasure at his success.

"Lost my temper," he said lugubriously. "Dashed at Barty. He jumped up roaring—made to fry me to a crisp—hit his head on the ceiling and fell over. Poor Barty! Still, he oughtn't to have said all that about Poggs!"

Georgiana glanced at the cage. Damerell had contrived to fashion a hammock out of the velvet cloak of a late princess, and it appeared to be occupied. It was not as though Rollo could have liberated his bondmate in any case, of course. She had seen to it that he would not have magic enough to do anything foolish.

"I suppose that still counts as a defeat of sorts," she said dubiously. "Our ancestors would not have hesitated to devour him in the circumstances."

"But Mother wouldn't like it if I ate Barty."

"Oh, your mother is a most irrational creature!" said Georgiana. But now that the point had been raised, she found she could not easily dismiss it. "Would it distress her greatly, do you think?"

"Certain to!" said the golden dragon. "She's no end fond of Barty."

The more Georgiana reflected upon the matter, the more it seemed to her that Rollo was right—a most unusual state of affairs, but then, it was a time for unprecedented occurrences.

"Yes," she said irritably. "Like as not your mother would declare war if you ate him, and we cannot afford a civil conflict in Threlfall now. You had best restrain your cannibalistic instincts, Rollo, though they do you credit. You may have the carcass if Bartholomew dies, but if he does wake you must let him alone."

"Pray don't speak so, aunt! I never thought of Barty's not waking." The dragon nudged Bartholomew's prone form with his snout, apparently in hope of discerning some flicker of life.

"I expect there is no harm done and he will only have a headache," said Georgiana. She continued, with a solicitude quite unusual in her dealings with Rollo, "Had not you better leave before you are overcome by blood-lust? Even I find it difficult to restrain myself when the urge is upon me."

"I don't feel as though I will be overcome," said the dragon, craning his neck to look down at himself. "I never could work up a good blood-lust, even as a dragonet. But perhaps I had better go. The rabbits will taste better *en plein air.*"

"I do not see why you did not eat them when you caught them."

The dragon was nearly at the threshold, but he said, "I thought I would see if Poggs would like one. But I had forgot he don't eat things that talk, and the rabbits are raw besides."

"Silly mortal prejudices!" said Georgiana.

In a moment the golden dragon would be out of the cave, but as she looked after him, Georgiana was struck by an odd detail.

"Why, Rollo," she said, "one of your rabbits has yellow hair on its head. Yes, yellow ringlets, I declare—like an elf, or a mortal! I have never seen that on a rabbit."

"I believe it is the new fashion," said the dragon. He stretched his wings, his haunches tensing as he prepared to leap into the air.

But something in his manner had piqued Georgiana's curiosity. She followed her nephew to the threshold.

"Stay, now," she said, her eyes alight with suspicion. "I did not notice it before, but you sound different today."

"Sore throat!"

"Do not you dare fly away, Rollo!" bellowed Georgiana. "You will give your aunt an answer, and you will drop those rabbits in your mouth while you do it!"

Her voice resonated through the cavern, drawing forth strange echoes. The very walls of the cave seemed to sag, as though they felt their weight, and all at once the golden dragon's feet were rooted to the spot.

"Why, aunt, what's amiss?" he said, turning his head.

The wide-eyed dismay, the apprehensive tone, were all Rollo to the life. They were enough to give Georgiana pause—but only for a moment. For despite the dragon's best efforts his eyes had acquired a ring of hazel that was rapidly drowning out the blue.

"You are not Rollo at all, are you?" said Georgiana grimly.

Before the dragon could answer, there was a piteous squeak from his mouth.

"I cannot keep hold of the spell," said the yellow-ringleted rabbit. "Oh, help—Mr. Damerell—Miss Muna—help!"

The enchantment unravelled. Out of the golden dragon's

mouth tumbled three small furry bodies—but they began to transform before they ever hit the ground.

Muna could not help, nor do more than gasp, as she changed back into a human being. Unlike Henrietta, she had adapted without difficulty to her metamorphosis. Her human body might have been no more than a costume. It had seemed just as natural to be a rabbit.

To be transformed again so abruptly was bewildering. She could not remember how to persuade her tongue to shape human speech, much less cast a spell to save them. Scream she could, however, and scream she did as she fell, until her collision with a warm body knocked the breath out of her.

Even having Muna's full weight land on him did not wake Rollo. He had reverted not to his draconic but to his human form, and he only stirred a little, snorting his sleep. Next to him Henrietta was sobbing, so distressed that she scarcely seemed to notice the impropriety of their position—entangled with a gentleman, none of them remotely fit for company.

A great leathery wing swept over them. Muna sneezed, and when she looked down on herself she was clothed again, in the robes she had worn before they were changed into rabbits.

"There!" said a kind voice. "You will be more comfortable so." A four-clawed foot planted itself on either side of her, Henrietta and Rollo, each large foreleg covered in scales. The same voice said:

"You will account to me, Georgiana, if any harm comes to these three!"

"You must be a stranger to Threlfall if you think you will intimidate *me*," said Georgiana disdainfully. "A gentledragon would introduce himself before making threats! You must be a shape-shifter of talent to have imitated Rollo so closely. I was very near being taken in. What do you call yourself?"

The golden dragon said nothing, but though Muna could not see his expression it must have betrayed him.

Georgiana said, in an altered tone, *"Oh!"*

A broad smile spread across her countenance.

"Well, well, well," she said. "Paget Damerell! I never suspected . . . but if the bond enabled Rollo to assume human form, why should it not have done the same for you, t'other way around? Foolish of me never to have thought of it! But who would suspect anyone of taking a mortal form by choice?

"Of course, there is Rollo," added Georgiana as an afterthought. "But he can hardly be taken as a guide to rational conduct. I'd always thought you had more sense, Damerell. If you are able to take this form, why do you ever spend any time in the other? You are far handsomer as you are now—there is no comparison!"

"You honour me," said Damerell. Sheltered as she was by his bulk, Muna could tell he was taut with tension, but he spoke with all his accustomed suavity. "I find my mortal form possesses certain advantages. Among other things, it is far easier to fit into a hackney coach."

"And here are your rabbits," said Georgiana, surveying Muna, Henrietta and Rollo. "How ugly Rollo looks without his scales! As for the other two—why, they are mortals! Mortal females, I do declare."

"They are friends of the Sorceress Royal and under her protection," said Damerell.

He seemed to mean this for a warning, but it had the opposite of the intended effect. Georgiana looked pleased. If she had had palms, it was clear she would have rubbed them.

"The Sorceress Royal's friends, you say? How convenient," she said. "This might have been my design all along. Indeed, I believe it was, for I must have guessed your friends would hear of what had befallen you, and I had the sagacity to see where *that* would end. Few mortal magicians can resist the allure of an adventure in Fairy!"

She lowered her head to inspect Muna and the others, her sulphurous breath gusting over them.

"You are a discriminating creature, Damerell," she said. "I have never understood what you saw in Rollo, for on the whole, I have no doubt you only befriend people of the best kind. You, now, with the yellow hair—I expect *you* are wealthy beyond the dreams of avarice!"

This succeeded in rousing Henrietta out of her waterworks. She sat up, dashing the tears from her eyes.

"You are mistaken, ma'am," she retorted. "I have not a penny in the world!"

"Oh, you cannot mislead these nostrils," said Georgiana. "Nothing can equal the Threlfall nose for detecting the scent of gold, and you stink of wealth."

"If so, the stench is deceptive," said Henrietta bitterly, but she might have remained silent for all the notice Georgiana took of her. The *naga* turned her gaze on Muna.

"I cannot tell what *you* are at all," she said contemplatively. "But that must be a sign of your powers, for there are not many mortals that can bamboozle me. We will say you are a renowned magician. That ought to satisfy the Fairy Queen, particularly since you are a friend of the Sorceress Royal. It has all fallen out very well! I shall substitute these two mortals for you, Damerell, and offer them to the Fairy Queen in your place."

Henrietta gasped.

"*What?*" said Damerell.

But Muna was on her feet in a moment, hope flaring. The words tripped off her tongue before she could stop them.

"You mean you will take us to the Palace of the Unseen—the Fairy Court, I mean?" she said breathlessly.

"That is just what I intend," Georgiana agreed.

"No!" said Damerell.

The dragoness's look of satisfaction dimmed. "Why, Damerell, I should have thought you'd be pleased."

"I am not and I won't allow it," said Damerell. His claws dug into the floor of the cavern, scraping grit from the stone. "I have been a sorcerer bonded to a dragon of Threlfall for more years than I like to recall. To suggest that two greenhorn girls would be a worthy replacement for me . . . do you mean this for an insult, ma'am?"

"I do not say they are exactly equivalent," allowed Georgiana, "but it is not as though the Queen will ever know she might have had you instead. I should think two Englishwomen would please her just as well. In her current temper, nothing will suit the Queen better than to do the British an ill turn."

"Very good," said Damerell. "*I* am English, so why should not I do?"

"You are being very strange, Damerell, I must say," said Georgiana, peering down at him in puzzlement. "Why should you wish to be eaten when we have two perfectly good replacements? Indeed, I never wished to sacrifice you at all. I've always been fond of you, you know."

"You are most kind," said Damerell frostily, "but still, I must insist—"

"I don't deny I held up my talons and squawked when Rollo first told us he had taken a mortal bondmate," Georgiana continued as though he had not spoken. "But I am not afraid of owning my mistakes. I am happy to say you are far better than anyone had a right to expect for an inconsequential runt like Rollo. I should not have proposed offering you up to the Queen, but there seemed no other course if Threlfall was to be saved. However, now there is no need for it."

"I cannot agree," said Damerell.

Muna did not think he was likely to sway the dragoness, for far from being convinced, Georgiana was beginning to look vexed. It was clear she was like all powerful people accustomed to having their way—to be resisted would only serve to annoy her.

Still, Damerell was an old, canny magician and he appeared determined that Muna and Henrietta's lives should not be exchanged for his. Left alone, he might well prevail upon Georgiana, and that would not suit Muna at all. She did not of course wish to be eaten by the Queen of the Djinns, but she meant to be taken to the Palace of the Unseen. Since Fate had granted her this chance, she could not pass it up.

"Don't be silly," she burst out, forgetting shyness. "You will not waste all our efforts to rescue you, sir? I call that disrespectful, after all we have done!"

"Hear her!" said Georgiana approvingly. "You had best attend to your rabbits, Damerell. They speak good sense."

Damerell gazed down at Muna with a look of surprise. "I mean no disrespect. But if I could abandon you—two mere girls, one of whom I have known since she was a babe in arms—I had far better be dead than alive."

Henrietta had been silent, watching the dragons quarrel with wide unseeing eyes, but now she bestirred herself.

"No, sir," she said. "Miss Muna is right. We came to save you, and we must see the job through. Britain could readily spare a Miss

Stapleton, but a sorcerer of your age and experience would be a grievous loss."

Damerell looked outraged. *They will argue forever if I let them!* thought Muna in despair. Then she saw what she must do.

She stepped out from the shelter of Damerell's body. Georgiana Without Ruth loomed over her.

Georgiana was built upon such lines as made it evident that Rollo was, in fact, on the petite side for a *naga*. From Muna's position the dragoness's teeth looked enormous, and it was necessary for her to swallow a lump in her throat before she could speak.

"Madam, I have heard that spirits will sometimes agree to a bargain," she said. She was relieved to hear that her voice was steady, if rather high-pitched. "I have one to propose. If you will take me and allow Mr. Damerell, Mr. Threlfall and Miss Stapleton to return to England, I promise to come quietly with you, and not give any trouble."

Georgiana let out a scorching plume of red flame, blackening the ceiling. Muna scuttled backwards, but after a moment she realised the *naga* was laughing.

"What a bargain!" said Georgiana. "Why, what trouble could *you* give me?"

What would Sakti say if she were here now?

"I shan't tell you, of course. That would only teach you how to guard against it!" said Muna, tossing her head. "But I would counsel you not to underestimate me. Have not you wondered how we contrived to gain admission to your home despite your wards? Everyone knows no one may approach the caverns of Georgiana Without Ruth unless they have Threlfall's blood in their veins."

Georgiana shook out her wings. "There is no mystery about that! You conspired with Rollo, of course." Yet there was a note of doubt in her voice.

"I had never met Mr. Threlfall before this day," said Muna disdainfully (it was not a lie, she thought, for surely a dream-meeting did not count—one met all sorts of unlikely people in one's dreams). "But if that is what you like to believe, far be it from me to disillusion you!"

Her air of superiority—assumed in memory of Sakti at her most exasperating—was somewhat punctured when a hand landed heavily on her shoulder and she leapt, yelping. But it was only Henrietta.

"Muna, you are brave—noble!" Henrietta's voice trembled. "But we could not let you sacrifice yourself for us. It was I who insisted upon coming to Threlfall. If anyone is to be offered up to the Court, it should be me!"

"So you will be," said Georgiana. "You will both be offered up. There is no need to quarrel among yourselves, for your opinion is not of the least consequence." She turned to Damerell. "You and Rollo will return to the mortal realm. Rollo will be safer there if the Fairy Queen decides to pursue him—and it will be a relief to be rid of his mumchance airs!"

She cast a discontented look at Bartholomew. He had yet to stir; indeed, both he and Rollo were still lost to the world, despite the hubbub around them. *The Sorceress Royal's charm must be very potent,* thought Muna.

This gave her an idea. If only the hairpin had not been lost in the course of her metamorphoses! Her hand stole inside her robes—and closed around what she was looking for.

"I suppose it is too much to hope that Rollo had anything to do with vanquishing his brother?" Georgiana was saying.

"That was the work of the fair hands of these ladies," said Damerell, bowing.

Georgiana sighed. "They will make worthy gifts, at least. It has been some years since any mortal has got the better of a Threlfall. Bartholomew will not know where to look when he wakes. Well, we had best be off! Come along, you two—what do you call yourselves?"

A breeze ruffled Muna's hair, and a golden wing descended in front of her and Henrietta, obscuring their view of Georgiana. The dragoness's incredulous voice could be heard, saying:

"Come now, Damerell, do not play the fool! You don't wish to quarrel with *me*."

"Let us go, Mr. Damerell," said Henrietta. Her voice was unsteady, but she lifted her chin and took a step forward with the air of a martyr. "We came to Threlfall of our own accord, and we are prepared to suffer the consequences."

"Don't be a gaby!" said Damerell curtly. "You cannot think I will allow either of you to come to harm."

"Oh, you need have no fear of that," said Georgiana. "I shall see to it myself that they are delivered to the Court without a scratch upon them. The Queen will not have them if they are anything less than perfect."

Damerell only growled in reply. Peering around the edge of his wing, Muna saw wisps of smoke rise from Georgiana's nostrils. Her jaws began to glow.

"You will leave me with no choice, will you?" said Georgiana. "You drive me to this, Damerell!"

We shall all be torched to a crisp! thought Muna.

"Step out of the way, ma'am!" she cried, addressing Georgiana. She did not wait for the *naga* to respond but stabbed Damerell in the wing with the hairpin she had found in her robes.

Damerell cried out and retracted his wing, glaring down at Muna. "Miss Muna, you are in danger of causing me to lose my temper!"

"I am sorry!" said Muna, whisking the hairpin out of sight. She had hoped some remnant of the Sorceress Royal's charm would have clung to it, but the magic had evidently faded. "But I had to try. Oh, sir, if you knew—!"

"I cannot understand you," said Damerell crossly. "I can only suppose you nourish romantic dreams of dying a spectacular death, for I do not know why else you should want to go to the Fairy Court, knowing . . ."

A distant look came over Damerell's countenance. He blinked, licking his lips.

"Knowing . . . what awaits you there . . ." he said. A shiver went along his person.

Muna seized Henrietta's wrist, whispering, "Mr. Threlfall—we must not let him be crushed!"

Henrietta nodded. The Englishwoman grasped Rollo's right arm, Muna his left, and they tugged him out of the way before Damerell collapsed to the ground, his eyes rolling back into his head.

"Good heavens!" said Georgiana as the dust settled around them. "I suppose that was the same chantment that knocked out Bartholomew and Rollo. I will have your weapon, if you please, miss."

"I have lost it," said Muna, for she had no intention of surrendering the hairpin, but:

"Oh, I think not!" said Georgiana. To Muna's dismay she found herself offering the hairpin to the *naga*. A large rough tongue swept it off her palm.

"A clever device," said Georgiana, when she had swallowed the hairpin. "You need not look so downcast—you could not have used it again in any event, for you would require a great deal more magic than remained in that to overpower me. It was well done in any event. Of course, I could have incapacitated Damerell, but not without doing him an injury, and I should be sorry to hurt him unnecessarily."

"And now we may go to the Queen's Palace," said Muna. As she spoke, Henrietta slipped a cold hand into hers.

Muna felt a spasm of guilt. It was hardly just to Henrietta that she should be dragged along to the Palace of the Unseen, simply because Muna had a mission. But Muna could not let her heart fail her now, when she was so close to seeing Sakti again.

She pressed Henrietta's hand but did not take her eyes from the *naga*.

"Yes, indeed," said Georgiana. "You will have your way!"

She gave Muna a quizzical look out of her great topaz eyes.

"I hope the Court pleases you, but I must warn you, you are not likely to enjoy it for very long. The Queen believes her doom has come upon her, and nothing makes a fairy more dangerous. I always said she would come to a bad end, given how she started—and now," said Georgiana ominously, "it has begun!"

17

Two days later
The Sorceress Royal's quarters, England

PRUNELLA

PRUNELLA'S LETTERS HAD always given her trouble since her infancy. Even now that she was Sorceress Royal and nominal head of a disgruntled thaumaturgy, her spelling had not improved, and since she knew this, she did not look up when the knock came on the door.

"Come in," said Prunella. She was still engaged in puzzling out the word "deuteroscopy" as the door opened and shut again. A brief silence ensued.

"I beg your pardon for interrupting, Mrs. Wythe," said Clarissa Midsomer finally. "I was told you desired to see me."

"Deuteroscopy" was abandoned. Prunella put down her pen, gazing at Clarissa across the polished expanse of her mahogany desk—the desk at which generations of Sorcerers Royal had sat, including two of Clarissa's forebears.

The Midsomers prided themselves upon that, but then Clarissa had not lacked for reasons to be proud when they had been girls together at Mrs. Daubeney's School for Gentlewitches. Clarissa had been a prize student—a gentlewoman and the scion of an old thaumaturgical family, possessed of such self-mastery that she never betrayed herself by indulging in magic. She had always looked down upon Prunella, for Prunella had then been a penniless charity case, so hopelessly magical that she was always setting the school by the ears with her antics.

What a change time had wrought! Prunella was not respectable even now—no female who practised magic openly could claim to be respectable—but she had a potent defence against any who might look down upon her, in the staff of the Sorcerer Royal. Her marriage with Zacharias Wythe meant she was comfortably established, and she had made magic fashionable—for if thaumaturgy did not love her, high society was delighted to receive a sorceress possessed of such beauty and vivacity. The whiff of scandal that trailed after Prunella only enhanced her glamour in the eyes of the *ton*.

The Midsomers, on the other hand, had suffered a decline in their fortunes since Clarissa's brother Geoffrey had left for Fairy in the wake of his failed bid to gain the staff of the Sorcerer Royal. Though thaumaturgy had been happy enough to throw in its lot with Geoffrey Midsomer when it seemed likely he would succeed, following his failure there was a general feeling that his manoeuvrings had not covered him with glory—that, in fact, he had not conducted himself like a gentleman.

Following his departure, his father continued to be one of the chief critics of Prunella and Zacharias's reforms, but he was rather more civil than he had formerly been. Geoffrey's mother had retreated from society in her distress at losing her son to an indefinite exile to Fairy, and she had neglected her daughter in consequence. Clarissa had had an unpromising first Season, and now, her debut past, it was a matter of some doubt when the Midsomers would be able to relieve themselves of her charge.

As she surveyed Clarissa, Prunella could not help feeling that it might be some time yet before any gentleman sought Miss Midsomer's hand in marriage. It was not that Clarissa was ill-favoured, nor that she committed any striking errors of taste, like wearing pink against that white skin and red hair. But she had an intensity that was liable to make gentlemen nervous.

Mortal gentlemen, that is, thought Prunella. Evidently gentlemen of the Fairy realm had quite different tastes. The Duke of the Navel of the Seas remained Prunella's guest, ostensibly for the purpose of investigating English thaumaturgy's complicity in the theft of the Virtu. But Prunella could not see how he was to find the Fairy Queen's talisman, with all the time he spent paying calls on Clarissa at the Academy.

"Yes. I am obliged to you for coming," said Prunella. "Pray have a seat."

Clarissa sat down unwillingly, looking as though she suspected the chair of wishing to take a bite out of her.

Prunella saw that this would not be a straightforward conversation. Clarissa might feel herself in need of Prunella's patronage now (and the reason for that was one Prunella had yet to puzzle out), but she seemed to like Prunella no better than she had done at school. Prunella had been sufficiently concerned, in fact, that she had taken the unusual step of consulting Zacharias on what she ought to do.

"If you will take my advice, you will say nothing to Miss Midsomer," he had said.

"But surely we have a duty to ensure that she does not go astray," protested Prunella. "We were the cause of the trouble. She would never have met the Duke if it were not for my ball."

But Zacharias would not be moved. "Even parents and guardians are liable to come to grief in these affairs. You can claim no such authority over Miss Midsomer. You are only likely to cause affront, and achieve nothing of what you intend."

Prunella had concluded that duty required her to disregard Zacharias's counsel, but she was conscious now of a lurking wish that she had listened to him after all. It was too late for regrets, however. She plunged on:

"How do you find teaching at the Academy, Miss Midsomer? I hope you find the scholars agreeable?"

"They are well-behaved enough," said Clarissa. Suspicion flickered in her eyes. "Have they complained of my lessons?"

"Oh no," said Prunella. "It was unfortunate Henrietta should have been called away so suddenly—I believe her aunt in Shropshire is *very* ill—but we are obliged to you for stepping in at such short notice." She paused. Perhaps a compliment would put Clarissa at her ease. "I must say, you have made remarkable progress since we were at school together! I never knew you had such magic."

"I *am* a Midsomer," said Clarissa stiffly. But she seemed conscious that her improvement required further explanation, for certainly she had never shown any sign of having unusual magical talent at Mrs. Daubeney's school. She added, "We have an extensive library of spells at home—one of the best in England. After Geoffrey left, I had a great deal of time to devote to study."

It was no good beating around the bush, Prunella decided. Since she would not win Clarissa over by flattery, she might as well resort to candour—a mode that came a great deal more naturally to Prunella.

"You will tell me about your studies in time, I hope, for your abilities are testament to their efficacy," she said pleasantly. "But I wished to speak with you about another matter. It concerns the Duke of the Navel of the Seas."

A violent pink flush tinted Clarissa's cheeks. "The Duke?" She cleared her throat. "What have I to do with the Duke?"

"Nothing, I hope!" said Prunella. "That is what I should counsel, in any event. For it has not escaped my notice that the Duke has been paying particular attentions to you. I do not say you have encouraged him, of course . . ."

With Clarissa Midsomer it had always been a short path from any emotion to anger. She snapped, "You would have no grounds for saying so!"

"But I have observed his attentions with concern," said Prunella, ignoring this. "If you will allow me the liberty, Miss Midsomer, it is clear you do not dislike the Duke. And why should you? There is no doubt he is a gentlemanly creature and desperately handsome—"

"What do you know about it?" Clarissa's face was now red enough to outdo her hair.

"Why, I have eyes to see, haven't I?" said Prunella. Clarissa's manners had not improved since they had known each other at school, she reflected. But Prunella had grown inured to incivility during her years as Sorceress Royal—many of her colleagues still could not endure that a female of obscure birth and native ancestry should presume to the honours she bore. Unruffled, she continued, "I don't fault you in the least. But it behoves us never to forget what the Duke is—not only a fairy, but the representative of a nation contemplating war upon ours."

"Dare you accuse me of forgetting it?" cried Clarissa. "I have more reason than any other to remember what we have to fear from Fairy. You think me a heartless creature, I suppose, who cares nothing for a brother exposed to all the perils of the Fairy Court!"

Prunella had in fact forgotten all about Geoffrey Midsomer.

"I did not mean to suggest you don't care for your brother," she began, but Clarissa had had enough.

"I know why you summoned me, Prunella Wythe," said Clarissa, sitting bolt upright and bristling. "It does not suit the Sorceress Royal that the fairy ambassador should pay attentions to anyone but herself!"

Prunella stared. "What?"

"You have become so accustomed to being flattered by all around you that it aggrieves you to find you are not universally admired! I am sorry for it, but I am afraid it is quite out of my power to assist. I cannot compel the Duke to feign esteem where he feels none. He is at liberty to direct his attentions where he will."

"My dear Clarissa," said Prunella, with genuine astonishment, "you cannot think I want that strange creature to court me! I am far too busy for coquetting—and even if I did desire a romance, I should not choose a fairy that introduced himself by declaring his intention to murder me and everyone I cared for. I spoke out of disinterested solicitude. I am sure your father and mother would not like you to set up a flirtation with a fairy."

"I am not setting up a flirtation," said Clarissa passionately, "and you need not think you can browbeat me with threats to betray me to my parents!"

Prunella had been resolved to be serene and superior, as befitted an employer chastising her underling. Instead she found herself crying out, with all the energy of a schoolgirl scolding another:

"You are most unjust! I was *not* threatening you. Perhaps it will surprise you, but I am not in the least inclined to seek out opportunities to speak with your parents."

Clarissa rose with a flourish.

"I think we have said enough," she said freezingly. "We understand each other, I believe."

"I do not think we understand each other at all!"

"If there is nothing else, I shall take my leave," said Clarissa. "Good day, Mrs. Wythe!"

The door shut behind Clarissa, leaving Prunella gaping after her.

Prunella's first thought was that Zacharias must not know anything of the exchange. Zacharias was never so ill-bred as to say, "I told you so," but he *thought* it very loudly.

She sank back into her chair, frowning.

The oddest thing about the conversation was that Clarissa should have stormed out without tendering her notice. Prunella would have thought that the first thing Clarissa would do upon being provoked was to resign in a huff. She had been much given to flouncing out of the room at school whenever anything did not go her way.

It seemed Clarissa wished to stay at the Academy—indeed, desired it strongly enough not only to submit herself to Prunella as her employer but to tolerate being advised by one she had always despised. But why?

"I *wonder* what she came for!" said the Sorceress Royal.

18

The next day
The Palace of the Unseen, known also as
the Fairy Court, Fairyland

MUNA

"I AM SORRY," SAID the fairy steward, not sounding sorry in the least. "But my instructions were quite clear. Her Majesty is not at home to visitors."

It was the first spirit they had seen since their arrival at the Palace of the Unseen. Georgiana had brought Muna and Henrietta through echoing corridors to the presence chamber, where those desirous of an audience with the Queen of the Djinns were received. They had not seen a soul on the way, and the presence chamber was empty.

The chamber was a large hall, such as might have been found in any mortal nobleman's residence. It was furnished in the height of European luxury, the walls hung with rich tapestries, and it was only upon closer inspection that one noticed its peculiarities. In the tapestry nearest to Muna, a crowned djinn composed of smoke and flame appeared to be presenting a lavish set of robes to an earthenware jug. The mirrors on the walls did not quite reflect reality—in the glass, the blazing wax candles that lit the hall were snuffed out; Henrietta's hair was dark; and Muna's reflection was covered in gleaming scales, instead of her own ordinary brown skin.

When they had waited for a time, Henrietta ventured to ask Georgiana if it was always so quiet. The *naga* shook her head, looking grim.

"Everyone with an ounce of sense is making themselves scarce," she said. "It is the best way of avoiding trouble when the Queen is on one of her rampages. And what with the loss of the Virtu, this is such a rampage as none will have seen since the Queen ascended to the throne!"

The steward who finally appeared seemed far from pleased to have been summoned forth. It looked like a tree that had contracted the notion that it would be amusing to walk the world as a mortal man but had got caught halfway through its transformation, so that it was neither wholly vegetable nor quite human. Nonetheless its countenance was perfectly expressive.

"I should advise you to go away and come again when Her Majesty is in better spirits," it said. "I should think her mood will have improved in around two hundred years or so."

Georgiana Without Ruth bridled.

"This is absurd!" she said. "It is not every day that the Queen is presented with such gifts as these. Her Majesty has not relished the taste of mortal flesh in a great age!"

Muna shivered, drawing closer to Henrietta. She was beginning to doubt whether it had, after all, been such a good idea to insist upon being brought to the Palace of the Queen of the Djinns. Henrietta's face was set and pale, but she touched Muna's arm.

She must be as frightened as Muna. She was certainly nearly as helpless; what magic she had could be little good here, in the beating heart of the Unseen Realm. Yet the light brush of her fingertips against Muna's skin was reassuring.

"A gift may be rare without being suitable," said the steward. "Perhaps you are not aware, ma'am, but fashions have altered in the Fairy Court. It is felt now that the practice of eating one's enemies lacks elegance."

This was encouraging. Muna allowed herself a spark of hope, but:

"What fiddle-faddle!" said Georgiana. "Her Majesty was planning to devour the Virtu at her banquet. Is it any less elegant to devour spirit-stuff encased in flesh than when it is imprisoned in an amulet? Besides, she's the Queen, ain't she? It's for her to set the fashion. If she wishes to eat mortal magicians, I should like to see the sprite that dared to disdain her for it!"

"The point is well made," said a voice behind them. "But which mortal magicians am I to eat?"

At the entrance to the hall stood a tall creature like a woman—a giantess, indeed, for she was taller than Georgiana, and the crown of her head nearly touched the high ceiling. Her face was indistinct and curiously changeable. At one moment it seemed to Muna she had the face of a European woman, forbidding but not unbeautiful—at another, her skin looked darker, her features more familiar—and then when Muna looked again she saw, with a shock, a snake's head with glowing eyes, its tongue darting out to taste the air.

The fairy steward fell on its face, crying, "Sovereign!"

The Queen of the Djinns was accompanied by a bevy of attendants of various shapes and sizes. Some were mere darting lights; others were shaped like beasts or plants, but yet others might have passed for human. Among these last was a girl who caught Muna's attention at once.

Her hair was covered by a neat green cap, her face daubed with red mud and her teeth blackened like a princess's. But Muna would have known Sakti anywhere. Her heart bounded in her chest, but she suppressed her exclamation, for Sakti immediately pulled a ferocious face that said, unmistakably, *Quiet!*

"So you are here, Georgiana," said the Queen of the Djinns. "What brings you to my court?"

As she passed the *naga*, the candles flickered, their flames bowing as before a breeze, and the windows and mirrors turned dark. Her attendants crowded around her as she collapsed upon an enormous ottoman—including Sakti, who had assumed an expression of courteous submission. It did not suit her in the least.

"I was here not a week ago, as you know perfectly well," snapped Georgiana. She paused, her eyes widening.

"Why, of all the absurd hoaxes!" she exclaimed. "Why did you raise such a commotion if you had the Virtu all along?"

She was staring at the Queen's head. It was only now, tearing her gaze from Sakti, that Muna noticed the ornament the Queen wore. A shock of recognition thrilled through her.

Nestled against the Queen's hair was a serpent made of bluish-green stones. It was nearly identical to the pendant Clarissa Midsomer had worn at the Sorceress Royal's ball—save that Clarissa's snake had terminated in a stub tail, whereas the Queen's ornament had two heads, one at each end, with ruby eyes and a red tongue.

Muna had scarcely begun to puzzle out what this could mean when the Queen gestured at her attendants. They scurried out of the room, Sakti going with them. At the door Sakti paused and turned her head, meeting Muna's eyes—and then she was gone, leaving Muna more confused than ever.

Sakti had looked at her with great earnestness. It was a look she had given Muna dozens of times before, when she had done something she should not have done, and desired Muna not to betray her to Mak Genggang. But what did the look signify now?

The Queen spoke only when the doors had shut on her attendants.

"This, do you mean?" she said, raising a languid hand to her hair. "It is only a replica. You of all people ought to be able to tell that!"

Georgiana coughed. "Of course! A remarkable imitation. It would not have deceived me, but I did not expect . . ."

"That I should be wearing a replica? Few in Fairy know that the Virtu is lost," said the Queen. "It would only cause anxiety among my subjects."

Georgiana nodded sagely. "I daresay you don't wish the loss to be gossiped about at your banquet, since representatives from Fairy Without will be present. It would certainly be awkward if *they* discover what a precarious position you are in!"

Muna felt this could have been put with somewhat more tact. The Queen said freezingly:

"The Virtu will not be lost by the time of the banquet. I have sent an elf to Britain to recover it—a person on whom I know I may rely, unlike *some others*."

Georgiana's tail lashed, but to her credit she did not rise to the bait, despite the obvious reflection upon Threlfall.

"That's as may be!" she said, mildly enough. "If your elf does not succeed, however, I should think you would be glad of a sensation to replace the Virtu."

She put out a foreleg, nudging Muna and Henrietta forward. Henrietta looked terrified, but she gave a respectable curtsey. Muna imitated this with rather less grace.

"Your Majesty," said Henrietta.

The Queen stared. "What are these supposed to be?"

"Gifts from Threlfall to its Queen," said Georgiana. "These two are *magiciennes* from England—rare creatures, for most English thaumaturges are male. They are not a patch on the Virtu, of course, but still it will make a remarkable impression if you devour two mortal witches at your banquet. Such a thing has not been done in many years."

The Queen's lip curled. "So this is how you seek to avert my wrath—by a sacrifice?" She swept the girls with a look of disdain. "What crimes have these wretches committed?"

"They are not wretches," said Georgiana indignantly. "Both girls are the finest *magiciennes* England has to offer. They are of unimpeachable birth and possess extraordinary magical powers, and what is more, they are intimate friends of the Sorceress Royal. She will be distressed beyond measure if you eat them."

"That is not true!" cried Henrietta.

"Hush!" said Georgiana. "Do not you know that food must only speak when it is spoken to?"

But Henrietta's interjection had served its purpose. The Queen squinted at her and Muna.

"Now that I look at the creatures," said the Queen, "they do not look so very English. Are not the English paler on the whole?" She pointed at Muna. "You now, you make an odd-looking Englishwoman. How do you account for it?"

"I am not an Englishwoman, Your Majesty," said Muna, curtseying.

Georgiana looked as though she longed to cuff Muna.

"Perhaps this one is not English," she allowed, "but she is a valued guest of the Sorceress Royal. And as for the other—"

"I am a revolutionary!" said Henrietta.

"Eh?" said Georgiana.

"What?" said the Queen of the Djinns.

"I swore I should die before the truth passed my lips, but you have forced it out of me," said Henrietta, speaking very fast so she could get it all out before she was interrupted. "It is true I was born an Englishwoman, but I shall die a spy for the French!"

"Nonsense!" snapped Georgiana. To the Queen she said, "I do not know why the girl is telling such falsehoods, but I have it on good authority that she is beloved by the Sorceress Royal."

"I grew to womanhood under the same roof as Prunella Wythe," admitted Henrietta. "But that only gave me a better understanding of all her defects. I could tell you, oh! such tales of her wickedness!"

This seemed to interest the Queen. She rose slightly on her ottoman, leaning forward. "Is that so? Pray recite them. Accounts of the iniquity of my enemies are always welcome at this Court."

Henrietta was not prepared for this. She shot a look of alarm at Muna. "Oh . . . well . . ."

"There, you see," said Georgiana in triumph. "She does not know any tales of the Sorceress Royal's wickedness."

"Miss Stapleton knows dozens of tales," said Muna, wishing to be helpful, and it did seem to Muna that Henrietta would not have to overexert herself to bear ill report of a friend as high-handed and quarrelsome as the Sorceress Royal. "She is only trying to recollect the worst."

"Yes," said Henrietta. Muna's encouragement appeared to stimulate her powers of recollection. "If you will credit it, Prunella once borrowed my favourite dress and spoilt it beyond repair! I had had it made up from a length of silk my father gave me, which was shockingly dear and Prunella knew it, but that did not detain her for a moment. She wore it to a ball and spilt claret down its front, and it has never been the same again. And it was most unjust, for I am fair and Prunella is dark, so the dress should not have suited her at all—the shade was far too pale.

"But it became her extraordinarily," said Henrietta, in tones of outrage. "She looked perfectly enchanting in it!"

"You turned traitor because your friend spoilt your dress?" said the Queen.

Henrietta flushed. "It must seem a trifle to Your Majesty, but . . ."

"On the contrary," said the Queen, "having the wantonness to risk the possessions of others is certainly the sign of a dishonourable character."

She gave Georgiana a meaningful look. Firing up, the *naga* said to Henrietta:

"I hope you do not expect *me* to believe you parted brass rags with the friend of your infancy for such a trifle. The honourable would not discard years of friendship and loyalty for a single error!" She turned to the Queen.

"Your Majesty, I beg you will not listen to any more of this!" said Georgiana. "What the girl means by telling such tales I don't know, but whether she is a spy or a maggot-pate is not of the least consequence. I wager she will still make delicate eating."

"I cannot concur, Georgiana," said the Queen. "It seems to me the identity of this female is a matter of the first consequence. You tell me you are making me a gift of two English magicians. Very well. But now it appears they are hardly English at all!"

She rose. If the Queen had feet, they were concealed by billowing skirts of black shadow. Where her skirts trailed along the ground, the surface blistered, turning dark.

"I ask myself," said the Queen, her voice growing louder, "why should Georgiana Without Ruth seek to deceive me? What can have prompted this gift? Why should Threlfall—for centuries, faithful friends of the English—be so anxious now to distance itself from England?"

Georgiana drew herself up. "I will not pretend to misunderstand you. You mean to accuse us. I own we have not covered ourselves with glory—my brother Harold ought to have taken better care of the Virtu, since it was in his charge. But though we have failed you, we have not been faithless. Threlfall has never yet betrayed its Queen."

The Queen raised an eyebrow. "You deny conspiring with Britain to steal the Virtu?"

Georgiana snorted, setting her whiskers a-flutter. "Why should we have stolen an amulet we have guarded on your behalf for so many years? This is nothing more than an ill-natured rumour. Indeed, Your Majesty, I would counsel you not to pay too much regard to the gossip in your Court. You keep your courtiers too idle, and in consequence they invent lies to amuse themselves. They will say anything to make a sensation."

"And what of the whispers of the return of the True Queen?" said the Queen. "You will claim those are merely the product of idleness, too, I suppose!"

Georgiana stared. "The True Queen? What has *she* to do with anything?" But even as the *naga* spoke, enlightenment dawned upon her. She said, "So that is the trouble! You fear the Virtu has fallen into Saktimuna's grasp!"

Muna had been determined not to draw any attention to herself. But her head whipped up at the sound of her own name and Sakti's in the *naga*'s mouth. She turned wide eyes on Henrietta, but all of the Englishwoman's attention was on the Queen; she showed no sign of remarking upon the name.

"Do you dare utter that name in my presence?" roared the Queen. The tables and chairs rattled and the tapestries lifted briefly away from the walls, but this did not daunt the *naga*.

"It has been many years since I have seen you quail at it," Georgiana observed. "But if you suspect your sister's powers have been restored to her, it is no wonder you have been acting so strangely."

"I should guard my tongue better if I were in your position, Georgiana," said the Queen in a warning tone, but Georgiana replied, unperturbed:

"A loyal subject may always advise a wise sovereign without fearing to give offence. Do not forget it was Threlfall who supported you in your bid to rule over Fairy Within." She sighed. "We scarcely thought then that our devotion would count for so little!"

"Devotion, indeed!" scoffed the Queen. "If you threw in your lot with me, it is only because you knew I would prevail."

"Of course," said Georgiana. "Why else would the greatest clan outside the Draconic Provinces have bound its fate to the younger daughter, forswearing the heir to the throne? We helped see to it that you were crowned."

"You need not think you can hold that over my head," snapped the Queen. "You have been amply rewarded for your services. If Threlfall was loyal because you profited from loyalty, you will not shrink from perfidy when it serves you!"

This proved too much for Georgiana's patience. Smoke spiralled from her nostrils.

"There is no reasoning with you," she said. "I tell you what it is. You ought never to have used your sister so ill, when she never did anything to provoke you. Usurping her throne, stealing her heart—and casting her out into the mortal realm! Everyone thought it was barbarous, and now you are suffering the consequences."

The Queen's eyes were glowing with a green light. Shadows gathered around her head, which seemed suddenly as distant as a mountain peak seen from the ground, wreathed with thunderclouds and lightning. "How dare you address your sovereign so?"

"If anyone had told you what was what *then*, you should not be so fearful now," said Georgiana. "If you wished to betray your sister, you ought to have done it properly. It was all very well stealing her heart and depriving her of the chief source of her magic, but it was pure silliness locking her heart in the Virtu and leaving the rest of her alive. You ought to have eaten her outright. That would have ensured that you absorbed all her powers, so she could never again give you any trouble. If you had acted with decision, no rumours of the True Queen could worry you now. "

"You are offensive, Georgiana," said the Queen of the Djinns. The floor quaked at her voice, so that Muna and Henrietta were obliged to clutch at each other to stay on their feet. "I have borne your insolence with restraint. But you are in want of a reminder of what is due to the Queen of the Hidden World!"

Whether it was the dragon's scale she had swallowed, or simply being in the Unseen Realm that was the cause, even Muna could smell the magic that set the air around the Queen crackling. It seared through her nostrils, bringing tears to her eyes. She felt Henrietta take her elbow in a firm grip. The Englishwoman's voice spoke into her ear:

"We must go at once, if we can. Will you lend me your magic, Muna?"

"I rather think *you* are due a reminder that Threlfall makes a better friend than an enemy!" thundered Georgiana. A gust of wind stirred the mortals' hair as the *naga* spread her wings above them.

"Yes, but how?" whispered Muna to Henrietta. The Englishwoman started murmuring a formula under her breath.

But she was never to complete it. The Queen snapped her fingers and the doors burst open. A motley crowd of spirits poured into the hall, swarming across the room and up Georgiana's sides with incredible rapidity.

Muna seized Henrietta's wrist. They bolted out of the way, pushing through the mass of spirits intent on the *naga*'s destruction and huddling against the wall. Muna strained her eyes, studying the crowd, but she could not see Sakti among them.

Georgiana reared up, growling, but the Queen's attendants weighed her down, forcing her wings back.

"You do not think these creatures will detain me for more than a moment?" Georgiana said. Her jaw unhinged, and from within the darkness of her maw shone a wavering blue light—the heart of a growing flame.

"Perhaps not," agreed the Queen, "but I shan't need more than a moment."

She snapped her fingers again. There was a rushing in the air, a furious roar from the *naga*—and Georgiana shrank. Muna blinked and saw the *naga* on the ground, reduced to the size of a civet.

"Whoever takes her heart may have a bite of it!" said the Queen.

Her courtiers set upon Georgiana at once, so that the *naga* was lost amid the seething mass of bodies. Her voice could be heard, screeching reproaches, and after a moment she reappeared, breaking through the crowd. She was snapping at the heels of a monstrous black dog with glowing red eyes and a hideous array of yellow fangs.

But Georgiana was now rather smaller than the dog. It evaded her without difficulty and ran up to the Queen, dropping a glowing object at her feet.

"Oh, you blackguard!" cried Georgiana in a high cheeping voice. She lunged at the dog, knocking it off its feet, but the Queen had already scooped up the shining orb.

Georgiana froze, her face a picture of horror. The dog took its chance, pouncing on her. Though Georgiana writhed and hissed, she could not throw it off.

"This is not her heart," said the Queen.

"Surely you don't think I would be so foolish as to keep my heart inside myself!" snarled Georgiana. "You will never find it. It is buried deep—far too deep!"

"Well, there will be time enough to search for it," said the Queen serenely. "Till then, this is enough of your soul-stuff to weaken you—and empower me."

She held the stolen light aloft, gazing at it. The skin on her hands began to blister, but she did not seem to notice it.

"It is potent stuff, Threlfall's magic," said the Queen. "If I had the Virtu still, I should add this to its store. Since I do not . . ." She pinched off a spark from the orb, feeding it to the dog, who ate it with every sign of satisfaction.

"Oh, you jade! Ungrateful hussy!" shrieked Georgiana in an infuriated chirp.

The Queen swallowed the rest of the orb, ignoring her.

Large as the hall was, it seemed to Muna that it was far too close and hot. The ceilings pressed down upon her. Her skin itched.

She had been here before. The memory lay under her hand; she could feel the shape of it, though it would not come clear. In just the same way, she had been betrayed and robbed of her power, her struggles and resentment all for naught . . .

"Muna?" said Henrietta's voice, penetrating her confusion. "Muna!"

"I am well," lied Muna. She reached out blindly, steadying herself against the wall.

The Queen of the Djinns had sunk back onto her ottoman, looking pleased with herself. She raised a hand.

"Take Georgiana of Threlfall away," she said. "And the mortals she brought with her. They are to be detained while I consider the punishment for their offences."

Henrietta and Muna shrank against the wall, but it was impossible to hide. Dozens of pairs of eyes were fixed upon them. Not one pair was friendly, and nowhere among them could Muna see her sister.

"I cannot finish the spell," whispered Henrietta. "Will you help me?"

"I cannot," said Muna. The hall was spinning around her. Her head hurt abominably, and her breath came short. Even if she could formulate an appeal to the fine ones in her state, all the spirits here must have sworn allegiance to the Queen; they were unlikely to help her and Henrietta. Still, guilt wrenched at her. "I am sorry!"

She did not know if Henrietta even heard her. Before the Englishwoman could answer, the spirits fell upon them, hurrying them towards the great doors at the end of the hall. The doors opened directly onto a tunnel—a narrow space shrouded in gloom, whose end could not be seen. A musty underground smell gusted from the opening.

The spirits rushed into the tunnel, jostling their mortal burdens unmercifully.

Muna's arm scraped against a rocky wall; her head was bumped against the ceiling. Cold water dripped on her face, and nightmarish visages surrounded her, hooting and shrieking. She drew in a terrified breath, but before she could scream, she was plunged into darkness.

19

UNA REMEMBERED THIS. It had happened just this way, once before. She had been caught like a fish in the net, while her sister looked on, unmoved . . .

She could not scream, for she could not breathe, but whether it was terror or magic that had taken her breath, she could not tell. Perhaps she was dying. But the thought did not bring relief, for if that was so, she had died before, and that meant one could die again and again; suffering did not need to have an end.

A hand clutched at hers, cold and dry, the skin soft. Muna recollected that there was another with her, no less frightened than herself. Henrietta—that was her name.

"Do not be afraid," Muna tried to say. She wound her fingers through Henrietta's.

The magic spat them out, and they tumbled onto a damp yielding turf.

Muna opened her eyes. There was a pale blue sky above, embroidered with leaves in brilliant shades of yellow, red, orange and burnt umber. She glimpsed Henrietta's pale blond hair out of the corner of her eye.

Trees with brilliant white trunks loomed over them. Thin gold sunshine poured into the glade, but the crystalline light did nothing to counteract the cold.

Muna sat up, rubbing her arms. She felt feeble, but her mind was clear.

"We were captured," she said aloud. The last thing she remembered was being seized and borne off by the Queen's attendants. Then she had been overcome by unconsciousness. They must still be in the Unseen Realm, but . . . "Where have they brought us?"

Henrietta started up with a glad cry. "But I know this place! These are my father's lands in Shropshire."

Muna could not have said why, but she was quite certain they were not in England, nor anywhere in the mortal realm. Perhaps it was the effect of having swallowed Rollo's scale; it had lent her a sense she had not possessed before, a feeling for magic.

Or perhaps it was something else. She thought of the serpent she had seen in her vision in Henrietta's classroom, slumbering beneath the sea.

"But the Queen will not have freed us," said Muna. "It must be an illusion."

Henrietta had arrived at the same conclusion as she looked around. Her face fell.

"Yes. It is only a glamour put on to deceive us. I wonder what they mean by it!" Still she looked about hungrily, as if she could not have enough of seeing, though she knew all she saw to be false. "This grove was my particular refuge when I was a girl. It was here I fled to evade punishment for mischief."

Muna rose to her feet, brushing twigs off her dress. She was still somewhat dazed, but Henrietta's voice was reassuring, an anchor to ordinary things. To keep her talking, Muna said, "Were you a mischievous child? You surprise me!"

Henrietta smiled. "I believe I was as obedient a girl as anyone could hope for—certainly my sisters were less biddable! But my minders were persuaded I could conquer my magical nature if I wished. They thought if I were spanked I should in time learn not to fly in my sleep."

"And did you learn?"

"No," sighed Henrietta. "I tried my best, for my family found my habits distressing, but it was no good. I did not stop floating in my sleep till I joined Mrs. Wythe's Academy. Mr. Wythe said it was because I had been obliged to suppress my magic during the day—it burst out at night when I slept and could not restrain it. But since at the Academy I began to make full use of my powers, there was no longer a surplus to be drained off. It vexed Prunella that I stopped; she had wished to study how I did it."

The reference to the Sorceress Royal seemed to give her thoughts a melancholy turn, for she fell silent. Muna was opening her mouth to ask why she looked so grave when a chill wind blew, making them both shiver.

"Does your father have a house here?" Muna said.

They saw it when they emerged from the grove—an imposing structure of pale gold stone, standing upon a rise in the distance. It was larger than any building Muna had ever seen, surpassing even the English king's house in Malacca. She would not credit it was the Stapleton family's residence until Henrietta had repeated herself.

"But it is even grander than the raja's house in Malacca!" said Muna in awe. She gazed at Henrietta with new respect. Nothing in her comportment suggested she was accustomed to such grandeur, but this explained Mr. and Mrs. Stapleton's high-handed manners.

The thought of her family's good fortune seemed to give Henrietta little pleasure, however. There was a shadow on her face as she gazed at the house. She said abruptly:

"I wish I had not said what I did of Prunella! We don't know what may happen. I hate to think of"—she swallowed—"of dying, with matters as they stand now—with no chance of telling her all."

"But you were only play-acting," said Muna, puzzled. "Mrs. Wythe agreed you should say what you must to persuade Fairy you were subverted by the French. It is not as though you said anything very shocking. Mrs. Wythe ought not to borrow her friends' clothes only to spoil them."

"She could have all my finery and be welcome to it, if only I could see her again!" declared Henrietta, with a sob in her voice. "She is my dearest friend in all the world, and she has no conception of what has troubled me for the past several months—does not know why I mean to marry a man for whom she does not have the least regard! I wish I could have told her. We had no secrets from one another at school."

"I am sure you refine too much upon it," said Muna. She was still distracted by the scale of the Stapletons' mansion. "Is this where you live, then, with your family?"

"In the summers," said Henrietta absently. "Shropshire is a considerable distance from town. We have a town house in London."

Muna gazed at her, round-eyed. "You have *two* such houses? Your father must be vastly wealthy."

"My father is ruined," said Henrietta flatly. "If he does not find a means of discharging his debts, he will be obliged to sell both houses."

Muna stared. Henrietta did not meet Muna's eyes, but the tightness in her shoulders had eased. She seemed relieved to have unburdened herself.

"I have not apologised for my mother's conduct at the Sorceress Royal's ball," she said after a pause. "You will have thought it odd—even offensive."

So much had happened since Muna's encounter with Henrietta's mother that it seemed remote and unimportant. Muna said politely that she recollected nothing in Mrs. Stapleton's behaviour to cause offence. "She seemed most hospitable."

Henrietta shook her head.

"My mother's manners do not always do her credit," she said awkwardly. "She has the best of intentions; it is only that my father's secret weighs upon her. My father has sought to hide the true state of his affairs, but it is impossible to conceal such a matter indefinitely. My mother fears we shall be debarred from the society to which we have always belonged. That is what makes her worry so about setting the fashion and—and all that sort of thing. It is *not* that she is eaten up with ambition, whatever Prunella says!

"And her fears are not groundless," Henrietta added. "Already there is a wounding decline in the attentions she and my father are accustomed to receive. If his creditors should find out, we are finished. Unless . . . unless something is done."

Understanding dawned on Muna. "This is why you intend to marry the thaumaturge of whom Mrs. Wythe disapproves."

Henrietta nodded. "Mr. Hobday is a friend of my father's. He has promised to settle my father's debts after our marriage—and to do it discreetly, so no one need ever know."

Indignation flickered to life in Muna at Henrietta's resigned expression. "But it is very wrong of your father to require you to marry for such a reason."

"Oh, I have not been forced into it. My father is not so gothic!" said Henrietta, trying to smile. "He would not have encouraged the union if he did not esteem Mr. Hobday and think he would make a good husband. If I had opposed the match, or"—Henrietta blushed, lowering her eyes—"or if my affections had been engaged elsewhere, then I am sure my father would not have asked it of me. But I am very willing to be married."

Muna did not know why she should feel so troubled by this pronouncement. Whom Henrietta chose to marry was none of her business—and yet it seemed to Muna there was something seriously amiss in the whole affair.

"You like the gentleman, then?" said Muna.

"I don't dislike him," said Henrietta unpromisingly.

Muna thought of Mak Genggang. The witch had always made it her business to intervene in any matches on the island that she suspected to have been forced upon one of the parties. She was wont to remark that she had liberated far more brides than she had educated witches.

"I don't dislike cabbage," Muna found herself saying, "but I should not consider marrying it. *Not* disliking seems a poor foundation for future happiness."

Henrietta would have been quite within her rights to tell Muna off for presuming to advise her, but the Englishwoman did not seem offended.

"For *my* happiness, perhaps," she said. "But there are my sisters to think of. It is Amelia that gives me the greatest anxiety, for she is to make her debut in society soon, and she is the prettiest of us all, everyone says so. I am afraid for her—she is so headstrong, she is bound to do something reckless if she is obliged to marry a gentleman she does not like. But if I marry Mr. Hobday, there will be no call for that. The girls could wed according to their inclination."

With each word from Henrietta, Muna's vexation increased. She said snappishly, "So you will sacrifice yourself! That is very noble, to be sure."

For all Henrietta's sweetness of temper, even she could be provoked.

"You are speaking as Prunella would!" she said. "I know she will enact theatricals over it—that is why I have not told her. But why should not I decide to marry Mr. Hobday if it serves my purpose? Dozens of girls do the same every day. And it is not as though . . ." She cut herself off, flushing.

Muna raised an eyebrow. "Not as though?"

Henrietta gave her a defiant look. "Well, it is not as though there is anyone I should prefer to marry."

"It is only that you have not met the man to whom it is your fate to be bound," said Muna sagely.

But Henrietta only looked thoughtful and a little removed. "No. Even when, in the past, I have conceived an admiration for a gentleman, I could never imagine being married to him, nor desiring it. Perhaps I was made wrong. As God gave me magic, He decreed that I should desire other things. Mr. Wythe says there are records of spinsters who devoted their lives to the secret study of thaumaturgy. Their connections believed them to be mere old maids, of no account, when in truth they were pioneers—Britain's first *magiciennes*! I believe I should have liked that—to have been married to magic."

Somehow Henrietta's declaration rang hollow; there was some part of the truth that she withheld. As Muna watched the colour deepen in Henrietta's cheek, a thought surfaced in her mind, like a crocodile emerging from a brown river.

Henrietta admires Mr. Wythe! Muna thought, thunderstruck.

It was a new idea, but immediately convincing. It was only natural for Henrietta to harbour a secret passion for Zacharias Wythe. He was not only handsome but a brilliant thaumaturgical scholar, with a command of magic that must be as much of an attraction to Henrietta as his person and manners. Was not Henrietta always quoting his sayings with a respect that bordered on reverence?

Certainly she blushed a great deal—the smallest thing set her off—but did not she colour with particular rapidity when she spoke to, or of, Mr. Wythe?

No wonder Henrietta could name no one whom she would prefer to marry. Her affections were indeed engaged—but their object was one she could not disclose to her father, since Mr. Wythe was so closely associated with the Academy, which Mr. Stapleton abhorred.

Muna was conscious of a sinking at her heart, but there was no reason she should feel either disappointed or surprised. When she was reunited with Sakti, Muna would never see any of these people again. And after all, she ought to be happy for Henrietta. For Muna had seen, in a flash, the solution to Henrietta's difficulties.

It was a delicate matter to interfere in affairs of the heart. Muna was not at all confident of her powers in this area, and yet the idea was so obvious and sensible that it could cause no offence to raise it. The first thing to do was to confirm her suspicion.

"But what if the gentleman you married were a practitioner of magic, who could teach you?" Muna suggested. "You could devote your lives to the study of thaumaturgy together."

Henrietta blinked. "I suppose . . . but few gentlemen would countenance their wives or daughters having anything to do with thaumaturgy. I shall have to give up magic upon my marriage, for I doubt whether I shall be able to conceal my activities from Mr. Hobday."

"There can be no question of your marrying him, then," said Muna, dismissing Mr. Hobday. She was now quite certain of her ground. "There is only one gentleman you can marry—Mr. Wythe!"

Henrietta gaped. "What?"

She looked so scandalised that Muna added:

"I don't suggest that you go behind Mrs. Wythe's back, of course. That would not do at all! But I don't see why she should object, once all is explained to her. Most men of substance take several wives, and I am sure she would rather her husband marry the friend of her youth than a stranger. You would not be obliged to wed Mr. Hobday, which you say she would not like, and since Mr. Wythe is wealthy, you would still be put in the way to help your family."

Muna thought her proposal a neat one, likely to be productive of happiness for all concerned.

But Henrietta did not receive it with the joy she had expected. The Englishwoman opened her mouth and shut it again, like a fish, then did this two more times. It was a matter of some doubt whether she would ever speak again when they were interrupted by the sky splitting open.

It did this with an enormous crash like thunder at the height of a storm. Henrietta jumped, clutching at Muna's arm. Muna returned her grasp, looking up in alarm.

There was a crack right across the sky, through which only darkness could be seen. But as they gazed upwards, the darkness receded, till it was surrounded by white. They were looking into a gigantic dark eye, peering through the fissure in the sky. Its owner drew back, so that they could see the bridge of a nose, and then a second dark eye.

"There you are," said a great rumbling voice, setting the leaves on the trees a-shiver. "Just a moment!"

A massive foot appeared through the crack in the sky, followed by another, and a giantess lowered herself through the gap. At first she was large enough that even as her feet touched the ground, her head was still among the clouds, but she was shrinking all the time as Muna and Henrietta watched her. By the time she turned to them, she was almost exactly of a size with Muna, save that she was a little taller.

Muna had forgotten that Sakti was taller than her.

"Muna, are you quite well?" said Henrietta.

"Yes," said Muna. She dried her eyes, but even so her vision was blurred with tears.

She went towards her sister, unsure of whether she wished to embrace Sakti or slap her. But none of the questions or reproaches that rose to her lips found expression, for Sakti spoke first.

"How came you to be so late, *kak*?" said Sakti. She was in the same outlandish dress in which Muna had seen her earlier, with black teeth and her face painted, but her impatient expression was wholly familiar. "I have been waiting for an age!"

Sakti was not quite so cross as her greeting suggested. While Muna was still sputtering in outrage, Sakti flung her arms around her, exclaiming:

"I had quite given up on ever seeing you again! I thought you must have been eaten by spirits, or perhaps the English had turned on you and thrown you in gaol. I nearly *died* when I saw you in the Queen's presence chamber."

"Why did not you speak to me then?" said Muna. Any vexation was rapidly melting away in the face of Sakti's delight in seeing her. "I thought—oh, I don't know what I thought! I feared you didn't wish to see me."

"I like that! When I put a spell on you just so you would come to me," said Sakti, indignant. "How could I have spoken to you with the Queen of the Djinns watching, pray? I have been doing all I can to avoid her notice! But why did not you stay there? I gave you a look so you would know you should stay where you were and I would come and find you when the Queen was gone."

Muna was almost as diverted as she was annoyed by this faith in her mind-reading abilities. "How was I to know that that was what your look signified?"

"It would have saved a great deal of time if you had paid attention," said Sakti severely. "I must have looked in dozens of trees to find you!"

"Trees?" said Muna, thinking she must have misheard.

"Did not you see them as you came in?" said Sakti. "All this"—she gestured around them at the grove—"is an illusion. We are inside a tree that the Queen cursed and turned to stone. There is a whole jungle of them, entombed in the caves beneath her Palace. They say the spirits of the trees offended her by their loyalty to a great spirit, her deadly rival."

Muna went still. In her mind she heard again the angry voices of Georgiana of Threlfall and the Queen of the Djinns, quarrelling about the ancient history of the Unseen Realm . . . but was it so ancient?

"The rival spirit you speak of," she said. "Was that the True Queen?"

"Why, I should not have thought you would have had time to learn the Court's gossip," said Sakti, impressed. "You had better not let anyone hear you call her the True Queen, however; it is sedition. It is safer to say 'the Great Serpent.'"

But Sakti did not linger on the subject of the True Queen; she was more interested in recounting her efforts to find Muna. "I should think there are hundreds of trees here. Most of the ones I looked in were occupied by languishing mortals, or spirits with the heart cut out of them, capable of little more than spitting and swearing. But there were a few demons that still had magic enough to make trouble, and I barely escaped from them with my hide! The prisoner in the tree next to you nearly bit off my head—it was a sort of monitor lizard that could breathe fire.

"But you know, *kak*, you ought not to have come directly to the Queen's presence chamber. The Queen does not even know *I* exist. There are such a number of spirits here, and all so different, that it is easy to avoid drawing attention to oneself. No one has even suspected me of being a mortal. Why did not you come by a quieter way?"

Muna had forgotten quite how exasperating her sister was. "It is not so easy to open a door from England to Fairy. And it is not as though I had a map!"

"Could not the *polong* help you?"

Muna began to answer, when she remembered they were not alone. When she glanced back she saw that Henrietta remained at a courteous distance, pretending she could not hear their conversation.

Muna and Sakti spoke in Malay, but who knew what powers of understanding the English *magicienne* possessed? It was not out of the question that she might have cast a translation spell . . .

But even as the thought passed through her mind, an image of Henrietta's countenance as she gazed on her father's house rose before Muna.

No, Muna thought with a certainty that surprised her, *Henrietta would not deceive me.*

Henrietta trusted Muna. Perhaps it was time that trust was returned.

Sakti had followed Muna's gaze. She frowned. "Who is that?"

"Henrietta," said Muna, beckoning. As the Englishwoman came shyly towards them, she said to Sakti, in English, "This is

Miss Henrietta Stapleton, an instructress at the Sorceress Royal's school for witches."

"I do not need to be told who this is," said Henrietta, smiling. "It is your sister, of course. The resemblance is remarkable!"

To Sakti she said, "I am afraid we had given you up for lost—we thought it so unlikely that a mortal swallowed up by the wilderness of Fairy should ever return. But it seems we underrated your resource, Miss . . . ?"

Sakti did not supply her name. It was Muna who said, "My sister is called Sakti."

"*Kak!*" protested Sakti.

"She is my friend," said Muna in Malay.

Sakti's look of misgiving did not change. "She is English."

"Even Mak Genggang has English friends!" protested Muna. "I tell you this lady may be relied upon." She turned to Henrietta. "My sister is about to explain what happened when she vanished in the jungle. Aren't you, *adik?*"

Sakti gave Henrietta a discontented look, but then a cheering thought occurred to her. She said in Malay, "After all, we can always abandon her here if she is not to be trusted."

"*Adik!*" said Muna reproachfully, but Sakti continued, in English:

"There is not much to tell. I found the enchanter that cursed us, that is all."

Muna's eyes widened. "You found the author of the curse?"

"The curse?" echoed Henrietta, no less astonished. "Are you under a curse, Muna?"

"Yes, we believe so. I will explain all in time!" said Muna hurriedly. She turned back to Sakti. "*Adik*, do you mean the curse-worker Midsomer was here, in the Unseen Realm?"

"*Midsomer?*" said Henrietta.

"No, not Midsomer," said Sakti, frowning. "What has Midsomer to do with anything?"

But then her expression cleared. "Oh, the spell in Malacca! That was a mistake. The magic must have gone awry. There is a Midsomer here—Geoffrey Midsomer, an English magician who married a spirit and heartily regrets it—but he is not our enemy. The author of the curse is a spirit, one of the Queen's attendant djinns. I don't know his true name, of course—he is far too canny to have let it slip—but he goes by some absurd title. The Earl of the Waters of the Nose, or some such . . ."

Muna stared. "You don't mean the Duke of the Navel of the Seas?"

"That is it! He is the one that cursed us."

"But that can't be," said Muna, baffled. "What makes you think so?"

"Why, he was the one who summoned me here," said Sakti. "That is how I came to the Palace. I arrived and he declared himself my master."

She paused, looking around, before performing a complicated gesture with her hands. A wall of white light sprang up around them, from which issued a faint buzzing, like that of bees.

"In case anyone is listening," explained Sakti. "You see, the—Duke, did you call him? *I* think of him as the thief, for he stole your magic and our memories, and that is not all. He has stolen a treasure belonging to the Queen—they call it the Virtu."

"That can't be!" Muna repeated. But then she thought of the turquoise pendant resting in the pale hollow of Clarissa Midsomer's throat, on the night of the Sorceress Royal's ball—the Duke's eyes, intent and full of wonder, fixed on Clarissa—and the eerily familiar ornament the Fairy Queen had worn, which had looked so much like Clarissa's necklace.

Muna's protests died in her throat. She pressed a hand to her temple, for impossible ideas swarmed in her mind.

All she was beginning to surmise could not be true, she told herself. She was going mad, perhaps. It was something in the air of the Unseen that was giving her such strange fancies. She must be sensible. And yet the suspicion growing within her would not be conquered by staid sense.

"The Queen thinks it is a secret that the Virtu has been stolen, but there are no real secrets in the Palace of the Unseen," said Sakti. "You never met such a parcel of old gossips as the spirits here! They all know the Queen is desperately anxious about the loss of her talisman, but since she means them to be deceived, they are obliged to collude in the pretence. She sees conspirators everywhere, and anyone who dares ruin the illusion would suffer."

"But the Duke was sent to Britain to recover the Virtu," Henrietta began. "*He* cannot have stolen it . . ." But her voice trailed off.

"Yes, it was clever of him, wasn't it?" said Sakti. "He went to the Queen when the news came that the guardians of the Virtu had lost it, and insisted he go to Britain on her behalf. He thought it best to be out of her way. I expect the Queen half-suspects him, but currently she suspects everyone of meaning her ill. There are rumours that her sister—the Great Serpent—will soon return. It seems *she* was the true heir to the throne and rightful sovereign of the Unseen Realms, and the Queen is only a pretender. It has made the Queen exceedingly cross; the Court is in a terrific ferment."

Glancing at Henrietta, Muna saw that the Englishwoman was near being convinced. Muna's own incredulity was dying away, for Sakti spoke with such confidence that it was impossible to doubt her. If she was right, it would certainly have been an astute move on the Duke's part to have accused another and volunteered to investigate the theft.

Muna shook her head in an attempt to clear it. The Duke who had summoned Sakti to his side had stolen the Virtu. The Virtu contained the best part of the banished True Queen's magic—the True Queen who was expected to make a return.

· It all pointed to an answer that Muna feared must be true, incredible as it seemed. But there was still a missing piece. Groping towards understanding, Muna said aloud:

"What makes you think the Duke stole the Virtu, *adik*?"

"Oh, he told me," said Sakti offhandedly.

Muna was mystified. "Surely it was very trusting of him to confide in you!"

"Well, he had lost half of it," explained Sakti. "That was why he summoned me. He desired me to steal the half he had lost.

"The creature is addicted to gambling, you see," she continued. "He owes parts of his soul to all sorts of persons. Everyone in the Palace knows that his affairs are hopelessly involved. I expect that is why he stole the Virtu—so he could extricate himself from his embarrassments. But it did not occur to him to stop gambling once he had the Virtu. He accrued further debts of honour and had nothing else with which to settle them."

"Do you mean to tell me that the Duke *gambled away* the Queen's Virtu?" demanded Muna.

"Yes, wasn't it stupid of him?" said Sakti, with some relish. "I was vastly encouraged when I discovered that! But the creature is not altogether witless. He did not surrender the whole of the Virtu to the winner—he broke it in two and kept half. But of course that meant he only had half the magic he had hoped for."

"So that is what happened," said Muna slowly. "It begins to fit together."

"What does?"

"Why did the Duke desire you to recover the lost half of the

Virtu?" said Muna, ignoring Sakti's question. "I mean to say, he is a powerful spirit. It seems odd that he should have summoned a mortal female to help him."

Sakti frowned.

"That is something I have not quite made out," she admitted. "I think his summoning spell must have gone awry. He used the Virtu to call me up. I believe he was hoping for a great spirit—a *mambang* or *naga* of renown. He seemed quite disappointed to find me so insignificant. He had nearly made up his mind to steal the lost half back from Midsomer himself, but then he was obliged to leave for England . . ."

"Midsomer!" Henrietta exclaimed. "You do not mean Geoffrey Midsomer acquired the other half of the Virtu?"

"Oh, do you know him?" said Sakti, looking at Henrietta with new interest. "He is not much of a magician, but it seems he has extraordinary luck at dice. The Duke is not the first spirit to have suffered at his hands at the gaming table. But no one can touch Midsomer, for his wife is a favourite of the Queen, and very short-tempered." Sakti sighed. "One can only search Midsomer's residence when she is away. I have not been able to find the missing half of the Virtu, though I have hunted high and low."

But she squared her shoulders, turning to Muna with an air of resolve. "But I shall find it, *kak*—never fear! And when I do, I mean to demand our freedom from the Duke. He is so desperate he will not be able to deny us. That is why I summoned you here."

"I am glad you did," said Muna.

She saw all now. It had been no accident that she had been granted that vision of the serpent floating in the waters. She had been led here for a reason.

"But you will not find the Virtu if you look for a hundred years, *adik*," she said. "You see, I know where the other half of the Virtu is."

Henrietta's head whipped around. "You do?"

"You know where it is too," said Muna. "Do you remember the necklace Miss Midsomer wore at the Sorceress Royal's ball?"

Henrietta's brow furrowed. She shook her head.

"There was such a great deal to think of that day," she said apologetically. "I scarcely saw Clarissa before the ball, and I missed most of it after the Duke appeared, for I was seeing to our guests."

"If you had been less preoccupied, you would not have failed to notice it," said Muna; though she addressed Henrietta, her eyes were on Sakti. "Miss Midsomer wore a gold chain. And hanging from it, a very fine pendant, in the shape of a snake . . ."

Sakti's eyes were round. "A blue snake, with red eyes and a short tail? The Duke's half of the Virtu was the same!"

"The replica the Queen wore in her hair reminded me of Miss Midsomer's ornament," said Muna to Henrietta. "And Miss Midsomer is sister to Geoffrey Midsomer, is she not?"

Henrietta saw what she meant.

"You think Geoffrey Midsomer gave Clarissa the half of the Virtu he won?" she said. "I suppose it would have been sensible. He must have known the Duke would seek to reclaim the article if it remained in Fairy. But if Clarissa wore it to the ball, the Duke must have seen it. He met her then, did he not? Prunella told me of it. She said he was fascinated with Clarissa."

"He was entranced!" said Muna, recalling the fixity with which the Duke had gazed at Miss Midsomer. "But what if it was because he had recognised the missing half of the Virtu in Miss Midsomer's pendant? It is no wonder he decided to stay in England. It was his best chance of retrieving what he had lost to her brother."

Henrietta looked troubled. "I cannot believe Clarissa knew what she had. If she did, surely she would have told Prunella and surrendered the Virtu. Even now the Fairy Queen suspects Britain of having robbed her!"

"This sister of Midsomer's is in England?" said Sakti. When Muna nodded, Sakti said, "Then we shall have to go to England to steal it back, I suppose."

"Yes," said Muna. "We must go to England." She took a deep breath, but it scarcely alleviated her nervousness at what she had to tell Sakti. She knew it would sound mad, for Sakti seemed to have no suspicion of the truth herself.

"For the Duke is there too," Muna continued. "And we must recover the whole of the Virtu, *adik*—the half he holds as well."

Sakti looked startled. "You wish to steal his half? So we may use its magic to break the curse, you mean?"

Muna shook her head.

For a moment she felt sick with dread. A part of her had known the truth since she had seen the replica of the Virtu perched upon the Queen's head. Perhaps she had known it even before—when she had asked the fine ones to grant her a vision of her sister, and they had shown her the serpent, half-asleep under the waves surrounding Janda Baik. But till now Muna had not dared to look directly at the truth.

"Because . . ." she said, but the words stuck in her throat. To say what she knew was to lose what was most precious to her in life—to accept that the connection she valued most was an invention of her fancy, founded on a mistake—to admit, finally, that she did not have a sister.

She looked into Sakti's wondering eyes. Muna could see that Sakti was impressed by her daring in declaring that they should steal the Duke's half of the Virtu as well as Clarissa's.

It heartened her absurdly.

It was not a lie, she thought. *I was her sister.*

For months Muna had defended and advised and borne with and worried for Sakti; *that* had been no sham. It did not matter if it was happenstance that had bound them together, rather than blood. Sakti had been hers since Muna found her on the shore.

"Because the Virtu is yours," she said. "*You* are Saktimuna, *adik*. You are the spirit they call the True Queen—the Great Serpent, sister to the Queen of the Djinns."

20

AMELIA

ANYONE MIGHT HAVE thought there was little in her circumstances to worry Miss Amelia Stapleton. At eighteen, she was blessed with beauty, wit and—apparently—fortune in equal measure, due to make a dazzling debut at a coming-out ball for which her fond mamma had spared no expense.

But Amelia was in fact burdened with anxieties large and small. She was ruminating on these one morning, a week after the Sorceress Royal's ball, when her sister Louisa burst into the room.

Louisa wore the air of importance of one who bears great news. Amelia half-rose from her chair, exclaiming, "Do not tell me—Henny is back!"

"No," said Louisa tragically. "Mr. Hobday is here!"

Amelia stared. "Here?"

"He is waiting in the drawing room with Papa," said Louisa.

"Porter told me. Papa sent her to bring Henny down to see Mr. Hobday."

They were gazing at each other in horror when the door burst open again, admitting this time the youngest Stapleton sister.

"'Melia, have you heard?" cried Charlotte. "Mr. Hobday is here and wishes to see Henny! What are we to do?"

It had been six days since any of them had seen their eldest sister, Henrietta. They had all grown accustomed to Henny's sudden absences—she had been given to them ever since Mrs. Prunella Wythe had founded her plaguey Academy—but she had never been away for so long before.

Louisa had even begun muttering about going to the Academy to try to find her, though they were all terrified of the Sorceress Royal. Everyone said Mrs. Wythe was an unwomanly creature, ruthless with those who got in her way. It was an article of faith among the Stapletons' set that Mrs. Wythe had exiled Geoffrey Midsomer to Fairyland, and caused the death of Matthew Bloxham:

"For Bloxham would never have retreated to the country and contracted consumption if Mrs. Wythe had not made it impossible for him to remain in London," said Mr. Stapleton's friends. "It is a scandal how she used him. It is not as though he had even *succeeded* in assassinating her!"

It was surprising that gentle Henrietta should be on intimate terms with such a female, but then there were a great many surprising things about Henrietta's conduct of late. None of her sisters had conceived that she would dare defy their parents as she was now doing, for she had always been the most tractable of them all. It was only in the matter of magic that she had ever given their father and mother a moment's concern, and even there Henrietta had not misbehaved deliberately—she simply could not smother

her magic, any more than she could stop her hair from being yellow, or prevent her fingernails from growing.

Yet for two years Henrietta had been doing what she must know their father and mother would frown upon. She was not practised at misconduct and she had never had any particular gift for deception. It had required the joint exertions of Amelia, Louisa and Charlotte to conceal the fact that Henrietta was practising thaumaturgy from their parents, though the sisters had never dared to betray to Henrietta that they knew her secret.

They had sought to preserve the secret from the servants, too, but in this they had not been altogether successful. Fortunately the labouring classes took a more kindly view of women's magic, for it was not uncommon for maidservants to rely upon enchantery to ease their labours. The servants thought it eccentric in Henrietta, as a gently born female, to wish to cast spells, but so far none had betrayed the fact to Mr. and Mrs. Stapleton; indeed, they did what they could to help the girls. But with the best will in the world, the maid Porter would not find Henrietta now.

With that thought Amelia came to a decision.

"We shall have to let out Not Henrietta," she said grimly.

Her sisters' faces fell.

"Oh, not that!" said Louisa. "Cannot we go to Mrs. Wythe and explain she must let Henrietta come back to us?"

Amelia shook her head. "Perhaps we ought to have done that sooner, but we haven't the time for it now. Papa will begin to wonder."

They had had to persuade their father and mother that Henrietta was unwell whenever she was called upon to make an appearance in the past few days, and they had been hard put to it to prevent Mrs. Stapleton from summoning an apothecary. Amelia did not like Not Henrietta any more than Louisa and Charlotte, but this was a time for desperate measures.

Before her resolve could falter, she went to her wardrobe and flung open the door. At the bottom of the wardrobe lay a long cylindrical object, wrapped in linen.

"Come," said Amelia, "we must get her out."

Louisa and Charlotte helped her lift the object and heave it out of the wardrobe onto the floor.

Steeling herself, Amelia bent and undid the cloth, grimacing when her fingers brushed against the yielding substance beneath. It was almost like flesh, but not quite; it always made Amelia shudder to touch it.

When she was done, a young woman lay on the floor, her blond curls fanning out around her head. Her eyes were shut, faint blue veins tracing the pale lids.

"Good morning, Henny!" said Charlotte loudly, making the others jump. "Wake up!"

The eyes snapped open.

"Good morning," said Not Henrietta. She sat up, smiling, just as though the three had not set upon her and bundled her into the wardrobe when, a few days ago, they had agreed that they could no longer endure her society.

Perhaps it was only to be expected that Not Henrietta would not remember. Amelia did not think she had a mind, or any thoughts or memories of her own. It was this that made it so awful to look into her eyes.

"Nobody could believe that is Henny," whispered Louisa.

"*You* did, once," replied Amelia.

At first they had all been deceived by the creature that took Henrietta's place at home when the original was occupied elsewhere. Not Henrietta was a tolerable simulacrum when the enchantment worked—she could pass as Henrietta for half an hour or so—and in earlier days Henrietta had not depended upon her as much as she later came to. The sisters had only discovered the deception when, one day, Not Henrietta had horrified them by losing an ear without seeming to notice it. Louisa had been persuaded that Henrietta must have been stolen away by fairies and replaced by a changeling. In her alarm she had been on the verge of giving the game away when Henrietta herself had returned and the simulacrum was banished.

But Not Henrietta was never gone for long. As the Academy took up more of Henrietta's time and her absences grew more extended, the sisters had seen more of the simulacrum. Yet they had never grown used to Not Henrietta. It was eerie to look at a countenance so familiar and beloved, and see behind it not even a stranger's mind, but a brute intention, bloodless and boneless.

"I should not think Mr. Hobday will notice any difference," said Charlotte.

None of them had a high regard for Mr. Hobday. He was proof, if proof were needed, of Henrietta's sense of duty. All three girls had burst into tears when Henrietta told them she meant to marry him. She had said it in such a noble manner: "Just like a martyr submitting herself to the lions," sobbed Charlotte.

Their distress was the chief reason news of the engagement had yet to be published abroad, for Henrietta had begged Mr. and Mrs. Stapleton to give Mr. Hobday more time to ingratiate himself with her sisters before any announcement was made.

Mr. Hobday had tried, but unfortunately his manners were not such as to overcome the girls' prejudice against him. He could not help betraying his consciousness that they—indeed, the entire family—were dependent upon his goodwill and fortune. He patronised Louisa and Charlotte, and made gallantries to Amelia that bordered upon the offensive. If Amelia was ever inclined to become impatient with Henrietta and her inconvenient secret, the recollection that Henrietta intended to marry Mr. Hobday for their sake always brought forbearance with it.

Amelia leant over the simulacrum. "Mr. Hobday is here and wishes to see you. Will you see him?"

Not Henrietta looked up with that horrible empty smile. Amelia had never realised what a strong mind Henrietta possessed under her appearance of pliancy, till she had encountered her sister's simulacrum. Not Henrietta was wholly yielding; she gave way wherever one touched her. The real Henrietta might be gentle, but her mildness was only a type of armour that disguised an indomitable will of her own.

"By all means," said Not Henrietta agreeably.

"I T is a bad business, what has happened with the Midsomer girl," said Mr. Hobday, shaking his head. "To think the rot could have spread so far! I should never have expected it of a family like the Midsomers."

Mr. Stapleton's powers of concentration were not what they had previously been. To lose all that was once the basis of one's self-estimation is a grave bereavement, and grief makes men forgetful. It took him a moment to emerge from his distraction.

"Miss Clarissa Midsomer, you mean?" he said, after a pause. "What has happened to her?"

"Have not you heard?" said Mr. Hobday, surprised. "It has been the talk of the Society. Miss Midsomer has joined the Sorceress Royal's school for witches."

Mr. Stapleton had been so preoccupied with his own affairs that he had paid little attention to the gossip in thaumaturgical circles. He was deeply shocked. "Does *Miss Midsomer* mean to study thaumaturgy?"

"No. She means to teach it!" said Mr. Hobday. "And the fact that Mrs. Wythe has accepted her suggests that she, at least, believes Miss Midsomer capable of it. The girl must have been studying magic in secret for years. One shudders to think how her family must feel! It requires a peculiarly depraved character to perpetrate such a long-running deception."

"I had no notion," said Mr. Stapleton; indeed, he could scarcely believe it. Clarissa Midsomer and Henrietta had been girls together at school, and unlike Henrietta, Clarissa had always kept a decorous distance from the Sorceress Royal. A memory of the infant Clarissa rose before him—a little redheaded, roly-poly creature, cowering behind her nurse when she was summoned to the drawing room to greet her father's friends. "The Midsomers did not suspect it?"

"No. You can conceive of their dismay. Midsomer will not say a word to anyone. Of course, no one has seen much of Mrs. Midsomer since the son was sent away, and this latest scandal is not likely to bring her out of her shell. If Miss Midsomer had cared for nothing else, she should have thought of her mother. Shocking!" Mr. Hobday shook his head.

"If it were my daughter, she would not be received at home again," he continued. "But Midsomer will not be drawn on whether he means to countenance her. I hope he does not. Thaumaturgy looks to him as the representative of one of our oldest families. He should not be seen to lend his sanction to such misconduct."

It was not as though Mr. Stapleton approved of the Academy, or its founders—Zacharias Wythe, brilliant but misguided, and the wild young Sorceress Royal. The displeasure of his last encounter with Mrs. Wythe was still fresh. Warmth rose in his cheeks at the recollection.

Yet though he understood Mr. Hobday's sentiments, he could not quite agree. Mr. Hobday had no daughters.

"Certainly one would not wish to lend one's countenance to such behaviour," said Mr. Stapleton. "But Miss Midsomer is very young, at an age when excitement and admiration mean a great deal. No doubt Mrs. Wythe seduced the girl with promises of a thrilling career."

"Or perhaps it was Mr. Wythe who carried out the seduction," said Mr. Hobday, leering.

Mr. Stapleton bridled. It was one thing to suggest that a high-spirited girl might be taken in by a dashing female, who was feted by the *beau monde* and possessed considerable personal charm—quite another to insinuate that she had been swept away by a married man. Fortunately he was not obliged to pick a quarrel with Mr. Hobday, for there was a knock at the door, and Henrietta appeared.

"Ah, Henny," cried Mr. Stapleton in relief.

It struck him at once that something was amiss. Something had often been amiss with Henrietta of late, though Mr. Stapleton could not put his finger on what it was. He watched Henrietta with more than usual anxiety, which was not soothed even though she greeted Mr. Hobday with all her usual quiet civility.

He was not so deluded as to think Henrietta bore any extraordinary affection for Mr. Hobday. It was not a love match, but Henrietta had been brought up properly. She would never have expected that her own inclinations would determine her choice of a husband; she knew she must marry to oblige her family.

But her inclinations were nevertheless a matter of some importance. Mr. Stapleton did not intend that his daughter should fall prey to the misery and vice that were often consequent upon an ill-suited union. He had hoped that Henrietta liked Mr. Hobday enough for marriage, and it concerned him that all the signs he could read suggested the reverse. She was always courteous to Mr.

Hobday, but there was a worrying detachment in her manner—an inner withdrawal of self, which he could only hope was attributable to maidenly reserve and spoke of no deeper antipathy.

Today there was no hint of that inner withdrawal. Somehow that was even more worrying.

"Your father and I were speaking of this sad business concerning Miss Clarissa Midsomer," said Mr. Hobday. "I daresay you knew her well at school?"

Mr. Stapleton might feel sorry for Clarissa Midsomer, but he had no wish for Henrietta to be associated with the erring girl in her affianced's eyes.

"They were never on intimate terms," he said quickly. "Is not that so, Henny? Your letters from school scarcely ever made reference to Miss Midsomer."

"Yes, indeed," said Henrietta. Though the import of her words was somewhat unclear, her tone certainly resounded with agreement.

"Oh yes," said Mr. Hobday. "As I recall, it was Mrs. Prunella Wythe who was your dearest friend at school!"

"Yes, indeed," said Henrietta with just the same enthusiasm.

"They were thrown much together as children," said Mr. Stapleton. "At an age when Henny lacked the powers of discrimination she possesses now . . . and of course she compassionated Mrs. Wythe, as an orphan living on the headmistress's charity. Henny had no means of knowing what Mrs. Wythe would become."

"No, indeed," agreed Henrietta.

Mr. Stapleton looked at her in irritation. This failure in tact was most unlike Henrietta; he would have expected her to have steered the conversation to safer waters by now. She returned his look with no apparent consciousness of having done ill; her expression was mild and attentive, betraying nothing.

"Was there anything of interest in the latest *Gazette?*" he said to Mr. Hobday. "I confess I have yet to glance at it."

But the wickedness of magical females was something of an obsession of Mr. Hobday's, and he would not be put off by so feeble a diversion.

"You must have noticed some defect in Mrs. Wythe and Miss Midsomer's characters even then," he said to Henrietta. "They could not have brought themselves to practise magic so openly if there had not been some canker at the root, which must have been discernible even in infancy."

"Yes, indeed," said Henrietta.

This rang a particularly false note, and Mr. Stapleton glanced at her, disturbed. Henrietta was a good girl, but if she had a fault it was an overly tender heart—a reluctance to sever bonds that should rightly be consigned to the past. She had learnt not to defend Prunella Wythe to Mr. Stapleton and his friends, but she would never usually consent to condemning her.

As always whenever he thought of his daughter's friendship with the Sorceress Royal, Mr. Stapleton reproached himself for not forbidding the connection. But with Henrietta it was difficult to forbid anything but that which was truly out of bounds. She was not like the other girls, who were perfectly happy to storm and scold. Henrietta only submitted and looked sad, so that it was impossible to tyrannise over her, unless one had a heart of stone.

"Are you quite well, Henny?" said Mr. Stapleton.

Henrietta bounced up, startling him.

"No!" she said, in a faint die-away voice that sat oddly with the vigour with which she had moved. "I feel most peculiar! If you will forgive me, sir"—this to Mr. Hobday—"I shall take my leave. I have a headache."

Mr. Hobday was all solicitude, but he had hardly begun to wish her a swift recovery when Henrietta clattered out of the room. He stared after her, disconcerted.

Mr. Stapleton cleared his throat.

"Miss Stapleton has not been herself," he said. He could not of course state his true suspicion, which was that Henrietta's odd behaviour likely arose from trepidation about her engagement. He reached for another excuse.

"Our circumstances weigh upon her," he said.

He was shaken by a pang of guilt, for there was truth in what he said, though it was not the whole truth. He had striven to hold his creditors at bay, to protect his family from the worries that besieged him. But it was he who had put them in this impossible position—his failures that exposed them to the wearing necessity of maintaining a facade, when they knew the family was on the brink of ruin.

The explanation served its purpose. Mr. Hobday's countenance cleared.

"That is natural," he said. "But that will all be dealt with soon enough!" He patted Mr. Stapleton on the back with a comforting hand.

It was impossible to forget what he owed Hobday, reflected Mr. Stapleton, and yet he had never before been so glad to see his friend leave. It struck him for the first time that Mr. Hobday as a friend, an equal, was a very different person from Mr. Hobday the benefactor and prospective son-in-law. Mr. Stapleton was not altogether sure that Mr. Hobday was improved by the change.

THERE was no response when Mr. Stapleton first knocked on the door to Henrietta's bedchamber, or when he tried again, though her sisters had confirmed she had retired to her bed. When a third attempt was no more successful, he pushed the door ajar.

"Henrietta?"

There was no answer. Henrietta lay on the bed, staring at the ceiling. She was under the sheets, but as far as he could tell, she was fully dressed.

"Are you well, Henny?" said Mr. Stapleton, beginning to be alarmed. "I could summon your mother . . ."

"Oh no!" said Henrietta brightly, without stirring. "I have a headache, but it will pass with rest."

She did not rise, or even turn to him. Clearly she wished to be alone but was unwilling to say so. She had never behaved in this fashion before, but perhaps he no longer knew his daughter. She was no longer a girl, but grown to woman's estate, old enough to be married—and rescue the family's fortunes.

Mr. Stapleton paused at the door, hesitating. He could not quite bring himself to go.

"Hen," he said abruptly, "are you quite certain you wish to be married?"

"Yes, by all means!" chirped the sunny voice from the bed.

Even now she did not look at him. Feeling like a man groping in the dark, Mr. Stapleton made a final attempt.

"I do not forget that your happiness is in my care," he said. "To betray that trust is the last thing I would wish to do. You know what the connection would mean for us, but if you dislike the idea . . . if you do not feel you can esteem Mr. Hobday enough to marry him . . ."

"I have the highest regard for Mr. Hobday," said Henrietta in the same unvarying cheerful tone.

"Then you do not mind it?"

"No, indeed."

"Good," said Mr. Stapleton.

Curiously, he felt disappointed, though he had dreaded any

other answer. He thought of the bills mounting on his desk, the creditors who rang the door at all hours. Just last week Mrs. Stapleton had gathered up the jewels he had given her, meaning to pawn them, before he had stopped her:

"We are not in such straits yet!" he had said grandly.

He had looked fine to Mrs. Stapleton and himself, but it had all been a lot of foolishness. They were well past the point at which they ought to have sold her jewels. Now, indeed, the sacrifice would scarcely alter their position. What they needed was a fortune—Mr. Hobday's fortune.

"Very good," said Mr. Stapleton.

21

CLARISSA

LARISSA HAD HAD a number of reasons for coming to the Sorceress Royal's Academy, but not least of these had been the desire to have time to herself.

Time and solitude were scarce commodities for the daughter of such a household as the Midsomers' had become. When Geoffrey had still been in England he had absorbed, as by right, the largest part of the family's energies and attention. His prospects—thaumaturgical and matrimonial—had been their chief preoccupation.

It had been just like Geoffrey to render all this loving deliberation superfluous by deciding his future in both regards without troubling to consult his family. After he had gone to live in Fairy with his wife, it was expected of Clarissa that she should devote herself wholly to her mother, for whom Geoffrey's departure was a grievous blow.

Clarissa shuddered at the memory of those long, dreary days—labouring at some futile piece of embroidery while her mother reminisced about Geoffrey, breaking off only to inveigh against the Sorceress Royal for her part in exiling him to Fairyland. Here, at least, Clarissa had been able to play her part with spirit, but even finding fault with Prunella Wythe lost its savour in time. However unscrupulous and immodest Mrs. Wythe was, she was certainly having a better time than the correct Miss Midsomer.

Now that Clarissa had thrown off correctness, swallowed her dignity and begged Mrs. Wythe for a place at the Academy, she was less bored. But it had been impossible for Clarissa to pursue her investigations as she desired, for it turned out that being a *magicienne* involved an extraordinary amount of work. Clarissa's days were wholly taken up with lessons—preparing for, teaching and recovering from them—as well as tending to the scholars, who were even more tiresome than Clarissa's own schoolfellows had been.

She had been at the Academy for almost a fortnight before she was able to attempt what she had come there to do. Zacharias Wythe had taken the scholars out for a lesson in cloud-riding. Henrietta Stapleton was still absent on her mission of mercy to an aunt in whom Clarissa only half-believed, and the Academy was otherwise empty for once. Clarissa did not fear being disturbed for the rest of the day, for Prunella Wythe came to the Academy only infrequently, giving out that she was occupied with the business of her office.

Ludicrous! thought Clarissa as she strode through the silent corridors of the Academy. It still filled her with wonder, and no small measure of indignation, that a penniless chit like Prunella Gentleman should now hold the staff of the Sorcerer Royal—the jewel of English thaumaturgy, coveted by the kingdom's finest magicians.

The change in Prunella's circumstances had evidently given her inflated notions of her own consequence. To think that *she* should dare to lecture Clarissa, as though Clarissa would be

overcome by the attentions of such a creature as the Duke of the
Navel of the Seas! She was no green girl, to be taken in by the
fairy's attentions. She knew a flirtation with her could only be a
passing amusement for such a being.

Still, her cheeks warmed with pride at the thought of him. It
was something to be courted by so handsome and charming a per-
sonage. It had certainly made Prunella wild with jealousy. It was a
pity neither the Duke's rejection nor Clarissa's rebuff was likely to
teach the Sorceress Royal her place.

That was the nature of the world in these forsaken times. People pushed into places where they did not belong, taking what they
had no right to, while those whose birth entitled them to those
honours were cast aside.

But Clarissa forgot these vexing reflections as she approached
the gallery. It had caused a great deal of talk when the Sorceress
Royal had moved the Society's collection of speaking portraits.
There was no illegality of which the Fellows of the Society could
complain—the Presiding Committee had agreed to the removal,
because the paintings were causing too great a disturbance in the
Society—but everyone knew there would have been no disturbance, and no need for the move, if not for Prunella Wythe. It
was she to whom the paintings had raised such clamorous
objection.

Zacharias Wythe had offered to house the collection—so he
could study the magic that animated the portraits, *he* said—and it
had ended up in the Academy, to the outrage of Clarissa's father.

But perhaps it was for the best, thought Clarissa. The collection
had formerly been housed in a part of the Society to which women
were not admitted, save for the Sorceress Royal. If the paintings
had not come to the Academy, Clarissa might never have had the
chance to see them herself.

She looked up at the painting for which she had abased herself to Prunella Wythe.

There had been two Sorcerers Royal named Midsomer, but in truth, only one had been of any importance—the gentleman whose portrait she now studied. (In former days, Sorcerers Royal had not been remarkable for their longevity, and the other Midsomer who had occupied the office had held the staff for only a matter of days before he was struck down by a rival's curse.)

"Mr. George Midsomer," she said aloud.

She had intended to draw his attention, but even so she jumped when the painted man stirred, fixing his gaze upon her.

George Midsomer looked remarkably like Clarissa's brother. Geoffrey had often vexed Clarissa, in his absence as much as his presence. Yet she found the resemblance comforting, though the look George Midsomer swept over her was scarcely friendly.

"I do not believe we have been introduced," he said coldly.

"Do you need to be?" cackled the neighbouring portrait. "Look at the two of you! Like peas in a pod, you are!"

His voice woke the other paintings. Murmurs and rustlings filled the room as the painted thaumaturges began to stir, but Clarissa Midsomer did not mean to address a crowd, and it was of particular importance that her consultation with her ancestor should not be overheard. She snapped her fingers, and the other paintings fell silent, frozen within their frames.

"Did my colleague speak aright?" said George Midsomer, looking at Clarissa with new intensity. "You are a descendant of my line?"

"Clarissa Midsomer, sir," said Clarissa, curtseying. "You may be acquainted with my father, Mr. Julian Midsomer. He is a Fellow of the Royal Society of Unnatural Philosophers."

Her ancestor's countenance showed no flicker of recognition, nor any increase in warmth.

"If you are a daughter of my line, how comes it that you are performing magic?" said George Midsomer. "Does this father of yours know you are here?"

Clarissa threw her head back. She would not be intimidated. He would understand once all was explained. "Sir, he does. And he . . ." It would be going too far to say Clarissa's father had approved of her scheme; he had opposed it passionately, only conceding when Clarissa's mother had dissolved into tears.

"He does not object," said Clarissa. "He knows my intentions in coming here."

She reached into her pocket. She had kept the article hidden on her person since the Sorceress Royal's ball, for she had received a thorough scolding from her parents for wearing it openly that night.

The recollection brought a rush of heat to her face. It had been reckless of her, but in truth Clarissa had been anxious about the ball. She had been determined that she would not be cast into the shade by little Prunella Wythe, and she had given in to the temptation to show away.

Since then she had exercised strict discretion, however. As she drew out the article now, the rubies that served as the serpent's eyes caught the light, and the bluish-green stones ornamenting its coils shone richly, striking her again with their extraordinary beauty.

"My brother gave this to me," she said, holding it up to the painting of George Midsomer. "He had it from a fairy."

Geoffrey had not of course told Clarissa anything useful about the article. He had said only that it was a talisman he had won from a fairy in a bet:

"He kicked up no end of a fuss, so it must be an object of considerable power," Geoffrey had said. "It was only when I said Laura would be dismayed to hear that the Queen's courtiers no longer honoured their debts of honour that he relented." Geoffrey made no pretence of controlling his wife; from his account, everyone in the Court lived in fear of her, including Geoffrey himself.

"But I don't trust the fellow so far as I can throw him," he continued. "If I keep it here, he is bound to take it back by some means. Will you keep it for me? If you offer it to the Sorceress Royal, I should think she will agree to arrange for me to come back to England."

Not for the first time, Clarissa had been struck by Geoffrey's wastefulness. He had a wife and familiar esteemed by the Fairy Court; all the wonders and terrors of Fairyland lay open to him. Yet all he did in his brief clandestine visits to his family—arranged by his wife at his insistence—was to bleat of his homesickness, and complain about the privations of his life in the Fairy Court—a Court dozens of thaumaturges had died longing to see! If Clarissa had had his opportunities . . .

But with the ease of long practice, she pushed the thought away, consigning it to darkness. Repining against one's fate as a female might do for a Prunella Wythe, who had no family, or a Henrietta Stapleton, who had no dignity. It suited Clarissa Midsomer ill.

She did not mean to do as Geoffrey had suggested, however. Surrender a powerful talisman to Prunella Wythe! Why, Prunella was no more to be trusted than any fairy. Clarissa had persuaded her parents that Geoffrey's proposal would not do. Instead, she would seek guidance from a more reliable source—her ancestor.

"The Sorceress Royal caused my brother to be banished to Fairyland," she explained. "He desired me to use this to free him from his bondage, and it is for his sake that I came here."

But George Midsomer hardly glanced at the article.

"If your father believed that cock-and-bull tale, he is a fool!" he sneered. "I saw you enspelling the others to silence. To think that my descendant should be casting cantrips like a village witch!"

"It was only so that we might speak undisturbed," protested Clarissa. "I meant no disrespect."

But her ancestor was unmoved.

"If you think I will lend any aid to your misbegotten enterprise, you are mistaken," said George Midsomer. "Go home and make over the talisman to one worthy of it!"

"But Geoffrey gave it to me," said Clarissa desperately. "We agreed I should keep it, to avoid suspicion falling on my father. No one would suspect *me* of possessing a talisman smuggled from the Fairy Court."

"I don't wish to hear your excuses. Tell your father to return with this talisman. I will speak with *him*."

Clarissa saw her chance slipping through her fingers.

"But he can't!" she said. "My father opposed the establishment of the Academy and he could never lower himself so far as to ask the Sorceress Royal to allow him to see you. Pray hear me out, sir! We are persuaded the article contains a great magic, if only we can contrive to unlock it . . ."

"You are mistaken there," said a new voice—a voice that did not belong to any dead thaumaturge. A voice Clarissa knew. She turned, her heart in her throat.

The person who emerged from the shadowy corner of the gallery was tall and elegant, robed in green velvet. His silvery hair shone as he stepped into the light.

"I am afraid your unmannerly ancestor will be no good to you, Miss Midsomer," said the Duke of the Navel of the Seas. "The properties of your talisman are a carefully guarded secret. No English thaumaturge could tell you how to draw upon its powers."

"Your—Your Excellency!" stammered Clarissa.

"I suppose your brother did not tell you what that object is called," said the Duke.

He had a knowing smile on his face—a smile that was kind, even flirtatious. Yet it sent a chill like ice water trickling down Clarissa's back. Realisation dawned upon her, locking her joints in place with horror.

"I . . ." She cleared her throat. "I did not know."

"No, of course not," said the Duke. "It would not have served my purpose if your brother had known that the article I was obliged to surrender to him was the Queen's Virtu."

"*You* stole the Fairy Queen's amulet," said Clarissa, clasping her cold hands. The stones of the Virtu scraped against her palm.

"Only because I desired it," said the Duke. He was no longer smiling. His eyes were searching, but somehow their expression reassured her, as the smile had not. "But I have a confession to make, Miss Midsomer. I did not surrender *all* of the Virtu to your brother."

He held out his hand. On his palm was a ruby-eyed snake, crafted out of stones the colour of green hills seen through a blue haze. At one end flicked a curling red tongue; at the other, the coiling body came to an abrupt terminus—for, Clarissa saw now, it was not meant to exist alone, cut off at the tail.

She opened her hand, bringing her talisman to meet the Duke's. Where the two halves fit together, no join could be seen.

"I believe we can help each other," said the Duke.

22

Beneath the Palace of the Unseen, Fairyland

MUNA

"THE MAGIC HERE must be making me ill," said Sakti. She shook her head violently. "For a moment I thought you said *I* was the Queen's sister!"

"I did," said Muna. It was a relief that the words were out, though Sakti and Henrietta both looked at her as though she had lost her wits. She did not blame them. *They* had not heard the serpent's drowsy thoughts. They did not know all Muna knew. "You are."

Muna could not remember when she had last seen Sakti anxious on her behalf. The expression sat awkwardly on Sakti's face. She touched Muna's arm.

"Do you feel quite well, *kak*?" she said. "Some mortals don't take well to the Unseen Realm. One hears of human magicians who run mad, or pine away . . ."

"Listen, *adik*. When I was in England, I had a vision—two visions," Muna corrected herself. "The Sorceress Royal hosted a celebration a few days after I arrived, and while I was waiting to be taken there, I thought I saw you in the halls of the Academy."

"So your malady began then!" said Sakti. She put a hand on Muna's forehead. "Do you feel feverish? What else did you see, or hear? Pak Husin heard voices when his brother-in-law cursed him."

"There are no voices; I am not ill." Muna removed Sakti's hand from her forehead, determined to finish her tale. "It was not you I saw. It was Miss Midsomer—I had mistaken her for you, though you look nothing alike. At the time I dismissed my error, but my vision was truer than I knew. I saw you in Clarissa Midsomer, because she wore the Virtu. My second vision came when Miss Stapleton taught us a spell for divining the present—"

"Surely divining the future would be more useful."

It seemed to Muna that Sakti was being obtuse. "I wished to know where you were," she said. "Miss Stapleton was so good as to adapt a divination spell for the purpose. I asked the fine ones to show me a vision of you, but they took me into the past, and I saw—Saktimuna!"

She lingered over the syllables, looking expectantly at Sakti, but there was no change in her sister's expression.

"What," said Sakti, "is Saktimuna?"

"Oh," said Muna, deflated—but there was no reason Sakti should know the name, or remember that it was hers. Sakti remembered nothing else, after all. "It is the true name of the True—of the Great Serpent."

"Yes," said Henrietta. "Georgiana Without Ruth referred to the Fairy Queen's sister by that name. It put the Queen in a horrid passion!"

"I am not surprised," said Sakti, impressed. "The true name of a great spirit is not a thing to fling about carelessly. No wonder the Queen is so afraid of Threlfall, if they dare speak the Great Serpent's name."

"*Adik*, do you remember the spell we found in the English

king's house in Malacca?" said Muna. "When you asked the spirits, *Whose magic is this?* the first answer they gave was *Saktimuna*. We thought it was a mistake, but it was the truth. It was only that we did not understand it. The magic in you was Saktimuna's—because *you* are what remained of the Great Serpent, after her heart was stolen by the Queen of the Djinns."

But even this did not convince Sakti. In her doubt she unbent so far as to give Henrietta a look, as much as to say, *Can you believe what she is saying?*

Henrietta said to Muna gently, as one might speak to a person seized by an ague, "You said you had a vision of this Great Serpent in our class. What did you see?"

"The Serpent was sleeping in the seas around Janda Baik," said Muna, not looking away from Sakti. "She had been thrown down there when her magic was stolen from her." She paused, recalling the wounded serpent beneath the waves and the great grievance of which it was only half-conscious. She understood now why its thoughts should have felt so familiar. Who knew Sakti better than Muna? "The Serpent was angry, but too weak to do anything about it. I don't believe she was properly awake."

"Georgiana did say the Fairy Queen exiled her sister to the mortal realm," said Henrietta slowly.

But if she was beginning to be swayed, Sakti was not.

"You may not feel ill, but I don't think you can be quite well, you know, *kak*," said Sakti, shaking her head. "We must leave this place as soon as we can. It's clear the air doesn't suit you."

Muna glared at her. If only Sakti would, for once in her life, accept Muna's authority as the elder! But that was an unhappy thought, for it reminded Muna that they were not sisters at all. In truth she had no authority over Sakti, nor any real bond to her. She was merely a mortal who, lost in the storm, had stumbled upon the

Great Serpent, with the result that the spirit had attached itself to her in its confusion.

"Why else would the Duke of the Navel of the Seas have summoned you, of all persons?" Muna demanded. "The Virtu holds the Great Serpent's heart. The Duke must have intended to call *her* forth."

Sakti chortled suddenly. "If he did, small wonder he was disappointed to get me instead! But this will not do, *kak*. If I were the Serpent, he would have known me."

"There is no reason he would have recognised you. After all, you lack the best part of your powers—your heart. That was taken from you and stored in the Virtu. You are only the remnants of the Serpent—the scrapings of spirit that were left after her core was hollowed out."

"That is complimentary!" said Sakti airily, but Muna could tell her resistance was weakening. Sakti looked vexed, as she always did when she suspected she was about to be bested in a disagreement. It was strange to be fighting to persuade her of an idea so unwelcome to Muna herself, but—Sakti was owed the truth. Muna pressed her advantage.

"When you first entered the halls of this Palace, did not you feel that you knew them?" she said. "From the way you speak of the Queen's Court, anyone would think you had passed a lifetime here, when you have known it for less than a fortnight."

"Oh, it is my fault now that I am clever and adaptable?" snapped Sakti. "And who are you meant to be? Saktimuna contains your name as well. Perhaps it is *you* who are the Great Serpent. You have not considered that!"

Muna had in fact thought about this. "Remember the night I found you? I must have been out on the sea when the storm came on. We were both cast upon the shore; you were confused, and you named me after yourself. It is not as though I could be the Great Serpent, when I have no magic at all!"

Henrietta had been too polite to interrupt before, but now she said, "What do you mean, Muna? You do have magic. I have seen it."

Henrietta's voice gave Muna an unpleasant start. She had almost forgotten the Englishwoman's presence, or she might have taken more care about her words. It was not how she would have chosen to reveal her deception to Henrietta, but she could hardly turn back now.

"That magic was borrowed," she said reluctantly. "I was only sent to the Academy as a companion to my sis—to Sakti. It was she who was Mak Genggang's protégée; I worked in the witch's kitchen."

"Oh," said Henrietta. It was all she said—she uttered no reproach—but the look in her grey eyes struck Muna to the heart.

"I am sorry to have misled you," she began, but Sakti said impatiently:

"What does it matter if my "sister" has magic or not? She is not obliged to tell you everything about herself. I am sure there is a great deal *you* have withheld from her!"

Distressed as Muna was, the word "sister" in Sakti's voice warmed her, but her pleasure in it faded at Henrietta's expression.

"No," said Henrietta. Her voice was precise and emotionless. "That is not so."

But Sakti had already turned to Muna, demanding, "Supposing I am the Serpent, *kak*, what do you wish me to do about it?"

Muna cast a desperate look at Henrietta, but the Englishwoman would not meet her eyes. This gave Muna a pang, more painful than she would have calculated on. But contrition, explanations, reconciliation must all wait. There were greater matters at hand.

"Only what I said," she said to Sakti. "We must recover the Virtu. You must have your heart back."

Sakti's eyes were wide. "But even if you are right . . . what happens once I have it?"

It was bittersweet to have Sakti look to her for guidance, as though they were sisters still. Muna took comfort in it, though with every word she spoke she knew she was severing the bond that meant most to her.

Whatever she decides, she thought, *it will never be as it was between us.*

Still, Muna's voice was steady as she said, "That is your decision. But you will be at liberty to make it. No one should have any hold over you."

Sakti stared at her. Then she flung her arms around Muna, making her stagger.

"I do not deserve such a sister," she said in a voice muffled against Muna's shoulder.

Muna returned her embrace, only raising a hand to dry her eyes.

"You do not!" she agreed.

"But how shall we get to England to recover the Virtu?" said Sakti. "The border is closed. The Queen's subjects may not travel to Britain, any more than the British are permitted to come here. I thought perhaps that was what had delayed you, though I put all my magic into my spell to summon you here."

Unexpectedly, Henrietta spoke.

"We were able to enter Fairy because of Georgiana Without Ruth," she said. "She is head of the clan of Threlfall and they have never paid any regard to the Queen's ban on travel to Britain. Mr. Threlfall resides in London, but he visits his relations in Threlfall regularly, and Georgiana seems to cross the border whenever the fancy strikes her."

"You mean we should ask Georgiana for help?" said Muna. "But she surrendered us to be eaten by the Queen!"

Henrietta still would not look directly at Muna, but she answered, "Georgiana is not likely to betray us to the Queen now that they have fallen out. And if Sakti can arrange for her release from prison, I should think Georgiana would be willing to help us in return. Fairies have a strict sense of honour, and they dislike being beholden in matters of life and death."

"Could you free the *naga* from her prison?" said Muna to Sakti doubtfully. "Come to that, how did you manage to come into our cell? Was not the entrance barred by magic?"

"Yes. But the cells are trees, as I told you," said Sakti. "All I did was tell the tree spirits that I had been sent by the True Queen. Hardly anyone has spoken to them in a great long while, save the Queen's Guard, who only give them orders. You would be surprised how pleased they are to hear a friendly voice!"

"I don't think I would be surprised," said Muna, thinking of the spirit who had granted her her vision of Saktimuna. "Ordinary civility seems a rare commodity among spirits!"

"As I recall, Miss Sakti, you said there was a fire-breathing lizard in the tree next to us," said Henrietta. "I suppose it did not happen to mention its name?"

IT was strange to emerge from the light of the grove into the darkness beneath the Palace of the Unseen. Muna had no recollection of the space, though she and Henrietta must have passed through it when the Queen's attending spirits had captured them.

They stood in a vast dim cavern, in the centre of which was a rank of pillars. Upon inspection these were revealed to be trees made of rock, with branching stiriae, like boughs. A delicate tracery of leaves was marked upon the ceiling, and a web of knobbly roots offered to stub the toes and bruise the shins of the unwary.

The only faint light was shed by lamps affixed to the trees. Muna glanced up at these and froze. Beneath the crystal shade was no wick, but a very small person—smaller even than the *polong*, for Muna could have held him in the palm of her hand. He was swathed in translucent drapery, which did nothing to preserve his modesty; its purpose was evidently to soften the harsh light shining from him, for his entire person gave off a silver glow. His countenance was blank, the eyes gazing sightlessly ahead.

"*Adik,*" whispered Muna. "What—who is that?"

"What? Oh, the lights," said Sakti when she followed Muna's gaze. "They are imps who once displeased the Queen. They are like fireflies—give a good light when they are well-fed. She has them all over the Palace." She frowned at the lamp. "They are usually brighter. I expect these have been starved for a dungeon-like effect."

The imp took no notice of them.

"Are they . . . alive?" said Muna.

"Oh yes," said Sakti. "Sometimes they weep."

Looking at Henrietta, Muna was a little comforted to see her own horror reflected in the Englishwoman's face. She had always known that Sakti could be callous, but it had never before struck her that perhaps Sakti's insensibility was on an inhuman scale.

"You will free them, I hope," she began, "when—that is to say, if—"

"This is the one that had the lizard," said Sakti, pointing at a tree.

She did not appear to have heard Muna, and Muna was glad of

it, for she had spoken without thinking. To require Sakti to adopt any particular course once she had recovered her heart was precisely what Muna meant not to do. Yet she found herself already assuming that Sakti meant to regain the throne—that she would wish to rule over the realms of the Unseen as their rightful Queen.

"I think we had better bring the lizard out here," decided Sakti. "There was a desert inside the tree and it was intolerably hot—most uncomfortable."

She laid her hand on the bole of the tree. A susurrant voice spoke, making Henrietta and Muna jump:

"Who approaches?"

"It is the emissary of your Queen," said Sakti in her grandest manner. "We wish to speak with the *naga* you hold. Pray discharge her."

The faint rustling voice said, "Give me the True Queen's blessing, mistress, and it shall be done."

Sakti traced a symbol on the bark. A grinding noise started up, as of stone scraping against stone.

"What blessing was that?" whispered Muna.

"I invented it," murmured Sakti.

The tree began to tremble, so that the vibration could be felt in the stone beneath their feet. A dark gap opened in the trunk, hot air blasting out from it. Distant roaring filled the air.

Henrietta retreated hastily, but Sakti remained where she stood, peering into the gap.

"Come away, *adik*!" cried Muna, tugging at Sakti's arm, but they did not move fast enough.

When Georgiana Without Ruth burst from her prison, she knocked them both to the ground.

"The nerve of it! The unspeakable cheek!" bellowed Georgiana, revealing sharp teeth in a terrible red mouth. "The Court will rue the day it dared to use a Threlfall with such contumely!"

She reared up, her claws pricking Muna's flesh through her clothes. This was not comfortable, but it was not as debilitating as it might have been, for the spell the Queen had cast on the *naga* was still in effect. Georgiana was as Muna had seen her last—no larger than a civet.

"I shall pay out that jumped-up hussy," cried Georgiana in a voice like the enraged clucking of a chicken. "I shall teach her *such* a lesson. If she thinks her stolen crown will preserve her from the vengeance of Georgiana Without Ruth, she will find she is mistaken!"

She fixed a red-eyed glare upon Sakti and Muna, so furious she did not seem to recognise Muna.

"But first," growled the *naga*, "I must have sustenance!"

"You can't eat us," said Sakti, undaunted. "It was me who freed you. It would be exceedingly ungrateful in you to devour me for my pains!"

"And who are you?"

"I should have thought you of all people would know me," said Sakti, with as much composure as though she were not sprawled beneath the *naga*. "I am the True Queen, of course. My friends called me Saktimuna in days of old."

"Nonsense!" sputtered the *naga*.

But Sakti's declaration operated upon her like a dousing in cold water. Georgiana lowered her wings, and the red light in her eyes died down.

Sakti took the opportunity to sit up and shove her off. Georgiana was so astonished that she slid to the ground without complaint.

"No," said the *naga*, "it can't be." But then:

"It *is* you," said Georgiana in wonder. "But reduced—oh, shamefully reduced! Your own sister would not know you."

"She did not," agreed Sakti.

"Why, a single swipe of the paw would kill you!"

Sakti's smile flickered.

"If it were *your* paw, mistress, there can be no doubt of that," Muna said quickly. Georgiana was plainly in no humour to help the Fairy Queen, but Threlfall had betrayed Saktimuna once before—they could not be too careful. "It would certainly delight the Queen of the Djinns if you were to deliver her sister to her. But it seems a shame when she has used you so ill. After you brought her gifts, too, and bore with shocking incivility from her attendants!"

"Did my sister do all that?" said Sakti to the *naga*. "How like her to have rewarded your loyalty so!" She shook her head. "Some people have no sense of their debts—do not know how to be grateful. Now, I have never failed to return a favour. Once I regain my throne, I shall not forget those who helped me. They will find in me a faithful and loving friend!"

"Of course we could not presume to advise you, ma'am," added Henrietta, raising limpid grey eyes to Georgiana. "But laying yourself out to please the Queen has not produced happy results so far. Might not it answer better to try disobliging her?"

Georgiana settled back on her haunches, crossing her forelegs and fixing a knowing eye on them.

"I see what you are about," she said—but she sounded amused. Muna and Henrietta exchanged a look of relief. "You need not think you will get around me with sweet words!"

"Even sweet words of vengeance?" said Sakti.

Georgiana showed her teeth, charmed. "You *are* Saktimuna! She always knew just what to say to get her way."

The *naga* paused. It was only once she had taken several moments to relish their apprehension that she went on. "It is true the

Queen was offensive. Her years of power have gone to the girl's head! But it is a heady brew. Who is to say you will not do the same?"

"I say so," said Sakti. "And if I know anything of this Court, my sister will even now be marshalling her troops to take Threlfall. She will wish to act before your absence has begun to give your clan concern."

"We have been prepared for an attack since the loss of the Virtu was discovered," said Georgiana. "Threlfall will not be cheaply won."

"No, I expect not," said Sakti. She sighed. "But it is a pity, when one thinks of the sad loss of life! If I were restored to my former glories, I could ensure that Threlfall's ancient title to its lands was respected."

"You do not have the Virtu, then?" said Georgiana. "Your sister feared you might."

"Not yet," said Sakti meaningfully.

"But we know where it is to be found," said Muna. "It is in Britain. Will you help us get there?"

"Only if you feel equal to the task, of course," said Sakti. "In your reduced state!"

Georgiana bridled. "I would counsel you, Saktimuna, to refrain from insulting persons from whom you desire aid!"

But it seemed Sakti had hit upon the truth, for the *naga* continued, "I shall recover my full strength in time. Your sister could not deal me any lasting injury, since I have hidden my heart away. You would have been wise to do the same! But if you desire me to open a way between the worlds now . . ."

Sakti glanced at Muna, who nodded.

"I think we should leave as soon as we can," said Sakti.

"I shall require a restorative," said Georgiana. Her amber gaze turned to Henrietta and Muna. "I do not need much. A dose of mortal spirit would suffice to recruit my energies. Which of these two can you do better without?"

"Oh, if a mortal will do, you may as well take the English-woman," said Sakti.

"*Adik!*" cried Muna, scandalised. Alarmed, Henrietta inched closer to her. Muna pressed her hand in reassurance. "Miss Stapleton is my friend. And," she added, when Sakti looked unconvinced, "she is a friend of the Sorceress Royal. We shall need help to recover the Virtu once we are in England. It would be injudicious to offend their arch-witch by sacrificing her oldest friend."

"The Sorceress Royal need never know," argued Sakti. "We could say we'd lost her friend in the Unseen Realm—tell her the Queen took her."

"No!"

"I could eat this one instead," said Georgiana to Sakti, nodding at Muna.

"Try it," said Sakti, her eyes flashing, "and you shall discover in me a temper even worse than my sister's!"

"Hush, *adik*," said Muna, though the sign of attachment pleased her.

"Then I can do nothing for you," said Georgiana, vexed. "We may as well all be reconciled to being devoured by your sister at her banquet. It will serve you out for your foolish obstinacy!"

"*Kak*, you must see that someone must be sacrificed," said Sakti in her most reasonable tone.

Muna shook her head. An idea had come to her, sparked by the faint gleam of light off Georgiana's scales.

"There is something else I can offer," she said.

After all, it was borrowed magic, she thought. *I must be able to give it back.*

Muna thumped herself on the chest. At first nothing happened, but at her second attempt she seemed to feel something dislodge inside her.

A third blow—gold light flickered at the tips of her fingers, and a cough rose in her chest, bringing tears to her eyes. Encouraged, Muna thumped herself yet again. This time when she started coughing she did not stop.

They were great, racking coughs; each rumbled through her body like an earthquake. Muna heard Sakti and Henrietta's voices raised in concern, but she held up her hand, warding them off. A crisis approached. She was almost at the point—almost—

She clapped a hand over her mouth, her eyes streaming, and brought up the scale.

"Stand back," she gasped when she could speak.

Muna straightened up, holding out her hand to the *naga*. Rollo Threlfall's scale gleamed wetly on her palm.

"That's disgusting!" exclaimed Sakti. "What is it?"

But before she could look closer, the *naga's* head darted out on her long neck. A rough tongue flicked over Muna's palm. Muna snatched her hand away with a cry, but fortunately her fingers were intact. Georgiana had only plucked the scale off her palm.

The *naga* swallowed and said, "This is Rollo's!"

"Yes," said Muna. Georgiana seemed less cross than might have been expected, but all the same Muna was glad Sakti stood between her and the *naga*. "He lent it to me so that I could find your cavern and rescue Mr. Damerell."

"That is how you got around my wards, is it? Let us go to Britain, by all means," said Georgiana grimly. "I am sure Rollo is there, and I shall have a great deal to say to him!"

"Have you sufficient magic now?" said Sakti.

"There was some good Threlfall magic in that scale," Georgiana allowed. "Still, Rollo was the runt of his litter. A whole mortal would settle the point beyond doubt."

She directed a hungry glance towards Henrietta and Muna, but Henrietta was looking away.

"Did you hear that?" she said.

When they had all fallen silent, they could hear metal chiming against metal, and the heavy tread of many feet—the noise of an advancing crowd.

"The Queen's Guard," said Sakti, turning pale.

"You have been betrayed," said Georgiana. She glared at the stone trees. "I'd wager it was one of these disreputable creatures that did it. I should set fire to the lot if I were you!"

Even as she spoke, Georgiana was transforming, expanding at a remarkable rate. First she was the size of a donkey, then a water buffalo, then finally a small elephant—though she stopped there, short of her original size.

"Come along, now," the *naga* said. "There is no time to waste!" As they stared, she added, "To ride a Threlfall is an honour not many people have survived. I shall expect a queenly reward for this, Saktimuna!"

"You shall have it," said Sakti. But she did not climb up onto the *naga*. Instead she said to Muna, "Go on, *kak*. I will come—after I have seen to the trees!"

"What is there to see to?" Muna protested.

But Sakti had already disappeared into the dark spaces between the pillars. Muna hesitated, wondering whether to follow her, but Georgiana snapped:

"Do you *wish* to be devoured by the Fairy Queen?"

"I shall only be a moment!" cried Sakti's voice from among the trees.

"Shall we go, Muna?" said Henrietta. Her voice was steady. She would not admit to being afraid, but her hand was cold on Muna's arm, and it trembled like a leaf in the wind.

They climbed onto the *naga's* back together, helping each other up as the army of spirits approached. Chittering voices could now be heard, interspersed with the occasional uncanny howl.

"Banshees!" said Georgiana. Her scales were dry and smooth, like those of a snake, covering muscles that quivered with tension as Muna crawled over them.

Sakti appeared in a gap between the trees, looking dissatisfied.

"It was not them who gave us away," she said. "Oh, this will vex me!"

"What does it matter?" said Muna. She leant over the *naga's* side, holding out her hands. "Come *along!*"

Sakti shinned up the *naga's* flank with a practised air; she might have ridden a dragon dozens of times before. Muna reached for her hand.

But all at once the cavern swarmed with spirits, their shrieks so piercing that Muna clapped her hands to her ears. In the darkness she could only see the spirits in brief flashes—here a ghostly visage framed by streaming hair; there a gaping mouth limned with blood. All else was a nightmarish muddle of bodies and limbs, hands and paws clutching at Georgiana.

But the *naga* was not to be so easily caught. Her muscles bunched and she leapt off the ground. Muna would have fallen from her perch if not for Henrietta. The Englishwoman had seized the *naga's* neck with one hand and Muna with the other.

Muna saw Sakti slide off the *naga's* back into the seething crowd.

"Adik!" Muna lunged forward, or tried to, but Henrietta's arm was like a band of steel around Muna's person.

"Wait, wait," cried Henrietta. "Mistress Threlfall, wait!"

Her voice was drowned out by Georgiana's roar. The *naga* unhinged her jaw, issuing a crimson jet of flame. The spirits fell back, wailing, and the *naga* rose in the air.

It seemed they must inevitably come to grief against the ceiling. Muna was distantly conscious of Henrietta flinching, but Muna was not afraid for herself. She was vainly trying to make out Sakti in the crowd below when the stone ceiling parted above them, as though it were nothing more than mist blown away by a gust of wind.

Georgiana's wings flapped once, twice, and then they were out—not in the Palace of the Unseen, but out of doors. Above them stretched a dark sky, with a few stars scattered across its surface. Half-veiled by cloud, the serene white face of the moon watched as Georgiana sailed across the sky, flinging off the weight of the Unseen with every powerful beat of her wings.

Muna saw none of this. She could only see Sakti's face, surprised and slightly indignant as she went down under the crush of spirits. She could hear someone weeping, making an extraordinary racket, but she could not spare any attention for them. It was of vital importance that she get down and find Sakti, but something held her in place—an iron grip.

As she struggled, she could feel the grip weaken. She would break free in a moment—

"Hold on to me, Muna," pleaded a voice. It was familiar, though distorted by distress. It was Henrietta who spoke.

"You must help me," said Henrietta, "or we shall both fall!"

The urgency in her voice penetrated through Muna's horror. Muna's vision cleared.

They were high in the sky—miles, at least, from the cavern where they had left Sakti. The Palace was nowhere to be seen. And it was Muna herself who was making that woebegone noise, something between a sob and a wail.

She stopped struggling. She could not quite suppress the noise, but she must have contrived to moderate it, for Georgiana said irritably:

"Has she returned to her senses? I never heard such a caterwauling in my life!"

Muna tried to swallow the caterwauling, but it stuck in her throat, unwieldy as her grief. She looked down. Her hands hung limp, shaking uncontrollably. Underneath them lay a slumbering dark country.

"This is England," said Henrietta. "We are home!"

Behind them was the night sky, the clouds bright with reflected moonlight. Muna could see no trace of the path Georgiana had opened from Fairy to England—nothing marking the boundary between the seen and unseen worlds. On the other side of that imperceptible border was Sakti—lost to her, now, forever.

23

The Lady Maria Wythe Academy for the Instruction of
Females in Practical Thaumaturgy, England

ENRIETTA AND MUNA'S arrival in England was attended by as much fuss and rejoicing as can be imagined. Perhaps it was Zacharias Wythe who was made happiest by their reappearance, for Mrs. Wythe's wild plans for rescuing them from Fairy's clutches had been the cause of domestic discord since Damerell and Rollo had returned from Threlfall, bringing the news of what Georgiana intended.

But Prunella, too, overflowed with delight. She was so glad to have Henrietta back, and to be relieved of the need to report Muna's disappearance to Mak Genggang, that it troubled her not at all when Georgiana declared her intention of remaining in England for the next few days:

"For Rollo and I have a great deal to discuss," she said, with a gleam in her eye that made Mr. Threlfall shudder.

"Certainly!" cried Prunella. "You must stay with us—or no"— she corrected herself at a look from Zacharias—"we have the Duke with us, of course. It might occasion some awkwardness if he knew you were in England. You will not mind staying at the Academy?"

"Best you do, aunt," said Rollo eagerly. "Far more comfortable for you!"

At once the Academy was plunged into the business of making Georgiana comfortable. Servants and scholars rushed around, their arms full of linens and spells respectively, for the Sorceress Royal thought it wise to fortify the wards around the Academy. Fortunately, accommodating Georgiana was an easier task than it would have been before the Fairy Queen had got to her—the journey to England had exhausted the remaining magic in Rollo's scale, and Georgiana had reverted to the size of a civet upon arrival.

The bustle passed over Muna as a wave of inconsequential noise. Later she would have little recollection of the evening, save the pressure of Henrietta's hand on hers, and Henrietta's voice, repeating patiently but with immovable firmness:

"Miss Muna is tired. She must be allowed to rest. We will talk tomorrow."

By some alchemy Henrietta contrived to detach herself and Muna from the Sorceress Royal well before Prunella was done feeding and exclaiming over them. She brought Muna to her bedchamber, lingering even as Muna sat heavily on the bed.

"I am sorry, Muna!" said Henrietta.

Muna only nodded. "Thank you."

Henrietta must have seen that Muna had nothing left to give. She said no more, but touched Muna's hand and—thankfully—went.

Muna ached all over. Her eyes were dry and burning. She longed for nothing so much as to collapse and forget everything, but instead she reached under the bed.

She felt a flicker of relief when her fumbling hand grasped the bottle—who knew if some conscientious servant might not have found it? She held it up to the light.

As ever there was no sign of the *polong*. Muna saw only her own face reflected in the glass. It looked young and unformed, but the expression was as old and tired as Muna felt.

"*Kur*, soul!" she whispered.

Though she had surrendered the magic she had borrowed from Rollo, somehow she did not doubt that the *polong* would appear.

Perhaps great need was a form of magic in itself. Red smoke billowed from the mouth of the bottle, coalescing into the *polong*'s trim figure.

"Now what do you want?" she snapped, but then she saw Muna's face. "Child! What has happened?"

"I went to the Palace of the Unseen," said Muna. "My sister was there. My sister—she—"

But this was as far as she could go.

The *polong* clicked her tongue, half in sympathy and half in censure, as Muna wept. "There, did not I tell you not to go to that wicked place? Now you are sorry, but the rice has turned to gruel, so what is the good of tears?"

It was just the same scolding tone Mak Genggang adopted when she wished to comfort anyone, but Muna was beyond being consoled by such small familiarities. When she continued to cry, the *polong* said, "What has become of your sister?"

"She was taken by the spirits in the Palace of the Unseen," said Muna. She scrubbed her eyes with her sleeve. She must not be diverted by useless emotion. "I must save her, if I can."

If there is anything left to save, thought Muna, but she could not attend to the counsels of despair, or she did not know what she would do.

"I need your assistance, *kak*," she said.

The *polong* looked alarmed. "It is a pity about your sister, but I told you I would not start any quarrels with the Queen of the Djinns!"

"I would not ask so much of you," said Muna. "It is a task you will not mind, I think. It is the sort of thing Mak Genggang would never command you to do."

A spark of interest flashed across the *polong*'s countenance.

"Indeed?" she said guardedly.

"Tell me, *kak*," said Muna. "Would not you like to commit a larceny?"

M UNA would not have believed that she could sleep that night. She had planned to wait for the *polong* to return from her assignment, which the spirit had accepted with a ready will. But England was colder than Muna had remembered. Waiting in an armchair by the dying embers of the fire, she began to shiver, and to keep warm she climbed into her bed.

Once she was there, weariness did the rest. She slept, and for a few hours forgot her troubles.

Golden sunlight was streaming through the window when Muna woke. For a fleeting moment she did not remember where she was. She lay gazing at the rectangle of sunshine on the floor, wondering that her heart did not rise at the sight, for it seemed to her that it had been some time since she had seen the sun.

Then she remembered. Her fingers curled on the sheet.

"Oh," said Muna. She turned her face into the pillow.

She only raised her head when the knock came at the door.

It was Henrietta. "May I speak with you?"

Muna looked back at the windows, still fogged by sleep and grief. With a sun so bright, the day must be considerably advanced. "Will not we be late for breakfast?"

"It is almost noon," said Henrietta. "We did not like to wake you. How do you feel? Would you like to take a sup of something?"

She was not asking about the state of Muna's appetite alone, but Muna was in no humour to talk about how she felt. She shook her head. "I am not hungry. What did you wish to speak of?"

Henrietta waited till Muna had shut the door to begin.

"I have spent the morning rowing with Prunella," she said. "But I have won my point—and she will be in a better mood presently. Once she has calmed down she will see it is all for the best."

"Is Mrs. Wythe quarrelling with you already?" said Muna in disapproval. "One might think she would be better pleased to have the friend of her childhood restored to her!"

"Oh, it is my fault," said Henrietta. "I ought to have waited to tell her what I intended. Mornings don't agree with Prunella. But I didn't wish to put it off, for I mean to leave as soon as I can get away."

"Leave?" cried Muna, briefly forgetting her various preoccupations.

Henrietta looked pale but resolute. "Yes. I promised I should not implicate Britain if I was discovered in Fairy, and I mean to keep my word. The Fairy Queen is bound to pursue us here. If she finds us in England, it will confirm her belief in England's guilt—so I must do what I can to direct her attention elsewhere."

"Where will you go?" said Muna. "Not France?" She knew nothing of France save that it was at war with Britain. Confused images rose before her, of grim-faced soldiers bearing guns and spears, people fleeing from burning villages . . .

"No. Lady Wythe has a friend in Scotland; I shall go to her first," said Henrietta. "But we shall put about a story that I have run away to France with a *Comte*—that will fit with what I told the

Fairy Queen. Then the news will follow that I was abandoned by my"—she cleared her throat, blushing—"by my lover, and Prunella will tell everyone I flung myself into the Seine!"

"Good gracious!"

"I thought a body should be found," said Henrietta. "I could create a simulacrum of myself for the purpose. But Prunella thinks it unnecessary. She says she would rather not see my corpse—it would distress her, even if she knew it was not real."

"But how will you return?" said Muna, wishing her wits were not so muddled. Things were moving altogether too fast. "If it is given out that you are dead . . ."

"It will make a return awkward," agreed Henrietta. "That was what made Prunella so cross. But I brought her around in time. She could not deny it is awkward for her to have us on her hands, with an irate Fairy Queen in hot pursuit. For myself, I shall not mind being in hiding. I shall assume a new name and disguise my features, and I mean to travel. I should like to learn more of foreign magics."

She glanced shyly at Muna, but Muna was still digesting the implications of the scheme.

"What of your relations?" said Muna. "It will give them a great deal of distress to believe you dead." This came too near matters she would rather avoid thinking of. Her heart contracted painfully, and she put her hand to her chest.

The light in Henrietta's face dimmed.

"Yes," she said soberly. "And if I run away, my engagement with Mr. Hobday will be broken. I believe Papa has already borrowed a considerable sum from him. But"—she clasped her hands—"it cannot be helped! I have thought and thought about it all night, and I believe my first duty is to my country. After all, my family would suffer as much as everyone else if Fairy were to declare war on us. Besides . . ."

She fell silent.

"Besides?" echoed Muna.

"It will sound strange!" said Henrietta. She had a distant look in her eyes. "It is not as though I *liked* being gaoled by the Fairy Queen. But visiting Fairy, tasting its magic and speaking with dragons on terms of near equality . . . it brought home to me the meanness of my existence here. If I remained in England with my family, still I should be obliged to live in hiding all my life. I could never call myself a *magicienne*, nor publish a spell in the *Gazette* under my own name. Why, I am *good* at devising spells! Better even than Prunella, for when she has done something new she can never tell you how she did it."

Henrietta paused.

"And if I stayed," she said, "I should have to marry."

There was something in her voice—the hopelessness of one speaking of a certain doom—that gave Muna a pang. She said:

"You need not marry Mr. Hobday if you do not like him."

Henrietta shook her head. "If it is not him, it must be another gentleman. And there is none I would marry."

Save Mr. Wythe, thought Muna. This gave her a worse pang, but before Muna could decide what to say, Henrietta went on, more cheerfully:

"But my own wishes are of little account. Duty requires me to leave Britain, so depart I shall. I only wondered whether you would be so good as to help me?"

"I will do all I can," said Muna. "What do you need?"

Henrietta hesitated. "Have you given any thought to what you wish to do now? You will be welcome here for as long as you should like to stay," she added quickly. "Prunella will come and tell you so herself, but she insisted upon my saying it too."

"That is good of her," said Muna. "I shall take advantage of Mrs. Wythe's hospitality for a little longer, if I may. But I don't mean to impose on her for long."

It was difficult to conceive of a future. Even when Muna put her mind to it, as she did now, striving to pierce through the darkness that pressed in on all sides, there was only her great intention—the charge she had entrusted to the *polong*. Beyond that, she could not tell what might happen.

If she lived, however . . . *if* she lived . . . what would she choose?

It was a question she had not asked herself before, but the answer came readily. Muna saw a substantial wooden house—a house sitting nearer the jungle than was quite comfortable, haunted by more than its fair share of ghosts, yet promising absolute safety to those admitted to its shelter. As she thought of Mak Genggang's house, its very smell came back to her—the scent of sun-warmed timbers, spices frying in the kitchen, and Mak Genggang herself, clean flesh and freshly laundered cotton.

"I should like to go home," said Muna. "To Janda Baik, I mean."

Henrietta nodded. "I thought you might. Prunella and I think it would be wise for you to take precautions, if so. You would not wish the Fairy Queen to turn her attention to your home."

"No, indeed!" said Muna. "What would you recommend?"

"We must account for you, you see," said Henrietta. "It is no good putting about a story that explains only my disappearance, when the Fairy Queen knows there were two of us. We thought we might say that I took you with me when I ran away. You would stay here as long as you liked, and go on to Janda Baik when you were ready, under a false name. Since you have no family here, and no one knows you, that misdirection should suffice. There is a spell we could use to give you a new face, for a time. You could put it off, of course, once the Queen had forgot us."

"That sounds sensible," said Muna. It was unlikely the Queen would soon forget her, or that Muna would ever be able to go home, but Henrietta did not need to know that. She was leaving soon, and would be spared the consequences of Muna's plan. "So I go with you to France, do I? But what do I do when you die?"

"Oh!" said Henrietta: it seemed her invention had not extended so far. "Perhaps you remain in France. You spied on Britain on their behalf, after all, and are entitled to their gratitude."

"No," decided Muna. "I think I had better dive into the river with you! I should not wish to be parted from you, since we had gone so far together."

This made Henrietta laugh, as Muna had intended. For a moment they sat smiling at each other.

"There is another favour I should like to ask," said Henrietta. "I know it would gratify my mother extremely—and I should like to give her pleasure while I can. But you must feel at liberty to decline if you do not like the notion."

"What is it?"

"My mother is hosting a ball tomorrow evening for my sister Amelia's coming-out," said Henrietta. "I know it would please her if you were to attend. She was very much struck with you."

"I remember," said Muna. The Sorceress Royal's ball seemed long ago now. She felt as though she had aged centuries since that evening; it was impossible to hold any grudge about Mrs. Stapleton's conduct then, or do anything but what would please Henrietta. "I should like to attend the ball, if you are sure I would be wanted."

"Oh, you will be a sensation!" said Henrietta. "I do not know why society should abhor an English *magicienne* but fall into raptures over a foreign sorceress—but there it is! I am very much obliged to you. It will not make up for all I mean to do, but my mother will be delighted, and that is something. And," she added, brightening, "I shall like you to meet my sisters!"

But then Henrietta seemed to realise this might be an unhappy reference. She flushed. "That is to say, if you would not mind my presenting them to you."

"I should be honoured to meet your sisters," said Muna gently. "Will you tell me about them?"

This was a well-advised question, for Henrietta forgot all awkwardness at once in the pleasure of describing her sisters. There were three: "None has magic, thank goodness! We have always been the greatest of friends, though I was sent away to school. Charlotte is the drollest, for she is not yet thirteen and still very much the child. Louisa is second youngest; she has the most sense, but it is Amelia people notice—she is the prettiest, and has the most *go*. I have not made up my mind which you will like best."

"That is easy enough," said Muna. "I shall like you best. What ought I to wear to your mother's party?"

A grave look came over Henrietta's face, for this was a delicate matter. "It must be something befitting an exotic, but not anything Mamma would deem improper. I believe . . ."

But Henrietta never had the chance to explain what Muna should wear, for then the *polong* reappeared, with none of the discretion Muna had asked for. The door burst open and red smoke poured in, making the women cough.

Henrietta leapt to her feet, whisking out a handkerchief and putting it to her nose.

"Do not breathe it in, Muna!" she cried in a muffled voice. "It may be poison!"

But Muna had heard what Henrietta had not—the clatter of an object dropping on the floor. Muna flung herself down and saw the gleam of red gems, set in a coil of bluish-green stones. She laid her hand on it just as the *polong's* voice boomed:

"Here is my gift to you, child—the Queen's Virtu and the heart of Saktimuna, restored to wholeness!"

24

HE *POLONG* EMERGED from the smoke, glowing with self-satisfaction, but she checked at the sight of Henrietta. "Who is this?"

"My friend," said Muna absently.

"Your friend?" echoed the *polong*. "You did not tell me you had friends among the English. Did not I say Mak Genggang wished them to remain ignorant of my existence?"

"Are you acquainted with this fairy, Muna?" said Henrietta. Then she saw the object in Muna's hands. Her eyes widened.

"You have found it," she breathed. "The Queen's Virtu!"

The object was the twin of the ornament the Queen had worn when Georgiana had brought Muna and Henrietta to her—a double-headed snake, its body made of turquoises and its eyes of rubies. And there was more.

"This is writing," Muna said aloud.

She showed the talisman to Henrietta, but Henrietta only looked confused. "I cannot see any writing."

"Look here." Muna's fingers traced the stones forming the serpent's body. Close to, she could see that the stones formed a pattern, and no meaningless pattern either. The words unfolded in her head. She murmured them aloud:

"Here is the inner heart and virtue of the villainess Saktimuna, who

was cast out of the Unseen. Whoever holds this shall master the Serpent, who is unworthy to be mistress of herself."

"What language is that?" said Henrietta. It was only then that Muna realised she had been speaking neither English nor Malay, nor any mortal tongue. Both Henrietta and the *polong* were looking at her strangely.

"That is Palace speech," said the *polong*, frowning. "The tongue reserved for the royalty of the Unseen. How comes it that you are able to read it . . . ?"

The spirit's voice trailed off. She stared at Muna, her lip trembling in outrage.

"That Woman!" spat the *polong*, startling Muna. "She must have known. The Great Serpent disappears in a storm and two girls are found on the shore the morning after, girls who have no memories, no family to claim them . . . of a certainty she knew. Of all the sly, mistrustful creatures! To think of her charging me with your protection and not telling me!"

"You mean," said Muna, "Mak Genggang guessed my sister was Saktimuna? She knew of the existence of the Great Serpent?" She did not know how to feel about this.

"Of course she did," said the *polong*. "The Great Serpent was old when Mak Genggang's grandmother was born. Where do you think Janda Baik drew its magic from? The Serpent was the source of the island's power—it was her magic that drew witches and lamiae and kings to its shores. The witches all knew that."

Sakti had not known it, thought Muna—but then, Sakti had only been an apprentice witch. No doubt the disclosure of a mystery like the Serpent was reserved for those who had progressed further with their studies than Sakti had had the opportunity to do.

She squatted so that she was nearer the *polong*'s level.

"Kings?" said Muna. "Do you mean the Sultan of Janda Baik?"

"The kings were before your time," said the *polong*. "They were always taking it into their heads that the Serpent was an evil spirit and trying to kill her—without the least success, of course. In time Mak Genggang was obliged to beg the Serpent to pretend she had been murdered, so that the kings would stop troubling us. There had not been a questing raja in our waters for many years when the Serpent disappeared."

"When was that?" said Muna—but of course, the *polong* had already said. The Great Serpent had disappeared in a storm—the storm after which Muna and Sakti had woken on Janda Baik, with no knowledge of who they were.

The *polong* would not say more in Henrietta's presence, but Muna thought she understood what the witch must have felt then. To lose the island's chief defence, at a time when the British were circling Janda Baik like kites . . .

"That was why Mak Genggang was so busy," she said aloud. "She scarcely had time to try to break our curse."

"She would have done better to devote more time to you, and less time to . . . other things," said the *polong*, glancing at Henrietta. "Perhaps she only suspected, after all. I cannot see why she should have sent you away if she had known what you were."

"She feared we might fall into the hands of the British," said Muna. For Henrietta's benefit, she added, "The raja of Malacca, I mean, who might not have been sympathetic. Now that I know my sister was the Great Serpent, I understand why she feared it!"

"Oh, Sakti was not the Serpent," said the *polong* offhandedly. "What can have given you that idea? It is both of you, I see that now! Mak Genggang would have guessed it, too, if she had known what had become of the Virtu."

Henrietta knelt by the *polong* while Muna gaped.

"You think Sakti and Muna are both parts of the Great Serpent," said Henrietta.

The *polong* looked at the Englishwoman with misgiving. "What do you know of it?"

"Nothing whatever," said Henrietta candidly. "But I know that a talisman as powerful as the Virtu cannot be broken up without dramatic results. I wondered, when Sakti told us what the Duke had done . . . but now I can guess what came to pass. When the Duke divided the Virtu in half, it must have split what remained of the Serpent in two."

The *polong* looked grudgingly impressed. "Yes. When the Queen took the Serpent's heart and flung her down into the mortal realm, that weakened the Serpent—made her more liable to be broken up again. That is how some smaller spirits are made. They spring from the destruction of greater spirits."

Muna looked incredulously from the *polong* to Henrietta and back again. They seemed to understand each other—and yet with every word they spoke, Muna's bewilderment grew.

"But, but," she stammered, "but I cannot be part of any spirit. You forget I have no magic."

"You are the Serpent's material part, of course," said the *polong*. She was matter-of-fact, just as though she were not saying the most extraordinary, inconceivable things. "A spirit of the Serpent's size requires an anchor to the mortal world if it is not to dissolve into lesser imps. You have seen the imps I mean—they are the fine ones who must carry out the orders of mortal magicians and greater spirits alike.

"Some spirits anchor themselves to human beings and become their familiars, but the Serpent tethered herself to Janda Baik. The island became a part of her, as she was part of it. When this Duke you told me of broke the Virtu, he will have divided the Serpent into soul and matter—spirit and insensate clay. You are the clay, and Sakti is the spirit, which is the same thing as magic."

"I can't be . . ." But Muna allowed her voice to trail off into silence, for she found she believed the *polong*.

Was that why the Serpent's thoughts had been so familiar in her vision? They had been her own.

"But if it is true," she said aloud, "Sakti is not . . ."

Not my sister, Muna meant to say, but she had known that already, when she had decided that Sakti was Saktimuna, the lost True Queen, and Muna herself a mere hanger-on. There was no reason she should feel so desolate now—and yet to know her attachment to Sakti had not been devotion to a sister, nor a charge she had disinterestedly assumed, but merely a sort of obsession with a part of herself . . . made Muna feel unmoored, cut adrift from the certainties that had buoyed her before.

"Yes," said the *polong*. "Sakti is not dead."

Her voice penetrated through Muna's haze of self-pity. Muna raised her head. "What?"

"The Duke may not have intended it, but he served you well by breaking you up," said the *polong*. "It will be far more difficult for the Queen of the Djinns to destroy you now—you cannot be extinguished unless she tracks down every part of you. It is like those magicians that hide their heart away, so they will be proof against any attack. So long as the Virtu survives, so will you—*all* of you."

Muna looked down at the gleaming talisman in her hands. "You mean I could use the Virtu to save Sakti?"

"Or revive her," agreed the *polong*. "Whatever they may have done to her in the Palace of the Unseen may have scattered her spirit, but since you have her heart, you ought to be able to recover what remains—so long as you find her before the Queen does. If the Queen realises what Sakti is—a sliver of the Great Serpent's soul—I should think she will devour her at once."

"What do I do?" said Muna urgently. "How can I find Sakti?"

"It will be easy enough once you have your magic back," said the *polong*. "You shall have to take the Virtu into yourself."

Muna understood. After all, she had absorbed Fairy magic once before.

She raised the Virtu to her mouth, but a hand seized her wrist, stopping her.

"Wait!" cried Henrietta.

Muna had nearly forgotten Henrietta was there. While she blinked, Henrietta turned to the *polong*. "But what will happen if Muna takes the Virtu into herself? Might there be any ill effects? Surely to absorb so much magic will alter her."

"Beyond recognition!" agreed the *polong*. "With the Virtu, she will be the best part of the Great Serpent. Once she has summoned Sakti, that will make up the whole. Saktimuna will be restored to herself, able to protect Janda Baik from its enemies."

"But will Muna be *herself*?" said Henrietta.

"Why, no," said the *polong*. "She will be swallowed up in the Serpent." The spirit seemed puzzled by Henrietta's agitation. "But Muna is not a real person, you know."

The *polong* seemed to intend this as reassurance, but it did not answer.

"She is a real person to me!" retorted Henrietta. She turned to Muna. "Don't listen to this creature. We must not be precipitate. There is surely another way!"

"Oho!" cried the *polong*, bristling. "The Englishwoman shows her hand, but you will not be deceived by her, child. It is clear she desires the Virtu for her own people!"

Henrietta flushed. "That is *not*—that is a falsehood, Muna, you must believe me!"

Muna was not listening to either of them. She looked at the *polong*. "If I swallow the Virtu, could I defeat the Queen?"

The *polong* spread her hands. "Who can say who will triumph in these battles between great spirits? But the Serpent always claimed that her powers surpassed those of her sister. She said she was overthrown only because she had not expected treachery from that quarter."

"Muna," said Henrietta. "Muna, do you hear me? If you do this, you will be absorbed into the Great Serpent; you will lose yourself in her. There is no call for you to make such a sacrifice. I beg you will not do it!"

She took Muna's arm, but Muna put her aside as gently as she could.

"There is no such thing as 'myself,' you know," said Muna. "So it is no great odds either way."

"If that is true, then there never was a Sakti cither," said Henrietta, "and nothing for which you need make a martyr of yourself!"

It was like being touched on an open wound. Muna flinched. "Don't! How would you feel, if it were your sisters? If I can ensure that Sakti lives—even if she is changed, even if we are both changed—what can I care for anything else?"

Before she could lose her nerve, she put the Virtu in her mouth. Henrietta lunged at her, apparently determined to pluck the talisman from her.

"Henrietta!" sputtered Muna. She contrived to fend the Englishwoman off, but it was not such a straightforward matter to eat something so unlike food. Even if Muna's mind was convinced of the need to swallow the Virtu, the rest of her was far from being persuaded. She was still choking on the talisman when the *polong*'s head whipped up.

"Put it away!" said the spirit. "Here she comes!"

"Who?" said Henrietta, but the *polong* was already dissolving in a swirl of red smoke.

The door blew open on a burst of magic, sending Muna and Henrietta staggering backwards. With its wild red hair and burning eyes, the creature that entered the room was scarcely recognisable as human—it resembled more than anything else a furious djinn.

"Thief!" screamed Clarissa Midsomer.

"Are you well, Muna?" said Henrietta anxiously.

Muna gulped. "Quite well!"

Her eyes were wet, her voice hoarse, but Miss Midsomer's spectacular appearance had achieved what her own efforts could not. In her surprise she had swallowed the Virtu.

"YOU wicked hussy!" cried Clarissa, advancing on Muna. "I know it was you that took my pendant. Where is it? Give it to me!"

Miss Midsomer's left hand hung by her side, clenched into a fist. A voice in Muna's head said, *The mortal is devising a curse.*

Muna was surprised to realise the voice was her own, though it hissed rather more than she habitually did. And the voice was right—in her hand Clarissa was weaving an enchantment, a curse bristling with malice and ill intention.

Swallowing the Virtu had wrought no great change in Muna herself, save for the Great Serpent's memories rustling at the back of her mind. It was the world—that wore a new aspect. It was as though Muna had for a time forgotten how to smell. Now that magic was restored to her she wondered that it had ever seemed mysterious.

Miss Midsomer's enchantment did not worry her; it was only a little mortal spell. She could have undone it with a thought, but it scarcely seemed worth the effort. She had other business to tend to, of rather more importance.

She reached for Saktimuna's powers. They surged to her hand, the air growing thick with the numberless imps of which magic was made up. She could see them with much more clarity than when she had called upon the fine ones in Henrietta's class—a multitude of faces, as insubstantial as smoke, but each individual.

If she had been the Serpent she might have rapped out a peremptory command, but she was still mostly Muna, who knew what it was to be insignificant and disregarded. She said to the fine ones, *I should be obliged if you would bring my sister to me. Will you?*

The fine ones were only too ready to assist—they seemed overwhelmed by receiving such courtesy from a great spirit. Once the spirits were dispatched on their errand, Muna returned her attention to the scene playing out around her.

"Clarissa!" Henrietta was saying, pink-cheeked. "What do you mean by charging in, in this ill-bred manner? You forget that Miss Muna is our guest!"

"She is nothing more than a thief!" Clarissa jabbed a bony finger at Muna. "You will stand my witness, Henrietta Stapleton! The native witch employed black magic to rob me. My pendant has been taken, and the spell I cast to discover where it had gone showed me her creature, making away with it!"

Henrietta folded her arms. "Do you say it was *your* pendant, then?"

"What do you mean?" said Clarissa. "Of course it was my pendant."

"Only that if you had come into possession of a valuable amulet—one for which the Fairy Court had been searching—you would have reported it to the Society at once, wouldn't you?" said Henrietta deliberately. "You would not be so disloyal as to keep such a secret when the Sorceress Royal was being accused of the theft—when the Fairy Queen was threatening war on Britain in consequence!"

The colour drained out of Clarissa's cheeks, leaving her white to the lips. "I—I do not know what you mean."

To Muna, with her new eyes, Clarissa looked very young: no villainess, but a mere girl, caught up in schemes and machinations beyond her understanding. Perhaps the same thought occurred to Henrietta, for she said gently:

"Clarissa, there is more at stake here than you know! Will not you trust us? Prunella agreed that you might join the Academy because we thought we could help you."

"Because she wished to keep an eye on me, you mean!" Clarissa flashed out. Abandoning her pretence of ignorance, she went on, "You need not read me any sermons on what is at stake, Henrietta Stapleton! You know nothing of the matter. You had no right to take the Virtu. I was holding it in trust for another, and he has grave need of it."

"If the Fairy Queen turns against Britain," said Henrietta, "your brother will suffer as much as any of us!"

Clarissa blinked. "My brother? What has my brother to do with it? *He* will be perfectly well whatever comes to pass."

Nonplussed, Henrietta said, "When you spoke of holding the Virtu in trust for another, were not you speaking of your brother?"

"No," said an unexpected voice. "She held it for me."

The Duke of the Navel of the Seas shut the door behind him, putting his back against it.

"Florian!" gasped Clarissa, in a tone that made Muna look at her sharply.

"Don't worry, my dear," said the Duke. "You will have taken the greatest care of the article, I know. My luck turned, that is all. But there is always another throw of the dice!"

He smiled at Henrietta. "Now, ma'am, where is the Virtu?"

Muna was still looking at Miss Midsomer. It was plain that the Duke had laid himself out to win Clarissa over upon discovering that she held the missing half of the Virtu. The way Clarissa gazed at him proved his attentions had not been in vain.

"It is wrong!" said Muna, indignant. She turned on the Duke. "It was very wrong in you to trifle with a young girl for your own ends. If you desired her half of the Virtu, you could have stolen it from her. That would have been dishonourable, but better than stealing her heart!"

Clarissa drew herself up, outraged.

"Thank you, but I do not need defending by the likes of you!"

The Duke patted her hand with the air of one soothing an excitable pet. "I have trifled with no one's affections," he declared, "but even if I were the greatest philanderer in the thirty-one worlds, that would be none of your business. Will not you surrender the Virtu to me and save the need for a quarrel? You should know that I am capable of being very disagreeable!"

"You will not find the Virtu here, sir," said Henrietta, for the Duke had chiefly addressed his remarks to her. "I would advise you to leave and seek refuge where you can from the Fairy Queen's vengeance—if, indeed, there is anywhere in the world that will serve! I cannot conceive what can have possessed you to deprive Her Majesty of her most valued treasure."

"What did you mean to do with the Virtu?" said Muna. "Did you think of taking the throne?"

"No, no!" said the Duke, in sincere horror. "That would be endless trouble. All I desired was a quiet life. You do not know what it is like to be a courtier in the Fairy Court," he continued, with feeling. "The ceaseless intrigues—the tests of one's loyalty—the wearying gossip! All of it trivial beyond belief, and yet a single error could doom a spirit to endless torment. I was obliged to endure it for hundreds of years!

"It made me willing to risk what might come of stealing the Virtu." The Duke's eyes gleamed. "And I am willing to risk a great deal more to recover it. Come, now, where is it?"

"I am sorry to disoblige you, sir, but it is as Henrietta said," said Muna. "We cannot return the Virtu."

"Because you want it for your own!" Clarissa burst out. The curse in her hand was fairly sparking, ready to be loosed. "You do not care that it will mean a life of subjugation for Florian! Well, I am not having it. Prunella Gentleman has ruined my life once before, by causing Geoffrey to be sent away and bringing disgrace upon my family. You shall not do the same, Henrietta Stapleton!"

"My soul!" exclaimed the Duke, but Clarissa lobbed her hex at them.

"Muna!" cried Henrietta.

She readied herself to dive in front of Muna, but fortunately there was no need for any such dramatics. Muna caught the curse out of the air and closed her hand around it, snuffing it out. It stung like raw chilli—a stronger spell than she had supposed. Clarissa must be a *magicienne* of considerable natural talent, though she was untrained.

"You ought not to play around with such spells," said Muna to Clarissa, in reproof. "You might have scalded yourself, and then wouldn't you have felt silly?"

The Duke looked at Muna as though he noticed her for the first time. "Who *are* you?"

"I am not altogether certain," said Muna truthfully. "Whoever it is, I have only been her for a short time. I expect you know her, sir, better than me."

Recognition dawned in the Duke's eyes.

"*No,*" he said, just as Georgiana of Threlfall had done. "No, you cannot be her!"

There was something niggling at Muna. Memories were heaped up behind her eyes, thick as leaves on a jungle floor. To rifle through them for any particular recollection was like searching for a brooch dropped in the undergrowth. And yet . . .

"Florian," she said aloud. "There was a page boy who attended on my sixth parent, who went by that name. Was that *you?*"

The Duke fell on his face. "Have mercy on an erring sprite, gracious Saktimuna!"

"You have the Great Serpent's memories, then?" said Henrietta. She gave Muna a searching look, but she must have found what she was looking for, for relief softened her face. "It is plain you have her magic!"

Muna nodded. "I remember."

It was not quite that the memories were her own. The Serpent slumbered at the back of her mind, as it had slumbered in the watery deeps for uncounted years. Now that its heart had been freed from the Virtu, Saktimuna would gain strength. Muna did not doubt it would overpower her in time—and then it was Muna who would be nothing more than a fleeting voice at the back of the Serpent's mind.

But she would not think of that now. It would not be long before her self, as she knew it, was consumed, but she still had time enough for what she wished to encompass.

His face pressed against the floor, the Duke was murmuring incoherent platitudes regarding their long acquaintance and the Serpent's great generosity. "You will forgive me, mistress, knowing how miserable I have been under your sister's tyranny. I have misled her for a time, but I cannot put her off forever. She will realise who must have taken the Virtu—she will pursue me here. It may only be a matter of weeks!"

"Oh, we shan't have to wait so long," said Muna. "I have called her here. I expect she will be along as soon as she can get away."

"*What?*" said the Duke, Henrietta and Clarissa.

"I have asked the fine ones for my sister," explained Muna. "If Sakti still survives, that will draw her to me. But if she does not, it ought to bring me the Queen."

"But, Muna, what can you want with the Queen?" said Henrietta. She looked appalled.

"What I have always wanted." And for once Muna and the Serpent spoke in one voice. "What she took from me."

25

AMELIA

ALL SEEMED TO augur well for Amelia's coming-out ball. Even Mrs. Stapleton, a woman easily fluttered by minor adversities, looked forward to the party with pleasurable anticipation. The revelation that Henrietta's friend, the native sorceress, was to make an appearance at her ball had put Mrs. Stapleton in good humour with the world, and she bore the ordeals of being a hostess with uncommon fortitude.

Amelia did not share her good spirits. Though Henrietta's inexplicable absence had finally ended with her return the day before, she had convened a conference that morning to inform her three sisters that she was going on a journey—a long journey. They must keep it a secret, but she wished them to know that she would be perfectly well. They might receive concerning reports of her, but they must not allow these to worry them.

"But where are you going?" cried Charlotte. "I think it is cruel, when you have only just been—"

Amelia squashed her before she could reveal all they knew of Henrietta's secret life, for she foresaw the hubbub that would ensue—explanations, tears, reproaches. They had only a little time before they were bound to be interrupted by a parent or servant, and what they needed from Henrietta was answers.

"When will you come back?" said Amelia.

Henrietta coloured, casting her eyes down; she was a pitiably bad liar. "I do not yet know. But I shall find a way to send you a message when I can."

"What of Papa and Mamma?" said Louisa, thinking of the trials they would endure in attempting to conceal Henrietta's absence from their parents.

"They shall know of my departure before anyone else," said Henrietta. "I know it will distress them, but you will be able to reassure them without giving me away."

"This is all very mysterious," said Amelia. "Cannot you tell us more? We would never betray your confidence, you know, Henny." She thought of Henrietta's engagement. "If it is to do with—with Mr. Hobday, I am sure Papa could be reasoned with. Nobody wishes you to be unhappy."

She had expected Henrietta to blush and disclaim any unhappiness at the prospect of being joined with Mr. Hobday. But her sister only blinked, as though she had forgotten all about her betrothed.

"Oh, Mr. Hobday!" said Henrietta. "We need not be in any haste to tell him. He will hear of my departure by some means or other. I hope he will not be too vexed with Papa, but I do not expect it will upset him unduly. You know, 'Melia, I am not sure Mr. Hobday was ever particularly attached to me!"

Henrietta's sisters were obliged to be content with this, for the conference was broken up by the entrance of Mrs. Stapleton. Their mother had heard from her maid that Lady Burrow's niece would wear a pink gown that evening. Henrietta's dress, too, was pink. Did Henrietta think it wise to wear her blue dress instead? But Mr. Hobday had declared himself fond of pink. Mrs. Stapleton did not know what was to be done.

When this dilemma had been resolved, a dozen more presented themselves for Amelia's attention, so that it was impossible to question Henrietta further. For of course she promptly vanished, leaving Not Henrietta in her place.

"I wonder if Henny will even bestir herself to attend the ball!" Amelia said bitterly to her sisters. "It is only my debut. Why should she consider it of any importance, compared to her magic?"

"Oh, don't speak so, 'Melia," said Charlotte, distressed. "What if Henrietta should never return? She looked so solemn this morning, and she would not be drawn on how long she would be gone."

Amelia had not seriously considered this possibility, but now that Charlotte had raised it, she was obliged to acknowledge that it seemed likely.

"It *is* provoking," said Louisa, "but we do not know what business takes her away. I hope it is nothing dangerous." She raised worried eyes to Amelia. "Ought we to say something? I fear we do wrong in not telling Papa!"

Amelia deliberated, but finally shook her head. "Papa is so burdened with care that if we can save him any worry, we should—and he would be so cross with Henny! We must speak to her again before we do anything. If we tell her we know all, surely she will confide in us."

"If Henrietta goes away forever, what will Papa do?" said Charlotte. "Perhaps Mr. Hobday would have you instead, 'Melia."

"Oh no!" said Louisa. "Bad enough that Henny was to marry him, but Amelia . . . !"

"I would never rub along with Mr. Hobday," agreed Amelia. "No, Charlotte, we shall have to find another way. I must find another wealthy gentleman, though," she added with feeling, "it will *not* be a thaumaturge! Just think if we had magical daughters! It is bad enough having a sister with magic."

"But so long as you could persuade your husband to allow it, there would be no difficulty," argued Charlotte. "It is not Henrietta having magic that is the trouble. It is Papa and Mamma's not being sympathetic."

But Amelia was in no humour to be sympathetic with her sister's inconvenient thaumaturgical leanings.

"I am not so certain!" she said grimly.

When Amelia descended to the ballroom that evening they had still seen neither hide nor hair of Henrietta. Her vexation began to be threaded through with apprehension. Perhaps Louisa was right. Everyone said the practice of magic was fraught with peril, even for gentlemen. How much more hazardous must be it for a female? Henrietta would never tell them if she was in danger.

Despite her anxiety, Amelia was determined to do her duty as a debutante. She was conscious of the expense that had been incurred on her account and knew that with but a little effort she might recoup it. She was in good looks and the reception from the gentlemen in attendance—a mix of thaumaturges and the laity, including several eligible bachelors with respectable fortunes— was encouraging.

Yet as the evening wore on, her conviction grew that something was amiss—something more than the substitution of the wholly inadequate Not Henrietta for the original. There was a strange note in the conversations Amelia had—a certain constraint, explained only when Emily Villiers came to press her hand.

"You look a very angel, Amelia," she declared. Emily was more Henrietta's friend than Amelia's, for she had been a schoolfellow of Henrietta's, but the families had been acquainted for many years.

She fixed a soulful gaze on Amelia. "We will not speak of it tonight—the night of your triumph! I only wished to assure you that your friends will stand by you, whatever comes."

Amelia's heart gave a painful thump in her chest. *Henny!* she thought.

Henrietta must have been exposed—or worse. But Amelia and her sisters had had ample practice in the art of concealing their emotions for the past several months, since Mr. Stapleton had told them about the parlous state of his affairs.

Amelia said, smiling, "You terrify me! It is most kind of you, but I was not aware I was in special need of friendship."

"Oh," said Emily, doubt crossing her countenance. "Perhaps I have misheard." But despite Amelia's suavity, some flicker of unease must have betrayed her, for Emily pressed her hand again. "You may trust I have told everyone there is nothing in the rumours! Where is Henrietta?"

Perhaps Henny had not been exposed for a witch. But what then could have made Miss Villiers look so tender and solicitous?

"Is it true she is to be married?" said Emily in a low voice. "Is there nothing else to be done? How I feel for her!"

Amelia was so overcome with relief that it was necessary for her to exert herself to suppress a broad smile. It would have been a highly unsuitable response, for of course her father's ruin was no matter to smile about. But the threat had been looming over one for so long that one had grown accustomed to it. To be ruined, after all, was a disaster one could imagine—whereas who knew what outlandish things might be happening to Henrietta even now?

Amelia must put Emily off—try to mislead her, for it was clear Emily had heard some rumour of how Mr. Stapleton's affairs stood now. Before she had decided what to say, however, Emily cried out:

"Ah, there she is!" Emily waved. "Henny!"

Across the room stood the chief source of Amelia's disquiet—Henrietta herself, not her unsatisfactory replica. She was accompanied by a native woman, attired in a primrose yellow satin dress Amelia recognised as one of the Sorceress Royal's.

"That must be the foreign sorceress," said Emily. A gleam of professional interest lit her eyes. Miss Villiers had nothing to do with the Sorceress Royal's Academy, as far as anyone knew. But she had known Mrs. Wythe at school, and if Henrietta was any example, in these times there was little that could deter a determined female from the practice of conjuration.

Henrietta seemed wholly unconscious that she might have given Amelia any reason to be discontented with her.

"You look ravishing, 'Melia!" she cried, embracing her. "Porter has outdone herself. Those curls become you wonderfully."

When Henrietta turned to her companion, Amelia noticed a faint rose hue colouring her sister's cheeks. "Muna, this is my sister Amelia. And this is Miss Villiers, whom Mrs. Wythe and I knew at school."

Amelia wished to study her sister's friend, for the native sorceress appeared to be of rather more importance than she had realised. But Miss Villiers pounced on Muna at once. The foreigner was whisked away, leaving behind little more than an impression of melancholy dark eyes.

Amelia took the opportunity to draw her sister aside, whispering:

"Henny, Miss Villiers has told me something extremely alarming."

Henrietta's eyes widened. Amelia said quickly, "She asked if you were to be married. Do you think she might suspect—about Papa, I mean?"

"Why, Henny," said Emily Villiers, breaking off from her interrogation of Muna, "I thought there was only to be *one* foreign sorceress here."

"What do you mean?" said Henrietta.

Amelia looked around to see that another native female had arrived. She looked very much like Muna, for the hue of her skin and the cast of her features were similar, suggesting they were of the same extraction. The new arrival was swathed in a gauzy material that made her look as though she were robed in mist. It was sufficiently opaque to preserve the proprieties, but the effect was nevertheless rather scandalous in a young female. The other guests were looking askance at her when a cry broke from Muna.

"*Adik!*" Muna hurled herself across the room, falling on the stranger's neck.

"Thank goodness!" said Henrietta, glowing with relief. "The spell summoned her sister, after all."

"Her sister?" said Amelia. The foreigners were engaged in a heated conversation, conducted in whispers.

"Muna was parted from her sister when they were—er—travelling in Fairy," said Henrietta. "She cast a spell to recover her, but I was very much afraid that . . . Well! All's well that ends well. I must congratulate them."

This left much to be desired as an explanation.

"Henny," said Amelia, frowning.

But Henrietta must not have heard her, for she was already starting across the room. Amelia followed her, but what with the press of the crowd, she had not reached the other end when the ball was interrupted by an even greater sensation than Mrs. Stapleton could have dreamt of.

SAKTI allowed herself to be embraced, but she seemed amused by her reception.

"There, there!" she said tolerantly. "Were you so worried? You should have known I would always land on my feet!"

Muna drew back, drying her eyes. "You were drowned by a wave of spirits! Is it any wonder I was worried?"

"Well, you may forget worry now," said Sakti. "For I have found us a place to live!"

"What?" said Muna.

"It is a pleasant country in Fairy Without, far from the regions governed by the Queen of the Djinns," said Sakti. "We will be safe from her there, for the people of that country defeated her so roundly in war that she has never ventured to trouble them again.

"You see, I have reflected upon the matter. Of course we had to tell the *naga* Georgiana that I meant to assert my right to rule, or she would not have helped us. And perhaps I *could* defeat the Queen once we recover the Virtu and I am restored to myself, but for what prize? From all I have seen of the Palace of the Unseen, the throne seems an excessively uncomfortable seat. What with you being mortal, *kak*, my enemies would always be seeking to threaten you, so as to frighten me into doing what they wished. It seems to me we would do better to get away from all of that.

"You will like the country I have found," Sakti added. "The climate is far more agreeable than Britain's, and even an improvement on that of Janda Baik, for they have no mosquitoes or leeches. They *are* plagued by a sort of small djinn, not very clever, but the djinns are said to be morbidly sensitive and can be kept off with insults to their appearance."

Her smile faded when she saw Muna's expression. "You don't seem pleased."

"Oh, I am," said Muna unconvincingly. "We will go anywhere you like, but *adik*, you do not know the whole of it. I found the Virtu—the whole article, unbroken—"

"How clever of you!" said Sakti. "Then there is no reason we should not go now." Sakti seized her hand, as though she meant to spirit them away at once.

"Wait!" cried Muna. "I promised my friend I would attend her mother's party. I cannot leave now. Besides—"

Sakti frowned. "*Kak*, need I remind you that you are pursued by the Queen of the Djinns herself? When I left the Palace she was ranting about pursuing Georgiana Without Ruth and her mortal slaves. And if she realises what *I* am, I shudder to think of the consequence!"

"What *we* are," said Muna, not without trepidation.

"I beg your pardon?"

"It is as you said, *adik*," said Muna, watching Sakti's face. "We are both Saktimuna. We were one soul before, but when the Duke broke the Virtu in two, it divided us one from the other. I took the Virtu into myself, and—"

"You took the Virtu into yourself," echoed Sakti. "You mean you ate it?"

At her tone the warmth of their reunion drained from Muna, leaving her cold and uncertain.

"Yes, but—"

"You ate it," repeated Sakti. She looked at Muna as though she could not recognise her. "I could not have believed you would be so selfish!"

"I can explain," said Muna.

But Sakti did not want explanations.

"Have you been jealous of my magic all along?" she said.

"No!" said Muna desperately.

She bethought herself of Rollo's scale and hit herself on the chest, but she knew even as she did it that it would not work this time—she would not be able to disgorge the Virtu. It had been one thing to bring up Threlfall's magic, which had never been her own. The Virtu held her own heart; she would not be able to surrender it so easily.

Muna tried again anyway. She would have done anything to take away the look in Sakti's eyes—the uncomprehending shock of a betrayed child.

But Muna had forgotten her summoning. The enchantment was still unfolding, and now it worked itself out to its conclusion.

Sakti was the first to notice the unrest spreading through the crowd. She turned away to see what was happening as the general chatter subsided.

"Oh no," breathed Muna.

At the entrance to the Stapletons' ballroom stood Saktimuna's sister, brought by the fine ones at Muna's request. The Queen of the Djinns looked around disdainfully, as though she were surprised to find herself in such company.

26

MUNA

THE QUEEN HAD elected to appear in the form of a woman crowned not with hair, but an enormous scarlet bud blossoming out of her head. The bud expanded and contracted with the steady rhythm of a heartbeat. From its core, cradled by fleshy petals, shone a light from which Muna hastily averted her eyes.

"There!" said Sakti, with sour triumph. "Did not I say she would pursue you? You ought to have listened when I told you to come away with me. Now it is too late!"

Muna shook her head, gripped with horror. "She would have found me wherever we went. I called her."

"You *called* her? What can have possessed you to do that?"

"I thought you were dead!" protested Muna. "I thought if I summoned my sister, either you would be restored to me, or—or the Queen would come, and I could at least seek to avenge you. I thought you might like to be avenged."

Sakti was still angry, but her expression softened. "You were prepared to challenge the Queen of the Djinns for my sake? Truly?"

"*Adik*," said Muna wearily, "when have I ever lied to you?"

Before Sakti could answer, the Queen's voice boomed out:

"There she is!"

The Queen was gazing directly at them. She was not alone, for by her side was a spirit rigged out in extravagant European style. Lace ruffles cascaded from his throat, jewels gleamed on the enormous buckles of his shoes, and atop his monstrous wig was perched a crown.

"The King of the Djinns!" whispered Sakti.

"But there are far too many souls about," said the Queen, frowning. "It is most distracting! Would you be so good as to silence them, my love?"

The King flicked his fingers. All noise was abruptly muffled, the guests freezing in place. Muna looked into the face of a nearby Englishman and saw the light from the Queen's head reflected in his dazed eyes. He was enchanted.

"You have taken the Virtu into yourself, I see," said the Queen. Her eyes on Muna were glittering. Potent magic wafted from her. "You should count yourself fortunate I have found you. The Virtu would have poisoned your blood in time. Its magic is far too rich a brew for any mortal to sup."

Muna knew she should run or perform some magic to defend herself and Sakti. But she was fixed in place, all her limbs trembling, for the Serpent had chosen this most inconvenient of times suddenly to rear its head.

Saktimuna's memories flooded her—painful memories, of the time when her heart had been torn from her and she had been banished to the mortal realm. It had been agonising to be deprived of the best part of her soul and magic. But worse than that had been the betrayal—for Saktimuna had loved her sister.

"I ought to have made certain of the Virtu long ago," said the Queen. "Only foolish sentiment held me back. But I shall not make that mistake again. First I shall consume you and the Virtu—and then all of England will know my vengeance!"

Do something! said Muna to herself, but even as the Queen bore down upon them, she was powerless to speak or move, overwhelmed by the Serpent's ancient grief. She shut her eyes.

The Serpent had been defeated once before. She would be defeated again. She, Muna, would die, and so would Sakti, and so would everyone else she knew and loved . . .

A warm hand stole into hers.

"Stupid woman," said Sakti into Muna's ear. "Can you believe she has not realised what we are? If you strike now, *kak*, you will take her by surprise. Do not be afraid!"

Courage flowed into Muna through the hand in hers. She opened her eyes. The Queen was nearly upon them, but Sakti's words had broken Muna's paralysis. Now she was able to reach inside herself, drawing upon the glowing core of Saktimuna's magic inside her.

The magic came awkwardly to her hand. It had been an age since she had last been mistress of such power—she was no longer accustomed to it. But as Muna gathered it up she began to remember what it was to be the Great Serpent.

The words of a long-forgotten spell rose to her lips. Searing light sprang from her hand and she hurled it at the Queen, knocking the fairy off her feet.

"My soul!" cried the Queen's consort, leaping to her side.

The enthralled guests stirred as their trance broke. The Englishman by Muna came awake all at once, stood blinking for a moment, then bolted for the doors.

"Let us go, *kak*," said Sakti.

But Muna shook her head. "I have only stunned her for a

moment." The King was lifting the Queen from the floor. The Queen's power was not quenched, only dimmed, and shortly she would wake, angrier than ever. "Go now, *adik*. Save yourself."

"And what will you do?" demanded Sakti.

Muna could not see Henrietta in the crowd. Perhaps Henrietta had fled, though it was her own house. That would be best, but Henrietta was not the only mortal who would be defenceless against the Queen of the Djinns.

"Perhaps I can draw the Queen away when she wakes," said Muna. "I cannot leave her to vent her rage upon these people."

"Englishmen and women!" Sakti looked around. As the guests emerged from their ensorcellment, they hurried out of the room, jostling Muna and Sakti in their haste to be gone. "I do not see them lingering in danger for *your* sake. You don't think you will be able to defeat the Queen, do you?"

"Not as I am," said Muna. "But it was my spell that called her here. I must see this out."

"You mean you will submit yourself to being devoured," said Sakti, "so she will have the Virtu at last, and her powers will be increased tenfold! Your English friends would not survive for long then. She is already incensed against them, and will blame them for having helped us. I beg you will not make a martyr of yourself, *kak*. You must see it will do no good!"

It was true, and Muna's course lay clear before her. A part of her had known what must be all along, but she had resisted it, dreading the prospect, for she had hoped only to sacrifice herself. Even now, with no alternative open to her, she could only bring herself to speak with difficulty:

"Then there is only one thing to be done, if we are to overcome the Queen."

"Oh yes?" Sakti's lip was already curled, mockery on the tip of her tongue.

"If we were reunited . . ." said Muna. "If we were Saktimuna again . . ."

The mockery faded from Sakti's face. She was silent for a time. "Could it be done?" she said.

With the insight lent her by the Serpent's magic, Muna could see how it would be done. It would be a simple matter, joining two pieces that had been broken apart. "Yes."

Sakti looked as serious as Muna had ever seen her. "If we do it, there would be no you or me any longer. Only *her*."

Muna felt a pang of pity. She had had more time to grow accustomed to the idea, so that it distressed her less. She ought to have faced up to it before, instead of springing it on Sakti now.

"I think she will be a great deal like you," she said, to reassure Sakti. "The *polong* said you were the magical part. I am only the material, and spirits are mostly magic."

Sakti frowned. "If that is true, there will be no you!"

"I don't mind it," lied Muna.

"*I* would!"

The guests had made it plain they found Muna and Sakti very much in the way of their escape, though being preoccupied they did not do more than brush against them pointedly. When Muna felt a hand on her elbow, she ignored it, till a familiar voice whispered:

"Muna, you must go!"

Muna jumped. Henrietta said urgently, "The Queen is stirring even now. She will be furious when she realises you are still here. Take your sister and flee!"

Across the ballroom the Queen was blinking in the King's arms, a faint light starting to filter from her head.

"*You* should flee," said Muna to Henrietta. "There is no need for you to be concerned on my behalf. I have the Virtu. What could the Queen do to me?"

"Don't be stupid," said Henrietta passionately. "Recall that Saktimuna had her heart when the Queen cast her out of Fairy!"

"Hear her!" said Sakti.

Muna touched Henrietta on the shoulder, meaning to send her away. But to her surprise her magic encountered resistance.

"This is my house," said Henrietta. "You cannot think I will abandon it!"

Still, Henrietta could not fend off the Serpent's magic for long. Given another minute Muna's spell would have caught, but they were not spared another minute. The Queen rose, shaking off her consort impatiently.

"Go, go!" said Muna, shoving Henrietta, but the Queen came towards them, snarling imprecations in Elfish. Henrietta was closest to her and the Queen reached out to seize her—but before the Queen could touch her, a ball of flame exploded beneath her hands.

The Queen fell back with a cry. Mr. Stapleton stepped between her and Henrietta, lowering his wand.

"I regret I must ask you to leave, madam," he said. He was wholly pale, his wand trembling in his hand, but his voice was steady. "You are incommoding the other guests."

He turned to his daughter. "Run along, Henny. Look for your mother and sisters."

"Papa—"

"You will not contradict my orders now," said Mr. Stapleton, raising his voice. "You are the only one who has magic, and I depend upon you to protect the family. You may set me at defiance at any other time, Henrietta—but on this one occasion you will do your duty, if you please!"

Henrietta's eyes filled with tears. She made an abortive move towards him, but then she choked out, "Yes!" Drawing her sleeve across her eyes, she darted off.

The Queen glared down at Mr. Stapleton in much the same manner as she might have looked down upon an insect that had dared to cheek her. "Who are you?"

Mr. Stapleton squared his shoulders, raising his wand. "I am the master of this house, and while I live you shall do no harm to anybody under this roof!"

"That is not to say much," said the Queen carelessly. "Mortals live for hardly any time at all."

Muna was glad Henrietta had obeyed her father, for it meant she was saved the sight of what happened next. The Queen waved her hand as though she were dusting away a mite, and Mr. Stapleton went flying. He hit the wall and slid down to the floor, where he lay unmoving.

When the Queen turned back to Muna and Sakti, there was a new sharpness in her gaze. An unpleasant smile spread across her face.

"I must have been blind, or distracted," she said. "I thought you were a mortal who had stolen the Virtu. But I see I was mistaken. I did not think to find *you* here, sister! It has all fallen out very well, I declare. I shall finish what I left undone all those years ago!"

Muna ignored her, meeting Sakti's eyes.

"Not against your will," said Muna.

Sakti looked grim. "It is not as though we have a choice. Will it hurt?"

"No," said Muna. The Serpent stirred within her, eager. "Give me your hands."

Sakti's palms were damp with perspiration, for she was afraid. Muna smiled at her for the last time, until Sakti gave her a tentative smile back.

To mend the break was simple, as natural as water flowing downhill, or a sapling reaching towards the sun. It hardly felt like magic at all. Muna drew Sakti towards herself and they ran together like drops of rain on a pane of glass.

H ENRIETTA opened the door to the nursery, confronting a red-faced fury waving a chair.

"Stay back!" it cried.

"Amelia," said Henrietta, "is my mother here? And my sisters?"

Amelia paused with the chair held aloft. Then she dropped it and flung herself on Henrietta's neck. Mrs. Stapleton, Louisa and Charlotte crowded around, scolding and questioning.

Henrietta had arrived at the scene of a lively disagreement. The first thing Amelia said when she could make herself understood through her tears was:

"Tell my mother she is not to go downstairs, Henny!"

"Oh, certainly!" said Henrietta, disentangling herself from her sister's embrace.

At the sight of everyone's tearful faces, she put aside her anxiety about her father and Muna. It was clear that a calm head was needed. "It is your duty to stay here with the girls, Mamma. There can be no question of your exposing yourself to danger."

Mrs. Stapleton protested, "But your poor father . . ."

"You need not fear for my father. I shall join him again directly, now that I know you are safe." Henrietta glanced back at the door. It was a good sturdy barrier, with wards woven into the very grain of the wood, that would repel even a fairy that sought to enter.

"I shall strengthen the wards," she decided, "and you must not let anyone in. Papa or I will come and let you out when it is all over."

"You don't mean to go down again?" shrieked Mrs. Stapleton. Her intention to share in her husband's fate was forgotten. She seized Henrietta's sleeve, insisting that Henrietta should remain in the nursery.

"But I am the only other Stapleton that has any magic," Henrietta said. "You will not let Papa stand against the Fairy Queen by himself?"

"What of the other gentlemen? I am sure we invited two dozen thaumaturges, at least!"

"They have run away. Papa is all alone."

"Mr. Hobday as well?" Mrs. Stapleton faltered out.

The last Henrietta had seen of her betrothed that evening had been his retreating back. "Mr. Hobday has taken his leave as well."

This could not but sway Henrietta's mother. Still she continued her remonstrances, though it was unclear whether these were intended for Henrietta, or for an uncaring Fate. "But your Papa is a gentleman and a thaumaturge, and you are so young! I do not doubt you are very clever, Henny, but you are not the Sorceress Royal. A year or two at her Academy is not the same as having two familiars. Besides, Mrs. Wythe is an orphan, who need only account for herself. You have your family to think of!"

Henrietta froze. But this was not to be the last of the surprises reserved for her.

Charlotte said, wide-eyed, "Mamma! Did *you* know Henny has been teaching at the Sorceress Royal's Academy?"

"It is one thing to teach, but quite another to meet the Fairy Queen in battle," said Mrs. Stapleton. "I should never have allowed you to remain at the Academy if I knew this was to be the end of it!"

"Mamma, you knew . . . ?" gasped Henrietta. She turned to her sisters. Guilt was written across all three of their faces. "You all knew!"

"A mother that does not know what is in her child's heart without being told is not worthy of the name," said Mrs. Stapleton. Despite her distress, being able finally to speak of Henrietta's secret life was plainly a relief to Mrs. Stapleton. With the air of one unburdening herself, she went on, "And that creature you conjured to take your place, Henny—I don't say she was disagreeable, for she was civil and obliging enough, but her understanding was not equal to yours! We could not be deceived for long."

"You mean my simulacrum," said Henrietta, feeling foolish. She had thought it such a clever shift!

"Not Henrietta is not in the least like you," agreed Louisa. "I wish you would dispense with her. I am sure we could manage without."

"If you knew all along, why did not you say anything?" said Henrietta helplessly.

"*I* said we should," said Charlotte. "But Amelia and Louisa would not allow it!"

"I have always believed a mother should not force confidences from her children," said Mrs. Stapleton.

"You meant it to be a secret," said Amelia with unwonted shyness. "We thought if you wished us to know, you would have told us. We hoped in time you would trust us with the truth."

"I never mistrusted you," said Henrietta, but there seemed to be something stuck in her throat, and her voice emerged faint and wavering. She swallowed. "It is only that . . . I thought you would mind my being a *magicienne*."

"But you have always been magical," said Charlotte, a little puzzled.

"You are our own Henny," said Mrs. Stapleton. "How could we mind anything that you were?" She caught Henrietta's hands in her own. "We shall tell each other all that is in our hearts, and forgive each other for the secrets we have kept!"

"Yes." But even as Henrietta kissed her mother, she freed her hands from Mrs. Stapleton's clasp. "So we shall—another time, Mamma."

"Henny, I forbid you to go!"

"I must, Mamma."

Mrs. Stapleton made a final attempt. "Your father would wish you to remain!"

"Then this is the last time I shall disobey his wishes, or yours," said Henrietta. She wiped the tears from her eyes and left, barring the door behind her.

27

THE TRUE QUEEN

SAKTIMUNA CAME TO herself in a strange place. She was no longer in the familiar warm waters in which she had slept for so many years. The air was dry on her scales.

When she raised herself to look around, she knocked her head against a ceiling. Recoiling, she broke a chandelier. Shards of crystal showered down around her.

Saktimuna lowered her head, hissing, and caught sight of herself in a glass. Scarlet eyes with black vertical slits of pupils gazed back at her. They were set in an elegant spade-shaped head, covered with shining scales of a deep blue-green, the same shade as the sea where it was deepest.

The sight surprised her.

"We are not quite gone yet," she said aloud. "It is not so bad!"

But after a moment she could not remember why she said this, or to whom it was addressed.

The puzzle did not detain her for long, for now she noticed the only other soul in the room worthy of her attention. For many years Saktimuna had longed to meet her again—had dreamt, as she lay half-slumbering beneath the waves, of setting her teeth in that very neck.

"Sister!" she hissed.

The Queen of the Djinns recoiled. The scent of terror rose from her. She stammered, "It is you! What a cheap trick, to hide from me!"

But then she drew herself up, drawing on bravado like a cloak.

"You need not think you will frighten me," said the Queen. "I bested you before, when I was little more than an elvet. Now I have ruled over Fairy Within for centuries. Dragons do obeisance to me. Mortals shrivel to dust at my approach! Do you think *you* pose any challenge?"

Saktimuna said in wonder, "You have not altered in the least."

Her sister had always been given to showing away, flaunting her powers and demanding the admiration of her friends. Saktimuna had loved her all the more for her frailty, knowing it had its source in her sister's want of confidence—for their parents had not been kind to those of their children they did not favour.

But love had turned to bitterness long ago.

"It has been so long," said Saktimuna. The Queen stumbled back as Saktimuna slithered towards her. The floor was cluttered with mortals and furniture, but these were no obstacle to the Serpent. She glided over them, scarcely noticing the mortals' cries. "I should have thought you would have learnt better by now."

"How dare you speak to me so?" cried the Queen. "I am the Queen of the Unseen Realms!"

She blasted Saktimuna with a curse, but the Serpent knocked it away. Diverted, the magic showered over the mortals scattered about the room—but they had no cause for complaint, for those that still lived died quickly.

"Not for much longer," said Saktimuna. She struck.

But Saktimuna's sister was still capable of surprising her. Even as she lunged, the Queen vanished. In her place was a small brown mouse, which shot across the floor.

The Serpent darted after the mouse, knocking over tables and chairs, rolling over inconsequential bodies. The mouse scuttled into an inconspicuous gap in the wall, and Saktimuna's jaws closed on air.

Furious, she butted her head against the wall. The house trembled around her.

She would bring it down if necessary. Her sister could not hope to evade her for long.

"Papa?" chirped a small voice.

It was a yellow-haired mortal who spoke. Saktimuna glanced at her without interest before returning to her task. She could hear the mouse scurrying behind the wall, pursued by Saktimuna's magic but just outpacing it. If it would only stop for a moment, she would have it.

"Try something smaller, my love!" cried the Fairy King. Saktimuna had not seen him before, for he was crouched behind an overturned bureau. "A wood-louse, perhaps. She will not soon find a wood-louse!"

The Queen's consort would have been wiser to stay silent. It struck Saktimuna that perhaps what she needed was more magic. The best means she knew of gaining more magic was by taking it from others.

The Serpent's head swung around, her tongue flickering out.

"Do not you dare—!" cried the Fairy King.

It was the last thing he ever said. Saktimuna's head darted out. She caught the Fairy King between her jaws, lifted him in the air and swallowed him down in three gulps.

"Good heavens!" cried the yellow-haired mortal.

H ENRIETTA clapped her hand over her mouth, kicking herself.

But she was too late. The Serpent turned, fixing gleaming

reptilian eyes on her. There was not the smallest spark of recognition in their ruby depths.

Henrietta could scarcely believe the destruction the Serpent had wrought during her absence. Bodies were strewn upon the floor—men and women she had known all her life, some of whom would never rise again. Towards the other end of the room lay her father, slumped against the wall. Henrietta could not tell if he was dead or alive.

The air seemed as thick as treacle. Her limbs were heavy with fear, but she forced herself to walk towards the Serpent, clenching her fists to still their trembling.

This was Saktimuna, then—the Fairy Queen's sister whose stolen heart, locked in the Virtu, had caused so much trouble. And somewhere inside the Serpent was Henrietta's friend.

Muna would not have wanted to be this great murderous monstress, with beautiful, pitiless eyes. Perhaps she was lost forever; perhaps there was nothing Henrietta could do to bring her back. But Henrietta had to try.

"Muna," said Henrietta. The name came out on a voiceless croak. She cleared her throat. "Muna!"

IT had been such an age since Saktimuna had last savoured fairy ichor that she had nearly forgotten its effect. It bubbled through her veins like champagne, granting exhilaration, forgetfulness of self—and a glorious infusion of power. To extract her faithless sister from her hiding place would require only a flick of the tip of her tail.

The mortal's voice was an unwelcome intrusion into a brilliantly coloured world. Yet it would not be ignored. It persisted, as monotonous as the screeching of cicadas in the evening, repeating, "Muna, Muna!"

Saktimuna could silence the voice, but she had no wish to dilute the taste of fairy ichor with mortal blood. She gave a warning hiss, but it did not deter the mortal. Instead, a small cold hand touched her scales.

"Muna!" cried the little voice again. "These people have nothing to do with your quarrel. They don't deserve that they should suffer for the wrongs done to you."

It was most irritating. Now that Saktimuna looked at the mortal, she could see that a faint light of magic flickered within its frame. It would not be wholly unprofitable to devour it. She would get the matter over with quickly. Then she could deal with her treacherous sister at her leisure.

Saktimuna dived, but to her astonishment a stinging hex exploded in her face. She reared back, hissing.

For a moment Henrietta gaped, stunned by the success of her feint. The spell she had employed was a mere childish cantrip, of the sort Mrs. Daubeney's young gentlewitches used to hurl at one another when they quarrelled, but it had one advantage she had not calculated on—its novelty. The cantrip was designed to give its target an itch. Evidently Saktimuna had never had an itch in her life, and she did not relish the experience.

The Serpent threw herself into outraged coils, neglectful of the people and furniture she crushed beneath her bulk. Henrietta turned and ran.

"Jade!" howled Saktimuna. "Impudent hussy! You will regret what you have done!"

Henrietta stumbled over a toppled chair, landing heavily on her wrist. The pain startled a cry out of her.

The interruption to her flight was fatal. When she rolled onto her back, she looked up into the Serpent's glowing red gaze. There was no hope of getting away.

Henrietta shut her eyes.

Because her eyes were closed, Henrietta did not see the brown ball of fur flash across the floor, as the mouse that had been the Fairy Queen chose that moment to make its reappearance. It transformed as it went, till finally the Queen straightened to her full height, her disguise thrown off.

"Ah!" said Saktimuna. "I am pleased you have decided to join us again, sister."

Henrietta's eyes snapped open. The Fairy Queen stood before Saktimuna in the form in which she had first appeared that evening— a woman beautiful and strange, more than mortal. Light beamed forth from the bud on her head, setting at defiance the dark shadow of the Serpent looming over her. The Queen raised her hands.

"I have been too kind," she said. "I should never have allowed you to live. I have not had a moment's peace since I ousted you. But let us make an end of this now!"

But even as the Queen spoke, Henrietta felt magic flood the room, like waters breaking through a dam—fairy magic, potent with centuries of stored-up spite. It was so strong that Henrietta could scarcely endure it. Her head throbbed, her vision blurring. Her hands flew to her temples, pressing down to still their aching.

The Queen paused, blanching. Her eyes widened as she started to choke.

"You have forgotten that we learnt all the same cantions at our mothers' knees," said Saktimuna.

This is the Serpent's magic, thought Henrietta, dazed. It was Saktimuna's hex that filled the room with this overwhelming pressure, stealing the Queen's breath and making her sway. This was the power that had lain in the Virtu all along. Little wonder the Queen had been so afraid when the Virtu was lost.

The Fairy Queen, who had once seemed so invincible, put her hands to her throat. Her face turned olive green, the veins standing out upon it. "You—" she gasped. "You—"

"Do not be afraid, sister," said Saktimuna tenderly. "Henceforth you shall have peace."

Saktimuna's graceful head plunged down. She plucked the Queen's head off, quenching its light, as delicately as one might nip a flower off a stem.

The Queen's headless body crumpled to the ground. Henrietta buried a scream in her hands.

This time it was the Queen's magic that roared through the room. Unlike the Serpent's magic, it was not harnessed to a directing will, nor aimed at a single target, and it spread out, altering the nature of everything it touched. The dead bodies on the floor shrank, so that they looked like broken dolls, their limbs splayed. The shadows on the walls came alive, hooting and revelling in the Queen's death. The few pieces of furniture that had not been destroyed scampered away—Henrietta saw a table, much prized by her mother, rush past on slender deer's legs.

Saktimuna was occupied with devouring the Queen's remains. Henrietta averted her eyes, but she could not shut her ears to the sound of the Serpent swallowing her prey. She rose, grasping at the nearest object to steady herself.

This happened to be a chaise longue, which was creeping slowly but with determination along the wall, though it was much the worse for wear. The splintered wood pierced Henrietta's palm. She snatched her hand away, yelping, but the twinge of pain was almost a relief, for it was real, no fever-dream brought on by magic.

The Serpent raised her head at Henrietta's cry. The ruby red eyes looked directly at Henrietta.

"Muna," said Henrietta, without hope. She limped backwards, step by tottering step, but her foot caught in the side of a warm body. She did not know whose it was, or whether they were dead or alive; she did not dare break Saktimuna's gaze to look.

There was nothing of Muna in those reptilian eyes. Hatred of the creature that had consumed her friend rose in Henrietta's throat. If only she had the right words—a formula that would reverse time and restore Muna to herself.

"Muna," she said, "come back."

Her voice fell thin and unconvincing on the air. She knew Muna was gone, absorbed by the Serpent.

I am pleading with a ghost, thought Henrietta.

Still she squared her shoulders, raising her head. She had shut her eyes earlier in fright, but now she was prepared, and she would meet her end with courage.

IN addressing Muna, Henrietta was seeking to raise a ghost. But in the Unseen Realm there is less of a distinction between the living and the dead than mortals tend to draw. After all, both fairies and ghosts are constituted more of spirit than of flesh.

The ghosts of Saktimuna's other selves still had a form of existence in her mind, for among spiritkind, to be named is to be. Even a shard of a name like "Muna" had its own power—and every time Henrietta uttered it, what was left of Muna stirred.

There was not much left of her. But what there was, was deeply concerned that Henrietta should live.

Even as Saktimuna had pursued the Queen, a very small part of the Serpent's mind, unbeknownst to the rest, was considering the possibility of dividing herself again. It seemed to the ghost that had been Muna that it would be possible for Saktimuna to split her own heart in two—to cleave herself into separate halves—so that each half would have the independent life it had enjoyed before. Though the ghost could not quite remember why, it felt this an outcome much to be desired.

But it must proceed with caution. The thing would have to be done with care if Saktimuna were not to break apart altogether, her spirit dissipating abroad.

The ghost held itself in readiness, watching for its moment. Saktimuna's mind was as busy and confused as most minds are. Most of her conscious thought was focused on her prey, and it was possible for even such a self-destructive impulse as the ghost harboured to remain unobserved amid the noise.

When Saktimuna sprang on the Fairy Queen, taking the Queen's power into herself, the ghost saw its chance. This was the time. With the influx of the Queen's magic, she could tear herself in two now and be tolerably certain each part would survive.

While the Serpent's conscious mind cast around for a new victim, the ghost fumbled for a weakness, a crack it could pry open.

It was not difficult to find the fault. After all, Saktimuna had been rent asunder before. This time she did it herself; the split was clean and it would last.

28

MUNA

MUNA CAME TO herself slowly.

She lay in a bed with clean-smelling sheets. A soothing repetitive noise filled her ears, like the sound of waves crashing against the shore. It took her a moment to realise it was snoring.

She touched her nose, wondering, and saw that her hands were a mortal's hands: brown-skinned and short-fingered, with squarish palms and pale half-moons of fingernails. Through the gaps between her fingers she caught sight of a figure—an old woman, dozing in a chair by the bed. The snoring came from her.

Muna sat bolt upright, electrified. "Mak Genggang!"

The witch stirred, snorting. "Eh? Are you awake, then?"

Memory rushed in upon Muna: the absorption of herself and Sakti into the Serpent, Saktimuna's rampage, Henrietta's intervention, and the final breach. She gasped, "Henrietta—how is she? Is she safe?"

Mak Genggang leant over her, her expression inscrutable. "I should have thought you would have asked after your sister first of all. She was always your chief concern before."

Muna blinked. "But I know what became of my sister. I devoured her."

Then she realised what Mak Genggang meant.

"Oh!" she said. "But Sakti is well, isn't she?" Sakti's flesh might have been divided from hers, but they were one soul still. This time the link between their minds had not been severed, so that Muna knew Sakti to be on the other side of the wall—intact, untroubled and fast asleep.

"But Henrietta is a mortal," said Muna. "And I was trying to *eat* her!"

"Well, you did not succeed, if that is what you fear," said Mak Genggang. "Saktimuna devoured no mortals. It seems she was on the verge of doing it, but according to Miss Stapleton, the Serpent was suddenly taken ill. She disappeared, leaving the two of you in her place."

That, Muna remembered. "And Miss Stapleton? You have spoken with her?"

Mak Genggang nodded. "She is unharmed."

Relieved of her anxiety, Muna settled back in bed and gazed at Mak Genggang. There was no trace of fear or awe in the witch's countenance. She looked back, frowning slightly, just as she would have looked at the mortal girl Muna had once been.

A great calm happiness bubbled up inside Muna.

"We are in England still?" she said in wonder. "When did you come, *mak cik*?"

"I arrived this morning," said Mak Genggang. "I should have come sooner, for Prunella asked for me when they could not wake you. But the Unseen is in a state of considerable disorder and I was delayed. You should have summoned me earlier, child. Surely you knew I would not withhold my help."

"I did not know how," said Muna. Her brow furrowed. "You have left Janda Baik undefended?"

Mak Genggang waved her hand dismissively. "Oh, the British will not dare touch us while I am in London at the invitation of their Sorceress Royal. What is more, I am attending upon the True Queens of the Unseen Realm. Tuan Farquhar may know little of the Unseen but he knows enough to fear the name of its rulers!"

"The True Queens?"

"That is your title now," said Mak Genggang. "Yours and that wilful child Sakti's. Devouring the incumbent is the traditional means by which the throne of the Unseen passes to its heir. Your usurper—she that was Queen before—consumed your six parents in order to gain the throne, after she had exiled you. And now you have consumed her."

It was only now that Muna became aware of the magic surging in her veins—not only Saktimuna's magic, but also that of the former Fairy Queen and her King, whom the Serpent had consumed in her wrath. The power coursed hot under her skin. She must fairly glow with magic to anyone who had the eyes to see it.

That was what the witch had come for, of course—the magic that had protected Janda Baik. Muna did not blame her. Mak Genggang's presence brought with it a vision of the island, extraordinarily vivid—its rich earth under the omnipresent sun, and the palms that fringed the shore. Suddenly she was overcome by the homesickness that had never really left her since she had set off down Mak Genggang's path through the Unseen. A wonderful idea came to her.

"I could come back to Janda Baik," said Muna. "Stand guard over it, as I did before."

Mak Genggang did not respond as she expected. The old woman only looked thoughtful.

"It is not that we would not be grateful for your protection," she said. "You know how we are placed. Without the magic you lent us for so many years, we shall be sadly exposed."

Muna met her eyes. "But . . ."

"But you cannot come back," said the witch. "And you know it." She was not unkind, but her tone was unyielding.

Muna had not expected the blow. Her happiness dissolved at once.

"You could not stop me," she said, gulping down her hurt.

"Who would govern the Unseen Realm?" said Mak Genggang. "You have not seen what I saw on my journey here."

Muna could imagine the chaos that reigned in the Hidden World following the abrupt removal of its monarch. Conspiracies, struggles for power, wars . . . the very idea wearied her. She would not have minded it as the Serpent who had been thrown out of Fairy. *Then*, the incessant intrigues of the Palace of the Unseen had been all she had known. But she had since spent centuries in cleaner waters.

"Sakti could be Queen," said Muna. "It would not worry *her*. She does not mind power—indeed, she likes it."

"And that means she will be just and merciful?" said Mak Genggang. "She will seek to resolve difficulties with patience, taking the winding path where it leads true, disregarding easier courses where she would come to grief? She will extend shelter to the weakest of her subjects—correct the wrongs your sister wrought?"

Muna was silent. She was remembering the imps imprisoned in the lamps in the caverns beneath the Palace of the Unseen, and the offhanded manner in which Sakti had said, *Sometimes they weep.*

"Sakti is not all bad," said Muna.

"No. But all that is in her is spirit and magic and love of self," said Mak Genggang. "The True Queen will need more than that if she is to put the Unseen Realm to rights."

"But why must I put the Unseen to rights?" Muna protested, even as the weight of the responsibility settled upon her shoulders. "*I* did not spoil it."

"Why ask such a question when you know the answer?" said Mak Genggang. "You know the rule that governs all magic. Nothing can be taken that is not paid for. Perhaps you might have evaded your duties if you had stopped at recovering the Virtu, but you could not consume the powers of your sister and her consort without incurring a debt. You owe that debt to your subjects—to the kingdom you have inherited."

Muna bowed her head, looking at her hands on the bed sheets. They were the old Muna's hands, but she herself was no longer the old Muna, bound to no one save Sakti.

For a time they were silent—as much as Mak Genggang had to say, she was practised, too, in silence, as all witches must be. It was Muna who broke it.

"Will you teach us?" she said.

Mak Genggang looked startled. "Teach you? Your Majesty knows a great deal more magic than I do now."

"I beg you will not call me that," said Muna, disturbed. "'Child' will do perfectly well. But I meant, will you teach us how to rule? Sakti and I are not quite the same as Saktimuna—and even she never learnt how to be a raja."

It was the first thing she had said that surprised the witch.

"Very well," said Mak Genggang, after a pause. "I will teach you what I can."

She rose, putting the back of her hand against Muna's forehead. "But now it is time for you to rise. You seem to have suffered little harm from your adventures. Will you take a meal? You will not need mortal sustenance anymore, but it will reassure your English friends to see you. Your Miss Stapleton has been wild with worry on your behalf. She would be here all day if her family could spare her."

Warmth rose in Muna's cheeks.

"She is not *my* Miss Stapleton," she began to say, before she realised how absurd it would sound to protest, as though she thought Mak Genggang was implying more than she could mean. She swallowed her words.

"I will come," she said instead.

Muna had indeed never felt healthier. She was wholly refreshed, full of vigour, and ready to spring out of bed. She sat up, and for the first time noticed something odd. She threw off the sheets and gaped down at herself.

"Did not you know?" said Mak Genggang.

"No!" said Muna faintly.

Stretched out on the bed, instead of her own ordinary legs, was a serpent's tail, covered in shining blue-green scales—evidence, if any were yet needed, that the girl Muna was gone forever.

29

One month later
The Lady Maria Wythe Academy for the Instruction
of Females in Practical Thaumaturgy, England

PRUNELLA

RUNELLA WAS GREAT with news as she clattered up the stairs. She took no notice of Damerell when she passed him in the corridor, though he started and blushed—a most unusual thing for Damerell to do. All Prunella thought of was finding Henrietta, for when one has received astonishing news, there is nothing more satisfying than imparting it to another for whom it has the same significance. On this occasion, no one but Henrietta would do.

"Henny, you will never credit what I have heard," cried Prunella, bursting into the sitting room.

It was a neat, pretty apartment, reserved for the use of the Academy's instructresses. Only Henrietta was there now, writing a letter. She started, dropping her pen. A look of guilt crossed her countenance.

"Oh, Prunella!" she said. "I thought you were receiving Georgiana Without Ruth."

"So I did," said Prunella. "She has just left."

"All is in order? The arrangements with Threlfall, I mean?"

"Oh yes," said Prunella. "She has agreed to dedicate a cavern for our use."

Left to herself, Prunella would not have required any reward for her intervention with the True Queens of Fairyland that had ensured that the magic stolen by their predecessor was restored to Georgiana Without Ruth. ("It can do us no harm to have Threlfall in our debt," Prunella had said.)

But Georgiana was punctilious about the debts she incurred. She had invited the Sorceress Royal to establish a wing of her Academy in Threlfall, where Englishwomen could study thaumaturgy in peace, untroubled by the oppressive concern of their fathers and brothers.

"Of course, the cavern has been furnished in the draconic style," said Prunella. "It is rather bare and draughty, but Zacharias has consulted with our scholars, and they have some clever ideas for how it may be adapted for their comfort. Miss Campbell has been particularly ingenious."

It was not the draughts that worried Henrietta.

"It is most kind of Georgiana to offer the use of her family's ancestral lands," she said. "But are you quite sure the scholars will be safe, set down among dragons? I say nothing against Mr. Threlfall"—Henrietta coloured as she said the name—"but he would be the first to agree that not all his relations are like him!"

"No," agreed Prunella. "Georgiana has guaranteed her family's good behaviour, but all the same I believe Rollo has some very reprobate uncles. I am sure they will not strain themselves to curb their appetites, if the opportunity to indulge them presents itself. But it will do the scholars good to learn to fend off hungry dragons. Magic is a dangerous business; we shall do our girls no favours by coddling them!"

Henrietta was not altogether convinced. Seeing this, Prunella said, "I do not think Threlfall more dangerous than England for a *magicienne*. At least dragons are not more likely to devour a female magician than a male. Whereas the conduct of our English thaumaturges has scarcely been such as to inspire much confidence!"

"They are not all beyond hope," said Henrietta softly. "We have seen that some are capable of reform."

Prunella tossed her head. "I shall believe that when your papa relaxes his restrictions on you! How does he expect you to do all you must with only three hours a day to devote to magic?"

"Papa only desires that I should not neglect my other duties in the pursuit of magic. He is quite right. I am a daughter and a sister, as well as a *magicienne*."

"Hmph!" said Prunella, who could never be brought to agree that Henrietta's family might be reasonable in desiring some measure of her society. "But you have not heard my news, Henny. It will make you stare!"

"Do tell," said Henrietta, dutifully preparing herself to be amazed.

"You know Mr. Midsomer told us Clarissa had gone to visit her relations on the Continent."

There had been some discussion of whether it was desirable for Miss Midsomer to continue at the Academy, after all that had passed. Prunella had seen no reason to dismiss her: "I should much rather have her under my eye than leave her to make mischief elsewhere."

As it happened, however, Miss Midsomer had withdrawn from the Academy herself. It was her father who had conveyed the message to Prunella. Clarissa's interest in thaumaturgy had only extended to how it might be employed to enable her brother's return from Fairy, he said. Since that plan had failed, she had no wish to have anything more to do with the unwomanly practice of magic.

"Yes?" said Henrietta now.

"It was a falsehood," said Prunella triumphantly. "Clarissa is not on the Continent. She has gone away, but you will never guess where she went!"

Henrietta was distracted, or she would have had too much tact to say, "Is she in Fairy?"

Prunella looked crestfallen. "How did you know?"

"Oh, it was only a guess," said Henrietta, collecting herself. "It is not really true? How extraordinary!"

But Prunella was not to be taken in. "I hardly need to tell you whom she went with, I suppose! You will have guessed she has eloped with the Duke of the Navel of the Seas."

Here Henrietta was able to recover for some ground, for her astonishment was unfeigned. She peppered Prunella with questions. How had Prunella heard the news? Were they really married? The Duke must have been sincerely attached to Clarissa after all, though everyone had supposed him only interested in the Virtu.

"It seems he did begin to court Clarissa because of the Virtu, but grew attached to her on her own account," said Prunella, mollified. "Georgiana told me all. It has occasioned a great deal of talk in Fairy. The Duke and Clarissa mean to settle in Fairy Without, beyond the reach of the Court, for of course the Duke has scarcely endeared himself to the True Queens."

"No," said Henrietta. "I suppose not."

The reference to the Fairy Court seemed to make her thoughtful. She went to the window, standing there, irresolute, before seating herself on a sofa.

She said, without lifting her eyes, "As a matter of fact I have news, too, Prunella. I meant to tell my father and mother first of all, but since you are here . . . You must have seen Mr. Damerell on his way out."

"Oh yes," said Prunella, though she had already forgot the encounter. "Did you speak about the lessons he is to give the scholars in necromancy?"

"No," said Henrietta. She pleated her skirts with nervous hands, refusing to meet Prunella's eyes.

Prunella said, with growing suspicion, "Why are you so pink, Henny?"

"As a matter of fact, I asked Mr. Damerell to come so we might speak of a—a personal matter," said Henrietta, adding in a rush, "He has been so good as to agree to marry me."

It would be an understatement to describe the Sorceress Royal as thunderstruck. Henrietta had never seen her friend at such a loss for words.

"You do not disapprove?" said Henrietta, worried.

Prunella opened her mouth, then closed it. She had yet to recover the power of speech when they heard the tap at the window.

When they looked towards it, they saw nothing but the green patch of garden that belonged to the Academy. After a moment, however, the glass rippled and grew dark. The small figure of a woman appeared in the glass, wreathed in red smoke.

Henrietta recognised the spirit at once. She rose, steadying herself against the back of the sofa. The colour was high in her cheeks.

"I bear a message from the True Queen of the Hidden Worlds for Miss Henrietta Stapleton," announced the *polong*. "Is Miss Stapleton at leisure to receive her?"

Henrietta's flush had faded as quickly as it had come. She was pale, but she said steadily enough, "Yes. Yes, I should be delighted."

"Which of the True Queens do you mean?" demanded Prunella, but the *polong* had already vanished. She turned to Henrietta in perplexity, but Henrietta said, with uncharacteristic shortness: "It is plain which one it must be. What reason would the other have to visit us?"

Prunella stared, for this was most unlike Henrietta, but before she could remark upon it, the True Queen herself appeared at the window.

Muna scrambled through the glass as though it were not there. She looked startled at the sight of the Sorceress Royal.

"I beg your pardon," she said. "The *polong* did not say Miss Stapleton had company. I would not have interrupted if I had known."

Henrietta had regained all her colour and seemed to have difficulty making any coherent reply. As she stuttered, Prunella stepped in, saying all that was proper: there was no need for apologies; it was always an honour to receive Her Majesty.

Muna nodded, but her eyes were on Henrietta. "May I speak to Miss Stapleton alone?"

MUNA was dressed in what had been her accustomed style since her ascension to the Fairy throne, with her shoulders bare above a bright *batik* sarong wrapped around her person. Out of the sarong emerged a serpent's tail, in which blues and greens shifted beneath the light. Stars gleamed in her cloudlike hair, and a soft light shone about her hands.

But her eyes had the same look they had had before—straightforward and a little worried. She had not altered in any important respect.

"You must be cold," said Henrietta. She reached for her shawl, anxious to be hospitable. She must be natural, for what reason was there to feel awkward at the visit of a friend? "Pray allow me . . ."

"There is no need, thank you," said Muna. "I do not feel the cold as I did before."

Henrietta felt foolish. "Of course not. Have you been well?"

Muna said, at the same time, "Have you been well?"

They were briefly mired in the exchange of apologies, but when they contrived to extract themselves from this, Henrietta said she expected that Muna had been monstrously busy. Muna confirmed that that was so.

"I could not get away before," said Muna. "But Sakti has promised to watch over the negotiations between the crocodile spirits and the weretigers—we have hopes that they will soon arrive at a truce—so I took the opportunity to come. I am afraid I ought to have given you more notice. I did not mean to interrupt." A faint blush tinted her cheeks. "I assure you I overheard nothing."

"Oh, I never would have suspected—in any case it was nothing I would not tell you," said Henrietta, flustered. It seemed of the utmost importance that she should not withhold the news, in fact; there was no knowing when she would have a chance to speak with Muna again. She blurted out, "The fact is—I am to be married!"

She could not bring herself to look at Muna as she spoke, but she raised her eyes the moment the words were out, scarcely knowing what she hoped to see.

Muna did not so much as bat an eyelash, to Henrietta's disappointment (*Why should you be disappointed?* Henrietta demanded of herself).

"What happy news!" said Muna, quite as though the intelligence made no difference to her at all. "I wish you joy."

But then she paused, looking far from joyful. Henrietta's heart leapt.

"Mr. Hobday is reconciled to your pursuit of magic, then?" Muna said. "I am glad of that!"

"No," said Henrietta. "Mr. Hobday has no desire to take a thaumaturgess for a wife—and I have no more wish to marry him than I ever had. I am engaged to Mr. Damerell."

This, at least, elicited a satisfying response. Muna's jaw dropped, all pretence of composure abandoned—for to Henrietta's great relief, she saw that it *had* been a mere pretence.

"*Mr. Damerell?*" said Muna. "But don't you—doesn't he—doesn't Mr. Threlfall . . . ?"

"It is surprising, I know," said Henrietta. She could not help but derive encouragement from Muna's discomfiture. It made it easier to explain what she had done and why.

"You see," said Henrietta, "since our adventure in Threlfall, Mr. Damerell has been saying how very much obliged he is for my efforts—*our* efforts—to rescue him. I put him off at first, but he would not give over. He insisted he must discharge his debt, as he called it, and I came to realise I would do him no favours in maintaining there was no debt. The laws of Fairy are extremely strict in this regard, I believe, and Mr. Damerell is subject to them in some measure, due to his connection with Threlfall."

Muna nodded. "He owes you his life. It is an uncomfortable thing for him, that you should hold that over them. Not, of course, that you would ever exploit it! But he and Rollo will be much happier when they have settled the balance."

"Yes," said Henrietta. She gulped, her trepidation increasing as she approached the main point. "I could not think of anything I desired, save to help my father. So I asked Mr. Damerell if he would marry me. He has a cousin who desires to leave him her fortune, only she will not do so unless he is married. Mr. Damerell has an independence of his own and has no need of money, but I do."

"Oh," said Muna. She was certainly surprised, but beyond that Henrietta could not tell what she thought.

"You are shocked," said Henrietta anxiously. "I know no modest female would dream of doing as I have done! But it is not as though it will be a *real* union—and Mr. Damerell does not mind. He thinks it a clever notion, and says he is just as glad to be able to please his cousin Elizabeth, for she is very old and has no other family."

"But what will Mr. Threlfall say?"

Henrietta wrung her hands. "That is the difficulty! Mr. Damerell assured me he would explain all, and he vows he did, and I tried to as well. But we cannot seem to make Mr. Threlfall understand."

"He is distressed?"

"No," said Henrietta despairingly. "He is *delighted*! It seems such arrangements are not usual among dragons. They often have more than one mate." She gave Muna a shy glance. "It is in Threlfall as it is in Janda Baik, I suppose. Mr. Threlfall thinks it a very good scheme, and wonders it never occurred to him before to find Mr. Damerell a mortal wife, for he says he has always wanted—always wanted *eggs*! And any eggs Mr. Damerell fathered would be his own too."

Muna was agog. "And will you lay eggs, do you think? I had not thought it possible for a mortal."

"I shall not," said Henrietta firmly. "I don't mean to be a true wife to Mr. Damerell. It will not be that sort of arrangement! He has no desire for a wife, and I—I don't wish to marry any gentleman. I told you so, you know."

Henrietta had half-feared that Muna would not remember, but she saw at once that Muna did. Muna did not seem to welcome the reminder, however. She had unbent as they spoke, her reserve falling away, but now it was as though a curtain had descended. She was all stiff courtesy again.

"Yes," said Muna. "I recall." After a pause, she added, with an effort, "Because you could not have Mr. Wythe."

This was Henrietta's moment—one of those moments that come but rarely, when what one does will set the whole course of the remainder of one's life. She must speak now or forever hold her peace. She said, hardly able to hear her own voice over the pounding of her heart:

"No! That was a misunderstanding. I never wanted Mr. Wythe. It is true I admired him when I was younger," she added conscientiously. "But it was only a fleeting fancy—a schoolgirl passion, soon burnt out. I would have told you so, only there was never the opportunity."

Henrietta raised her chin. She was terrified, but she would see this through, whatever came of it.

"In truth," she said, "it is because I could not have *you*!"

A dusky glow rose in Muna's cheeks. Henrietta met her eyes—only for a moment; then Henrietta was obliged to look away again, embarrassed and delighted in equal measure by what she had seen. Her courage was rewarded; her gamble had paid off. Henrietta would have dared far more for that exquisite moment of understanding, when she had seen all her own feeling reflected in Muna's dark eyes.

She would have asked for no more, brief as the moment had been. Muna was a Queen of Fairy now. There was no reason they should have anything more to do with each other. Yet more was to be given to her.

"Then maybe . . . !" Muna stammered.

To Henrietta's astonishment, Muna took Henrietta's hand and pressed a kiss to it. Greatly daring, Henrietta bent her face towards Muna's.

For a time there was no need for conversation.

Eventually Muna disentangled herself, patting down her hair, which was somewhat dishevelled by their activity. She cleared her throat.

"I came to ask if you would come to us in the Palace of the Unseen—the Fairy Court, I mean," she said. "I very much regretted the necessity of terminating my studies in English thaumaturgy before I had made any progress. And Sakti would like to understand it better as well.

"We would reward you for your service, of course," she added hastily. "And you could learn more of our magic too—the magic of the Unseen."

"Oh!" said Henrietta.

For a moment she was transfigured with joy, but then the weight of all that bound her to her life came down upon her.

Her realisation that she must reject the offer must have made itself evident in her face. She had said nothing, but Muna released her hand, stepping back.

"You need not feel obliged to agree," said Muna.

"No," said Henrietta in a stifled voice. "It is such an opportunity as every magician dreams of. And to go to *you*—!" She cut herself off before she could say anything unwise, but already

Muna's face was brightening. Henrietta hated to snuff out that light, but she compelled herself to go on:

"I could not leave my family. I hope I do not seem ungrateful, Your Majesty . . ."

"I beg you will call me Muna," said Muna, looking relieved. "Of course I did not mean you should leave England, or your family. I know you could not be spared for long, but when the girls go home, in the summer, could not you come to us for a month or so? You could return to England when the new term began—and come to us again the next year, if you wished. Sakti and I are not in the habit of detaining anyone who does not wish to stay in the Palace.

"It has freed up a great deal of space," she added. "You would not know the Palace if you saw it now! We have liberated the imps held captive in the lamps, and the trees in which you and I were imprisoned. Most of the trees have returned to the woods to which they belonged, on the edge of Fairy Within, but a few have chosen to stay in the Palace gardens. They are flourishing—Mak Geng-gang says she has never tasted such fruit. I should like you to see them."

Henrietta stared at Muna, disbelieving—but it could be done. A month in the summer, perhaps even two . . . her family would not object to that. Even if they did, their objections could easily be overcome with Prunella's support—and Prunella would certainly be in favour of a scheme so calculated to improve relations with the Fairy Court.

"That would be wonderful," breathed Henrietta. Yet still she hesitated, not daring to trust that she could enjoy such happiness. "But would not you rather have the Sorceress Royal, or Mr. Wythe, or Mr. Damerell? They know far more of thaumaturgy than I do."

"I would not rather," said Muna decidedly. "Having experienced your style of instruction, I must be trusted to know my mind, and I should prefer you to any other. Will you come?"

Henrietta smiled. Having started she could not seem to stop, and there seemed no call to try, for Muna smiled back.

"I should like it of all things," said Henrietta.

ACKNOWLEDGMENTS

For their hard work on behalf of this book and the last, I am grateful to Caitlin Blasdell, Rebecca Brewer, Bella Pagan and Diana Gill, as well as the wider teams at Ace and Pan Macmillan.

Thank you to Martin and Bernadette Auger for the Tate membership. A room to write in has a sort of talismanic power, and the Tate Modern Members Room was the birthplace of much of the matter of this book.

While writing, I complained to a great many people, including Aliette de Bodard, Tade Thompson, Victor Ocampo, Vida Cruz, Mia Sereno, Kate Elliott, Cindy Pon, Maxine Lim, the Concordians especially Tai Cheh Kuan, the Idlers by Bamboo, and my family. I am indebted to them all for their unfailing patience.

Thanks are due above all to my husband, Peter Auger, for everything, and to Rachel Monte, for being this book's earliest and best friend. This book would not exist without their love and support.